CRIMSON RAGE

ENJOY !

MATTHEW G. HANSON

Published by
Fideli Publishing, Inc.
119 W. Morgan St.
Martinsville, IN 46151

www.FideliPublishing.com

Special thanks to my sister Megan for editing,
daughter Gwyneth for final proofreading,
Doctor Cunningham for the science,
Debbe, Aiden, Mom and Dad for your support.

PRELUDE

CHAPTER 1

ASSASSINATION

1865

Wisps of smoke danced from the edges of the slats lining the barn as Sergeant Corbett pushed tight for cover against the crackling wood. His sweat-soaked faded blue uniform, soiled with blood from countless battles, crusted as he inched along the side of the barn.

With the excitement surrounding his return home after his time in Appomattox, Sergeant Corbett had all but forgotten his war-torn uniform discarded in the corner of his bedroom. If not for the arrival of midnight orders to join the hunt for an assassin, neither he nor his wife may have even touched the deleterious mass of cloth for weeks. Still, perhaps now, he thought, the crushing heat surrounding him might just engulf the loose material clinging to his body and eliminate the need to maintain the uniform ever again. Worse yet, perhaps his luck at returning home unscathed would finally change, and he'd die like so many others in the colors of his nation.

Lieutenant Colonel Conger flipped out the cartridge of his revolver to ensure each chamber held a tiny piece of brass. His nerves tensed as he watched layers of confidence shed from Sergeant Corbett as the time to engage the assassin drew near. Conger had relied on Sergeant Corbett countless times in battles near Petersburg, yet now questioned whether a few days back home had taken the fight from his most trusted soldier.

Wide-eyed young men wanting to fight for their country, for a cause, always brought excitement and fear to each battlefield at first. As months passed and conflicts raged on, excitement turned to mindless acceptance of each task assigned and the knowledge that death waited at every turn. Perhaps Sergeant Corbett's time home with his wife and family had permitted fear, once more, to return to the Sergeant's life.

When co-conspirator David Harold fled from the barn at the first flick of fire, Sergeant Corbett and Conger were convinced their mission might end without a fight. The actual assassin, though, the man they had tracked for weeks across state lines, resolutely remained inside the barn to test the will of the soldiers and hellfire.

Conger pushed the pistol's chamber into place, pulled back the hammer, and nodded to Sergeant Corbett. The sergeant drew in a deep breath, slid his finger onto the trigger of his weapon, and thrust his body against the barn door.

He stumbled.

As the door slammed against the barn wall, Sergeant Corbett shuffled his feet to find stability, dropped to one knee, and scanned his rifle's sight. Conger took position behind Sergeant Corbett.

In the back of the barn, a dozen rows of burning tobacco strands dangled from underneath a hayloft, while a dozen more had yet to catch fire. For now, the loft remained untouched by the flames, but a dusty mist hung about the structure's interior, as what tobacco had been consumed created a tavern-like smog. The sweet stench of Virginia tobacco forced Sergeant Corbett to squint as he scanned the room, finally training his rifle on two shadows outlined by the yellow flames.

"Let us see those hands!" Conger yelled as his revolver selected a target.

The strangers stretched their open hands high into the air with their backs to Conger and Sergeant Corbett. Their surrendered postures expanded their holocaust cloaks, and not until they slowly turned to face the armed men did they expose a lifeless figure strewn across a broken bale of hay. At their feet, unconscious, was the fugitive Conger and Sergeant Corbett had spent the last two weeks tracking along the east coast.

"We have this matter in hand," said one of the men, his hands turning sideways as his shoulders lifted.

"And you are?" Conger asked.

The stranger pointed to his chest, received consent from Conger, then reached into his jacket pocket. He pulled out a piece of rolled parchment and extended the item. As Conger stepped forward and grabbed hold of the paper, the cloaked man held onto the red ribbon that bound the document. While Conger unfurled the paper, the red binding drifted on the waves of heat delicately to the ground. After reading only a few lines, Conger's posture eased.

"This is happening…here? Now?"

The men dropped their hands.

Sergeant Corbett stepped forward towards the men, rifle ready, but stopped at the touch of his commander's hand on his chest.

"Not often planned out in an orderly fashion, sir. You know that." Conger's head nodded as he took in a breath, returned his hand to the parchment, and continued to read.

Like many men, Conger had enlisted as a private at the start of the war and wished for nothing more than a quick ascension in the ranks to lead men and return home a hero. Early losses to the Union opened up plenty of promotions, but slots went to men exhibiting great valor or heroism during battles where they often were the lone survivor. At first, Union soldiers found confidence in following the bravest and strongest men, but after several mishaps and losses of life due to brashness and bravado, the Union began seeking out men that could lead.

Although Conger did not find his opportunity to prove himself in battle, he volunteered immediately for a mission behind enemy lines just before a fight near Manassas. His initial task to contact southern sympathizers for information on troop movements soon morphed into espionage-focused tasks that made him one of the most trusted spies in the Union ranks. He could pose as a slave owner interested in observing battles up close to explain his presence on front lines or fake his heritage by rattling off prominent names from southern communities. Over time, his work was invaluable, and Union victories soon followed. As happens to almost every spy over time, however, the lies eventually caught up with Conger forcing him to find work elsewhere or risk losing his life.

Rather than lose a man with such skills to the wind, the United States government tapped him to work for a top-secret program that made him, and the two men in the barn, irreproachable. And while he eventually left the secret group after a few years at the behest of General Grant, he knew the tasks to which these men were assigned were of the utmost import and that they were given absolute discretion to remove any obstacle that stood in their way. On this day, thankfully, the fact that he and Sergeant Corbett were still alive to even have a chance to review the orders in his hands assured that his and Sergeant Corbett's deaths were not on the agenda.

Colonel Conger pointed to the man on the ground.

"He's one of them then?"

"Of course, sir." The stranger's voice formed a yell as the fire grew louder and consumed the hayloft.

"Why didn't you come to me with this when you arrived? I would have been of assistance."

"Too many men that don't know about us," the man thrust a hand in the direction of Sergeant Corbett.

"Of course, of course."

"And we assumed you would be the one watching the door, colonel, but when we approached in the darkness, we were greeted by your Captain Uhl."

"He give you any trouble?" Conger asked.

"Initially, he was not an agreeable sort, but once we pulled him back and showed him our orders, he relented."

"His men saw you come into the barn then?"

"No, sir. Captain Uhl pulled his men back so only he, you, and this fellow with the rifle still pointed at my head know we're here." He shot a look of disgust. "Think you could order your man to stand down?"

"Drop your weapon!" Conger said over the loud pops of exploding wood. Sergeant Corbett eased off his rigid stance. "So, how are we to handle this?"

"We need the sergeant's weapon." Corbett stepped back as the agent that had yet to speak approached, grasped the barrel of Corbett's rifle, and pulled.

"Relinquish your weapon, sergeant," ordered Conger.

"But sir?"

Corbett tugged.

"Now, sergeant! These men are in charge here."

The silent agent forced the weapon from Sergeant Corbett's grip, ensured the gun was loaded, spun, and pointed the barrel at the fugitive in the hay. A thunderous report from the rifle forced blood from the man's neck. The agent turned around, nodded to ensure Sergeant Corbett was paying attention, and tossed the smoking weapon back into his grasp.

Corbett struggled to control the rifle.

"Sergeant Corbett," said the agent who fired the weapon, "if anyone enquires about this situation, you are to say this man raised his pistol, and you had to shoot him. Do you understand?"

Corbett gazed at his weapon, then to the bleeding man.

The agent pulled back his coat, un-holstered his sidearm, and pushed it against Sergeant Corbett's temple. The cold steel formed an appreciable ring against his searing skin.

"Sergeant Corbett, do you understand what I have just said to you!?"

"Ye…yes, yes, I understand!"

"And should your story ever change, your family dies first, and then we come for you."

The muzzle pushed harder against his skull.

"Do you understand?"

"Yes…YES!"

"Lieutenant Colonel Conger," the other agent stepped closer, "you will publicly disavow Corbett's action in shooting the suspect…".

"I know what needs to be done."

"…and you are to ensure no real punitive action is ever taken against Sergeant Corbett."

"He will face no discipline," Conger said.

"Thank you, colonel. Now…if you would oblige," the agent pointed first to the fugitive, then to the exit of the barn. Conger moved towards the dying man and grabbed his legs.

"Take hold of his arms Sergeant Corbett," Conger said as the agent with the revolver pushed open the barn door. "We need to get out of here." Sergeant Corbett was slow to respond as he slung his weapon over his shoulder then searched for a way to avoid the cerise stains pooling on the dying man's shirt.

"We're coming out," yelled the agent at the door.

A portion of the loft holding the tobacco strands crashed to the ground as Conger quick-stepped through the door trailed by Sergeant Corbett.

"We need some help," Conger shouted. Uhl's men appeared from the darkness, descended upon them, and relieved Sergeant Corbett and Conger of the body's weight. Captain Uhl pushed through his men and ordered them to carry the fugitive to the nearby farmhouse. Uhl stood in front of Conger awaiting further orders, but with a simple wave, he was released to follow his men into the night.

A smatter of raindrops fell on Sergeant Corbett's face, and the cool sensation was welcome after the events in the barn. Cheers from the procession echoed across the valley and died out slowly as all of the soldiers disappeared into the darkness. Once free of prying eyes, Sergeant Corbett turned towards the crumbling barn, searching for the agents.

No one followed.

"You understood what happened in there?" Conger said, pulling in a deep breath.

Sergeant Corbett nodded.

"They will come for you if you ever speak truthfully about this day."

Corbett nodded, stared at the ground, and began to shake.

CHAPTER 2

LOOSE ENDS

April 27, 1865

The knock on the door was welcome as United States Attorney General James Speed had grown tired of staring at the same old intelligence reports.

"Come in!" His command echoed up into the miniature carved wood statutes of various Roman philosophers located atop the molding in each corner of the room. The great men were alit only from the angle at which they were exposed to the raging fire behind Speed's desk with words such as honor, justice, and humility inscribed at their feet. A stout courier moved into the room, his candle lighting the darkened sides of the statutes, as the creaking door and the depth of the room drowned out the last whispers commanding him to enter.

"Confidential dispatch for you, sir." He handed the attorney general the scroll.

"Thank you, Simpson. You are excused."

The messenger turned on the spot and returned to the door.

"Oh, and Simpson, could you set up some coffee? I think this night shall be a long one."

"As you wish, sir."

The tight seal opened as the attorney general ran a tiny steel blade across the top of the envelope. The oak door clicked shut behind Simpson as the letter slipped from its cover. Recovering his spectacles from amidst a pile of documents, he began to read.

> Sir,
>
> Booth intercepted and killed. Corbett took the shot, and former Agent Conger witnessed the act. Both understand their role. Having chased Booth for days after the assassination, we met with all persons Booth contacted while on the run, including Samuel Cox, Thomas Jones, Thomas Harbin, and William Bryant. All are unaware of Booth's visions. We have, however, taken Booth's friends Surratt, Powell, Herold, and Atzerodt into custody. I have spoken with Seward's assistant, who recommends their immediate removal as they know of Booth's visions. We have left clear evidence of their part in a conspiracy to kill the President. Prior history of Booth's desire to kill Lincoln through his diary and friends made covering reasonably easy. We will modify his diary and other papers found in his home before releasing them.
>
> ROBE
> Agent L

Attorney General Speed leaned back in his chair, holding the letter closer to his face as he reread it. Satisfied, he pushed forward to his desk and wrote down the names Surratt, Powell, Herold, and Atzerodt on a small piece of paper followed by the word 'hang.' He exhaled, pushed back his chair, rose, and approached the fireplace. His right arm leaned against the mantle as he grinned and tossed the confidential dispatch into the fire. The paper curled as Simpson shuffled back into the room. Drifts of steam from the coffee trailed. Speed welcomed the tepid cup into his chilled hands.

"Send out a post," Speed said. Simpson pulled a notebook and pencil from his jacket pocket.

"When you are ready, sir."

"To General Hancock. We need to meet tonight regarding the conspirators in Lincoln's death. The captured on this list shall remain in solitary confinement with limited contact by only you and your most trusted guards and are to be hung most urgently." Speed handed Simpson the note with the scribbled names, and Simpson turned towards the door.

"I know it is late, Simpson," he turned back to show his attention, "but wake Hancock if you have to. I want him here before my coffee is cold!"

PART 1

UNEXPLAINED 2009

CHAPTER 3

FLUSH

G abe smiled at his former college roommate as he twisted the top from another beer and handed it to his friend across the card table. Mike took a sip and formed a crude and exaggerated face of disgust.

"I know beer's supposed to be warm in some countries, but geez..." Mike said.

"Just pulled it out of the cooler," Gabe said.

"It's just," Mike stuck out his tongue, "gross."

Gabe chuckled at his oldest friend and even welcomed Mike's whining as he knew it was a clear sign Mike, once again, possessed a weak hand. Typically, a stoic and relatively quiet man in his daily life, Gabe discovered early on in their relationship that whenever Mike was struggling, he moaned and complained. Mike's attitude dimmed, and his voice turned doughy and raspy each time, whether with a teacher utilizing the Socratic Method to debate a topic or in conflicts with a referee in an intramural basketball game during their freshman year. As if those tells were not enough for Gabe to pull hundreds of dollars from his oldest friend but, as he aged, Mike formed distinctive crow's feet around his eyes and temples that pulled tight and most deep at his most significant moments of stress. Voice cracks helped Gabe fund his meal plans throughout college and now past knowledge and father time helped Gabe pay his utility bills. Still, on this night, it was not Mike that presented the challenge to Gabe's standard of winning but rather a new player Mike had invited.

The new guy, Tommy, a senior at Texas Tech who was an intern with Mike for the summer, had set a trap for the players. Introduced to the bespectacled college kid just a few hours earlier, with his pale pudgy cheeks and slight, unassuming smirk, Gabe and his friends anticipated when the twenty-something boy asked how to ante; they would walk all over him. Tommy further set the stage by tanking the first eight hands and losing over half his stack of chips. The others at the table bit hard, flooding chips into the pots and consuming beer after beer to celebrate what was shaping up as a night of profound victory over Tommy. In a perfect procession, the players' bravado increased, the smack talk grew, and by the time any of them were paying close attention, Tommy had not only recovered his losses but had won eleven hands in a row. Too late for much else than to watch the plan unfold, half the table was broke an hour earlier in the evening than ever before. As had been his routine for well over two hours on this night, Mike took one more pained sip of his beer and dropped his cards.

"I fold," he said, pushing his hand to the middle. Gabe's gaze moved to Tommy.

"Whatcha gonna do?"

Gabe watched for any tell. Tommy's Steelers cap set low over his brow and covered most of his face. Gabe noticed Tommy's lips purse as he looked up. Gabe's goofy grin reflected in Tommy's Oakley's, revealing nothing more. Gabe had always believed himself to possess a stare rivaling Clint Eastwood's and tried hard to look through the young man. While he didn't share the features of the famed actor that oozed intensity and grit, it wasn't until the release of an animated film in the late 2000s that most of his friends burst his bubble by likening him to the main character Flint Lockwood in *Cloudy with a Chance of Meatballs*. Elongated somewhat from the waist to the top of his head with short stubby legs, Gabe took a long look at himself after that and had to admit a likeness to Flint, not Clint. Not as awkward or geeky as the comical character and possessing a solid chin and nose that fit on his long and lean face, he by no means was a bad-looking man. Still, even with the slight faults with his features, they were overcome by his outgoing personality and penchant for never meeting a stranger. While his charm and deep blue eyes often worked to pry out information from others, his attempts to reveal any crack in Tommy's stoic veneer were failing.

Tommy fiddled with the unstacked mound of chips set in disarray in front of him.

A half-minute passed.

Tommy revealed a slight grin.

"All in," he said, brows jumping above the rim of the sunglasses.

Gabe's free hand caught his forehead as he dropped his cards on the table and looked up at Tommy. He circled the cards on top of one another in hopes that something other than what he had might appear. He peeled back the corners to look again and leaned low. Nothing had changed. More confident with his nines and fives before the pot tripled with Tommy's call, Gabe cringed at the genuine danger of a flush in Tommy's hand. He had already lost two days' salary to the kid and wasn't sure he could take a hit on a third. He cupped his hands and raised the cards for one more desperate look. The cards left Gabe's hand in disgust and fell to the middle of the table.

"Take it, newbie," Gabe said. Tommy stretched his arm across the table and swept his winnings into a plastic bag he had gotten from Gabe an hour earlier. Gabe watched the money fall and turned to Mike.

"You rarely ever show leaving us a player short, and when you finally do get here, you bring this guy!" Gabe's hand waived over Tommy's entire body. "On top of that, you never bring drinks or snacks and yet have the audacity to complain about the frostiness of the free beer when you get here. I need to reconsider our friendship."

"You always leave games early," Doug said as he pushed his chair away from the table, stood, and collected the two dollars he had remaining on the table.

"And you always show up without enough cash," said Phil, who, as usual, sided with Doug in every attack. Although Gabe called them "the twins," they were anything but by appearance as Doug was a bullish five-six while Phil was tall and lean. Still, the two had been best friends since they were in first grade in El Paso and even married two sisters that were one-third of the only sextuplets their high school had ever known. Dedicated to their families and one another, the girls insisted they all live near one another, setting Doug and Phil three houses and a holler out the door away from one another. Gabe first met the pair in the dog park, and the three hit it off immediately as Gabe embodied the bachelor life they both insisted they missed every day. The conversations turned to friendship and the friendship into poker nights as the men convinced the sisters that the boys needed at least one night every other week for their own time.As kids replaced canines, the bi-weekly games became routine, and Doug and Phil brought with them a contrived bitterness about being tied down. Despite their protestations, Gabe knew that they both took great pride in their families, their lives, and most of all, in their children. They were good dads, hard-working men that toiled in the hot sun constructing houses around El Paso, and while they claimed to be envious of Gabe's life, their claims that they resided in the eighth level of Dante's inferno were far from the truth. In addition to the white noise, cheap beer, and stacks of cash they brought to each game, harassing the arrogant Doctor Mike was a pastime that had become a tradition.

"You ever thought of hitting the grocery store on the corner for a bag of ninety-nine-cent chips?" Doug said.

"Maybe something from your house?" Phil said.

Mike smiled. "Maybe I just don't like you guys."

"I like 'em," Tommy said as the last coin dropped from the table into his bag.

"You keep out of this," Gabe said. "Just sit there and play with your green."

"And what exactly did you contribute to this event, new guy?" Phil turned his attack.

"And what kind of name is Tommy anyway?" Doug said. "Shouldn't you be a Tom or even a Thomas by now? You're not in fourth grade anymore."

"If you want to tell your wives and friends tomorrow about being embarrassed by a little fourth-grader named Tommy tonight, be my guest."

"Won't look good on the playground," Mike said.

"And besides," Tommy continued, "Tommy was just part of the ruse to pull you suckers in. You guys all bought into the 'dorky kid with glasses who doesn't know how to gamble' routine faster than anyone I'd ever tried to pull this on." The men stared, unamused. "And from now on, all you guys except Doug here can call me T or Tom. You, Doug, need to call me sir or your eminence since I pretty much own you after tonight." As the group began to catcall at Doug, he stood up, smiled, and wandered into the living room to a recliner.

* * *

As the earliest hour after midnight neared, Gabe ran his foot along the back of his Labrador, Stump, who was lounging beneath the table. "This was a good night," Mike insisted, "I need to get to these games of yours more often."

"Stop bringing friends." Gabe smiled.

"I didn't know he was any good."

"At least you didn't win my dog tonight," Gabe said to Tom.

"I can't have a dog. The landlord doesn't like pets." Tom pointed at Mike. "So, Stump's safe for now."

"Stump doesn't like you anyway. He picks up on deceitful types…you know, card sharks and such. That's probably why he growled at you so long when you walked in tonight." Gabe said.

"He's only my roommate for the summer," Mike said. "Once I teach him all about the fine art of being an eye doctor, he's got to go back to college for another semester to finish up his studies."

"Ah, college," Gabe said, "now I had fun back then."

"You two were roommates, weren't you?" Tom asked.

"Yeah, but after our freshman year, I never really saw Mike. He just grew up all of the sudden and never was much for poker or anything involving after-hours' revelry."

Mike shook his head. "Now wait for just a second; I did play with you guys…"

"Once or twice a semester, doc. From time to time, we'd tell you about the game, and when you didn't show up, we'd go looking for you at the library or the chem lab." Mike smirked. "He'd set up camp in different areas so that we couldn't find him. He was and is an extraordinary nerd."

Tom nodded.

"While that nerd title might be a little true, it might be best if you show your mentor just a little respect, Tom. After all, you did just finish taking a week's salary from me."

"I'm sure you'll get it back from me somehow," Tom said.

"I do have to admit, though, it was good to see someone besides Gabe walk away a winner." Tom raised his beverage to meet Mike's glass.

"I'm just happy to know two eye docs just in case I ever need a second opinion," Gabe said as he clinked Tom's glass and smiled.

"You about ready to go?" Mike stood up, reached for his jacket, and kneeled to give Stump a final pat on the head. "Gabe, my man, great to see you," said Mike extending his hand.

"You know you're always welcome here, Mike, but you might want to leave the card shark at home."

"Somebody has to drive his drunk butt home," Tom said as he dropped down the steps into the yard.

"We'll see you both in two weeks then, I guess." Gabe waived as he closed the screen door and began to pick up debris. Stump let out a long sigh.

"Come on, old man, get up and get outside." Stiff joints crackled as Stump headed outside. Gabe moved to the front window to ensure his pup made it off the porch as the phone rang. Late phone calls never meant good things for an FBI agent. Gabe grabbed the phone, took two long strides, and dropped onto the sofa by the window.

"What could you possibly be up to at this hour?"

"Your phone etiquette is horrible."

"When it's this late, it's usually bad news, you, or both," Gabe said.

"And I do so enjoy every one of our after-hour conversations," Detective Rebecca Ryan said.

"What is it, Ryan?"

"We've got another body, Gabe. Similar MO to our last two but with a new twist that the chief wants us to check out."

"I'm assuming you won't tell me more unless I pick you up again?"

"You know I can't help it that the El Paso police department garage refuses to fix my vehicle promptly. And since they paired us up and you have a working vehicle, you remain my only choice."

"No cab service out that way?" Gabe smiled as he watched Stump make his way across the yard.

"My department took thirteen months to get me a computer with software from this century, Gabe, and thanks to their continued ineptitude, I've even thought about giving up working for the EPPD and giving your FBI gig a whirl." Gabe chuckled. "The FBI has functioning cars, has to have better benefits, and the small amount of work you put in relative to what you get paid is a crime."

"I work when I need to, Ryan."

"You're not the laziest I've ever seen, but I could do the work of two agents in a day and still have five or six hours of free time before dinner."

"Ouch."

"Sorry," she paused. "I'm not being very nice. Come get me, and I might even bring you out some of those cupcakes I made for the office yesterday."

"You didn't make those, Ryan; I saw the receipt in your purse."

"I still have a few left…"

"Well, I just got done eating a bunch of chips, but I guess I could use some calorie clumps. Have 'em with you when I get there."

"Will do," Ryan said.

"See you in twenty."

Gabe hung up the phone, corralled Stump inside, and went to get dressed.

CHAPTER 4

NEW PARTNER

G abe dropped into his bureau-issued white Chevy that offered little to the eye for a car enthusiast on the outside and evenless for riding comfort on the inside. Nothing about his vehicle excited him and was just one more example of the rigid and lifeless standard issue equipment provided to agents in smaller cities. Not that he missed being a target for every trigger-happy wanna-be sniper in Iraq, but the toys he was issued as a member of the special forces would make any young man smile.

Eighteen months earlier, Gabe had arrived in El Paso to a spacious office overlooking the river valley to work as a field agent with seven other agents for the Federal Bureau of Investigation. Although the agents wished to treat him like a pledge by tasking him 'cat in the tree' cases, it wasn't long before he was caught up in a rash of gang-related murders along the Rio Grande. Yet where other agents failed to solve the cases, Gabe immersed himself into the world of the drug cartels, unearthing leads and suspects, and was instrumental in the takedown of one of the most prominent drug families controlling the western corridor of Texas. His reputation and involvement in solving complex cases established, it was no surprise the FBI loaned him to the El Paso Police Department to assist with a rash of unsolved murders.

As he pulled into Ryan's subdivision, Gabe cringed as remnants from construction sites kicked up noisy junk into the wheel wells. Ryan's house was easy to find as hers was the only house amidst three dozen empty lots lining a cul-de-sac. Gabe looped to his left in the middle of the street and honked his horn four times. The front porch light flickered on as Ryan burst through the door, waving her hand at the darkness.

As was the norm, even in the early morning hours of a new day, Ryan was dressed in her black slacks, a grey t-shirt, and a custom-made black jacket with a hood. Since the day they met, Gabe ribbed Ryan about her enhanced hoodie that seemingly was nothing more than a lost relic from the 'Members Only' craze that consumed his high school years. Ryan was immediate and consistent in her defense of the custom-made accouterment, eagerly revealing secret pockets for supplies, ammunition, and other knick-knacks. She would be ready for anything that came her way, and despite her insistence that she only possessed two such hoodies, Gabe discovered over a dozen waiting for duty in a front closet during one early morning pickup.

She wrestled with the lock on her front door that always stuck. Gabe hit the center of the steering wheel. Her tight ponytail whipped around and caught her in the cheek as she grimaced at Gabe. Even when displeased, she had a soft demeanor about her, and although he had never thought about her as anything but a partner, he had to admit her antics when frustrated verged on adorable.

"Your horn broken!?" she yelled in a whisper as she rushed towards the car.

Gabe shrugged.

"You can't see them at night, but I've got some crotchety neighbors in earshot who'll call the cops if you don't stop." Ryan pulled open the passenger door, fell into the seat, and pulled the door closed.

"What neighbors?" he asked as he hit the horn once more. She pointed randomly into the darkness while refusing to catch sight of Gabe's expression of ignorance.

"On the other side of the road there, Gabe. They can hear everything."

"But we are the cops." She punched him on the arm.

"Ouch! Take it easy, you little gorilla."

"Just drive...oh, and here are your cupcakes." She dropped a box onto his lap and proceeded to find her seat belt. The Kroger sticker on the bottom of the box stuck to Gabe's pants as he pushed them off to the middle console.

"Don't know where I'm going."

"Head back towards town," she flipped open her notebook. "We're heading to 1512 Montana Avenue just south of the Sierra Medical Center." Gabe punched the numbers into the GPS on his phone.

"What is all this junk?" Ryan leaned over and picked up a stack of papers impeding her feet. "Hoarding newspapers?"

"I had to pick those up earlier today, Ryan. It's just some local papers I read...just throw them in the back." Curious, she punched the dome light and leafed through the foot-high stack of papers as Gabe pulled away from her home.

"These aren't even in English."

"A couple of them are. There might even be some with pictures for you if you dig deep." She refused to look at him.

"I don't get it," she said as she flipped through pages of odd words, letters, and characters, "what's local about any of these?"

"They're from places I've lived, Ryan."

"How'd you get all of these?"

"Woody, the news guy outside your police department, collects them for me."

"You don't honestly have any clue what these say," Ryan held up one of the papers.

"There's an article about General Patraeus on the front discussing how some of his reforms in the courts in Iraq have come to fruition." Ryan frowned, held the paper close to her eyes, and found the general's name.

"I can read his name on here too, Gabe. That doesn't mean I understand this," she said.

"There's another story in that stack," he tugged on a faded pink strip of paper, "there, right there...it's about a poisoned water well in a small village in Afghanistan and how the locals had to rely on non-governmental sources to bring in water. The article reveals their frustrations with the government efforts."

"And what language is this exactly?" she asked.

"That's Pashto."

"Never heard of it," Ryan said. "I'm pretty sure you're making that up?"

"Why would I lie?"

"Just how many different languages are represented in this stack of papers, Gabe?"

"A few."

"Five, ten…?"

"Fourteen or so."

"Fourteen!"

"It's not a big deal, Ryan. Languages are just something I get."

"And you didn't think this little skill of yours is something you should have shared with me; you know, since we're partners and all?"

"Other than where you live, what you wear every day, and your work ethic, I know nothing about you, Ryan." Her lips pursed as no reply could be found. She continued to shuffle through the stacks.

"So, this is the great mystery of Agent Moss then…you know, your thing?"

"My thing?" Gabe's forehead creased.

"The thing that separates you from the wheat and chaff that got you into the bureau," she said.

"Well yeah, I guess that along with my military…"

"Lots of agents were in the military, Gabe…I knew there had to be something more to you."

"Well, thanks. I guess? Always full of so many compliments, Ryan, I'm not sure how to…"

"Wait, wait, wait, you told me you were a horrible college student. I recall you bailing on some math calculations a week or so back claiming you were a…and I quote…'piss poor student.'"

"Never was the best Ryan, but I honestly had no clue about my ability with languages until I was in Iraq."

"You just go to Persia one day and realize you can speak with the natives? Some descendant of Abraham touch you with a magic tongue for languages?"

"It was just Arabic at first, Ryan, don't be a wise ass."

"He was born over there, wasn't he?"

"Yes, Ryan, Abraham was born in Nasiriya, but no, I didn't meet him, Jesus or God for that matter, and none of them 'touched' me."

"So how'd this happen then?"

"It wasn't a big deal," he said. She looked down at Gabe's phone tracking their path.

"Says we have ten minutes…do tell." Gabe shifted in his seat, pulled back a hand to rest on the window, and pulled in a breath.

"My unit was charged with finding missing soldiers, and like most field units, we had an interpreter assigned to us. His name was Raza, and just as you work with me, he was our partner on almost every mission. He shared his dreams with us, ate with us, took us to his house to be with his family, and lived with us when we weren't near his home. He was immersed in every meeting, confab, visit, and raid we went on, and I was around him for every conversation we had with Iraqi citizens for over a year."

"So, you learned it from him then?"

Gabe shook his head.

"Not exactly, you see, one day while on patrol, Raza took a round in the shoulder from a sniper. As our unit medic made his way towards us, another shot rang out, and a specialist took the sniper's second shot to his head. Priority dictated the medic work with the head wound, so I did my best to bandage up Raza. I pulled him up against me to calm him while putting down cover fire to try and protect the specialist and medic. In between changing out mags, I peppered Raza with questions about all of the places I was going to have to take him when he came to see me in America just to keep his mind off his pain."

"Odd to just be there talking like that, wasn't it? I mean, in the middle of a firefight and all?"

"Seems surreal now that I look back on it, Ryan, but absurd things happened all the time in theater. Looking back, the conversation was as normal as the one we're having now. Nothing hurried, nothing urgent…just two friends bantering back and forth."

"Not normal, Gabe."

"Matter of perspective, I guess. You did what you did in the moment of the fog, and while my training kept me reloading and popping off suppressing fire, my concern over my friend kept me focused on keeping him alive as well.

"He survive?"

"Yeah, after the soldier with the head wound was evacuated and the gunfight died off, my commander ordered both of us into the back of a Humvee to return to base. Once back at base Raza had his shoulder patched up, and thankfully, he was good as new in a few weeks."

"I'm glad for your interpreter friend Gabe but what does this have to do with learning languages?"

"Well, later that night, my commander found me in my bunk and handed me orders to report to Arifjan in the morning for language immersion."

"Kuwait?"

"Yeah."

"So, he sent you off to get trained as the new interpreter?" Ryan asked.

"No, not exactly. While I was taking care of Raza during the battle, and then during our trip back to the base, we spoke in Arabic the entire time. Other guys in my unit heard us during the gun battle and then on the Humvee. I had no idea." Ryan smiled and tilted her head.

"That's a pretty cool way of discovering something like that."

"Yeah, maybe, but when they say immersion training, they mean complete immersion. I did so well in those initial classes in Kuwait that they sent me back to Washington for training in even more languages. It wasn't until after another whole year of classroom work that I could get back over to Iraq and then follow that with another deployment to Afghanistan, which provided me the opportunity to learn several more languages. Languages consumed my life for several years, Ryan, and on those tours, I became the go-to guy for interpreting at village meetings and high-level workshops with citizens."

"So, as I said, that's your thing?"

"I guess if that's what you mean, yeah, since just being a soldier was never going to get me into the Bureau. You indeed have to have something more, be it an engineering background, legal training, or political pull…my ticket in was languages." Ryan pulled out two papers from the middle of the stack.

"But why have German and Spanish papers in here then?"

"In my spare time, I've picked up other languages. First Latin, then Spanish, French, Italian, and finally German. I've been working on Russian for some time now and should have it cleared up in a few weeks."

"Are you able to read and speak all of these?"

"The speaking part is what I get quickly, Ryan, but it doesn't take long for me to pick up the written word as well. Of course, I haven't tackled Chinese yet, and I hear those characters are a real nightmare." Ryan ordered the stack of papers then looked back to Gabe.

"I think that's fascinating," Ryan stated, "but with all of those abilities, how'd they let you end up here in Texas?"

"After years of interpreting hundreds of thousands of pages of documents and transcripts and doing some other top-secret work around the globe, I was given a choice of what I wanted to do, Ryan. Washington was too hectic, and oddly enough, I'm able to find peace in the desert."

"And your assignment with me?"

"No idea other than someone out there either thinks I'm good at tracking down murderers or..."

"Or what?"

"You have no idea what you're doing." Ryan smiled as she placed the papers into the car's back seat.

"Just try to pay more attention to helping solve these murders piling up and leave the news of Somalia in Somalia."

"Not to worry, I don't speak Cushitic...yet," Gabe whispered as the tempered female voice from the GPS indicated their destination was three miles ahead.

"So what exactly are we in for up ahead?"

"Dead body was all I was told."

"Have you found out anything new on those other bodies from the last few weeks?" Gabe asked.

"I put the notes on your desk this afternoon."

"Had to get to game night," Gabe shrugged, "what'd they say?"

"It was about John Doe number one that I worked on alone three days before you were assigned to the department. His name is Todd Harris, and he just returned from a tour overseas in Kuwait. We finally got hold of his phone..."

"Wait, I thought you told me Doe number one...sorry, Todd Harris didn't have a phone," Gabe said.

"Well, that's what I knew at the time."

"Go on."

"Dimwit new guy, Patrolman Sanchez, called me yesterday and apologized for contaminating the Harris scene."

"Really?"

"Sanchez was the first to find Harris, and as he was checking for a pulse, in all of his wisdom, he collected up some of Harris' items, including his wallet and phone."

"Not the best crime scene integrity?" Gabe shook his head.

"He's twenty-one, Gabe. The younger generation has lost focus on taking the time to do things right. He tried to claim he was freaked out overseeing his first dead body, but I know damn well his focus is just like that of his entire generation."

"Which is?"

"Gotta save the cell phone!"

Gabe nodded and smiled. "So apparently, this guy not only picked up those two items but dropped them into his jacket pocket, and it never dawned on him, before he left, to turn those items over to detectives when they arrived."

"No one ever asked if he had touched anything?"

"They did, but he claims he felt the items in his pocket and, of course, assumed they were his."

"We all screw up sometimes, Ryan."

She wasn't satiated. "And to make matters worse, this guy takes an extended leave after finding the body due to his delicate psyche and forgets all about the phone and wallet in his jacket."

"And he never messed with the jacket after that night until he got back from leave?"

"Claims he got some blood on it and threw it in his trunk…and there it sat for well over a week."

"So, how'd he know you were looking for it?"

"During his first roll call back, I was asking for any help on trying to tie up the Harris murder with Bryan Caldwell's body we had just found the night before and started running through a list of things officers might have seen, including phones. It was only then he remembered Harris' cell phone was still in his jacket and still in the trunk."

"Well, while it sounds like he might need a little re-training, at least he brought it up after he messed things up," Gabe said.

"These kids are probably the reason they had to bring you in…at least you play like you're an adult at times."

"Thanks, mom!" Her fist returned to his arm. "So enough of the 'world according to Ryan speech…what's so special about Harris' cell phone?" Gabe asked.

"Once we powered up Harris' phone, we were able to find one rather strange number on both his phone and the phone we found on Caldwell's body."

"Why strange?"

"It was a bunch of sevens."

"Sevens?"

"Yeah, and as you might expect, when we dialed that number back, nothing happened, so I've tasked Jenkins with running down the source of this number to determine who these guys knew in common."

"Sort of sounds like a dead end."

"Any lead's a good lead." Gabe frowned. "What?" Ryan asked.

"Well, the phone lead doesn't help tie up the other guy you found first with his kidneys filleted. What was his name…?"

"Mallon."

"Right, Charles Chip Mallon. Well, at least since you were the first on that scene, we should have no worries about a cell phone showing up." Ryan nodded.

"He might not have had a phone, Gabe, but both Mallon and Harris were killed with a knife, so there's that."

"Yeah, but we know Caldwell died from blunt force trauma to his head. No knife or other weapon nearby…for all we know, he could have just fallen off a ladder."

"Didn't find a ladder, Gabe."

"You know what I mean."

"But at least we have one connection tying each dead body to at least one other dead body," Ryan said.

"Still not a single strong tie grouping the three though, other than they were all found dead in the street within a block of one another," Gabe said.

As instructed by the computer voice, Gabe veered slightly right and approached dozens of red and blue flashing lights that danced around inside his car. Stopping at the curb, Ryan collected her notebook, pushed open the door, and got out of the vehicle.

CHAPTER 5

MODUS OPERANDI

T he lights from the emergency vehicles cast an eerie orange and yellow glow off the colorful stucco houses. Ryan stopped in the driveway to speak with the officers to establish the chain of command while Gabe made his way to the entrance of the cordoned-off home. She scribbled down names in a notebook, learned that one of the homeowners was in the kitchen with an officer, then she followed Gabe inside.

The atrium was small, with a staircase just off to her right that curved up to the second floor. The space seemed more significant than it should have due to the high ceilings and long chandelier light above her. The entrance lacked the warmth of many homes she had been in due either to the white-wash walls or the absence of photographs, paintings, or even a clock for decoration. To her left was a dining room with a small wooden table and two chairs, and down a narrow hall to the right, she could see the living room. A pair of splayed-out legs on the living room floor froze her gaze as she closed the front door and approached the room.

"What are you doing…," Ryan said as she walked into the room. Gabe raised his finger to his mouth. Her brow furrowed, then eased as she reminded herself of Gabe's penchant for routine. Even though they had been at two other murder scenes together, Ryan still had yet to get used to Gabe's ritual with dead bodies. She had asked Gabe about his quirk with the first body they worked on together and even joked with him that it was just his medically untrained way to check for life. While he laughed at her hypothesis, he was serious in response.

At a time when violence was at its height in Iraq, Gabe's unit came upon a scene that he declared to be 'the most life-altering thing he'd ever experienced.' While out on patrol on the first day of April, Gabe happened upon two young soldiers missing for several days. Other than their tattered uniforms with the American flag still intact, they were unidentifiable by any usual standards as fingers, noses, and every other loose appendage had been removed from their stripped-down and filleted corpses. Their condition invited immediate assistance from first responders, but the urge to aid them was halted when Gabe noticed dozens of colored wires sticking out of crevices.

Despite every instinct in his body screaming to help these men, all he could do was hover over the bodies and take in the horrors frozen indelibly in their unclosed eyes. After long minutes he finally stood and stared into the distance. Some members of his unit wept; others yelled in anger, demanding vengeance. He cued up his mic, called the EOD team, and cordoned off the bodies. His mind cascaded with images of the unimaginable pain, fear, and loneliness the dead men felt in their final minutes. Enraged beyond thought for effective action for the first time in his life, he resolved to find every missing soldier quickly before they could suffer similar fates. After four hours of detailed precision to remove the explosives from within each man and the daisy-chained IED's surrounding them, Gabe returned to base, marched into his commander's office, and demanded that he and a unit of hand-picked soldiers be assigned only recovery missions thereafter.

His specialized unit of men made a name for themselves among the Jihadists after that horrific day, and rumors exploded that Gabe and his 'almuharibin mulahhid' or 'godless warriors' exacted revenge most sadistically upon finding the culprits that killed any American. Little effort was made by the men in his unit to temper the stories, and instead, they nurtured each tale to strike fear in the heart of the enemy and make them consider their actions with captives. As the accounts grew, the fear of retribution struck at the hearts of the enemy, and the stories were credited with vastly decreasing the level of torture Gabe and his men had witnessed that April Fool's Day.

Even as the level of savagery lessened, with every corpse Gabe and his men discovered, he continued his routine of hovering over each deceased…a chance to reflect on the first bodies he found…a moment to say a prayer for the dead…for an opportunity to say goodbye. And while Ryan knew the hovering itself offered no way of saving any of the men he found in Iraq, or even this woman laid out on the floor, she realized his routine offered him inner peace and a chance to resolve the mind-numbing memories that would drive most sane men crazy.

He leaned over the dead woman, perhaps no more than a foot from the side of her head, his eyes as still as hers. After a few moments, he followed her frozen gaze to the fireplace then followed the length of her body from head to toe before releasing a heavy breath. As he rose, he scribbled in his notebook, pivoted, and caught Ryan's stare.

"Okay to talk now?" she asked.

"I'm good."

"You know I'm still not used to the floating over the dead person shtick you do with these bodies, right?"

"We've all got our quirks Ryan…even you." She smiled. "Come on," he said as she pointed to the kitchen. Gabe passed Ryan as she put a hand on her hip.

"Excuse me?"

"Come on," he said with a grin.

"Who's in charge here?" Ryan raised her left eyebrow. Gabe turned to face her, placed his hand across his chest, and leaned over in a pose of contrition. Ryan's posture notably improved as she passed. Gabe followed on her heels but took just three steps before Ryan stopped abruptly, forcing Gabe to grab the wall to avoid a collision. A troubled man in his mid-twenties sat askew in a wooden chair in the kitchen. His eyes were wide as he recounted his arrival at his home.

"And then I just found her laying…" He noticed the pair in the hall. The officer taking notes stood up.

"Oh hello, Detective Ryan," said the officer. "I didn't know you were here." The young man was nervous.

"We just arrived, Officer Taylor. Not sure you've met Agent Gabe Moss from the FBI yet?"

"No, ma'am, I have not." Officer Taylor extended his hand. As they exchanged introductions, Gabe nodded toward the man in the chair.

"And who's this?" Gabe said.

"Sorry," said Taylor. He flipped a few pages on his notepad. "This is Roger Farr, and he owns the home. He arrived here about an hour ago and found his wife lying in the living room. He called us, and I was the first one to arrive. I've been with him ever since."

"Sir," Ryan said. "I'm Detective Ryan, and this is Agent Moss. We're going to need to talk to you here in a bit, but first, I need a moment with Officer Taylor outside." Farr nodded as Ryan rested her hand on the man's shoulder. "I'll be right back, but if you have any issues, you can ask the officer over there." She pointed to an officer standing in the hallway leading to the front door. "Is that alright?" He nodded.

Ryan led Officer Taylor into a room just off the kitchen while Gabe's attention was caught by flashes coming from the living room. While Ryan was all about the witnesses and story, Gabe was more hands-on. He excused himself from Mr. Farr.

"You done with stills of the victim yet?" Gabe asked the cameraman.

"Just getting some finals, sir," the technician gave a thumbs up. Gabe pulled out a pair of latex gloves from his coat and leaned over the body to get a better look at the woman's eyes. Her head rested on her left arm and short blonde locks stained reddish-brown cascaded over her face, partially covering her open right eye. He noted her right eye was unremarkable while the left was dilated wide. As he moved her head, a substantial pool of blood framed her skull and expanded on the Persian rug as liquids seeped from her mouth. Gabe moved over the right side of her head to the back of her neck and saw a curved handle made of bone protruding. He leaned back towards the front of her neck and squinted. The tiny glint of a blade emerged from the woman's voice box.

"Her husband called 911 when he found her," Ryan said as she came into the living room with Officer Taylor.

"Got a time of death yet?" Gabe looked to the technician.

"Have to wait for the coroner, but this was pretty fresh when we got here," the tech said.

"You think the husband could have done this?"

"He was appropriately hysterical when Taylor got here, and he hasn't found any indication thus far that the husband had anything to do with this," Ryan said.

"Still, the time…"

"Doubtful, Gabe. He came straight from work, and yes, before you ask, Taylor checked it out already. The time it took him to get from work to home to when he dialed 911 fits very tight. Seems likely he just walked in on this."

"What else have they found?"

"Taylor and I talked to some of the other officers that inspected the house, and best they can tell, there's no point of forced entry."

"Anything taken?" Gabe asked.

"Not a thing. They checked the drawers, the jewelry, a safe that Mr. Farr directed them to, and even took note of a couple of hundred dollars on the kitchen counter. None of it has been touched."

"So, she knew the person and let 'em in?"

"Would seem so."

"Where'd the crime scene tech go?" Gabe asked.

"I'm over here," he said, standing by the fireplace. "I'm just putting in some new film."

"What else have you done besides the stills?"

"We dusted the place for fingerprints, collected blood samples from the carpet she's lying on, and looked for any foreign fibers around and on top of her body. Honestly, anything left for me is up to what you need."

"Let's roll her over and get a better look at this wound then. I want to make sure to get some solid close-ups of the entry and exit point." Gabe directed the photographer as he shifted the body. "You got a decent macro capability on that thing?" The photographer nodded, speaking in monotone from behind the lens.

"I could capture the fillings in your teeth in low light with this baby."

Gabe grinned.

"Taylor also told me…"

"Hold up, Ryan, kids' right there. Let him tell me." Ryan's lips pursed as she turned and nodded to Taylor.

Taylor took in a deep breath. "Well, as the detective said, there is no sign of forced entry, and other officers have been talking to the neighbors for the last half hour or so. Honestly, but for the dead body lying there, there is simply nothing out of the ordinary."

"Any suspicious persons or suspects yet?" Gabe said as he pulled on the corpse's weight to get her high onto her left side for a better shot of the knife.

"The Farr's are new to the neighborhood, so nothing yet indicates they had any friends or enemies nearby."

"I've got it, agent," the photographer said. Gabe nodded, rolled the body slowly back onto her side where she started, then peeled off his latex gloves.

"Go ahead and take her out of here and make sure to fingerprint the entire knife once it's removed. The last tech put his prints all over the murder weapon and destroyed any lead on the killer."

"I'll supervise the removal myself," the technician said.

"That'll be great. Hey Ryan, I think we ought to get the husband down to the station…" Ryan stood by the fireplace and tilted her head. He walked over, looked into her eyes, and followed her gaze to a box frame containing a folded American flag along with over half of a dozen medals. Photographs of the dead woman in fatigues covered the mantle.

"She just got back about two months ago," Mister Farr said as he entered the living room. They turned to face the widower. Gabe made an effort to direct Mister Farr's attention from the zipper of the black bag closing over his wife's face, but Mister Farr shook off Gabe's arm. "She was a hero," he said. "Why would anyone do this?"

"I recognize some of the backgrounds in these photos," Gabe pointed to the mantle. "She was in Iraq, right?" Gabe waived away the men preparing to remove the body.

"For over a year. She spent most of her time in Baghdad and got outside the wire a time or two. She was involved in a rollover, hit two IEDs, and got one of those medals for surviving a firefight." Mister Farr held his hand up to his mouth and took a deep breath.

"So she was stationed at Fort Bliss then?" Ryan asked.

"No, we just moved here after her contract expired. They demobilized her here at Fort Bliss, and she liked the area so much that when they offered her a full-time position to work with outgoing units as an independent contractor, we jumped at the chance."

"So, she was a trainer then?" Gabe asked.

"Yeah," he said, "and decorating the fireplace was the first thing I did when we moved in. She was a little angry when I put all that stuff up there, but I am so…was…so…proud…"

"You see her yesterday morning?" Gabe asked.

"Yeah, I got her up at seven."

"Was there anything out of the ordinary that she said or did when she got up?"

"No."

"Was there anything different about her normal morning routine?"

"No, it was just like every other day. She got up, showered, got her uniform on, grabbed her phone, kissed me, and headed off to the base."

"Did you guys talk at all while she was at work?"

"Not once."

"When did you see her next?" Ryan asked.

"I saw her when she got home from the base yesterday afternoon around four, and then I headed to work."

"What time did you get home from work then?" Gabe asked.

"I work from five in the afternoon to two in the morning down at the grocery store, so I usually get home around two-thirty to two forty-five in the morning. Being the new guy, I get the worst shift."

"But you came home just after one tonight." Officer Taylor said. Gabe glared at the young officer. He stepped back into the hallway and flipped notes.

"Well, she called me about six or so and told me she wasn't feeling well. She had a massive headache, and I told her to call a doctor since her migraines are pretty severe and only go away with a prescription." He paused a moment. "You know…I guess she did say something about her eyes giving her problems in addition to the pain in her head."

"What kind of problem?" Gabe asked.

"She wasn't too clear, but it was something with her eyes she'd never had before. I'm not sure if you've ever had migraines, but these little invisible worms seem to dance in your vision when they get terrible, but these weren't like that. She said they were more like distortions…or colors…I can't remember."

"That's alright," Ryan said.

"But she was pretty worked up with what was going on, so that's when I pushed her to call her doctor. I was behind on unloading a produce truck, but I told her I'd call her back. I tried to call her again a few times, but she didn't answer, so a little before one, my boss noticed my concern, and he let me go home early."

"Do you know if she called the doctor?" Ryan asked.

"I assume she did."

"Where's your phone?" Gabe asked.

"We don't have a landline, but her cell phone is in the kitchen. I saw it when I got home." The group moved into the kitchen, and Officer Taylor pointed to several plastic bags on a table. Gabe sifted through the bags and picked up the one marked 'kitchen cell.' Donning a fresh pair of gloves, Gabe reached in, pushed the green power button on the device, and waited. The screen lit up, exposing a photograph of Farr holding an M4. Gabe punched the menu button and began checking recent calls.

"What's your number, sir?"

"765-3440, why?" he asked.

"And what time did you say she called you?"

"It would've been around six." Gabe clicked on the husband's phone number on the screen, and the phone's memory indicated a call was made to the husband at 6:09 p.m. the day before. Gabe clicked some more.

"Shows you made four more calls to her that went unanswered between 9:30 p.m. and about 12:40 a.m. last night. That sound correct?"

"Yeah."

"Alright," Gabe said, "and she made just one more call around 11:30 p.m. or so that lasted around twenty-five minutes."

"Must have been the doctor," Farr said.

Gabe turned the phone slowly towards Ryan. "It's a bunch of fours."

CHAPTER 6

EYE OF DEATH

The fluorescent bulbs cast a stale white aura across the decomposing bodies. Gabe was not accustomed to seeing a morgue full of patrons, but it had been a tough week on the El Paso police department as growing conflicts from drug trafficking spilled over the border from Mexico. Less than twenty-four hours earlier, an elaborate wedding turned gunfight on the south side of town brought ten corpses to the room. Gabe had seen the reports of the massacre and knew the instigator, a lone gunman, had been killed along with nine other revelers. Most likely a gang hit or a drug deal gone wrong, it was sad to see so many innocent victims caught in the crossfire.

Gabe walked past a body riddled with tiny holes, evidenced by straws sticking out in various directions to show entry angles. A few feet further was what remained of a toddler who had suffered grievous wounds to his torso and face. As Gabe approached the farthest part of the room, the soft hum of a band saw tearing crisply into a skull caught his attention. A misty white powder dashed away from the saw and instantly danced into the air around the men conducting the autopsy.

"How far have we gotten?" Gabe asked as the doctor set down the saw and turned. Having completed far too many autopsies together in the past few weeks, the doctor shot Agent Moss a disheartened look then motioned across the room to the entrance.

"You must stop bringing her in here if you want us to be friends," the pathologist said as he stared at Ryan, who was still at the door. "She's going to make a mess of my pickle bucket," Doctor Cunningham frowned.

Ryan began to heave.

"Honestly, I didn't know a human could hold that much food inside. You two stop at a buffet on the way here for an early breakfast?"

"No doctor, we swung by the office and then came straight here." Gabe watched as Ryan and the pickle bucket made their way into the hall then turned back just in time to catch the doctor pick up a pancake, roll it, and pop it into his mouth.

"Guess it's just you and me eating what I brought for us then," he pointed to the stack of cakes. While the acrid smell of death never bothered Gabe as it most often did with Ryan, the casual segue from watching Ryan chuck to the doctor eating pancakes brought about a slight bit of regurgitation. Gabe made a distracting move towards the subject on the table.

"Anything of interest yet?"

The doctor's attention returned to the skull in his hand. He tugged with no success.

"You haven't missed much." Cunningham grabbed a small chisel, placed it against the line along the skull, and tapped with a tiny mallet. With immense focus and routine precision, he worked his way around the cut in the skull to sever remaining connections. The doctor's penchant for disappearing into the immediate task at hand always unnerved Ryan. She found him distant and absent-minded when he set about any particular task and was bothered further by his inability to hold a normal conversation during those times he did speak. When he wasn't silent, the doctor made off-color comments and jabs at Ryan that Gabe recognized as a budding crush, one which the doctor had no clue how to develop. His awkwardness around Ryan could be found in the halls of most junior high schools, but typically older men figured their way out of difficulties around women in their early teens.Unbeknownst to either of them, the problems at personal relationships with the living bore more deeply into Doctor Cunningham's persona.

Once one of the most prominent heart surgeons following his gradua-tion at the top of his class from Johns Hopkins, he struggled to find his way through residency as he could not create any bonds with superiors and those around him. After initial setbacks with non-sedated patients, he found a home in the silence of surgery and built a reputation for carrying out ground-breaking procedures that saved many lives. As his reputation expanded, so did his duties, and soon he was no longer able to avoid speaking to families before and after surgeries. Following one such unsuccessful experimental procedure on a ninety-year-old man, his elderly wife voiced her displeasure in a crude diatribe before dozens of people in a waiting room. Cornered by her words, he let loose on the old woman, costing him not only his job but his future with pioneering surgery. More than anything else, he wanted a return to the silence of surgery. Eventually, he found solace in the mortuary sciences, pulling parts from subjects that would never talk back.

With his task of freeing the skull completed, Gabe saw his opening to reengage. "So you didn't start with the chest this time?"

"No, we decided to open Ms. Farr's chest last since it's impossible to roll her fully on her back with the knife handle in her neck," Cunningham said with a noticeable glare. Gabe looked away and noticed the evidence tech that had been at the crime scene standing just over the shoulder of one of Cunningham's interns.

"Just had to make sure the doctor and I didn't screw up with the knife, didn't you?" the tech said.

"I trusted you...just not sure I trusted him," Gabe pointed at the doctor. The crisp sound of the skull pulling cleanly from the head drew Gabe's attention back to the dead woman.

"Nothing abnormal there," Cunningham said as he circled his gaze around the exposed parts of the brain, looking for trauma. He pulled out a long knife and stepped around the edge of the table, sinking the instrument deep along the radius of her skull to sever any matter holding the brain in place. Setting aside the knife, he tugged the pink mass from its casing, exposing the interior walls of the skull. He inspected the parts of the brain that had been unexposed on his initial review as he moved towards a scale. Satisfied with no evidence of trauma, he placed the brain in a tray and instructed his intern to catalog the weight. Returning to the body, Cunningham bent over and examined the skull's interior with a small flashlight. He reached once more for a thin knife on the tray and began to cut away at the base of the woman's neck to open up the space leading to the murder weapon's location. The gap widened as the doctor chiseled.

"That is fascinating!" Cunningham waived Gabe over to look, and Gabe gestured to the tech to snap photos. Matter blocking the view gone, Cunningham's flashlight glistened on the blade at the base of her throat.

"Take a look at how the blade is blocking almost the entire throat cavity!" Gabe was surprised by the doctor's excitement. A man who'd conducted hundreds of autopsies over his career should hardly be impressed by a simple knife wound through the back of the neck.

"Let's see what sort of damage this baby did." Cunningham turned the woman further onto her stomach, grabbed a ten blade, and made four individual cuts around the base where the blade had entered at the back of the woman's neck. He instructed his intern to work on two of the cuts as they both peeled back the skin, cut down through the muscle and sinew, and opened the space around the blade's entry like a blooming flower. The intern suctioned out some dried-up blood that remained along the interior of the throat to clear the view as the doctor stepped back to give ample room to the photographer. Following a dozen flashes, the tech stepped back, and Gabe took his place alongside the doctor.

"Looks like it might have worked through the C1 and C2 vertebrae doctor and might have shattered the dens," the intern said from over Gabe's shoulder. Doctor Cunningham cut away a tiny bit more at one of the points.

"Does seem to have taken that out and worked right through there rather cleanly, doesn't it?" Cunningham said.

"Translation, please?"

"Sorry, break that down as simple as you can for super-agent here." The intern moved next to Gabe as the doctor stepped back. He pointed.

"The entry point at the back of the neck was right between the two vertebrae on top of the spinal column." Gabe's light wandered around the hole.

"I got that, but what did you say about the shattered part?"

"Do you mean the dens?"

"Yes, the dens."

"The dens is a little bone like a tooth that sticks up and allows the head to pivot." Despite its size, the bone is quite strong. If you look in there…" the intern shined his light, "…you can see what I'm talking about. It's obliterated. In the absence of some genetic abnormality, that normally takes a great deal of force to break that little bone."

"How much force exactly?" Gabe asked.

"Crashing a race car at a hundred and fifty miles an hour into a wall with no restraints; violent helmet to helmet contact in a football game. Something like that ought to do it," he said. Gabe nodded and noticed Cunningham ingest another pancake.

"Nice explanation," Cunningham said with his mouth full. "But as one of those causations is not evident here, whoever did this knew what they were doing."

"Why do you say that?" Gabe asked.

"Every centimeter the blade traveled as it went in caused one of a half-dozen catastrophic interruptions in this woman's body, any one of which could have killed…"

"Of course," Gabe said. The doctor's look indicated he wasn't finished.

"…her. The person doing this is a professional trained to place this blade precisely where he did to cause maximum damage. This wasn't some run-of-the-mill thief. This guy wanted her dead."

"An assassin?" Gabe asked.

"She's tough…" Cunningham pulled up her sleeves and pressed on her muscles, "…so this wasn't some street thug that pulled this off. Due to the lack of bruises on her along with no signs of struggle with her fingers or hands, and how this knife is situated, someone trained in the fine art of assassination carried this out."

"A few more shots of the body right now before you tug that out?" the tech asked, holding up his camera. The doctor nodded. Gabe, the doctor, and his intern stepped back from the table as the tech started snapping photos at her feet and moved up along the corpse to her neckline. He streamed two dozen shots of the cuts around the base of the knife before settling at the top of the skull. Gabe watched as tiny flashes of light from the camera poked through the incisions around the base of the blade. The tech rose and nodded to the doctor.

"Let's see what we've got here." The doctor tugged on the knife handle as the tech streamed photographs.

The knife didn't move.

"Little bugger's in there pretty good." Cunningham picked up a pair of forceps, reached down through the skull's open cavity, and began working both his hands. "I think some of that shattered bone trapped part of the blade in there."

"That could be why the killer left it in there," Gabe said.

Cunningham nodded. "And if that's true, we can surmise the killer was in a hurry to get away when the husband arrived home.

"Unless the husband was the killer," Gabe said.

"I thought it was clear her husband was at work?" said the tech.

"Everyone's a suspect…"

"Assuming then for the detective's sake that the husband didn't do this," Cunningham said, "had he arrived even a few minutes earlier, he might be laying here alongside her." After over a half-minute struggle, the blade came free. Cunningham held it up for all to see.

"Looks like a standard seven-inch blade," Gabe said as Cunningham motioned to his intern to get the tape measure.

"You familiar with these types of knives?" Cunningham asked as he pointed to a box of gloves for Gabe to don before handing him the knife.

"Well, I collected knives for years during my time in the service, but I've never seen anything with a handle like this before." The curved handle was smooth in Gabe's hand as he held the tip of the blade between two of his fingers and rotated the grip in his right. Despite excessive amounts of caked blood covering the blade and parts of the handle, the white of the grip was quite distinctive. "If I didn't know better, I'd say this handle is whale tooth."

"Whale tooth?" asked Cunningham. "They use that?"

"Teeth from sperm whales were used all the time before all those treaties in the 1970s, but yeah, today for the right price, you can still find this. We should still have this tested, though, to make sure what this is."

"But what's that?" Cunningham shined his light along the blade, exposing part of an inscription partially covered in crusted blood.

"Looks like writing." Gabe reached for a towel on the table and rubbed the length of the blade. With some force, the last remnants of blood detached. "In search of monsters to destroy," whispered Gabe.

"What the hell does that mean?" the tech asked. Gabe shook his head and rotated the blade as photos were taken. Once turned over, Gabe used the towel to expose a diagram of an eye adorned with light rays shooting in all directions.

"The eye of providence," said Cunningham coolly.

"The what?"

"The eye of providence," he repeated. "It's on my college fraternity crest. We learned more about that eye than you would ever want to know."

Gabe couldn't imagine the doctor would have been permitted anywhere near a fraternity during college, and the doctor caught Gabe's doubting glare. "It's on the dollar bill Gabe, you know, over the pyramid on the back. There are dozens of variations, but I'd gamble my salary the one right there is the eye of providence."

"So, what does it mean?"

"Generally, the eye of God," Cunningham said.

"So, tell me then, wise one, what does the eye have to do with the writing on the other side of the blade here?"

"I just cut 'em up, agent. I don't get paid to solve 'em," he smiled.

"Here you go," Gabe handed the knife to the tech. "Have them run the phrase and get me some more information about the eye of providence."

"Got it," the tech said. He dropped the knife into a clear bag marked on both sides with biohazard symbols before placing the open end into a heat sealer. Gabe walked back to the body as the doctor and intern prepared to open Farr's chest.

"Just a few more questions before I get out of here, doctor?"

"Shoot."

"Is there any way you can determine if those cuts on Mallon or that John Doe guy we brought in here a few weeks back were made by a blade like that one?"

"Now, which John Doe are we talking about here? I assume you mean the one that Ryan brought in here by herself two weeks ago and not the one you two brought in last week that we haven't figured out an exact cause of death for yet?"

"Ryan's Doe. The first one with the knife wounds. His name is Todd Harris. We just got his ID back yesterday."

"Well, I took pretty good notes on the Mallon and Doe, sorry, Harris autopsies, and if I remember correctly, the blade cuts had some similarities to one another, so I might be able to come up with something for you." Cunningham grabbed a blade.

"Sorry," Gabe raised his hand, "but I do have one more favor to ask of you if I might."

"Shoot again."

"This may not be possible, but is there any way you can determine if Farr here was suffering from severe migraines or a problem with her eyes at the time of her death."

"I don't follow," Cunningham said, taking the time to grab one more pancake amidst the questioning.

"Farr called her husband last evening before she died and said she was suffering from something worse than a migraine…some sort of…"

"There's nothing I could find that would indicate…"

"…images or distortions."

Cunningham took a moment to swallow the pancake. "I'm not even sure where to start. I'm not an eye doctor," Cunningham said, "and I've got seven bodies the D.A. needs carved up by the close of business today. I'll be lucky to get a half-hour break between now and then."

"I understand," Gabe said, "but if you have time?"

"Yeah, sure," he waived as he turned back to the body, "I'll see what I can do."

Gabe nodded. "I've got some more work to finish up at the office today before I head home to get some sleep, so buzz me if you find anything," Gabe said.

"Will do," Cunningham said. "Oh, and make sure Ryan gets me my pickle bucket back…oh, and it better be clean!"

PART 2

PATHS

CHAPTER 7

FRESH LEADS

Stump's warm tongue worked its' way across, over, and along Gabe's cheek. He rolled over onto his right shoulder and pulled his pillow close, trying to escape the unwelcome bath. Loose change vibrating on his nightstand caught his eye first and his ears next. When he was asleep, calls were never welcome, but he realized the hour was likely a reasonable one upon noticing a hint of daylight creeping through the blinds. He flipped open the noisemaker.

"Yes?" he said.

"You know you could have called to check on me."

"If my mother were hurling into a bucket like that, I might not call her for days," Gabe said. "You're strong woman. You don't need my sympathy."

"Well, then you could have at least called with a report on the autopsy."

Gabe pushed his pup away, sending him out of the room. "I was beat, Ryan, and I had no desire to interrupt you from your quality time with the toilet."

"I went to the doctor after I left you at the morgue, Gabe. I ate something bad."

"Whatever, Ryan, I figured we'd catch up after we both got some rest. What time is it anyway?"

"It's after noon."

"No?"

"Yes, you slept away most of yesterday and a good chunk of today." Gabe grinned. "And now you need to get over here so we can move on some of these leads I've got brewing." Gabe flipped on his television to check the time. The insipid cheeriness of the weatherman on the noon news verified his partner's claim. He made his way into the bathroom.

"So what've you got, Ryan?"

"I called Cunningham myself this morning, and he told me you asked about tying up the knife wounds on Farr with some of our other bodies."

"Thought you'd like that."

"I did. So anyway, when I called, Cunningham had just finished with his notes after reviewing his report on Mallon's and Harris' knife wounds."

"And?"

"The wounds on both of them came from a blade of a similar length as the knife used on Farr."

"How similar?"

"In his opinion, the holes in each body matched the diameter of the blade exactly. Also, the depth of the cuts into Mallon's kidneys and Harris' chest suggest at least a seven-inch blade."

"That's pretty helpful."

"Best he could do without having the bodies anymore, and I told him he did a good job even though he kept apologizing for cremating the bodies. Guy just doesn't see the big picture sometimes. He does well, I compliment him, and still, he finds a way to get all defensive about not doing more. I don't get him." Gabe caught his phone as it slipped from between his shoulder and ear as he fought with a stick of deodorant. "You alright over there?" Ryan asked.

"I'm trying to make myself smell good with this phone stuck to my ear, and I'm losing the battle."

"I'd be more worried about your wardrobe than your body odor."

"We all can't have a closet full of hoodies for each occasion." Ryan was silent. "So did Cunningham tell you if he found anything with Farr's eyes?"

"Nothing." Her anger often seeped out in short and stiff sentences.

"Not a thing?"

"Nothing," she said again. Then her curiosity won over. "Why…what was he doing with her eyes?"

"It's probably nothing, but I asked him if he could find any evidence of problems with Farr's eyes when she died."

"He didn't say a word."

"I'm sure he'll let us know if he finds anything," Gabe said as he dropped a cup of kibble into Stump's bowl.

"If you're about done over there, I would like to get to Fort Bliss for that appointment we set up regarding John Doe number two we found the other week."

"Yeah, but hey, now that we have named our first John Doe Todd Harris, can we just call John Doe number two, John Doe? It'll help keep all these bodies straight."

"Sure, Gabe, John Doe number two is now just John Doe."

"Thanks. So, anything new I need to know about Doe and his connection to Fort Bliss?

"As I was telling you just before my head ended up in a pickle bucket, a first sergeant over at Fort Bliss called me after reading a blog article about John Doe."

"A blog article?"

"That's what I said. One of our retired officers has a blog site where he discusses and dissects murders around El Paso."

"Really?" Gabe said.

"It's a popular site and has been useful in solving some of our cases over the last few years."

"How?"

"Well, the blog discusses the deaths and dives into the manner and methods in which people are killed. When something remains unsolved, or we have an anonymous body, departments often give out certain information to the blogger, and from time to time, someone that reads the blog comes forward with relevant information."

"Sounds like a resource all police should have," Gabe said.

"Maybe, but it's hard to find bloggers you can trust with certain information. So as I was saying, a first sergeant at Fort Bliss thinks John Doe might be one of his soldiers that went AWOL."

"They usually do a good job of knowing where their guys are," Gabe said.

"Well, I don't know about that, but he didn't hesitate to invite us to the base to speak with his commander, Captain Kyle, in building A23."

"So what time are we heading to Bliss?"

"As soon as you can pick me up." Gabe grinned. He should have known the answer.

"I'm leaving now." He flipped the phone closed and tossed it onto his bed as he made his way into the bathroom. A muffled buzz emanated from the bed.

"What?" Gabe answered. "You need some donuts too?"

There was a long pause.

"Agent Moss?" the male voice said. Gabe winced.

"Sorry, sir, I thought you were someone else."

"Does that mean I don't get donuts?" Ryan's boss said.

Gabe didn't answer.

"So you and my detective been hiding out at the Donut Hut then? That's why I don't get any updates from you two? And here I thought that was just a lingering urban folklore, cops and donuts. Didn't know the joke applied to the FBI as well?"

"No, sir, we've been busy. I can assure you of that," Gabe said.

"Well, when I don't hear from either of you in three days, and Ryan's not answering my calls, I get annoyed. So, tell me, Gabe, where are you two on figuring out why bodies are piling up in my town?"

"We have some leads," Gabe said, "including a knife found lodged hard in a victim yesterday and a possible new lead from Fort Bliss regarding John Doe number two we found a few weeks ago. We also know similar knife wounds were the causes of death on Mallon, Harris, and now..."

"Who the heck is Harris?"

"The first John Doe we found in the street with the knife wounds in his chest a few days after I arrived."

"I wasn't told we had a name on the first John Doe. See," the Chief said, "this is the kind of stuff I need to know!" There was a moment of silence. "Go ahead."

"So anyway, this knife we found last night might be the same one used to kill Harris and Mallon. We also have found a common phone number on the cell phones of Caldwell and Harris and another similar number on a phone last night. We're not entirely sure how that ties into anything at this moment, but we're working on it."

"You know I don't like this," the Chief said.

"Sorry?"

"I'm not sure if it's you or Ryan, but I'm thinking maybe you're a bad influence on her." Gabe frowned. "She's never been one not to call me before."

"I think we're both a little overwhelmed at how fast this is all happening," Gabe said.

"The great savior from the FBI can't handle it?" Gabe fought the urge to reply as he wanted.

"We're processing a ton of leads, sir, but I can assure you we are on top of it."

"You need more help?"

"We can handle this, sir, and no…we don't need any more help."

"You know the only reason I allowed you in on this was that some bigwig in Washington called the Mayor of El Paso and demanded it. They insisted you were the best at answering the unanswerable."

"I have no doubt you could be doing this by yourself, and I appreciate the opportunity to assist, so let us keep at it, and I promise you'll get results."

"Don't patronize me, son. I just want my detective to fill me in from time to time…that's all. Tell Ryan I need to hear from her every forty-eight hours." The voice started to fade. "Hell, I didn't even know Doe had a name for God's…."

Gabe heard a click.

* * *

At the gates of Fort Bliss, Gabe held his identification and badge out the window as a young sergeant stared at the picture of the clean-shaven man and strained to find similarities with the figure behind the wheel. The sergeant copied information on a clipboard while other guards wandered around Gabe's vehicle. Gabe chuckled to himself as Ryan struggled with her wallet as she insisted to a specialist that she did have identification.

"Nervous?" Gabe asked.

"Um, no," she fumbled. "There," she pinched the card tight between her fingers. "I knew it was in there." The guard grabbed hold of her license and copied down her information. When finished, the guard returned the license to Ryan, who slid it behind her badge. "I'll remember it there."

"Sir," said the guard at Gabe's window, "if you could follow the specialist and pull over there for a quick sweep of the vehicle." Gabe nodded and followed the walking soldier from under the large brick archway to a white awning that shaded his vehicle. Another soldier approached Ryan's side of the car and asked them both to step out. Gabe checked messages on his phone while Ryan, who had little experience with the military, was transfixed by the scripted dance. Gabe noticed from her body language that questions about this process were building up in her mind.

"Please place this up there on the dash of your vehicle," the specialist said, handing a placard to Gabe when the search was complete.

"Thank you, specialist," Gabe said. The pair got back in the car and drove onto the main road.

"Is that a joke?" Ryan asked. She pointed to a giant sign flashing '0 days since our last OWI'.

"No, I'm afraid it's not. Those are operating while intoxicated signs that are put up at every base so everyone can see the military is serious about drinking and driving."

"No, not that, I mean what it says. That can't be true?"

"You think this base has a bunch of saints on it?"

"Well, no, but come on, zero days since they caught someone for drunk driving?"

"Back at Fort Leavenworth, we had one of those signs, and I can't remember a time when the number showed more than six days."

"That's incredible."

"They're training for war," Gabe laughed. "What do you think we do to release stress?"

The roads did not follow any north/south designations, and as they moved further into the base, Ryan inquired about every building, acronym, and vehicle the pair passed.

"I've never really spent much time around the military," Ryan said. "This place is fascinating."

"And if you keep asking questions," Gabe said, "you'll learn everything you need to know about this place in an hour when what I really need you to do right now is to look for building A23."

Ryan paused with her questions from the tour and searched for building numbers as Gabe's car crept along. The five-floor brick buildings that came into view on her left, with basketball courts between them, reminded Ryan of the cookie-cutter college dorms at Evansville. Among them was their destination.

CHAPTER 8

JOHN DOE TWO

"Sorry to keep you waiting," a young captain said as he opened his office door and worked his way around the desk, "but I was trying to instruct one of my lieutenants on knot tying. He's heading to air assault school in a few weeks, and he's a bit nervous."

"No problem," Gabe said. "I know they kick you out if you make more than two mistakes on tying or identifying problems with knots. The kid should be nervous."

"That's right, Agent Moss," the captain extended a hand, "my first sergeant told me you were former military."

"I spent about seven years with various MOSs and did a few tours overseas before starting with the FBI. I never made it to jump school, though. They don't need as many guys dropping from planes anymore."

"In that, you are correct." The captain sat down and directed the pair to join him. "So, I've been told something on a blog site might have led you to discover where my AWOL soldier's been hiding out. Where'd you find him, down in Tijuana...running around in New Orleans?"

Ryan leaned forward and extended her hand. "Detective Rebecca Ryan with the El Paso police department."

"Oh, sorry...here I am rushing things." The captain shook Ryan's hand while looking at Gabe. "She the lead?"

"She likes to think so," Gabe nodded.

Ryan glared. "We're a team."

"Good enough then. So, what're you guys doing with my AWOL soldier?"

"We found an African American male, mid-twenties, with a big scar from his temple to his chin on the right side of his face."

"Sounds like my guy. Where's he at?" Ryan handed the captain a photo and a manila envelope. He studied the picture then pulled out a death certificate. The captain looked up slowly into Ryan's eyes as the certificate faltered back onto his desk.

"Is that him?" she asked.

"Yes," Captain Kyle replied, "but my first sergeant's email said you found him…never anything about him being dead." Creases on Captain Kyle's forehead formed, and his face paled as his lips pursed.

Ryan fidgeted in her chair and looked at Gabe. He pushed her gaze back to the captain.

"I'm really sorry about this captain," Ryan said. "We assumed your sergeant told you that the blog site was about unsolved murders in El Paso."

"Lines of communication clearly crossed up there, captain; sorry to spring this on you," Gabe said.

The captain nodded and pulled in a deep breath.

"Marlin," Captain Kyle pointed at the photograph partially covered by the death certificate. "That's Marlin's scar, no doubt." The captain chuckled. "All the glory of scars and marks from war, some inside, some outside. He got to bring his home for all the world to see.

Ryan's mouth opened for another question, but Gabe grabbed her shoulder and shook his head. She retreated.

"There's nothing really glorious about the whole damn thing. One day out on patrol with the sun beating down on us like every other day, and he just trips." The captain smiled. "Hundred days of patrols through the most dangerous streets in the world, close calls with IEDs, sniper fire a few times, half a dozen intense firefights, and the jackass just trips on some trash. We're all standing around laughing at him lying face down on the ground…gun trapped under his gut…fifty-pound pack on his back…sort of looked like a turtle in the sand squirming around." The captain shook his head. "He started laughing, and we could see puffs of that damn grainy crap they call sand sifting up into the air with each giggle that trickled out of his mouth. He just laid there for a minute as we all cut loose, then finally rose to expose blood covering his entire face. The laughing ended, medics ran to him, and we all took cover out of fear that some random sniper round happened to catch our friend in the head. Turns out no bullet though, just an old busted up bottle lying on the ground that gouged into his cheek and carved this distinctive mark down the side of his face." The captain's finger followed the scar in the picture.

"We're really sorry about your loss, captain."

"I've lost men Agent Moss…as I'm sure you have as well." Gabe nodded.

"Anything you can tell us about what Marlin was doing when he went AWOL. Where he's from, where he was going, why he left?" Gabe paused as the captain pulled in another deep breath. "We can take a few minutes if you want."

"No…just give me a second. I've just never lost a man here in the States. I'll be…I'll be fine," the captain spun around and grabbed hold of a large brown folder from a pile of papers on his desk. He turned back around and opened it. "Specialist Marlin Wade is from Detroit and joined the military five years ago. Not married, no children, and his mother is his only next of kin listed."

"How long has he been stationed here?" Gabe asked.

"He did his advanced infantry training here and then joined up with my artillery unit not long after. He was with me when we went to Iraq last year, and we returned together a month and a half ago. After we finished with our refrad process…"

"Sorry, what?" Ryan asked.

"Sorry ma'am, our return from active duty."

"Thanks."

"As I was saying, when we got back to Bliss, most of the guys took off on leave for two weeks. Only the first sergeant and I, along with three unlucky specialists who ran into civilian legal trouble, stayed behind. Marlin left with the rest of the soldiers in our unit, but when he didn't return, we put out some feelers with law enforcement in hopes of dragging him in." Gabe nodded.

"So, you coded him as AWOL?"

"Had to. You know how it is, sir. No one keeps in contact with us while on leave, and we don't usually hear from any of the soldiers until the day they get back on base. Still, sometimes after an overseas deployment, a unit has difficulty getting every soldier back from leave on time, and we have to code them properly…good soldier or not."

"Did you have any problems with Marlin Wade before?" Ryan asked.

"None," the captain said.

"Did he tell you exactly where he was going?" Gabe asked.

"He signed out and was heading home to Detroit. He gave us his itinerary," Kyle handed Gabe a sheet of paper, "and he was to fly back into the El Paso airport exactly fifteen days after he left. We called his mother's house initially when he didn't return but got no answer."

"If you could get us that number?"

"Sure, ma'am. Hell, guys in my unit always joked around overseas that it was safer there than it was on the streets of Detroit. Guess I didn't give that saying much credibility until now."

"What'd you say?" Ryan asked.

"Detroit. The mean streets…the gangs…I assume he got caught up in something bad. He always told us he lived in a rough neighborhood, but…

"No captain…he was found right here in El Paso," Ryan said.

"Here?"

"Just a few miles from your front gate."

"That…doesn't make sense," the captain said.

"Any reason you can think of why he might stay here? Gabe asked. The captain stared over the shoulders of the detectives and began to shake his head.

"I can't come up with a single reason why he would have deviated from his plan to return to Detroit. Besides, even if he did decide to stay here, he was a squared away soldier who would have informed us of any change."

"Is there anyone he was close with who might know why he stayed here?" Ryan asked.

"No," the captain said. "None of my unit is from around here, and everyone who was allowed to go on leave made an effort to distance themselves from this place and each other."

"If you think of any names, can you call us?"

"Of course. So, if you don't mind, sir, how exactly did he die?" The captain looked at Ryan, and she turned to Gabe.

"Well, captain, we're not really sure just yet."

"How is that possible, sir?"

"He was found in an alley with no visible signs of injury."

"No signs of injury? Heart attack then...a stroke?"

"All I've been told after the autopsy is there is no evidence of foul play and no cause of death that could be determined. Every unnatural cause was excluded as well as most natural causes, but we're still awaiting his toxicology reports to shed some light on this hopefully."

"This just seems all so surreal," the captain said.

"As he said, we're looking at all possible causes right now, and we'll find out how this happened," Ryan replied.

"What unit was he with overseas?" Gabe asked, hoping to shift the conversation back to the practical.

"He was in the five of the fifty-second ADA Battalion, under my command," Kyle said. "We had a smattering of military intelligence guys from the 204th and some other National Guard units attached to us as well."

"What was the mission?"

"We trained for an air defense mission in northern Kuwait and ended up doing a little bit of everything around a base on the south side of Baghdad. The closest town was a village full of shattered clay houses known as Tuwaitha."

"I've never heard of that," Ryan said. Both Gabe and the captain laughed.

"Should you have heard of it, Ryan? Honestly, how many people can name a city in Iraq other than Baghdad? Heck, I was there for years, and even I've never heard of it."

"Neither had I," Captain Kyle said, "but I looked it up online before we left and saw it was one of the places Iran bombed the heck out of not long before our war started. Thanks to those bombings, the village was full of hardened and distrusting people that fought with the Marines for an entire month when we first arrived. Like most villages, after time, they realized the Americans were not leaving, and backroom deals were made to end the violence which permitted us to set up a tiny base along what became a major supply route. After the first year or so of the war, things were rather peaceful in that part of the region."

"So, what exactly did you do there in Tuwaitha?"

"We mostly carried out a Mayor's cell mission."

"I don't follow," Ryan said.

"The mayor's cell runs a base," Gabe said. "They act like a mayor's office would for a small town. They keep the food coming in, the lights on, and the bathrooms from overflowing."

"Exactly," Captain Kyle said, "but in addition to those duties, our group also conducted some missions outside the wire doing convoy security and pulling patrols of the town every couple of days."

"Were you in command of the entire base?" Gabe asked.

"My unit made up most of the base, sir, so technically yes, but for operational reasons, there was a lieutenant colonel in charge. Overall, we had about a hundred soldiers at the base, so I knew pretty much everyone."

"Did you have a Master Sergeant Kay Farr in your unit?" Ryan asked. Captain Kyle looked over Ryan's shoulder in search of answers. He returned to her sightline with his head moving side to side.

"Not a name I recognize, but I can do some checking to see if she might have been attached to us for a time."

"What about a Todd Harris?"

His head continued side to side. "Name isn't one I recognize either agent, sorry."

"No problem, captain, but if you could look, that would be great," Gabe said. He looked down at his notes then over to Ryan. She shook her head and began to rise.

"We truly are sorry for the loss of your soldier," Ryan said.

"Thanks, ma'am."

"I'll forward over a copy of his death certificate and his personal items that were on him as soon as we've processed anything we might need for evidence," Gabe said.

"That would help us get our paperwork moving along, thanks."

"Also, even though you've identified our John Doe as Marlin Wade, we'll need his mother or another relative to fly down here and make an identification before we can wrap things up from our end and release the body," Gabe said.

"I'll have my first sergeant contact you later this afternoon to get that going. We need to make some calls to our casualty assistance people so they can notify his mother." Ryan waived slightly as she moved towards the door, and Gabe extended a hand to the captain.

"Do me a favor?" The captain's grip tightened.

"Sure," Gabe said.

"When you find out who is responsible for this…you let me know?"

"You bet."

* * *

The detectives shared only the sounds of their footfalls as they walked down the hallway and descended the stairs leading to their car.

"It would have been helpful if the first sergeant told the captain the soldier we were coming to see him about was deceased," said Ryan. Gabe's keys rattled as he removed them from his pocket.

"We weren't even sure John Doe was their guy, Ryan. We shouldn't go around delivering damming news before we have to."

"But that look on the captain's face. That was just…"

"He's dealt with death before in Iraq, Ryan, but yeah, this is different. You spend your days in Iraq praying no one dies under your command, and then you come home to the safety of the States only to have one of your guys get killed. It'll take him some time to process this one."

Ryan stared back at the building as Gabe slid into the driver's seat. She didn't rush to get into the car.

CHAPTER 9

UNSOLVED MYSTERIES

A steaming glop of beans fell onto Gabe's plate as he pulled the Coney dog away from his face to admire the mess of food that, for once, was not on his shirt. Chewing the Midwestern comfort food he'd loved since childhood, Gabe was mildly self-conscious of the childish humor he felt watching the bean goo as it slid out of the back of the bun each time he took a bite. It had been several weeks since he'd been able to experience such juvenile entertainment in anonymity and knew it was only a matter of time before someone would interrupt this low-rent yet deeply satisfying culinary moment.

"There you are," Ryan's voice broke his dining spell.

Gabe didn't look up.

"I've been texting you for the past half hour. Where've you been?" Gabe exposed a grin and shrugged his shoulders.

"Hiding," he smiled.

"What?"

"I was trying to get away for a while. You know, hiding."

"So you got my messages?"

"No," he said. "Well yeah, I'm sure they're on my phone there, but it's off."

"What if there was some emergency?"

"If I saw you bolting out of the PX looking all panicked, I would have figured it out." He broke the last remaining bit of the chili dog into two pieces.

Ryan shook her head as she sat down, slid the yellow note pad across the table, and rotated it for Gabe to read.

"Well, while you were dodging me, I spent the last twenty minutes writing down everything that ties up our dead..." Gabe's raised finger forced her to pause. He stood up, finger still erect, and walked towards the chili dog stand. Ryan's brow lowered as she watched Gabe joke with the vendor while dropping a hand into his pants pocket to retrieve a wad of money. Gabe handed the cash across the counter and received in return a large bowl of fried potatoes drenched in cheese. "You're going to eat those too?" Ryan said as he returned.

"Not for me, Ryan." He placed the mound on the yellow notepad and slid both items over to her.

"That's kind of you, Gabe, but I think I've had enough frozen potatoes and processed cheese for a lifetime."

"Then sit and look at it. YOU need to relax. This is one of the things I do to relax."

"I don't always have..."

"We have the time, Ryan, so eat. Honestly, detective, now that I think about it, I can't recall a single day where I saw you just sit back and turn off that brain of yours. I don't want to talk work right now, so either eat or sit and stare at the food for as long as it would have taken for you to eat it."

Ryan's pursed lips gave way to a slight smile as she uncrossed her legs, scooted the bench closer to the table, and pulled at the less cheesy pieces of potato.

"I do relax sometimes," she said.

"Work isn't relaxing, Ryan. That's all you do. What do you do for fun?"

"Re...lax...ation and I don't get together very often."

"That doesn't make any sense. Why not?"

"Well, I don't plan it in my day, Gabe...I just sometimes catch a Cowboys game and have a beer with some chips, those sort of things," she said.

"I can honestly say that's the first I've ever heard you even like football or beer."

"Well," she looked down and began to fiddle with a french fry drowning in cheese, "there's just not enough time for all of it."

"I don't get that. See here," he held up his chili dog, "this little baby has given me around fifteen minutes of joy without even saying a word."

"It's just that those happy moments, you know, those times when there's nothing to do or discover just don't seem to come around that often."

"What do you mean?"

"It's what we do, Gabe. Shootings, stabbings, rapes, bodies...it just doesn't end."

"As you said, Ryan, it's the job we are doing right now." You can walk away from this at any time and move on to something more docile. You know that, don't you?"

"No, Gabe, I can't, not when after what hit me again today reminded me of why I do this."

"I'm not following."

"That look on Kyle's face Gabe. The complete loss of trust in humanity... the part of his soul we pulled out of him today when we told him about his dead friend. I've been there...I lived that."

"We see death all the time Ryan."

"We pull up to scenes with dead people, Gabe. A body is just lying there, no pulse, no words, not even a breath. It's final. It's over. Cops are usually around snapping photos, interviewing witnesses and often have spoken with a victims' family. We basically just arrive and have to figure out the mystery. How often have you been the one that had to inform a loved one of their loss? Have you ever been at the apex of seeing that life shattered? Of being the person to tell another that they will never see their friend, brother, father, mother, son...or sister again?"

"You're right, Ryan. I can't say I've ever had to do that." She pulled a large fry from the mass and watched as an overflow of cheese cascaded back to the pool of yellow.

"When I saw Captain Kyle's face today when we told him about his friend, it only reinforced why I am the way I am."

"Which is?"

"I lost my big sister..." Ryan looked off into the distance.

"I'm sorry, Ryan, I didn't know."

"No one around here knows." Her gaze moved back to Gabe. "It's just not relevant."

"That's fine. You don't have to say..."

"No," she paused. "I think I'm okay talking to you about it."

Gabe nodded.

"I was twenty-one and in my last year of college. Linda, or Lindy as we called her, was five years older and had been married for three years to her high school sweetheart, Mark. She was pregnant with their first child, and my parents and the entire town were ecstatic about a grandchild. I was raised in a little Indiana town where whatever you didn't find out in church on Sunday, you would learn at the diner sometime later that week, so everyone was involved in the new addition to the population."

"Sounds like the small town could get a little annoying?" Gabe said.

"At times it was, but looking back on having so many people truly caring about me, it was great. You took the good with the bad, just like with any other big family."

"Well, that's true."

"So anyway, one weekend, I came home for a baby shower that Lindy's friends put together for her at the local diner, and we all took part in decorating the place. Someone let Lindy purchase the decorations, and she bought the most God-awful purple and green tablecloths to go with bright gold and silver centerpieces for the party. It's kind to say she would never qualify as a party planner or master of home decor."

Gabe smiled.

"I sent Lindy out on some errands to keep her from seeing what we did with some of her more atrocious decorations, but about a half-hour into the party, Lindy hadn't returned. When my mom showed up, she said Lindy had come home to grab some more family photos around three-thirty and then was heading to the diner from there." Ryan paused for a moment and pressed her fingers into the corner of her eyes.

Gabe offered her a napkin. "Sun makes me tear up from time to time, Ryan."

"Thanks." She smiled and dabbed. "So," she took a deep breath, "by six o'clock, my parents started to panic, and Mark and I offered to drive over to his parent's home in case she had gone there and maybe had some sort of car trouble. On the way there, I remember seeing two Sheriff's vehicles on a side road with their lights on, but we passed so fast I never really got a good look at what they were doing." Ryan's tone dropped, and Gabe strained to hear her words. "At Mark's house, before we could even get out of the car, the Sheriff pulled up in the driveway behind us. He fidgeted with his hat in his hands as he walked up to Mark. They had found Lindy's body in a cornfield just off of State Road 40. She'd been stabbed multiple times, and both she and the baby were dead."

"God, Ryan, I'm so sorry."

She shook her head. "It was the worst moment of my life."

"I can't even imagine," Gabe said.

"You've had to fight your own demons at war, Gabe…I think you understand…I guess that's why I'm telling you this."

He nodded. "So, this is why you're a cop then?" Gabe said.

"Not entirely, no." She pulled a few fries into her mouth and took long moments to chew. "While that feeling I felt that day, and again today with Kyle, was a motivating factor, it was not the only one."

"What more is there?"

"They investigated for two years and never found the killer."

"Oh…?"

"Hold on…there's more. Even though I was away at college, the Sheriff was a family friend, and he let me come home every weekend and help with the investigation. Early signs of a budding detective, I guess." Gabe smiled. "I was around the town police department so much that the local marshal even gave me a little office to work out of at the station while I sifted through the evidence."

"No luck, huh?"

"Actually…I solved it."

"But I thought you just told me they never found the killer?" Gabe said.

"They didn't. I did. But I never said anything."

"You've lost me, Ryan."

"It was her husband, Mark."

Gabe put his sandwich down and reached across to Ryan's hand.

"Jesus Ryan…and you never told anyone about this?"

"I was a kid Gabe. Cops had looked over the same stuff I had and never came to that conclusion. I had special access to the kids in the town, you know, witnesses that wouldn't have come forward if I was wearing a uniform. When I look back, I realize it was crazy the amount of information I compiled that the police never could. Still, when I was done, it just seemed so impossible. I mean, who the hell kills their wife and unborn child and then sits there in the driveway when the Sheriff told us Lindy was dead and acts the way he did. It was crazy…he was crazy…hell I was crazy."

"But you were sure he did it?"

"I had no doubt, Gabe. In all my weekends of work, I had uncovered a relationship my sister was having with the son of our town minister. I was able to determine quite clearly that the unborn child was his, and Mark found out."

"And you didn't come forward?"

"I was scared, Gabe. Was I right? Could he have done this? Mark was so in love with my sister and so excited about having the baby that it just didn't seem possible."

"So, he's still out there then…the killers on the loose, and being a cop is what, your penance?"

"A few weeks after my suspicions were solidifying and I was getting up the courage to say something, Mark returned to the sight of Lindy's death. He stood right there on the spot where he took her life and ran a blade up both his arms. Some hunters happened upon his body a few weeks later."

"Wow," Gabe said.

"And after that, I guess…it's just that I don't like unsolved mysteries, Gabe," she said. "They shatter people."

"As it did you," Gabe said.

Ryan nodded. "Learning of Lindy's death was the beginning of the end of my peaceful life as I knew it, but knowing what I uncovered and never telling anyone is just something I never want to happen to anyone else… ever again."

"And then I assume again you never said anything even after Mark's death?"

"My parents were a wreck along with most of the rest of the town, and the tiny little place where I felt so protected and loved was changed forever. We had lost my sister, I had uncovered a scandal that would have shredded the entire town, and the townsfolk were at least left with the belief that Mark had returned to the sight of his beloved to be with her. The truth was far worse than what was believed."

"I see the dilemma."

"Maybe I should have said something, Gabe. Maybe I should have given resolution to the unsolved murder. Thanks to both Mark's actions and what I never revealed, a bunch of suspicious, untrusting, and isolated people live there now. The innocence is gone, and perhaps I am to blame for letting the whole town suffer like that."

"I don't know what to say," Gabe said.

"You don't have to say anything. Honestly, it's nice to talk to someone about this after all of these years. But yes, Gabe, to answer your question about relaxation, I don't find time for it because I don't want to miss a clue or keep a question lingering out there too long. You saw Kyle's reaction today, and that is something I had hoped I would never see or feel again. I'm obsessed with making sure no one; no other town, family, husband, wife, or child has to go to bed without resolution."

"You know you're gonna kill yourself if you don't break away sometimes," Gabe said.

She grimaced. "I guess that's why I've got you." Caught off guard but warmed by her trust in him, Gabe returned her smile then raised one eyebrow as he surveyed her empty plate.

"I do like cheese fries," Ryan said as she smiled.

"You ever play cards?"

"Dabbled a little; why?"

"Because from now on, I'm going to take on the role as your personal relaxation assistant and drag you to our bi-weekly card game."

"No, Gabe, that's for you and your friends. I wouldn't feel…"

"No, no, no, I'm gonna make you a deal. You can be super Detective Ryan, and I will bust my ass helping you solve cases, but you have to promise me three things."

"Shoot."

"First, we have downtime for fifteen or twenty minutes at lunch each day where we can sit down and tune the world out."

"I think I can do that," she said.

"Second, I'm not going to call you Ryan or Detective during our time-outs from the world, so I guess it's either Rebecca or..."

"My friends called me Becca in college..."

"Good enough...Becca. And finally, you have to come to our card games which are every other Saturday night."

"I guess I can probably do that as well," she conceded.

"Besides, we have a new guy that took all my money last week, and I might need your help taking him out if he comes back again."

Ryan laughed.

PART 3

FRIENDS

CHAPTER 10

PUZZLES

The room seemed colder than usual as the sun remained hidden behind rain clouds for the second day in a row. The floor-to-ceiling windows along the tall eastern wall typically provided so much warmth that it was an odd day when the heaters kicked on in Gabe and Ryan's makeshift office. The room was meant for storage, but the only space available for Gabe when he arrived was amidst the worn-out chairs, broken desks, and EPPD's evidence too large to store in closets or drawers. Gabe didn't mind the isolation from the rest of the department chopped up into noisy cubicles, and even Ryan enjoyed the break from her assigned desk in the main room.

It had been two days since any helpful information on the recent deaths had come across Gabe's desk. Given the lack of solid leads, Gabe convinced Ryan to individually and privately chart out the facts they did know in hopes of establishing a more straightforward course of action. During the long rainy hours in silence, they first posted the names of the deceased on their cork boards in the center of the room. Once each board listed all the dead, they turned their boards, placing them back to back so neither detective could see what the other was thinking.

Ryan began her work by positioning the photos of the bodies in a perfect square with one name in each corner. The two on the left, Bryan Caldwell and Specialist Marlin Wade, died from different causes of death but were found around the same date. The two on the right side of the board,

Chip Mallon with his kidneys sliced and Master Sergeant Kay Farr with the blade in her neck, died from similar weapons. The fifth, Todd Harris, was in the middle of the board with a red sharpie line connecting him to the other pictures in the four corners. The red line leading to the left said 'phone #,' and the red line leading to the right said 'stabbed.' Ryan drew one giant green box around all of the photos and began pasting sticky notes inside the enclosed square, covering everything from marital status to their last meal eaten. Ryan's process kept the focus on the possibility of all the killings being related and forced every clue she posted up inside the box to be considered for each of the deceased.

Gabe placed the photographs chronologically by date of death. He felt it was essential to keep the dates in order and let the more minor details flesh out below each picture. Although many placement methods were acceptable for clue boards, he found it difficult to keep facts and bodies straight if they weren't in a sequenced line.

After a while, the posting of notes became a game between the two. Gabe would scribble something down, grab a red pen and make a grand gesture of tacking it up on his board. In return, Ryan would scratch something down, rush to the board and grin back at Gabe. The fun wore off after a few hours, and soon, the pair were taking extended coffee breaks as the board manipulation trudged along. On the morning of the second day, Ryan returned from her daily 'brain run,' and the conversation devolved into questions about why she wore her work shoes rather than running shoes to exercise, followed by pressing questions about how and why her ponytail remained perfect even in the driving rain. Moments after the earth-shattering topics were concluded, Gabe realized it was time the process ended.

"I guess I'll have to talk to you at the card game tonight," Gabe declared, his feet kicked up onto his desk as Ryan flushed down a bottle of water.

"What?"

"Tonight. The game. You're coming, remember?"

"No, I mean yeah, wait, are we done?" she asked.

"My brain is dead, Ryan. We're talking about your psychoses, it's getting close to lunch, and I haven't posted anything new in quite a while, so yeah, I'm done." Ryan's shoeless feet raced across the slick floor as she moved towards Gabe's half of the room. She slid before stopping halfway across the invisible wall they had constructed between them.

Gabe smiled and raised a hand to direct her to stay on her side. "No, let's start with your board."

"Ok." Ryan stepped back as Gabe got up and crossed into Ryan's side of the room. He dropped into a chair in front of her desk and wheeled himself to the front of her board.

"I like your grouping. It shows we don't think alike, which is good." His head fell to the side. "And these stick figures are outstanding, Ryan. Art major, right?"

"Don't hate Gabe. Those masterful renderings keep me focused on certain issues lacking immediate relevance but which could come into play soon enough."

"The cell phone there is obvious," Gabe pointed, "but what is this, Texas?" He pulled the diamond shape diagram off the board and held it up.

"It's Iraq, Gabe. Funny you don't recognize it. You sure your tours there weren't a cover for some cushy desk job in Germany?"

"Okay, it's Iraq, but why Iraq?"

"It's where Master Sergeant Farr and Specialist Wade spent the last year of their lives before ending up dead. Maybe there's something there?" Gabe nodded but knew Harris had been in Kuwait, while neither Caldwell nor Mallon had any history in that part of the world.

"What about this giant circle thingy with lines coming out of it under Kay Farr? Looks like the sun."

"It's the eye thing from the knife," she explained.

"Ah, of course."

"And it also represents Kay Farr's complaint about her vision."

"Speaking of Farr's vision issues, did you ever follow up with Doctor Cunningham about that?"

"Cunningham, the possessor of all knowledge of those now departed, alas, had some information but no pertinent clues," Ryan said.

"What information?" Gabe asked.

"He said there was something abnormal with Farr's eyes…a scarring on the macula of some sort, but he was in the middle of something else and couldn't recall the exact term. I, of course, asked Cunningham what sort of doctor couldn't remember a simple medical term, which shamed him into hopping on the internet. It didn't seem too difficult to remember," Ryan said, "I mean, come on, he dissects brain hemispheres and untangles spinal columns all day; you'd think a medical term for what causes a scratched eyeball would be a piece of cake to remember?" Gabe laughed as Ryan walked over to the coffee maker. "He told me Farr had histoplasmosis capsulatum."

"Capsa-whatum?"

"To the best of his knowledge, it's some sort of problem with the eye caused by a fungus from birds or bats."

"Birds or bats?"

"Yeah," Ryan said, "and apparently, it's quite common all across the world. I put a stop to his explanations, though, when he got into a bunch of terms I'm pretty sure even he didn't understand."

"And how did he find this histoplasmosis?" Gabe asked.

Ryan returned to the notes on her desk. "The histo left its mark inside the eye by way of parapapillary atrophy which disrupted the tissue around the eye, and then there were small circular scar lesions around the retina as well." Gabe laughed. "Clear enough?" she asked.

"I think I'll run this by my friend Mike tonight at the card game, and maybe he can give us more insight."

"Oh, and you're assuming one of your poker buddies will have more insight into this than our friendly medical examiner?"

"He's an optometrist, Ryan. I thought I mentioned him before?"

"Oh yeah, you did…sorry."

"Of course, he'll tell you he knows just as much as real eye doctors who've attended school more than four years, but we'll see."

"Can't hurt," she said. In anticipation, Ryan pointed around her board to Gabe's side of the room. He nodded and leaned back in his chair for another view of Ryan's board as she scampered across the room and took point in front of his board.

"There's nothing on here but your first pictures Gabe." He chuckled. "Where are all the sticky notes you kept posting up?"

He tapped his head. "All up here," he said. "Besides, I get more out of seeing what you put together over here than anything I could put down over there."

"This some joke to you?"

"No, Ryan, I honestly cannot think like that. They forced us to do this sort of thing at the academy, and as I said, I do take in more just seeing what others have done."

"I don't like the fact that you fooled me into trying to keep up with you with all those sticky notes."

"Sleight of hand, Ryan. I kept putting up the same one over and over. It's your nature to compete, so I was just trying to keep your brain moving for you."

"Not funny," she came back over to her side of the room and glared.

"So, what exactly have you been doing this whole time?"

"Well, most of the time was spent putting information into the AIS system I told you about, including a picture of that knife you have so prominently displayed on your board here."

"The FBI site?"

"Yeah."

"Well, you told me about a site, but I didn't recall you giving it a name."

"A.I.S., Advanced Information Systems."

"And so, while I have been slaving away on my board, have you obtained any useful information from A.I.S.?"

"Nothing since I posted the photo, but you need to keep reminding me to get on there, especially now that our little game of post-it-note is over."

"Can't remember to do that yourself?"

"Kind of a pain, Ryan. The system won't ping any email I can get on this phone when information arrives, and it takes about ten minutes just to get to the main page of the server to log in, so unless I am just sitting here like we've been doing the past day and a half I'll forget to check it."

"So, this super-secret website isn't too handy after all?"

"No, it's beneficial as long as other agents around the globe take the time to get on there and compare evidence or clues to help one another. But most of them, like me, don't have the time to sit around and wait for the thing to load…thing's somewhat of a nuisance."

"Well, we need to utilize whatever tools we can to figure this out, Gabe. I could get on there every night if you'd show me how to run it."

"Top secret, Ryan, and of course, we relax at night, remember?" Gabe said.

"Right, right," Ryan said. Satisfied he had gathered enough information from her board, Gabe pushed his chair back and stood up as Ryan's phone rang behind him. She pushed him aside, still frustrated at the lack of anything on his board, and grabbed the phone.

"Detective Ryan...yeah, go ahead and put him through." She covered the receiver. "It's the captain from Fort Bliss who we spoke with about Specialist Wade the other day." She placed the receiver on the phone and pressed the speaker button. Gabe perched himself on the side of the desk next to Ryan as the line clicked.

"This is Detective Ryan."

"Detective, this is Captain Kyle with the 5-52nd ADA Battalion at Fort Bliss; we spoke a few days ago."

"Yes, I remember; hello, captain. I have Agent Moss here with me on speaker too."

"Oh, hello, sir."

"Hello captain, what can we do for you?" Gabe asked.

"Well, I came across some new information."

"About Specialist Wade?" Ryan asked.

"No, this is in regards to the other soldier you asked me about."

"Warrant Officer Todd Harris?" Gabe said.

"No, you know, the female master sergeant you asked me about."

"Master Sergeant Farr?"

"Yes...I mean no, well...wait, sir, just let me try and explain."

"Go ahead," Ryan said. She punched Gabe in the arm and hushed him to silence.

"Yesterday, I received a request from a unit out of San Antonio for pay status information regarding a Master Sergeant Farr who was reported deceased. I sent an email back to the San Antonio unit since no one by that name ever served under me, and later that day, I remembered you brought up her name when we spoke. I did some more digging and telephoned San Antonio personally to learn more about Master Sergeant Kay Farr. It turns out it was Sergeant First Class Palmer, Kay Palmer, and yes, I do know her."

"And how is that?" Ryan asked.

"She was assigned to us from a National Guard unit out of San Antonio a few weeks before we deployed, so I never really had the chance to get to know her. During the call to her unit, I discovered that she went and got married when she was on leave. When she returned to Iraq, she was promoted, but with just a short time left in theater, it would have been almost impossible to get her name changed in our DEERS system before redeployment, so she chose not to get that done. Therefore, none of us ever knew her as Farr or by the rank you mentioned to me."

"DEERS?" Ryan asked.

"It's a system for personnel tracking for pay and insurance and tells us information about a soldier and his family."

"Okay."

"So, when we got back to the states, she changed her name and was offered some full-time job with the military as an OCT at Fort Bliss…"

"Sorry, again, what's an OCT?" Ryan asked.

"OCTs are trainers who work with units getting ready to mobilize soldiers to head to war. Farr moved to El Paso with her new husband just a few weeks back to start work at Fort McGregor and Bliss. I had no idea she was even here in El Paso until I received the inquiry from her unit in San Antonio. Sorry I didn't realize she had been one of mine."

"No, it's understandable," Gabe said. "I know how fast those units get tossed together. Heck, I didn't know half of the guys I was over there with, and they were covering my back."

"That's how it goes, sir."

"So that I am clear," Ryan said, "now you're telling us both Master Sergeant Farr-Palmer and Specialist Marlin Wade were both part of your unit overseas?"

"Yes, ma'am, they both were under my command and located at our base for most of their time in theater." Ryan grabbed a sticky note, scribbled down some information, and moved back to her board. Gabe watched as her new note replaced the third-grade rendering of Iraq she had initially posted.

"Do you ever recall Farr and Wade hanging out at all?" Gabe asked.

"No more than anyone else. There was no special relationship between them that I noticed, and I'm pretty sure they weren't even in the same chain of command, so it is possible they might not have ever met one another."

"I appreciate you calling us with this captain," Gabe said.

"If there's anything else you come across, please give us a call," Ryan said.

"Anything else, in particular, you're looking for, ma'am?"

"Other disappearances in your unit would be a start."

"Absolutely."

"Or any odd behaviors displayed by your soldiers who were overseas with you," Gabe added.

"What sort of behaviors, sir?"

"Anything out of the ordinary. Guys acting nervous, depressed, excited, or just out of their normal sorts."

"Sounds like a lot of my soldiers," the captain said.

"Sure, sure, but you know what I mean. Any unique or strange behaviors that separate one soldier from another or even from himself."

"Well, come to think of it…" Captain Kyle paused.

"Sorry?" Ryan moved from her clue board and leaned over the phone.

"I guess," Kyle paused, "we have one guy who's gone off the reservation a little."

"What do you mean by that?" Gabe asked.

"This stuff is confidential, sir…I…I'm just not sure we can talk about this over the phone." Gabe stiffened in his resolve, placed the palms of his hands on either side of the telephone, and leaned to within inches of the speaker.

"Captain, you and I both know you need to do what is best for your soldiers."

"I know, sir, but you're aware we have rules about confidential information."

"True, but right now, we've got two dead soldiers from your unit, and there is clear evidence that at least one of them was murdered. Any information you can get to us timely may lead us to find the killer."

"I understand, sir, but my job…" the captain said.

"I know you know your job, captain; now let me do mine. I'm only interested in finding a killer. I want this accomplished as fast as possible for you and your men, and honestly, this isn't the time for military red tape."

A long silence filled the line.

"Well, sir," the captain said, "we have a soldier who was locked up today for attacking three other soldiers. We've got him under guard now for what they're calling disruptive ideations."

"What sort of ideations, captain?"

"It was reported that he was seeing things just before he began threatening those that were there with him. He lunged at someone with a pocket knife, and after he was subdued by some nearby MP's, he began to threaten them as well. They put him in a straightjacket."

"One of your guys from Iraq?"

"Yeah. In fact, it was the lieutenant I was working with on the knots when you guys showed up the other day."

"He ever do anything like this before?" Ryan asked.

"No detective. Up until he pulled the knife and began threats against the MP's, he was as solid as they come."

Gabe shot a stern look at Ryan and whispered. "Just let me do this." She nodded. "So where is your soldier at right now?" Gabe asked the captain.

"Locked up over at the Provost Marshal's in an observation room."

"I need you to get us in to see him?" Captain Kyle did not respond. "Captain!?" Gabe said.

"I'm just not sure…"

"Let us help you, Captain Kyle. I can guarantee you the military doesn't want any more soldiers dropping like flies. We need to get in to see him."

"You can come over here tomorrow," the captain said quickly, "and I will see what I can do."

"But we need to see him now…"

"0900 tomorrow, sir, that's the best I can do."

"Understood, captain. We'll see you…" The call disconnected.

"Sorry I hushed you there, Ryan, but I wanted to keep his focus on the whole duty and honor to his troops thing. He's not supposed to report mental health issues to civilians, so he was a little out there on what he told us and what we are asking him to do."

"I got it…no worries," Ryan said.

"I know there are protocols in place which he's going to have to circumvent very carefully to get us in to see this guy tomorrow."

"You think he can get it done?"

"Guess we'll see," Gabe said. "Hey, we've been at these clue boards for too long, and it's just before lunch. You think we can bug out of here a little bit early to get ready for the game tonight?"

"I guess so," Ryan said as she grabbed her purse.

"So, you're not miffed at all about me shushing you up there with that call?"

"I'll let you know tonight."

CHAPTER 11

CARD SHARK

"I told her you'd act like gentlemen," Gabe said to the players in his kitchen. Doug grunted as he rooted around in the cooler for another beer. Unsatisfied with his initial selection, he dove back in as Gabe watched displaced chunks of ice fall onto his floor.

"I don't know what you're looking for, but I can assure you they've all got hops and barley."

"Yeah, but if I'm gonna impress the new girl, I need to have the right drink in my hand when she gets here."

"It'll take a lot more than that to make you look good," a voice from outside the screen door said.

"Oh, great, it's Tommy," Doug said. "I'm so glad you were able to make it back. Have you spent all of the money you stole from me last time?"

"Last of it paid for the drinks in here," Tom grinned as he held up a cooler.

"It's not gonna happen like last time. I'm ready for your little mister innocent routine, and it's alllllllll about business tonight."

"We'll see," said Tom. He dropped his cooler onto the floor and extended a hand to his verbal combatant. Mike followed through the door, dropped another cooler, and let two chip bags dangling from his mouth fall onto the poker table.

"So we're all gentlemen tonight, right?" Gabe said.

"Can't make any promises, Gabe," Phil said as his chest expanded and his voice deepened, "but I'll try to keep the charm under control when..."

"Keep your charm," Ryan's voice filtered through the screen door, "I'm just here for your cash."

All eyes were on Ryan as she pulled open the screen door. She worked off her unzipped sweatshirt and tossed it on the black leather couch, exposing a yellow t-shirt bearing an image of the Tower of London. Sporting a khaki pair of pants falling to the middle of her shins, with flip flops exposing professionally manicured nails, Gabe did a double-take to ensure the attractively dressed female was his partner. Not only had her standard uniform changed, but her hair also hung unbound around her shoulders. Doug punched Phil in the gut to deflate his still aped physique.

"Sorry about him," Doug said. "Phil's been acting that way since junior high." Ryan laughed as Doug extended his hand.

"I'm Rebecca," she said with a smile. Mike and Tom pushed past Doug on their way to greet her.

"I'm Mike!"

"Gabe's eye doctor friend," she said.

"The one and only, and this is my intern, Tommy." Tommy stepped forward.

"Please, call me, Tom."

"I'm Detective...sorry, Rebecca," she gave a little queen's waive to the others in the room as everyone else began to migrate to the table.

"My name is Phil," he said sheepishly. "Sorry about the flexing thing when you walked in. It's great to have you." She smiled as he pulled back a chair for her.

"Quit sucking up Phil, and let's get this show on the road," Gabe said. "I silenced Becca earlier today and got her mad. She insists she's here to bleed us dry." Hearing her old college nickname brought a soft smile to Ryan's face. As the shuffling of chairs ceased, for the first time in a while, she felt relaxed and at ease as the cards were dealt.

"Ah, so you irritated your co-worker today?" asked Doug.

"That's so out of character," Mike said.

"Work issues, guys. Sometimes I step on her toes and forget she's the lead." Ryan's head nodded. The guys chuckled at the thought of Gabe taking a back seat to anyone.

* * *

Three hours later, discarded potato chip bags decorated the kitchen floor. The empty coolers had been converted into side tables to keep the pizza within reach, and bloated bladders were the only cause for significant movement. Gabe had not done well so far this night. He sat back with a six and five of hearts and, utilizing the pool cards on the table, had the chance at a flush draw that might win some of his money back on the final hand. He looked across at Becca, who remained impossible to read.

"I'm in for fifty," she said.

Doug tossed his cards in. "Aaaannnnddd I'm out."

"What's the call, card shark?" Phil asked Tom.

"I lost that title tonight, guys; the lady there has it now." He nodded toward Rebecca. "She's got to come back next week so that I can get my money back. I'm out." Phil followed and slid his cards across the table. Mike took in a deep breath and tossed in another fifty before Gabe called, hoping for a heart on the river. Gabe took his time flipping over the final card, the king of hearts, and he strained to contain his excitement. With the queen, six, five, nine, and now king of hearts, he was sure he had a winner.

Gabe looked at Ryan as her lips pursed. She tapped the table, and Mike thrust another fifty into the pot. Mike's voice cracked as the chips dropped, and Gabe moved quickly to raise the bet.

"A little rich there, doc, but I think I'm in." Gabe threw down a fifty. Everyone turned to Ryan, who exposed a broad smile.

"I call and raise it another fifty." Phil and Doug, long since removed from the action, were reinvigorated by her brash bet and turned their attention away from the television and back to the table.

"You're about to get schooled, doc," Doug said.

"She set you boys up," said Phil.

Ryan smiled wider. "Wellllll?" Ryan said as Mike's fraught look indicated his hand was not worth fifty more dollars.

"I'm out," he tossed his cards to the middle and let out a guttural moan.

"I think I'm in." Gabe threw another fifty into the pot.

Before his money settled on the table, though, Ryan turned over her cards.

"Flush ace-high Gabe. You have something better?" she asked with a raised brow. Gabe sunk in his chair.

"That's just sad," Gabe said as he threw his cards face down on the table.

Mike reached to turn them over, but Gabe quickly intermixed his hand with the others. The losers at the table began to collect up their trash.

"You took us for a ride there tonight, Becca," Mike said. Busy stacking her bills, Ryan nodded. "And here I thought Tom was the player to reckon with. You really know your stuff."

"Well…I used to deal some," she said.

"What?"

"I worked at a casino in college dealing cards." She shrugged her shoulders.

"Dang lady, how'd you keep that one under the cuff?" said Doug.

"Shouldn't be surprised," Mike laughed.

"That's just great," Phil said as he pushed back from his chair and motioned for Doug to follow. "Come on, Doug, I need to get you home before your wife finds out you lost your kid's private school tuition again this week."

"She does get mad about that," Doug mumbled as he walked through the screen door being held by Phil.

"See ya next time, boys," Phil said.

"And girl," Doug said as the screen door shut.

"I should've seen it."

"Why do you say that, Tommy?" Gabe asked.

"She was too good. I don't lose that often, and man, she took a lot of cash out of my pocket tonight. I just should have known something was up." Mike patted his intern on the back and pointed Tommy to the couch. He shuffled over to the living room.

"So what school were you at where you had access to a casino?" Mike asked.

"I went to Evansville for college. They had a riverboat down on the water, and I worked there my junior and senior years."

"The Aces?" Mike asked.

"Yeah, the Purple Aces."

"Those guys had some great hoops teams back in the nineties. Were you there then?" Mike asked.

"I was and went to the games all the time when I wasn't working," she said. "They were good, but I didn't think many people out West knew about them."

"Not everyone living out here is from out here," Mike said.

"You guys get to a lot of basketball games during college?" Ryan asked.

"No!" Gabe said. He returned from the sink and sat down as Ryan counted her money. "I don't remember one game the good doctor ever made it to…at least after his freshman year."

"Watched them on television," Mike said. Gabe's feet couldn't find his favorite footrest, so he peered under the table and found Stump lying under Ryan, her flip-flop-less feet working across his smooth black fur.

"Traitor," Gabe said. Ryan smirked. "Anyway, Mike," Gabe turned to his friend, "we have a burning issue we hoped you might be able to help us with."

"Oh yeah," Mike sat up. "Becca said something a little earlier when the pizza arrived. What's up?" Gabe grabbed a spiral notebook from the counter and flipped through some pages.

"The medical examiner called us the other day and told us the pupils of one of our dead people had some scarring," Ryan said, not in need of notes.

"Did he tell you what the scarring was from?"

Gabe nodded. "He used the term Histoplasmosis capsulatum. He said the eyes exhibited signs of some trauma from that."

"It's pretty common stuff, really," Mike said.

"How common?"

"Well, histo can be found in almost anyone's eyes. It comes from bird droppings and is most often found in people who reside along river basins or on farms," Mike said.

"And so, this bird poop can actually cause eye problems then?" Ryan asked.

"Well, it's typically ingested by inhalation and first damages a person's respiratory system before moving into more remote parts of the body. But yes, given time, it could cause problems with a persons' eyes."

"Could it cause someone to see strange images, colors, or distortions?" Gabe asked, finally done reading through his notes. "One of the victims complained about vision problems to her husband before she died."

Mike's head started shaking. "I've never heard of histo causing any vision problems with colors or creating images, but I guess there could be wavy or crooked lines or even a blind spot appearing if the scarring went untreated."

"Think we could send you some of the finer details from our medical examiner and see if you can find anything he could have missed?" Ryan asked.

"If he's asking," Mike pointed to Gabe, "no, but for you, Ms. Ryan, I'd be happy to. I'll even put Tom on it. He's always looking for a challenging project to keep him busy." Gabe glanced at the young intern who was passed out and snoring on the couch.

"Then I am asking, and I would really appreciate it."

Mike scribbled on a business card and slid it to Ryan.

"Email me the information tomorrow, and if I can sober him up in the morning, we can get on it."

"I will, thanks. So, Mike, while I understand how that one came into your life." Ryan pointed at Tommy, "Gabe here doesn't let on much about his personal life. How'd you two meet exactly?"

"Guy saved my life," Mike said. Gabe scooted back in his chair and was quick to respond.

"It wasn't that dramatic; tell her the truth."

"Maybe not for you," Mike said, "but it was for me."

"How so?" Ryan asked.

"Our freshman year, we were both invited to a rush party at one of those off-campus frat houses that never abide by the rules regarding dry rushes. I was being taken around by a brother of the house, and pretty much everyone there was drinking and dancing…wasn't much room to maneuver. So anyway, one of the really drunk brothers started knocking lit candles from the bar onto the floor. As you might expect, the puddle of booze on the ground ignited, and some of the flames caught onto people's shoes and pants. What followed was a lot of screaming and panicking, and before I knew it, I got knocked over."

"Scrawniest kid at the party," Gabe said, "Kid just tripped.

"I got trampled by the mob Gabe."

"Clumsy guy…shaky hands…that's why I don't trust him with my eyes." Mike waved at Gabe to be quiet.

"So when I was knocked to the floor, my back got soaked with alcohol, and within a matter of seconds, the flames moved onto my shirt. I'd love to say I was calm, but honestly, I started freaking out until Gabe picked me up, pulled me towards the door, and started rolling me on the ground. Once the flames were out, he threw me onto his back, dropped me on the lawn, and headed back in to help others. It wasn't until about thirty minutes later when I saw him face down being carried out on a stretcher."

"Face down?"

"He'd burned his butt."

Ryan cringed.

"It wasn't my butt," Gabe said. "At least get the story right."

"Sorry, man, I was just trying to save you some dignity," Mike turned to Ryan, "he really burned off his…"

"Mike!" Gabe shouted, then laughed. "I got burned along my upper back. Just my back, Ryan. Not my ass and definitely nothing else important."

"Story was much better the way I was telling it."

"Was it bad?" Ryan asked.

"Some scars are still there but nothing unmanageable."

"Anyway," Mike continued slapping Gabe's knee, "this guy had gone back in and gotten over a dozen people out. The following week, Gabe was being lauded as a hero around campus, and he got bids from almost every house, but he wanted nothing to do with the limelight and nothing more to do with drunken frat kids. The whole episode sort of made him close up, and he decided not even to rush a fraternity."

"That's sort of sad to let all that go," Ryan said.

Gabe shrugged.

"I think he did it to avoid all the butt jokes," Mike said. "So anyway, I sought Gabe out to thank him for getting me out of the fire, but he didn't want to hear any more of it."

"I've noticed that," Ryan said before smiling at Gabe.

"Well, maybe it didn't affect Gabe that much, but the whole thing changed my life. It instilled in me a focus on my school and on career goals that I hadn't had before, and along the way, we eventually became friends and then roommates."

"Yeah," Gabe said, "but he never knew I only kept hanging out with him because he and some lab nerd created this excellent cream out of some funny-looking plants that soothed my burns."

"I didn't discover the stuff, Gabe. I told you it turned out to be nothing more than a lotion Procter and Gamble had discovered years before but was never marketed. Probably had some sort of poison in it, or it left horrific stains on its' users."

"Well, it was still genius, and from what I recall, you and your plants got along quite well until you abandoned the whole idea of a career in horticulture for the eye thing."

"Not a bunch of money in plants, Gabe and the eye gig has made for a good living."

"But once he abandoned the life of plants," Gabe returned his focus to Ryan, "is when the good doctor dove into his books and disappeared from hanging out with his friends."

"Maybe if you had just let me see your butt back then to see if the lotion..."

"I think it's about time for you to go home," Gabe said. He called out to Tommy, who stirred to attention and ordered him to take his dead weight boss home. As he rose, Tom wobbled and began patting around his pockets.

"We're good," Tom said as he finally pulled out the keys and jingled them.

"No, I'm good...and I'm driving," Mike said as he grabbed for Tom's keys. Tom conceded and boyishly waived at Ryan, proclaimed his undying respect for her card skills, and was hustled through the front door. Mike gave both Ryan and Gabe a hug.

"Get me that information, and I'll find out what I can about those eye issues."

"No problem," the detectives recited in unison. Gabe watched as his friends stumbled off the front porch and into Tom's car. Tom waved as they pulled out of Gabe's drive and headed down the street. Returning to the table, Gabe saw that Ryan had found her way beneath it to wish Stump good night. The giant Labrador moaned as she pinned back his ears. Leaving Stump to his massage, Gabe grabbed another empty chip bag and three half-empty bottles of beer from the table. As he poured the remaining contents into his sink, Ryan finally rose and wished Stump a good night.

"I had a great time," she said. "I needed this, Gabe, thanks."

"Good. I, for one, am glad you came tonight, and I know I can speak for all of us when I say we'd love to have you come back next time too." Ryan smiled and accepted his offer.

"Gabe," she said, reaching into the sleeves of her jacket, "I think you are a hero."

"Think so?" he said.

"I do. For lots of reasons." He made his way towards her and held open the screen door. As she passed, she made a tiny wave and shared a smile.

CHAPTER 12

COMPLETE STRANGER

The sun's sharp rays cut around Gabe's two hundred and fifty-dollar sunglasses at every curve of the road, and he cursed the cloudless weather. Although he loved the way the distinct frames looked on his face, the designer glasses offered no serious protection from anything other than direct light. They were a poor choice for mornings with hangovers.

"You keep moaning. Are you alright?" Gabe nodded as the car crested the mountain ridge and descended towards Fort Bliss military base to meet with Captain Kyle. The soft dulcet tones of Barry Manilow danced from Gabe's right pocket as he grabbed his cell phone, checked the digital display, and tossed the phone to Ryan.

"Is it Don Ho?"

Gabe snarled as she caught the phone.

"It's some number from your office," he said. "I can't drive, keep this sun out of my eyes and deal with your cracks about my ringtone all at once. See what they want."

"Hello, this is Detective Ryan." She listened a moment then whispered, "It's Jenkins."

"About time your genius lab tech got back to us. I hope he's got something."

"Usually does." Wedging the cell phone between her left shoulder and ear, she scribbled down notes as Jenkins talked.

Although Gabe was shocked by his appearance when first meeting Jenkins, the baby-faced whiz kid, he had to admit the youngster possessed an intellect beyond his years. He tackled every challenge with vigor, hacked any technology device without fear, and made technology work for the EPPD in ways Gabe never knew was possible. As a member of the 'me' generation, he was a rare find in a sea of youth who only thought about themselves first and foremost and never put forth more effort than necessary. Similar to Doctor Cunningham and other great minds that spent too much time inside the intricacies of their enhanced brains, Jenkin's personality lacked some fine-tuning. Still, unlike the good doctor, Jenkins' awkwardness was endearing. He was not oblivious to his shortcomings in relating to other humans and was able to laugh at himself in a manner that put everyone around him at ease. Even without the gift of personality or gab, Gabe enjoyed speaking with the young man that wore a different Yankees ball cap every day of the week, and he looked forward to seeing just what Jenkins would do next to amaze him.

"Are you sure?" Ryan asked. A garbled response followed. "How does someone do that?" Returning to her pad, Ryan forced down every word, and her notes grew more extensive. "In English, please Jenkins, not geek!"

A half-minute later, she stopped writing. "You're still the best. Talk to you soon." She dropped the phone back into Gabe's lap.

"So, what's he got?" Gabe asked.

"Remember the 444-4444 number and the same number of 7's we found on those phones?"

"Yeah, did they get a trace?"

"No," she said, "but they found similar numbers on Wade's broken phone as well." Gabe's car slowed as his full attention shifted to Ryan.

"So along with Farr, we now have four of our five dead people that all have a set of identical numbers on their phones that they dialed at some point before they died?"

"Yes, Gabe, and although both Harris and Caldwell dialed the odd numbers at some point in the past on their phones, these numbers were exactly the last ones dialed by both Farr and Wade before they died."

"So, whose numbers are they?"

"Jenkins just said these numbers don't exist."

"I assume he tried to dial them?"

"Yes, and he also had his computer run a scan on the numbers for every single area code existing in the world and found nothing."

"How is that possible? They've got to be foreign numbers?"

"He checked Gabe. They are not working numbers anywhere."

"So who or what were all of these people dialing then?"

"He couldn't say, but he had a theory."

"Which was?"

"Hang on." Ryan filled in her notes with details she'd been unable to capture during the call but that were coming back to her as they spoke. She made some underlines, drew some arrows, and then continued.

"So here is what I got from him once he dummied it up for me. The numbers were not actually dialed but instead are the result of a jamming system that might have been utilized on the receiving end."

"What?"

"Just stay with me here. So, Jenkins has read about machines that send out high-level pulses across telephone lines forcing the computer, aka phone, on the other end of the line to reflect a set of unintelligible words or numbers."

"Like a scrambler?"

"Sort of."

"So, if I call you and you have one of these machines, you can hit a button, and my phone will show some mixed-up words or random numbers to cover up the actual number I dialed?"

"Apparently," Ryan said.

"And Jenkins knows who has this technology?"

"No."

"No?"

"As I said, what he told me was merely a theory. He says this information came from one of the black market computer hacker magazines he gets from time to time to keep up with the fringe of the computer world. He claims he doesn't know of a single such system that is operational and stressed that it might just be a conceptual idea from some screwball hacker."

Gabe's complete focus returned to the road as he pulled sharp on the wheel, having almost missed the exit leading to the front gate of Fort Bliss.

"We'll need to dig down into that theory a little more before we give it any real credence Ryan. That sounds a little out there."

"I know, Gabe. I'm just the reporter here. Maybe we can swing by the station when we got done with Captain Kyle and talk to Jennings a little more about what he's come up with."

Ryan nodded as Gabe reached into the back seat and grabbed the military placard for his car that he'd received days before.

* * *

Ryan and Gabe walked up the steps to Captain Kyle's office. Turning left down a long hallway, they spotted him walking briskly towards them.

"Captain Kyle, it's good to see you again; sorry we're running a little bit..." The captain raised his finger to his mouth then flattened his hand, signaling them to remain in the hallway outside his office door. Ryan peered around the door as the captain entered his office and struggled with his laptop's electrical plug attached to the wall. He folded down the screen, shoved the computer into a bag, and patted his left and then right pants pockets. He approached the detectives, pulled his door closed, and signaled for them to follow. Once reaching the steps, he shuffled down two at a time.

"Is your car nearby?" he asked Gabe.

"Yes, are we going somewhere?"

"Where is it?" Kyle said, finally slowing.

Gabe pushed past the captain and led him across the lot. Once close enough to his commission Gabe raised his hand, and the car's lights blinked twice. Gabe jumped in the front seat as Ryan held the passenger door for the captain, who struggled with his computer bag. Ryan marveled at the change in the captain's demeanor. So crisp and refined the last time they met, Kyle now was disheveled and skittish.

"Where are we going?" Gabe asked as he pulled out of the parking lot.

"Take a left out here onto Chaffee and just keep going north."

"Just out for a little drive today?" Gabe asked, trying to bring a little levity to the car.

"Please, sir, just do as I ask. It'll only take about five minutes and will give me time to get this set up." The captain fiddled with the computer and kept glancing at the passenger side mirror. Gabe checked his rearview mirror butonly saw Ryan shrugging her shoulders. Gabe continued north as directed and drove past a small airline facility used to ship troops in and out of the base. After a sharp turn to the right, then up and over a slight rise, the road turned sharp left and paralleled a train yard containing a half dozen train tracks. Over a mile down the road, the captain spoke.

"Just up ahead," he exclaimed without looking up.

"Is that where I'm headed?" Gabe pointed to an open space in the fence encircling a dusty storage yard full of connex's.

"No, drive past the entrance and park down where the road ends along the fence line."

The car slowed.

"Right here is great. You can stop there." Gabe parked and began to roll the windows down.

"Keep them up, please," the captain said. He didn't break focus from his computer screen. The car windows reversed their direction.

"He's dead."

"Sorry, who's dead?" Gabe asked.

"Lieutenant McCollum, the guy you were coming to see today."

"What happened?"

"That's why we're out here."

"What do you mean?"

"They say he killed himself, but I don't buy it."

"Why not?"

"I can't say for certain, sir, but I'm..." The captain's index finger rubbed hard against his thumb.

"Take a breath, captain," Ryan said, "...and tell us what you do know."

"After I hung up with you two last night, I called the legal department to make sure you'd be cleared to visit today. I spoke with the JAG in charge of Lieutenant McCollum's prosecution. He didn't have any problem with you guys visiting, particularly after I informed him you were investigating Specialist Wade's death. The JAG and Wade knew each other fairly well since they both grew up in Detroit, so with his permission, I called my NCO to put you two on the visiting list."

"Sorry, NCO?" Ryan said.

"Non-commissioned officer," Gabe said. "Most soldiers start as enlisted and eventually work their way up to the rank of sergeant and keep all of the enlisted soldiers in line. They run the day-to-day business of each unit."

"Yeah," Captain Kyle chimed in, "this particular NCO is my most trusted soldier, and I had him monitoring McCollum after he started acting up. Just before heading home last night, my NCO called and said McCollum was acting even crazier as the day went on. McCollum got so out of control at one point they moved him from an observation room into a padded cell and called in a doctor who was scheduled to arrive sometime after midnight."

"Psych doctors, I assume?" Gabe asked.

"I would assume so too, but I'm not completely sure."

"Well, what did the doctors have to say?" Gabe asked.

"That's part of the problem, sir; I don't know whether they ever got there to see McCollum."

"So, why all the mystery if we don't have all the information yet?" Ryan asked.

"So sometime around midnight, when I knew my NCO's shift was about to end, I called to ask him to burn a copy of the video that was being taken of McCollum while he was in restraints. I thought today it might be a good thing for all of us to see the drastic changes for ourselves."

"So, he made a copy?"

"Yes, and he brought it over last night when his shift ended and left it in my desk drawer. When I got in this morning, I realized the copy he made was burned onto a secured disc which could get my NCO in trouble if anyone found out, so to avoid issues, I converted it to a non-secured disc with a burner I had installed on my computer when I was in Iraq."

"I didn't think you were allowed to transfer secured items to a non-secured source?" Gabe said.

"You're right, sir. Technically we're not supposed to, but we had all sorts of problems in Iraq with non-secured information getting put onto secured discs, and we often didn't have time to go back and ask for the problem to be fixed correctly. My burner may be illegal by Army rules, but it was the right thing to do to short circuit all of those unworkable security measures."

"Smart thinking," Gabe whispered as the captain removed a shiny red disc from its case and popped it into the waiting drive on his laptop.

"A little over two hours ago, I got a call from a colonel who ordered me to turn over all of the information I had on Lieutenant McCollum. He wanted McCollum's entire personnel file, all of his personal effects…and the disc."

"How'd he know about the disc?" asked Gabe.

"My NCO could have told him, but I have no idea. Still, that's not the point. The urgency of the full request from the colonel was what bothered me."

"And why is that?" Ryan asked.

"Not normal protocol, ma'am. It just left a funny feeling."

"So, let me guess, you kept a copy of the disc, didn't you?"

"Yes, ma'am, I kept the secured one and gave them the non-secured copy I burned this morning. You're not going to believe this." The whir of the disc drive filled the car. All three stared at the screen as it burst to life, revealing a man draped in an untied straight jacket seated at a metal desk. Although the jacket did not bind the man's arms to his body, metal belts on his arms were looped and locked to the table. He sat alone for long minutes; his left cheek pressed on the cold steel table; his eyes open wide as he stared through the two-way mirror. A soldier entered the quiet room.

"Bernie, I came to drop off some food and see if you needed anything."

"That's my NCO who burned the disc," the captain said.

"Bernie," the NCO called again.

"…the hell out of here!!!!" Lieutenant McCollum shot up and kicked back his metal chair. The arm binds held him close to the table, and leg irons which were not previously visible, clanged as they strained. Ryan began scribbling notes.

"It's just gotta end top; I've gotta put a stop to it."

"What does he mean by top?" Ryan asked.

"Top is just another name that soldiers call the highest-ranking NCO," the captain said. Ryan watched as the NCO rubbed his hand along his forehead and took two steps into the room.

"What the hell are you talking about, Bernie?"

"You can't hide it any longer, top. You can't get away!" Metal strained on metal. "I don't know how long you've been part of this, but I'm gonna end it!"

"Who's that?" Gabe asked as a young female entered the room and walked towards McCollum with a food tray.

"She's a new private just out of advanced infantry training. I'm not sure what her name is."

"He acts like he doesn't even know she's there!" Ryan said.

"Yeah, but it gets better."

The young soldier walked over to McCollum and set down a tray along with a plastic cup. McCollum turned to her.

"Thank you, private; I appreciate you bringing me something to eat."

"Not a problem, sir, but I have to wait here until you're finished." Lieutenant McCollum nodded and watched her as she moved into a corner and stood at parade rest. His attention turned to his food for a moment before McCollum again began to berate his NCO.

"I'm gonna kill you!" Bernie stammered as he heaped food into his mouth. "I see the evil in you top," he gestured with his plastic fork before rushing it back down to the potatoes.

"I'm sorry you feel that way, Bernie. If you need anything…"

"Your blood on my hands!" he shouted with his mouth full of food. The NCO exited the cell shaking his head, and Lieutenant McCollum returned his focus to consuming his meal. After a time, he struck up a bit of conversation with the young private, and once finished, McCollum apologized for taking too long. She collected the items and exited without incident.

"That's unbelievable," Gabe said.

"It goes on from here, but you'd just see more of the same."

"Did your NCO go back in again?" Ryan asked.

"Once more, then after that, it's some other sergeant who checks on the lieutenant with the same resulting outburst. I've known Lieutenant McCollum for four years and never knew him to raise his temper. What's worse is he's known my NCO you saw on there even longer than he's known me. The crazy guy you see on this tape is a complete stranger. It just doesn't make sense." The captain's face tensed as he closed the laptop.

"When does this tape end?" Gabe asked.

"My NCO burned a copy of the whole six hours of his shift, so it ends just after midnight."

"And what time frame was the piece you just showed us?" Ryan asked.

"At about ten-fifteen last night." Ryan made a note.

"Have you found out when the lieutenant died yet?"

"I was told that it happened around four in the morning."

"So, any chance of getting us into the autopsy?" Ryan asked.

"That's not possible."

Ryan looked to Gabe.

"Aren't they always done when a soldier dies in the line of duty?" she asked.

"That's correct, ma'am, but not this time."

"I don't understand," Ryan said.

"You know the colonel that called me this morning wanting all of McCollum's stuff?"

"Yeah."

"He wanted all of it in his hands by zero eight hundred?"

"Ok," Gabe said.

"He had a runner in my office at zero seven fifty-five to make sure I handed him all of the information."

"So?" Ryan exclaimed.

"Well, at zero eight-thirty, our post-wide internet broke the news of Lieutenant McCollum's suicide."

"Suicide?" she said. "So, then they already did an autopsy to determine the cause of death. I don't understand; what's the big deal?"

"One of my soldiers remained outside the medical wardroom where they had McCollum's body from the time he died until zero seven forty this morning when they picked him up, ma'am. Nobody did an autopsy. There wasn't enough time. Someone made sure there wasn't going to be one," Kyle said.

"And you're sure about the timeline when the body was finally released to military authorities?" Gabe asked.

Kyle nodded.

"The soldier watching the body is my little brother. I do not doubt the timeline."

"We've got to try and find out what the colonel knows about all of this," Ryan said.

"Suicide's pretty common now, detective," Kyle said. "Still, I've never seen a declaration of death without an autopsy or investigation. Even in Iraq, where proper channels were rarely followed, a declaration of death would never be made so fast. Five days, possible. Fifty minutes...no way in hell!"

CHAPTER 13

ANONYMITY

Giant shadows cast by the Franklin Mountains danced across the military base as the sun struggled through the cracks in the range separating North El Paso and Juarez. The detective's visit lasted hours longer than anticipated as the three watched the entire six-hour videotape of Lieutenant McCollum. Once finished, they drove back to Kyle's office, where the detectives asked more questions about the dead soldier. Difficult at first, Captain Kyle soon found the questioning cathartic as the discussions enabled him to share good memories of his friend. Exhausted at the end of an hour of stories detailing qualities of a grounded, durable, and tactically proficient man, Ryan, Kyle, and Gabe agreed there was at least one obvious conclusion. There was no way Lieutenant McCollum had killed himself.

Ryan and Gabe decided to remain at the base PX for dinner and found a lone table where they could sit out of earshot from the food court. True to their practice over the past week and a half, no business was discussed. Atypically, the two said little about anything to one another as they each reflected on the disturbing revelations of the day. Neither of them spoke until they had finished eating and had driven a few miles off base.

"I keep thinking about Tuwaitha," said Ryan as they crested the mountain ridge and began to descend toward their offices along the Rio Grande.

"Sorry, what?" Gabe asked.

"Tuwaitha. In Iraq. You remember, the city where Captain Kyle's unit was stationed."

"There might be something there," Gabe shrugged, "but our two dead civilians, Caldwell and Mallon, have never been in the military, and I doubt they've vacationed in Iraq."

"That's true, Gabe, but now we have Lieutenant McCollum, Wade, and Farr all having been there together under Captain Kyle's command…"

"Hold on, Ryan. You're jumping the gun a little on lumping McCollum into our parade of carved-up bodies and odd telephone numbers we've been finding. The official word is suicide for now, and until we can find something to prove it's not, that's what we've got."

"True. And I guess we don't have any videotapes that show the rest of our dead people thrashing about and acting insane like McCollum."

"Well, I guess it is possible the guy was seeing things before he died, though?" Gabe said.

"Why do you say that?"

"Not sure, but it might explain some of his behaviors."

Ryan nodded. "I assume from that you're trying to tie in Kay Farr's eye issues and headache before she died?"

"Well, other than McCollum being in the same unit as some of our other bodies, the odd behavior might be caused by visions and might be all we've got," Gabe said.

"While I guess it could be possible Lieutenant McCollum might have been seeing things, the greater concern was his desire to kill the people around him."

"Except for that one young new recruit."

"And I don't ever recall Farr's husband saying anything about his wife having a split personality like that and wanting to kill anyone," Ryan said.

"Sure, but like you just said, we had the benefit of watching the lieutenant devolve into a raving lunatic, and what's to say the same didn't happen to Farr? She wasn't around other people when she was on the phone with her husband. Maybe if she had been in a group, she would have regressed as the lieutenant did? Maybe the visions caused the lieutenant's crazy behavior?"

"Can you think of any way we might be able to get some sort of report about McCollum's cause of death?" Ryan asked.

"Any time there's any sort of negative action, offense, or soldier death in the military, a 15-6 investigation must be conducted."

"You're talking military again, Gabe."

He smiled. "A commander with an issue or concern appoints some lower-ranking officer to investigate."

"Easy enough."

"And then when the report gets done, the commander can take further action or no action based on the findings of the officer."

"But that takes time..."

"Yeah, Ryan, it takes more than an hour to complete, and that's why I'm pretty sure we won't find any 15-6 was or will be done anytime soon."

"Can't they get in trouble for skipping protocol?"

"No. Honestly, they can just create one after the fact or even find several other ways around this if they want to."

"So, we just call and ask for a copy of the investigation then?"

"They aren't available to the public, Ryan, and there are privacy considerations to take into account. Captain Kyle might be able to get something, though, but the only thing for a cop to do is to call the base commander and try to get some answers. Sounds simple and stupid, I know, but it's the next available step here."

"So, when they tell us there is no report and hang up, what next?" Ryan said.

"We do a little more than that, Ryan. Play up the angle that we're investigating all three deaths from the same unit and then throw in some basic questions about McCollum's suicide. The base commander should have collected some information about McCollum by now, and what he tells us can be compared to what Captain Kyle said. No one knows we saw the video or that we have any specifics at all about McCollum's death."

"Do you really think we could find out something?" Ryan asked.

"At least we'll get a sense if they're trying to hide anything. It also can't hurt to offer our services by way of an autopsy or additional manpower."

Ryan agreed and was quick to convince Gabe that she should be the one to call with no former military experience and more feminine wiles. Gabe dropped Ryan off at the front door of the police station before pulling around the building and parking in the underground garage. Required to drive down several levels to find a parking spot and then taking a moment to check voicemail messages from Cunningham, Ryan had a good ten-minute head start.

* * *

Pulling open his office door, he smiled as he heard a syrupy giggle come from Ryan as she tried to pry information from the base commander. While she worked her angle, Gabe rolled a chair over to his desk to make good on his promise to Ryan to check the AIS email. Anyone he cared about hearing from knew he only communicated by texts or calls, never email, so Ryan was right when she pressed him to check the AIS system daily. Gabe looked up at her as she hung up the phone.

"No luck?"

"Depends on what you mean by luck. That guy is my dad's age, but I think I've got a date tomorrow night," she said.

"You were laying the sultry voice on a little thick," Gabe said.

"Oh, thanks," Ryan raised an eyebrow. "I was trying to act innocent and naïve."

"That was not a Catholic school girl I heard on that line," Gabe said. "So you got nothing?"

"Not much. They pushed me through to his personal cell phone, and I think he might have been out tossing back a few drinks with some friends. His response was pretty canned as he said they already did an autopsy to determine a cause of death, so they didn't need our help."

"We know that's a lie."

"Truth or lie, it was well-rehearsed."

"Nothing else then?"

"He told me they'd have a medical report ready in a day or two and that I was free to pick it up personally from his office if I'd like."

"So, you'll get it from the commander then?"

"Yeah."

"And you'll wear the old candy striping outfit you keep hidden in your closet?"

"You think that might help loosen him up?" Ryan smiled as she fell into the chair behind her desk. Gabe's attention was caught by a blinking 'AIS' in the upper right-hand corner of his computer screen. His right index finger clicked twice on the mouse, and the icon rotated. The word 'loading' appeared.

"I think I might have something on my email about the knife." Ryan stood and walked towards his desk as Gabe held up his empty water glass and shook it.

"I'm your maid now?"

"This might take a minute. Agua, please?" She grabbed his cup, strolled over to the fountain, and began to fill it. Gabe made an odd grunt.

"Huh…never came up that fast," he said as she walked back to his desk with his glass half full. Gabe clicked on a file tab labeled El Paso, and a flashing red password box under the word 'sMail' appeared. Gabe pulled out a small piece of plastic, the size of a credit card, and set it next to his keyboard.

"You forget your password?"

"No, Ryan, I don't have the four passwords memorized."

"Four?"

"Well, one of the four, yeah."

"I don't get it."

"The security on this site is kind of crazy," he said. "When we were sworn into the FBI, we sat in a room for half a day setting up this AIS email account which required four different sets of five letters for our passwords."

"Why not just make one password?"

"Every time I try to access AIS, I'm prompted to enter one of the five-letter sets."

"That doesn't sound too tough, so what's the problem?"

"Well, I have to enter the exact five-code sequence after the five-code sequence I used when I last logged into AIS."

"And you don't remember which one you used?" Ryan said.

"Here," he gave Ryan the plastic card, "thanks to my recent activity logging in, I'm pretty sure it was the bottom password, so now I go back to the top and enter the first five letter password on the card." Gabe typed in X Y Z Z X.

"You're typing it in wrong, Gabe," Ryan said, pointing to the card.

"More security Ryan. We have to enter the code backward. If you enter the letters as they read, the computer will flag the entry, make it look like you are given access to the site, but will firewall off anything rated top secret or above."

"Why do they need to do that?" Ryan asked.

"If we're under duress and are forced to enter a code, putting these in as they read rather than backward will fool whoever is trying to get into the system and also permit the bureau to find us through a backtrace." Ryan nodded. "I still hope I've got the right one, though."

"Does your computer crash if you enter the wrong line?" she asked.

"Not quite Ryan, but you only get two chances at it before you have to call a tech in D.C. to unlock the system." He rolled across the screen to the word 'sponsor' and clicked twice. Gabe looked back at Ryan, smiling once more at her confusion, and explained he essentially hit the 'enter' button. The screen went blank, and then the email opened.

> *Agent Moss,*
> *I have information about the eye in the center of the day.*
> *Truth or Consequences: 19 holes of golf are a pain in the butt.*
> *Respond ASAP.*

Gabe read the email four times while Ryan scribbled the cryptic note on a pad of paper. His right hand held tight to his chin as he repeated it aloud.

"Let me work on this," Ryan said. "It can't be that complicated."

PART 4

WANDERING PATH

CHAPTER 14

ELEPHANT BUTTE

Gabe didn't wait around long while Ryan deciphered the email. In fact, in light of the card game the night before, and the goings-on at Fort Bliss, he was tired and quick to dismiss himself for the night. Although he made Ryan promise to leave early as well, he knew her nature would never permit her to shut down before the task was done. His phone rang just before 6:00 a.m. The caller ID indicated it was from the EPPD.

"Didn't go home, did you, Ryan?"

"I probably beat you home last night since the email didn't take me long to figure out. I just got in early this morning to get you moving."

"Get moving?" Gabe asked.

"You've got a meeting at noon today," she said.

"And you woke me up super early so I'd have time to primp for it?"

"You've got some driving to do, and I want you there early in case we've got more deciphering when you arrive."

"And where exactly am I going?" Gabe found a pencil on his nightstand.

"Up into New Mexico. A little town called Elephant Butte."

"And how did you figure that?" Gabe asked.

"The Truth or Consequences part was pretty easy to discern, but it took me a while to come up with the fact the "e" stood for both butte and had a meaning itself. I spent fifteen minutes on the internet searching cities or towns with the names truth and consequence in Texas and then New Mexico and finally hit on a town with both words in the name. After pulling up a map, I discovered a little town called Elephant Butte near Truth and Consequences."

Gabe wrote down the name of the towns.

"And where exactly am I going in this little town?"

"You'll be heading to a little bar called the 19ᵗʰ hole, which is halfway between the two towns. It's a hangout for golfers when they get done playing golf in either Elephant Butte or Truth and Consequences. Both cities have courses."

"Any idea who I'm meeting?"

"Well, I got back into your AIS system."

"Ugh."

"Sorry, but you left your card on the desk last night, and since I watched you input your last code, I knew which one to use."

"While I am sure no one would figure out it wasn't me, just please don't get on there without me present."

"Sorry."

"No, really, it's ok. It's just that my butt would be on the line if anyone found out it wasn't me accessing the system."

"Understood. Anyway, I replied that you would be at the 19ᵗʰ hole at noon today, and within about ten minutes, there was a confirmation reply."

"So, how long will it take us to get up there?"

"Not us…you."

"You're not coming?"

"The return message stated no tracers, phones, weapons, or partners."

"Well, I guess I can do two of the four," Gabe said. Trained from the day he first joined the FBI, Gabe never let a piece leave his side. In Iraq, it was at times a matter of life and death, in the FBI a point of constant preparedness, and today, on a wild goose chase like this, it was a necessity.

"I figured you wouldn't leave without your weapon or your phone," Ryan said. "Better get moving; you don't want to be late."

"My GPS says it's a two-hour drive, Ryan; I'll head out around nine," Gabe said. "I'll call you when I get there."

* * *

Gabe headed north across the Texas state line into New Mexico and got lost in his memories of his trips into the vast Iraqi deserts. He had to admit it had been some time since he felt that odd peace moving into the vast openness of the desert and away from the violence of the Persian cities. Yet unlike his time in the sand, trapped in a third-world country with technological advances forty years behind the U.S., there were few locations in the States that could not be reached. He picked up his vibrating phone.

"I'm not there yet!" he greeted Ryan.

"I was just..."

"I didn't want to worry you, mother, so I left very early. I'm already in New Mexico," Gabe said.

"No need for the sarcasm Gabe, but thanks for feeding my neurosis. Besides, that's not the reason I'm calling."

"So, what's up?"

"I got a call from Cunningham this morning about Specialist Wade's cause of death."

"What'd he say?" Gabe asked.

"He died from poison."

"What kind of poison?"

"Cunningham found it fascinating to discuss the scientific process of figuring that question out, but after about three minutes of nonsensical terms, I had him break it down to its simplest level."

"And?"

"Mushrooms."

"Mushrooms?"

"Yeah, Gabe, mushrooms."

"So, the guy ate some bad mushrooms and died? No doom and gloom? I guess we can scratch him off our list."

"Well, not just yet."

"Why not?"

"Because these aren't mushrooms found nearby."

"So, it was some exotic fungus from an Asian restaurant in Juarez, so what?"

"Well, Cunningham is sure these mushrooms do not grow around here, and they are not served in any nearby restaurants."

"Okay."

"And what's more, Cunningham also found the poison in Mallon."

"Mallon? The guy with his kidneys cut open?"

"Yeah."

"Why didn't our resident medical examiner catch that one before now?"

"He said since both of Mallon's kidneys were cut open, there was no fluid left for him to test."

"Then how'd he go back and verify the presence of the mushroom in Mallon so many weeks after his death?" Gabe asked.

"Cunningham still had a vial of blood from Mallon's body stored around in that creepy room he has next to his office, and once he knew what to look for, he found a trace of the amatoxin."

"The whatatoxin?"

"Amatoxin is what he called it Gabe, but let's just keep it simple and say mushrooms."

"Much easier. So, was he able to check for this in any of our other bodies?"

"He did check for the poison in Harris and Farr but found nothing," Ryan said. "He also checked over his records for Caldwell…"

"The guy with his head crushed in?" Gabe asked.

"Yeah, but he didn't have any indication from the tox screen that he had any poison in his system either."

"So, what does this mushroom do?"

"The mushroom attacks the liver and kidneys in some manner, but Cunningham didn't have all of the exact science off the top of his head."

"Where would someone find these mushrooms?"

"As I said, he didn't know too much, but he said he'd hook us up with a Mycologist friend of his for some answers."

"A what?"

"A person that studies fungus. Cunningham said she'd be the person to talk to, so save your questions until then."

"So, until we know more, though, at least now we have this common bond between Mallon and Wade of this poisonous…?"

Gabe went silent.

"Did I lose you?"

"No, sorry, I was just thinking that maybe whoever cut open Mallon's kidneys knew he was ingesting the mushrooms?"

"Yeah, I had that thought too. After all, the incisions flushed out all of his fluids that would have made it easier to discover the poison in the first place."

"Of course, if that's true if the same person killed Mallon and Wade, we still have to explain why they didn't cut open Wade's kidneys to hide the poison as well?"

"Yeah," Ryan said. "And then we also need to figure out if both of these men were going to be dead in a matter of days from ingesting this poison anyway; why would someone need to kill them?"

Gabe's forehead creased as he tried to form an explanation.

"Either way, now we've got something tying those two guys together, and along with the knife wounds and the odd telephone numbers, perhaps we're getting somewhere," Gabe said.

"Little bits of information tying up lots of bodies but making little sense," Ryan said. "I don't feel much better."

"We're getting there, Ryan. Perhaps today's meeting will close some loops. I should be arriving in the heart of the town in about a half-hour, and when I hit route 181, I'm going to turn off this cell phone and tuck it under the seat. I've already had my annual proctology examine, and since I'm going to be keeping my weapon, I'm afraid if they find two things they asked me not to bring, I might be in line for another."

"Way more information than I need," Ryan said.

"I'll text you if I find anything more out about these mushrooms. Just check your phone when you get the chance."

"Will do," Gabe said.

"Be safe," Ryan said before Gabe flipped his phone closed. He reached into his glove box, retrieved his weapon, and placed it on the passenger seat. His excitement increased as a tattered wooden sign with John Deere green letters informed him the 19ᵗʰ Hole Bar and Tavern was twenty miles ahead.

CHAPTER 15

PARANOID

G abe arrived at his destination and glanced at his watch. He was twenty minutes ahead of schedule. He climbed out of his vehicle and pulled off his sunglasses to get a better look. 'Town' was perhaps the wrong designation for this place as there was nothing more than one four-way intersection with a stoplight and a few faded brick buildings on three of the four corners. The parking lot on the southwest corner of the intersection where he stood was the only corner without a building. On the northeast corner was an old boarded-up building with the initials I.O.O.F., while the northwest corner housed a movie rental store. A brick façade building with five long rectangular windows consumed the southeast corner and above the door to the establishment was a faded wooden sign indicating he had found the 19th Hole Bar and Tavern.

Gabe pulled open the glass door and was noticed by half of the patrons affixed to stools. Gabe nodded, smiled, and turned to the booths lining the glass windows to his right. Three waitresses moved back and forth with coffee and clear purpose, and although he could not see the cooks, gruff conversations emitted through a small space behind the counter. A twenty-something waitress dressed in tan shorts and a bright pink collared shirt approached. Her dyed blonde hair was pulled back in a ponytail which stuck out over the top of a sun visor.

"Morning, cutie, you by yourself today?" she said.

"I am meeting someone, but if I could get a seat now, I sure would appreciate it."

"Sure thing, we'll put you in a booth if that's ok?" Gabe followed the young girl to a table directly across from where his car was parked. He slid across the leather seat on the side facing the tavern entrance as the waitress took out her order pad and tapped her pencil.

"Joe made up some biscuits and gravy this morning for the special, and we've got some homemade pies if you prefer to start with dessert today. That's what most of our customers do when the pies are fresh. They are good!"

"Just coffee would be great for now, thanks."

"Black?" She set her pencil behind her ear.

"Only way to take it," Gabe smiled as she headed for the counter. Gabe looked over the menu, and in less than a minute, the waitress returned to his table carrying a white mug which she flipped over and filled from a whole pot of coffee.

"Need some more time?"

"Yeah, I think I'll wait until my friend gets here," Gabe replied.

"Okay. I'll keep an eye on you. Just holler if you need something."

"Thanks," Gabe nodded as he picked up the cup and sipped.

"Shit!" He spit back the liquid, glanced up, and smiled back at the glaring patrons. He held up the cup in hopes they would understand. Several nodded as he went about soaking up what spilled on his pants. To avoid eye contact with anyone else, he dabbed away with multiple napkins and checked his timepiece as just two minutes remained until the designated meeting time. His heart pounded faster as he formed a pile of brown stained napkins on the table and pushed them to the edge. Finished, he set his sights on the front door.

Two plates of steaming food dropped onto the table from over his shoulder.

"What's this?" Gabe asked as he broke from his trance.

"I didn't know this when you walked in, but your friend called earlier and said he was running late and didn't want you to go hungry." The mound of sausage, fried potatoes, and eggs looked appetizing as she set down silverware in front of Gabe and another set next to his visitor's waiting plate.

"He did tell Joe you were picking up the check, though," she winked at Gabe and scribbled on her receipt pad. Handing him the receipt, she turned it over. "I put a phone number where your friend could be reached on the back of the receipt there. He gave it to Joe when he called and said it was a new cell." Gabe reached for the bill as she grabbed the soaked napkins.

"I appreciate that," Gabe said as he stared at the number.

"Seems if he's late, he should be the one paying?" she said.

"Sorry? What?"

"Oh nothing, just teasing. Is there anything else I can get for you?"

"No, thanks," Gabe said. "I guess uh…he'll be along in a minute." She turned and walked away.

Gabe reached into his empty jacket pocket in search of his cell phone. He looked across the street and debated whether to retrieve the device from under the seat. Eyes were likely upon him. Gabe scooted to the aisle, stood up, and walked towards his waitress, who was cleaning off a table.

"Do you have a payphone I could use?" Gabe asked.

"If it's a local call, you can use the one by the counter over there?" She pointed towards the cash register.

"Thanks." Gabe took a few steps past the front door to the other side of the cash register, where he picked up the receiver to an old rotary dial phone and smiled. He loved such historical artifacts. After entering the numbers, the line switched several times, indicating the call was being relayed.

"Agent Moss?"

"Yes."

"Pay for your breakfast, take your receipt, and make your way to the golf range in the back of the tavern."

"I'm not sure I'm in the right place," Gabe said. "There's no beer and nary a peanut in sight."

"Ask for Tyler and give him the receipt in your hand." The line dropped, and Gabe set the receiver back on the base. Gabe pulled out his wallet and handed the receipt to a more senior waitress. The perky young girl waiting on him came up and told the older woman she would ring out her customer.

"Everything okay today?" his waitress asked.

"Great, everything was great." Gabe scanned the room.

"You sure you're okay. You didn't eat anything?"

"Yes, I know, you were great; it's just my friend decided to skip breakfast and is going to meet me at the golf range. Now…where…is that exactly?"

"Just right through the door to your left there, and after you go through the bar area, you'll see a neon sign for the golf range out back."

"You've got a bar and a golf range back there?" Gabe said.

"Sure. It's kind of just hidden behind our little diner here, but it's all owned by the same guy."

"Take this," Gabe handed her a ten-dollar bill. "I appreciate your time." The waitress smiled and waved as Gabe turned and leaned against the large wooden door. Pushing it open, he found himself in a dark and cavernous two-story room across which hung a red neon sign reading 'Golf Range.' His black tactical boots clacked on the wooden dance floor, and he could make out a large stage about one hundred feet to his right. Located in the center of the room was the silhouette of a circular bar with white lights running the circumference of the wooden structure. Ringing the walls around the second story was an expansive balcony adorned with dozens of tables and chairs offering excellent dance floor and stage views. Gabe walked under the neon sign and wandered down a narrow hallway. A few yards from the door, Gabe came upon a window beneath a 'Range' sign.

"Hi," Gabe interrupted an old man sitting behind the counter, "I'm supposed to meet Tyler here." The old man raised a finger, rose from his seat, and shuffled through a noisy door. Gabe backed away from the counter and walked to his right to a large glass window overlooking several stalls comprising a driving range. He could never have imagined so much was located behind the tiny diner. Out of the corner of his eye, Gabe noticed the old man return.

"Tyler will be up in a moment," he said. "You're his first today." Gabe nodded and paced around the tiny waiting area, examining several golf pictures. Most were stock photos of famous players, but a few expressed a local flavor with '1965 Club Champion' and 'Longest Drive, 345 yards' written in white ink across the bottom. Without warning, a door leading to the hitting stalls opened wide. An imposing blonde man dressed in a bright red polo shirt and tan pants held open the door and waved at Gabe.

"So great to see you and right on time." This man, whom Gabe assumed was Tyler, smiled and reached forward to shake hands.

"Tyler, good to meet you."

Gabe handed Tyler the receipt from the restaurant. Tyler smiled and nodded.

"We're testing those golf clubs I told you about on the phone back here in the computer simulator. You'll notice a difference in your distance with these babies. Follow me!" Gabe followed Tyler out the door and past the row of hitting stalls. Tyler held open the door to a white trailer about twenty yards from the old man, and Gabe ducked inside.

"Stop when you get to the hallway there," Tyler said.

Gabe walked a few feet before coming to a wall. Tyler closed the door behind them, pushed past Gabe, and then moved down the hallway to Gabe's right.

"We're going to the simulator in here." Tyler led Gabe through a tinted glass door and into a rectangular room. "Take a seat on the bench," Tyler said. He moved to the opposite side of the room and began making a racket with a set of golf clubs in a large bag.

Gabe noticed a green hitting mat in front of him and a video projector hanging from the ceiling, from which a computer-generated golf course hole was cast on the wall to his right. The din of clubs knocking into one another stopped as Tyler knelt, unzipped a large pocket on the golf bag, and pulled out a wand.

"I need your jacket, watch, phone, keys, and wallet," Tyler said.

"I don't…"

"Jacket, watch, phone, keys, and wallet," Tyler said. "Agent Moss, this can't possibly surprise a man with your experience."

Gabe tossed Tyler his wallet first, keys next, and then unzipped his jacket.

Tyler placed the items on the table and waived the wand back and forth as Gabe removed his wristwatch. A range of whines and whistles cut the room's silence, causing Tyler to pry into various pockets of the jacket.

Gabe placed his watch on the table next to the wallet.

"What about your cell phone?" Tyler asked.

"Left it in the car."

"You know I'll find it if it's on you."

"Why do you think I used a payphone out front?" Tyler shrugged.

"I assume you still have a weapon," Tyler said.

"It's on my ankle," Gabe pulled up his right pant leg.

"I'm going to need that."

"Do you always make your golfers give up their pieces?" Gabe asked.

"Only those with special forces training." Tyler smiled, and Gabe felt unnerved. He reached down and popped the snap holding an old revolver tight to his leg.

"Do I get that baby back?" Gabe asked. Tyler pushed out the cylinder holding the bullets and dumped the shells on the table. Flipping the wheel closed on the revolver, he pushed the empty weapon across the table and back to Gabe.

"Are you wearing any tracking devices?"

"I've got nothing…"

"What about on your phone in the car?"

"I haven't used the phone for over a half-hour."

"We know," Tyler said. "My question was about a tracking device."

"Negative. It's my personal phone, not an issued one. There's no GPS on it." Tyler moved the wand over Gabe without a single whistle.

"Satisfied?" Gabe asked.

"Just about," Tyler directed Gabe back to the bench. Once Gabe was seated, Tyler flipped a switch on the wall, which prompted a holographic golf professional to appear on the screen to Gabe's right. The digital man exclaimed how Stevenson golf equipment would change Gabe's game forever. Gabe paid no attention to the presentation. Instead, he focused on Tyler, who leaned against the wall with a cell phone. After a few moments, Tyler closed his phone and took a seat next to Gabe as the video presentation continued.

"Take these keys," Tyler said. "You'll find a red station wagon out the door of this trailer and down to the left." Gabe did not take the keys.

"Aren't you the person I was supposed to meet?" Gabe asked.

"No, Gabe, I'm just here to clear you." He pushed the keys into Gabe's hand again. "You're going to need these to get where you're going."

"And where exactly is that?" Tyler pulled out a black sharpie and wrote '25N to 83W to 285N to E Country Club' on Gabe's arm.

"Look for a bright green Pontiac just east of the train tracks."

"Roswell?" Gabe surmised, thanks to two personal interest visits in the recent past to the Mecca for all things unidentified. Tyler nodded. Gabe stood up, and Tyler handed him his wallet, jacket, and watch. He moved towards the door but was stopped once more.

"You'll need this when you get to the car." Tyler pulled a two-iron from the demonstration bag and handed it to Gabe. "Don't lose this. You better get going. You have until three-thirty to get there."

It was now twelve forty.

"What about my phone and my car?" he asked as Tyler held open the door.

"Don't worry, you'll get all of your stuff back after the meeting," he said. "Oh," he continued, "and I strongly recommend you don't stop and try to make contact with anyone."

Gabe pushed open the trailer door, turned left, and saw the red station wagon. After pulling open the car door, Gabe threw the two-iron into the back seat. As the car started and Gabe shifted it into gear, Tyler appeared next to the trailer and waved. Gabe returned the awkward wave, drove away from the back of the tavern, and found his way onto State Road 25.

CHAPTER 16

SVETLANA

G abe knew from his time in the military that Tyler and his friends were more than just some rag-tag group of government employees looking to reveal some worthless information about the knife. He was sure they were trained in covert operations and were military or security specialists in possession of secrets that someone with a substantial amount of power would rather not have them reveal. Their damning knowledge set the stage for the gamut now being run in the middle of the New Mexico desert. Lost in his thoughts of all the possibilities that awaited him in Roswell, he didn't immediately notice the red and blue lights in his rearview mirror.

There hadn't been much traffic to pace with on his way to Roswell, and Gabe had no clue how fast he was driving. Gabe pulled over next to a Roswell city limit sign and pulled out his wallet. As the dark tan SUV pulled into the space behind him, Gabe noticed that the officer was towing a dirty four-wheeler, often indicating a conservation officer. The officer pulled himself slowly from the vehicle and placed a curve-rimmed baseball cap tight onto his head. Catching a spot of dust on his right calf, he slapped at his leg, causing a cloud to release from his pants before checking once more over his attire. Primped now, as he moved towards Gabe, his right hand settled tight over his holster. Gabe rolled down the passenger window.

"Good afternoon, conservation officer," Gabe said as he fixated on the cop's long handlebar mustache.

"Afternoon, sir, could I trouble you for your license and registration?"

"Not a problem, officer. Here's my license, and let me see if I can find the registration." Gabe pulled open the glove box and shuffled through papers, finding nothing. Gabe turned and smiled at the officer before once more resuming his search. The officer's patience waned.

"Wait here a second." The officer turned and walked back to his vehicle with only the license.

"No problem." Gabe pushed the loose papers back into the glove box and noticed the clock on the dash indicating he had less than an hour to arrive at his destination. He cursed under his breath for not being a little quicker on his feet and pulling out his badge. Abusing his authority was never something that came easy to Gabe, but if ever there was a time to utilize his trump card, it perhaps should have been now. The officer did not stay in his vehicle for long, and in his rearview mirror, Gabe saw the officer step from his squad car, weapon drawn.

Gabe froze.

"I need you to step out of the car," the officer said. Gabe put both hands out the window. Keeping his right hand raised, he lowered his left hand down and opened the door from the outside handle before exiting the vehicle.

"Hands-on your head, please, and lean against your car."

Gabe complied with the instructions. As Gabe rested against the hot metal, the officer got behind him and secured his wrists with a twisty band similar to the ones he used in Iraq. Once bound, the officer turned him around.

"There's a report of this car being stolen," the officer said.

"It's a rental I just got back near Truth or Consequences. I have a meeting in Roswell at three-thirty, and then I was heading back there tonight. I'm with the FBI, and I'm doing an investigation. I guess I should have told you that first, but I must get there on time."

The officer shook his head.

"Well, I'm gonna have to take you in until this all checks out," the officer said as he turned Gabe around. "We take stolen cars pretty seriously around here. Hold on a moment." Gabe watched as the officer rolled up the station wagon's windows, removed the keys from the ignition, and grabbed the golf club from the back seat.

* * *

The sun was blazing at its zenith as the police vehicle continued on interstate 70 past every entrance into Roswell. He felt more at ease with each missed exit and believed this 'stop' might just be another step to his ultimate meeting point. After twenty minutes, the vehicle turned into a cookie-cutter neighborhood east of Roswell.

"Officer," Gabe asked. "Is there any chance you might tell me where you're taking me?"

"We'll be there in a minute," the officer said. Gabe leaned back and watched out the window as dog walkers, stroller pushers, and yard sprinklers went about their daily routines. They all ignored the conservation vehicle as it rolled slowly past their homes.

"Little off the beaten path here, aren't we?" Gabe asked. The driver said nothing. "You nature guys keep your headquarters in one of these three-car garages?"

"Uh, no," the driver said. "In fact…we're here."

They stopped at the dead-end of a cul-de-sac. Each lot on the circle had a house, except one empty but well-groomed lot with an asphalt path stretching from the road into the woods.

"Agent Moss, I presume?"

A petite dark-haired woman dressed in an obnoxious pink shirt pulled open his door and motioned for him to exit. She grabbed hold of Gabe's arm, aiding him from the back seat, and spun him around.

"Agent Moss, my name is Svetlana. I'll have you free in a moment," she said as she snipped the binds. Gabe rubbed his tingling hands together as he turned to face her.

"We out here for a quick nine?"

"Depends," she said. The driver pushed the two-iron out his window, and Svetlana grabbed it tight.

"Thank you, officer."

"That's Officer Argyle to you, Ms. Uppel," he said. Svetlana frowned, and her head turned side to side as the car window closed.

"Would you like to get in agent?" Svetlana gestured to the golf cart parked just off the street. "Or do you have someone else you want to visit out here in suburbia?" Gabe shook his head and climbed into the passenger side of the electric cart.

Svetlana possessed sharp and detailed features that were most evident thanks to her fine black hair pulled back in a tight ponytail. At first glance, she reminded Gabe of Ryan, but upon closer inspection, despite the colorful pink and yellow golf ensemble that was immaculately pressed, it was not enough to ease her rigid core. The wrinkles on her forehead and the leathery appearance of her skin aged her well beyond her biological years, and the seriousness in her eyes made it evident her life's work had not been kind.

They drove down an asphalt path, past a sign reading 'To the 9ᵗʰ hole' as Svetlana handed Gabe the two-iron. "So, what was this all about?" he asked, holding up the two-iron as they pulled onto a cart path near the 9ᵗʰ tee box.

"What can I say? My guys get a kick out of making up these characters and routines for our missions," Svetlana said. "They try to have some fun with their work."

"So, Tyler and Argyle work for you then?"

"No, Agent Moss, we're a team. We support one another."

"You can call me Gabe."

"Good enough then, Gabe. Those two and their ridiculous gimmicks," she shook her head and revealed a smirk.

"What do you mean?"

"That stupid club you're holding there and this get-up I'm wearing. They create and run the meat and potatoes of every operation like this outfit and pacing you through the wringer today to make sure you weren't followed."

"Posing as a conservation officer was their bright idea?"

"Who questions a conservation officer Gabe? Those guys look for people hunting armadillos out of season with lead shot-tipped arrows for fun. That's probably the most outwardly unassuming law enforcement role you could ever take on. Hell, you could probably fake being one of those guys for months before any local enforcement types might ever catch on." Gabe smiled.

"So, you're never part of the setup crew then?" Gabe asked.

"They don't ever tell me anything other than where to be and at what time. And with every operation comes their own special brand of shenanigans so later they can have a good laugh."

"I can assume then they are not Tyler and Argyle?" Gabe smiled.

"No," Svetlana said as she broke a grin. "And I'm not Miss Upple."

"I don't get it."

"Think about it, Gabe, Miss Upple, or 'Supple' to go with Tyler with a T and Argyle with an A. T and A for…"

"Uh yeah…" Gabe cut her off, "…I get it. So, what's your part in all of this game then today besides James Bond's latest lover?"

Svetlana broke a wide smile.

"Nothing to do with love today," she said. Svetlana continued past the ninth tee box and pulled off onto a mulch path, traveling for twenty more yards before stopping at an overlook. Below, Gabe could see two golf holes running parallel to one another, each covering a distance of well over four hundred yards. The crisp green fairways stood out against the desert foliage and brown sand that enveloped both of the holes, and Gabe couldn't imagine the amount of water necessary to keep the course looking so fantastic.

Svetlana killed the golf cart engine and placed her arm on the padded seat behind his head.

"You found quite an interesting knife there in El Paso, Gabe," Svetlana said. "I'm pretty sure it's the first time one has ever been left at a scene."

"The knife belongs to one of your guys?" Gabe asked.

"We're better than that. We don't leave weapons behind. But I do know where it comes from. Well, I can't tell you who exactly that knife belongs to, but I generally know to whom these particular knives are entrusted."

"So, you must know what's engraved on the knife then?" Gabe said, testing her.

Svetlana smiled.

"In search of monsters to destroy," she said. "It's from a speech John Adams delivered when he was Secretary of State. And I assume you already figured out the eye on the handle is the Eye of Providence?"

"Yep," Gabe said. "My medical examiner friend had a similar-looking eye on his fraternity crest in college. He surmised the eye on the knife was the same. And the handle…"

"Is made of whalebone," she said. Svetlana reached into the small black satchel hanging on her shoulder and produced her own whalebone-handled knife. "Comes to us all the way from India," she handed it to Gabe. "It's given as a gift of sorts when people like me finish our training."

"And you're comfortable just handing me this right now?" Gabe asked as he turned over the blade to see the inscription.

"I know all about you, Gabe, and like you, I'm always prepared. Take a look up on the hill." Gabe saw nothing at first as he scanned where Svetlana was pointing. Then, just past a deep ravine about half a mile away in an opening among the trees, he caught the glint of something refracting the sun's rays. It was either a 300 mm National Geographic camera lens or a scope atop a sniper rifle.

"They're out there for you," Svetlana said. "My friend Argyle likes to shoot when he gets the chance, but Tyler never misses, so I'm guessing A is the one stuck ranging out the distance to your skull. As long as you don't make any sudden moves, you're safe."

Gabe grinned. "You don't need to worry."

"Just never know," Svetlana said.

"So, if my knife didn't belong to your team, who exactly does it belong to? Just how many teams like yours are out there?"

"I'm not sure. We've always assumed there were more teams, but until you found the knife, we never had any actual proof."

"How could you not know others were out there doing similar work to yours?"

"We were trained in a vacuum Gabe…just the three of us. So, until a picture of your knife popped up on the AIS system, we only had our theories about other teams like ours."

"So, this group you work for has a top-secret human resources department?"

"You could say that."

"And the name of this secretive bunch?"

"They're called ROBE," Svetlana said, "and before you ask, it stands for red, orange, blue, and emerald." Even though Gabe's top-secret clearance provided him the chance to partner with dozens of the most legendary operatives and clandestine groups in the world, he knew there were still secrets of the United States government he would never know.

"A rainbow coalition?"

Svetlana was unamused.

"Never heard of them before," Gabe said.

"Few have."

"So, what does this polychromatic gang do?"

"We collect persons deemed dangerous to the American people."

"By collect, you mean kill?" Gabe said.

"No, not that often. In fact, the majority of the time we're called out, we're simply given the name of a person to find, we capture them, and then turn them over to ROBE."

"So, who is it that calls you exactly?" Gabe asked.

"Come on, Gabe," Svetlana said. "You think they're going to hand us their social security numbers as well? All of our communications are conducted with these phones ROBE gives to us." She held up a cell. "They don't reveal names, it's never the same person, and we don't ask for anything other than our target's name, residence, and other pertinent tracking..."

"Wait, wait, wait," Gabe stopped her. "Just a second ago, you said you don't have to kill that often. How often is not that often?"

"There are occasions when the people we're sent to detain are at risk of hurting other people or have already killed someone before we can get to them. If they're already too far gone, sometimes we have to eliminate them. We make hits only when necessary, but our immediate orders are to grab them and bring them in alive."

"So, these people you find and collect, what is it that makes them so dangerous?"

"They're called Seers, Gabe. They're people who acquire the ability to see all living things' life force or aura. The ability to see various energetic levels of life force. At least that's how my team and I describe it."

"Doesn't sound too problematic..."

"The problem with this modification in their vision, though, is that throughout history, a large percentage of those afflicted tend to become psychotic and turn homicidal."

"So, ROBE taught you that these aura readers pose a threat to society?" Gabe said.

"Yes, Gabe. Our training explained that Seers were prone to have instantaneous homicidal tendencies towards anyone surrounded by a red aura. The other three colors a Seer can make out bring on limited emotional changes and are therefore unimportant. We spent several weeks in a mine in West Virginia training to become agents of ROBE, and they spent a vast amount of time discussing the national security elements or our job and little on the mechanics of the affliction."

"National security?" Gabe asked.

"We were told ROBE most often catches Seers before they become dangerous, though there have been times where Seers have carried out some prominent murders before they were identified or caught. Over the centuries, famous men and women have been killed along with many average citizens. It was impressed upon us quite clearly how imperative it was to stop these Seers before they get the opportunity to kill."

"This sounds insane." Gabe raised an eyebrow. "How on earth would these Seers never have come to the attention of the general public? Every conspiracy theory…every potential real and completely improbable angle of the Kennedy assassination, has surfaced. You can go online and read dozens of theories about the twin towers. How could any trace of this have stayed under the radar?"

"I didn't go through all this today just to drag you here and fill your head with a bunch of fairy tales," Svetlana said. "We were taught that up until the turn of the century, maybe only two to seven people a year were discovered to be afflicted with this vision problem and corresponding homicidal tendencies."

"So, you're telling me since the eighteen hundreds people have just been popping up with vision problems, and when they see someone in red, they try to kill them?" Gabe asked.

"In a nutshell."

"And there's only been a few of them every year?"

"Yes…until more recently."

"Hold on a second. When you're grabbing these people and turning them over to ROBE, what are they doing with them?"

"Our training in the cave led us to believe there was a cure for the vision problem and ensuing madness…" Svetlana looked down.

"But now you're not so sure what they're doing with the Seers, are you?"

Svetlana nodded. "We learned about a scientist named Atticus Heacox who suffered from the vision affliction back in the seventeen hundreds. He worked on a cure in a cave in Pennsylvania for several years as, for some reason or another, he never became psychotic or homicidal even though he had the visions. He found a cure…at least, we believed that until a few weeks ago."

"What changed?" Gabe asked.

"A month or so back, you found a man in the streets, half-naked with some major fractures along his skull."

"Caldwell," Gabe nodded.

"Yes, Bryan Caldwell. And around the same time, you found another man with a bunch of knife wounds in his chest alongside yet another body, who until recently, you were calling John Doe."

"Yeah, John Doe, sorry, Marlin Wade, and yes, he was found the same time as Todd Harris, who died from knife wounds in his chest."

"We collected those men for ROBE a week or so before you found them," Svetlana said.

"All three of them?"

She nodded. "All within two days."

"So, if ROBE had you collect them up to cure them, how'd they wind up dead in the street?" Gabe asked.

"We don't know."

"Where did you hand them off to ROBE when you captured these Seers?"

"Each of the drop-offs was near the produce district on the north side of El Paso, but in different locations. All of our exchanges are done from car to car and never are done in the same place twice."

"And you have no idea where ROBE took them after you handed them over?"

"None," Svetlana stated. "But there's more Agent Moss. Do you recall the grizzly massacre at a Mexican wedding a few weeks after you found Caldwell, Harris, and Wade? A slew of people and a couple of kids got mowed down in the firefight?"

"I saw those bodies in the morgue the morning when we pulled the knife out of a lady's neck, but what does that have to do with this?" asked Gabe.

"Go back and check the bodies from the massacre," Svetlana said. "You'll find First Sergeant Benito Mazar among the dead. He's another Seer we picked up about two months ago at Fort Benning. He had just arrived back from a stint in Kuwait."

"Another soldier?" Gabe shook his head.

"Yeah, another soldier." Svetlana's face turned red. "That's the main reason we're here talking today, Gabe. We think these Seers are being used by ROBE. With the knife you found, the three dead Seers showing up on the streets after we collected them, and then Mazar, there's more going on here than we've been told. We no longer want any part of our soldiers being used."

"Used to do what?" Gabe asked.

"We can't say Gabe, but it seems evident they're not being cured. Something's not right."

"So, it's just these recent events causing you to question your bosses?"

Svetlana nodded.

"And none of this doubt entered into your minds before now?"

"Not really, Gabe. We just went about doing our job like good little soldiers."

"What do you mean, not really?"

She looked at Gabe. "Since we started doing this line of work, there was only one time that any of us questioned what we were doing. About a year and a half ago, we caught up with a soldier in Bend, Oregon, that had just returned from Afghanistan. As with most of our targets, we got to him without incident and turned him over to ROBE. A few months later, Tyler was visiting some family in Florida. He swore he saw a picture of the same soldier in the newspaper as a suspect in a fatal shooting of an American with ties to Al-Zarqawi. The next day Tyler read another article about how the suspect killed himself in jail awaiting arraignment. For some reason, Tyler never thought about telling us what he read until these recent incidents got us all talking."

"And was it the same guy you had taken from Oregon?" Gabe asked.

"We did a search on the web and discovered the same soldier we picked up in Oregon, Specialist Carlisle, was listed as a suicide, and his place of death was Florida. We couldn't find any other newspaper article with any pictures of Carlisle, but we don't have a doubt today that the specialist was the same guy we tagged for ROBE up in Oregon."

"So, you think ROBE is using these Seers to kill people?" Gabe said.

"The Florida killing and then the Mazar wedding incident started us thinking. Of course, neither of those explain the three dead Seers you found in the street or what's happened to the dozens of other Seers we've gathered for ROBE over the years. With what's been happening in El Paso, along with this knife, there are a bunch of growing questions about what ROBE really had us doing."

"Any idea why all of these soldiers are popping up as Seers?" Gabe asked.

"None. However, over the past few years, we're often called out to military bases and get half a dozen or more Seers to pick up whenever units return home from tours in Iraq and Afghanistan. We still get calls to pick up non-soldiers at times, but soldiers make up a great majority of the ones we've been collecting recently. We've always hated corralling a bunch of war heroes, but now that they're turning up dead around El Paso, our work has become untenable."

"So, what do you expect me to do with all of this? Other than this knife, you haven't given me anything concrete to work with here."

"I'm hoping we can help each other," Svetlana said.

"What do you propose?"

"There's more information Gabe, but you're going to have to get it."

"Why can't you?" Gabe asked.

"As you have probably guessed, we're now on the run from ROBE. A couple of days back, just after we dug up information on the Oregon kid, we got a call to pick up some soldier at Fort Bliss who had threatened some MP's. Before ROBE called, the three of us agreed we were done collecting Seers, so we refused to pick him up. A few minutes later, some other ROBE official called back and ordered us to do what we were instructed or start digging our graves. I'm sure you can guess we don't get to just walk away from ROBE and return to our civilian lives. We had no choice but to go underground to protect ourselves, and we've realized this isn't ending until we're dead or we expose ROBE."

"You didn't get very far away from El Paso if you're trying to hide," Gabe said.

"We're in Roswell Gabe. Aliens live here, remember? Enough crazies and kooks are running around that we're pretty sure this is a safe place for us…at least for today." Gabe smiled. "We had to meet with you, and once we say goodbye today, you won't see us again unless you solve what's going on."

"And where do you suggest I look for this information?" Gabe asked.

"There are some notes and records of Atticus Heacox from when he was studying the Seers, located at a tiny library in Renovo, Pennsylvania."

"And how do you know those records are there?"

"You and I worked for some of the same people in the document distribution business for Uncle Sam before we started our more recent gigs." Gabe raised an eyebrow and nodded. "One of my jobs was to put those particular items there."

"And how can you be sure that these items are still where you say they are?" Gabe asked.

"A friend in Washington verified the records have not been moved since I delivered them there four years ago. However, he's being followed now, and it's apparent ROBE knows we've been in contact. I can only imagine they're somehow watching the documents located there, so it'd be too obvious if any of us that are familiar to the group showed up to get the items."

"How do you know your friend didn't already take the documents, is lying to you, and is waiting to see if you show up?" Gabe asked.

"It's someone I can trust with utmost confidence. That's all you need to know," she said.

"So, what are you hoping these records contain?"

"We hope they can help you," she said. "First to prove ROBE exists, and second to provide some insight into what the group is doing with the Seers. They're the only records we know of proving this group even exists."

"And you think those records will be enough to bring ROBE down?"

"Those records, in addition to the testimony from the three of us, ought to rattle enough cages to get some answers and perhaps put an end to ROBE's apparent misuse of Seers."

"So, what makes you think ROBE's not onto me yet?" Gabe asked. "I'm the one who posted this knife on the website for all government types to see?"

"They're too cocky, Gabe. They figure this will blow over in a few weeks, and the knife will just be dismissed as a murder weapon used by some eclectic killer. Besides, as you said before, no one has uncovered ROBE's actions in the last several hundred years, and I doubt they think someone is going to do it now. Today, we played out this elaborate scheme to verify you were not being tailed. Still, though, they might have some feelers out around your workplace or even at your home, so you need to stay alert."

"Makes me feel safe, Svetlana; thanks for the confidence booster."

She shrugged.

"So, I get my hands on these documents, and then what? Are you going to turn yourselves in? Are you going to lead us to the secret ROBE facility where they trained you? Are we going to find some Seer farm where all of these people have been kept?"

"We'll cross that bridge when it comes," she said.

"What about your phones?" Gabe asked.

"These?" she held up her cell.

"Yeah, why don't you let me have that phone from ROBE, and we can run some traces on it."

"ROBE utilizes some sort of scrambler. It sends out a return number…"

"Of a bunch of fours or sevens," Gabe said.

"You've seen those before?"

"Often enough that it gives a lot of credibility to this entire story you've just told me. I just hope there's more evidence out there than your word and a two-hundred-year-old diary. Wait," Gabe paused, "…what do you know about mushrooms?"

"I like mushrooms."

"No, I mean about poisonous mushrooms?"

"Nothing Gabe. Why, is there something I should know?"

"No, no, just asking about something we found in Wade's system and another victim in El Paso. I didn't slip you anything, so don't worry."

Svetlana smirked. "Renovo is where we need you to start, Gabe. Go there and find out what you can. We'll be in touch after you return."

"Another game like today?" he asked.

"I'll tell them to avoid the golf theme next time."

"That would be great."

Svetlana pushed the cart into reverse. The two didn't speak as Svetlana drove them back along the paths of the back nine until they arrived at the main parking lot of the golf course. Slowing as she rounded a slight bend in the lot, Gabe saw his government-issued vehicle.

"All of your stuff and your keys that we took at the golf range are inside the vehicle, Gabe." He pulled himself from the cart. "There's also an envelope with some instructions that might come in handy. We'll be in touch." She depressed the gas pedal, turned back onto the cart path, and disappeared around a bend of trees.

CHAPTER 17

RENOVO

With a full tank of gas, Ryan and Gabe hit the road and spent the first several hours dissecting Svetlana's story by comparing details from their unresolved deaths to her tales. While Ryan accepted the deaths of Mallon, Farr and Harris were all likely caused by a blade belonging to ROBE members, the other deaths by different means did not tie in as easily. The traces of a poisonous mushroom found in Wade and Mallon left more questions than answers as both men might have simply eaten at the wrong restaurant before they died. Both detectives agreed Lieutenant Bernard McCollum was the soldier Svetlana and her team refused to pick up at Fort Bliss. As well, the behaviors the pair had seen on the tape made it reasonable to assume he was suffering from the eye problems ROBE was created to handle. Still missing, however, was evidence of the aura's that Svetlana had talked about. While McCollum could have been suffering from eye problems similar to the ones Kay Farr had complained about, they had little evidence of the existence of anything regarding sudden visions causing madness. Finally, while they had a pile of bodies that might have had eye issues and a possible ROBE detainee lying in the morgue amongst a slew of dead wedding guests, it was still a substantial leap of faith to show that maniacs with eye problems were being corralled and utilized as assassins as Svetlana had proposed.

On top of what little they did know, Ryan's logical attempts to digest that a group of assassins worked for an organization named after a rainbow was enough to push her over the edge. She questioned her sanity, was stymied at explaining ROBE to her superior, and therefore had done her utmost to avoid calling her boss. If a maze of bodies, loose connections, and fanciful stories of ROBE weren't enough to strain Ryan, Gabe not only would not tell her where they were going but revealed their search might place them in grave danger. On the morning of the third day of driving, her patience was waning.

"We're just about there," Gabe stated as he pulled the car back onto the road after filling up on gas.

"We're just about where Gabe? We've been in Pennsylvania for a couple of hours now." Gabe responded with a relaxed smile and raised eyebrows as he brought the car up to speed. It wasn't more than two miles before Gabe reached across Ryan's body and pointed to a green road sign.

"Renovo," Gabe broke his silence. "We're here."

"Ah, of course, Renovo, and what's there, some secret ROBE village with all the answers?"

"It's where we'll find what we're looking for," Gabe smiled. "Hopefully."

"Did you just say 'hopefully'?"

"Yeah, Ryan, hopefully. It could have been moved by now."

"So, we've been traveling for two days more than I packed for, and I'm sporting brown teeth and itchy new granny underpants because you thought it might be fun to follow a hunch?" Gabe winced, remembering how awkward he'd felt waiting in line while Ryan purchased a three-pack of women's underwear from the Outdoorsman Outpost in the backwoods of Pennsylvania. He noted even now she was doing her best to remain calm while her emotions simmered underneath.

"Well, Svetlana and I used to do the same kind of work."

"What kind of work?"

"Secret squirrel type of work?"

"Secret what?"

"Sorry, secret squirrel. Overseas that was the name we gave to the CIA and NSA types that moped around the base in camos without nametags and long beards. They were responsible for the movement in the shadows, the torture by waterboarding we heard so much about at the start of the war, you know, the dark side of things."

"Ok, and you're saying you used to do that?"

"Not that exactly Ryan, but anything covert or off the map is what we refer to as 'secret squirrel' work."

"So you two worked together?" she asked.

"No, just worked for the same people."

"What people?"

"We both distributed declassified documents to public places so citizens of the United States could access that information. That was the company line anyway." Gabe pulled the steering wheel hard to the right as the vehicle rolled around the off-ramp onto PA-144.

"When was this, Gabe?"

"When I returned from my second stint overseas and was burned out on translating, I was approached by some people from the Department of Defense who offered me generous sums to complete a project. Touring the country in a blue van and decked out in civvies, I just had to deliver boxes of declassified documents to various libraries, old warehouses, and schools across the United States."

"Come on, Gabe, with FedEx and UPS covering even the most remote parts of China now, there must have been something pretty special in those boxes. You didn't ask any questions?"

"As I told you, I was releasing declassified documents and papers so people could have access. I had no real reason to question the company line and didn't give much thought to what was inside any given box. Super easy job, great pay, and the belief I was making our government more transparent. I called that a win."

"So, what changed this belief?"

"After a couple of loops around the country, I asked my boss a few questions about why we were putting out so many boxes into so many different places. It seemed like such a simple question over some drinks, and he casually told me the documents were being released as part of the Freedom of Information Act to make sure the public had proper access to government materials."

"Which, of course, doesn't seem like a bad thing?"

"It's not a bad thing if we were releasing complete and relevant documents to a location where members of the public could readily locate and identify them."

"Sorry, I'm not following," Ryan said.

"I was hiding documents for the government."

Ryan squinted.

"Alright, say, for example, the government has a damning report about interrogating witnesses in Iraq, and they don't want it to get out to the public."

"They can just make it top secret," Ryan said.

"Sometimes, but even top-secret documents can be declassified during a congressional witch hunt or over the simple passage of time."

"Sort of the like the Kennedy assassination documents they released on the twenty-fifth anniversary of the shooting?" Ryan said.

"Right, so anyway, at times to avoid the eventual congressional declassification and release or the fruitless fight against a Freedom of Information request, these documents are scattered across the country at different locations, so they're deemed available."

"But if you took this stuff to public locations, then why now all the creeping around, dismantling the car GPS, and destroying my phone before we left? If the stuff is there for us to grab, what's the problem?"

"Well, first, Ryan, I never stated I released complete and relevant records. You're assuming this job I carried out was with good intentions on the part of my employer. It wasn't. After the chat I had with my boss, I got curious, and on my next loop across the country, I started leafing through the boxes at night."

"And?"

"We mixed a few relevant documents with a massive amount of junk."

"What kind of junk?"

"We'd put a twenty-page report on illegal interrogations into seven or eight different boxes along with studies on ketchup residue runoffs or the purification efforts on cow manure and then go even further by dividing those boxes between different facilities across the United States."

"And none of these documents are on digits to be found on some computer file?" Ryan said.

"No, Ryan. Top secret files, notes of questionable acts, and all reports about those questionable acts are always in writing only. Besides, many of these documents I was disbursing were written way before the typewriter was even invented."

"So, none of these important documents are all in one place?" Ryan asked.

"Exactly. This way, our government avoids FOI requests and can say with a clear conscience that they do not have those documents when asked."

"But if this information is in this library, why can't some resourceful person just look it up in the catalog or on the internet and find it?"

"In addition to hiding these documents in plain sight and mixing them with other studies, Svetlana affirmed what I always thought. My bosses even mislabeled the boxes under titles very few on this planet care about. Therefore under 'coal mining data' or 'flu shot records from the 1700s', you might find documents about the Mai Lai Massacre. Even if people have a hankering to look at data on coal mines, they'll more than likely ignore four to five pages of what seems like non-relevant information and push it back into the box. On what ended up being my last trip around the country delivering boxes, I found Iraq interrogation materials in with 'Yarn Fiber Studies' and 'Drywall Rot.'"

"But if our government has some dangerous documents they don't want out in public, why not just burn them?"

"Well, Ryan, they're too arrogant and proud of what they've done at times, and history is all we have once we're dead and gone. Shred a document here or burn a document there, and then there's no proof that this person or that person was involved in some great event that happened in history. Great people are often judged by what they did while they were alive. We're a society that loves to read about fascinating things from the past, and one hundred years from now, details about what truly happened in Iraq will make for some great reading."

"That seems rather sarcastic," Ryan said.

"But it's so true."

"So, what makes you think the ROBE items are still here in Renovo?" Ryan asked.

"Svetlana had a friend in Washington verify the items she delivered to Renovo are still on site."

"So, these mislabeled boxes are just going to be lying about in this little library then?" Ryan asked.

"Well, no, Ryan, but I checked online, and this building has just two stories, a basement, and the main floor, and from my knowledge in where I placed documents, these are likely not on the main floor."

"And we're just going to waltz in there and rummage through these things? You don't think anyone will be watching?"

"I'm not sure," Gabe said.

"Don't worry; we can just take out the librarian or raid the place and hold her hostage." Gabe laughed. "You know, if you'd maybe told me about the need for a plan an hour ago, it might have made this easier," Ryan said.

"Sorry."

"It's ok; I'll come up with something." Her gaze focused on the thick forests outside the car window as she rattled through a half dozen ideas for storming the library. They crested a hill after a few miles and passed a tiny blue sign welcoming them to Renovo. Gabe eased off the gas as he rolled into town and searched for the library.

"Tiny town," Ryan said. "Guess we've got some entertainment for later," she laughed, pointing to the single-screen movie theater showing a film that had been released over a year ago in modern suburbia. Gabe checked the map in his hand. He accelerated to twenty miles per hour as they reached the end of the downtown buildings and passed a half-dozen single-story homes searching for a street sign. Not a half-mile from the center of downtown Gabe eased off the gas and veered to the left. Traveling another hundred yards, Gabe saw a circular white building in the distance to his left, shielded by a group of pines. Once around the giant firs, the road ended into a large cul-de-sac providing parking for the library.

"That's a library?" Ryan asked. The drab block building sat on the edge of a river winding around the backyard. Rusted gutters hung down on both sides of the building, and acid stains from the dense foliage surrounding the building marked the shingled roof. Technological advancements had not been kind to the libraries of the world as cell phones, tablets, and laptops eliminated the need to leave your dining room to find a significant literary work. While it was doubtful the founders of Renovo foresaw such technological advancements, this particular building was an example of a relic that soon would be a thing of the past. They pulled into an unmarked space in front of a dozen stairs leading to the front door.

"I'm leaving your ass and taking the first tuk-tuk out of this town if this is a dead-end," Ryan said as they ascended the stairs. Gabe pulled Ryan into him with his arm around her shoulder.

"Aw, come on, detective, it's an adventure!"

CHAPTER 18

GENEALOGY

Ryan watched Gabe as he spun in place to take in all of the ceiling murals, only ten feet from a desk where an elderly worker anticipated their questions. Ryan shook her head, decided it better to continue without him, and walked to the counter.

"Hi," Ryan said to the old woman.

"Well, hello, young lady, how can I help you today?" Gabe stopped, pointed up, and tried to direct Ryan's gaze. She stared at him, unamused, forcing him to leave his spot and engage with the librarian.

"He's always fascinated by old buildings," Ryan said to the librarian in a hushed tone.

"Sorry…I just…you know," Gabe pointed up again.

"I told you," Ryan rolled her eyes.

"It's ok; it's ok, dear. You should embrace that curiosity, young man… you might find it helpful someday," the librarian said. Gabe's 'told you so' nod was ignored by Ryan. "So, what can I do for you folks?"

"We're on a search for some lost ancestors," Ryan said. "We're kicking around the idea of getting married, and his family has this thing about knowing where I come from."

"Worried about soiling the good name?" the librarian smiled.

"Something like that, yeah," Gabe said. An elbow jabbed at Gabe's ribs.

"I was adopted years back, and all that we've been able to discover so far is that some of my ancestors lived here in Renovo for a time."

"I've lived here all my life, dear; I'm sure I might know them," the librarian said.

"Well, it'd be helpful if we knew their full names." The librarian cocked her head. "We've been at this genealogy stuff for months now," Ryan said, "and while we have the last name, all we keep coming up with are lots of misspelled, partially readable, and many missing first names, in many towns across Pennsylvania. After a recent visit to Pittsburgh, we tracked down the old social worker on my adoption case, and she led us here to your little town. It's not my parents who were here, though; it's my great-great-grandparents. The Millers?"

"I remember some Millers from around these parts," she said, "but don't recall any of 'em giving away their grandbabies."

"Well, we're just trying to find what we can," Gabe said.

"So anyway, we're here for a few days to churn through old birth records, census records, divorce, marriage, you know, just about any historical records you might have. Think you can help us?"

"Anything for young love," she said, sliding off her wooden stool. "Besides, we don't get too many visitors in a day, so you two will give me something to do." She pushed open the swinging door at her waist and signaled for them to follow.

"Nice story, darling," Gabe smirked as they followed the old woman to the back of the library, "but how'd you know genealogy was in the basement?"

"Sign by the door Gabe."

"Yeah…of course…I saw it."

* * *

Ryan's plan worked too well. In the hour after their arrival, Ethel pulled out every box, file, and book in the basement on the history of Renovo. Entire rows of shelves were vacated as the four long tables set up in the basement were covered in material Ethel insisted they review. Although the basement was as large as the main floor, the shelving units, fitting floor to ceiling, consumed the remainder of the space not utilized for the stairs and the tables. Counting free floor space and table space, little more than two shelves could be cleared and placed around the open parts of the room before it was necessary to return the boxed items to the shelves to retrieve more. While the trio worked their way through the first row of shelves nearest to the tables and the detectives feigned interest in the vast number of Millers that had graced Renovo, Gabe grew impatient with the pace, the space, and the inability to do what they came to do.

"I've got to walk around a bit," Gabe told the girls as he pushed back from the table and into two boxes.

"There's a lot to look through here, dear," Ryan laid it on thick.

"My back injury from Iraq, honey, you know how it is. I'll stay down here and just walk up and down the aisle if that's okay with you?"

"Don't go too far, dear," Ryan said.

Gabe chuckled as he strolled down the central aisle feeding the smaller aisles fifteen or so yards in length to his left and his right. Each aisle contained rows of books and boxes from ceiling to floor, which ended against the building walls on both sides. The basement was an obvious fire hazard with only one small window at the far end of the central aisle and the staircase for exits. As Gabe neared the white block wall and tiny window at the end of the central aisle, he looked back to ensure Ethel had not followed. He turned, raised his arms, and leaned back to crack his spine, catching a distinct red light of a surveillance camera in the aisle to his right. He turned his head slowly to his left and then, at the same speed, back to his right and shrugged his shoulders before moving back towards Ryan. Unsure if he had missed camera lights in the other aisles, Gabe continued to slowly rotate his head and react to imaginary pops in his spine to ensure a view down each aisle. He completed his head turns, found no other lights, and returned to the women sitting at the tables.

"Hon," he said to Ryan. "I need to get some paper out of the car, along with those other records we picked up in Pittsburgh. Do you need anything?" Gabe raised his eyebrows.

"Sure…I um…I actually could hit the restroom if possible?" Ryan said.

"I can show you, dear," the old woman said.

"Honestly, Ethel, if you could just tell me, I think I can find it." Ethel nodded and gave Ryan directions as Gabe loped up the steps.

"We'll be right back," Ryan said. She smiled, and Ryan tried to catch up to Gabe.

"Hold on." Ryan tugged at Gabe's fleece pullover at the top of the stairs. "What's up?" Gabe pulled her towards the front desk and out of Ethel's earshot.

"There's a camera downstairs," Gabe whispered. "They're watching the files."

"You found the information we need?"

"Well, no, not yet, but in the very last stack in the back, there's one security camera covering the row. None of the other aisles have one, so I think we've got it, but I need to get something out of the car."

"What am I supposed to do?" Ryan asked.

"Go to the bathroom," he turned, "oh, and keep Ethel busy."

* * *

"What do you think about the colored toilet paper I ordered for the lady's room?" Ethel asked as Ryan dropped down the final step into the basement.

"Mint green," Ryan said, "quite lovely, and just where did you ever find the monkey-shaped soap dispenser?"

"That's my own little touch," she said. "Just something I found at a garage sale on the other side of…oh!" The fluorescent bulbs overhead flickered and died, forcing a small emergency light at the base of the staircase and another at the end of the central aisle above the window to click on. A loud beep echoed through the basement stacks.

"Oh drat, not again." Ethel slapped her forehead and groaned. "Darn generator out back is supposed to kick in," Ethel said. "It never works like it's supposed to!"

"This happens a lot?" Ryan asked.

"From time to time, sweetie, I've got to check on it. Are you going to be okay here?"

"I think so," Ryan said.

"I'll be right back then." Ethel turned to walk away and collided with Gabe at the base of the stairs.

"Are you two alright?" Gabe asked, out of breath and grasping Ethel.

"Just a power problem," she assured him, "but I can handle it. Can you watch over your girl there until I get back?" Gabe released his grip on Ethel, and she smiled.

"I'll make sure she's well protected," Gabe said as Ethel trotted up the steps.

"I'll make sure she's well protected," Ryan mocked and reached out to grab for Gabe like he grabbed Ethel.

"Oh, calm down…you started this whole charade."

"You don't have to sink so far into it."

"You want me to play the part of the weak and helpless female in this game?"

"Of course not. You can be the man…for now." Gabe pushed past the tables and headed down the central aisle with the aid of the emergency light. Pushing her chair back to follow, Ryan had to jog to catch up.

"A little brash of you to cut the power to the generator?"

"That was nothing," Gabe explained. "Disabling the mainline into the power room was the real feat."

"Why'd you hit both?"

"When I was outside, I saw the backup generator and figured I'd kill both that and the main just to make sure we'd have sufficient time to look down here. Besides, I didn't want to take any chances the camera had a link to both power sources."

"Why's that?"

"The camera leads to a monitor located behind the front desk. The monitor had more than one line running away from it, and I followed it outside as well. The line from the monitor just buries into the ground and not in the general direction of the generator, but I'm guessing someone outside of this facility is watching that feed. While there could be an independent power source, I felt it was still just best to take out any I could find. Now keep your voice down. There could be other tracking or recording devices in these stacks."

"Are you sure the camera is off?"

"If there's no red dot, then we're good." The words barely out of his mouth, he reached the final aisle, put out his right arm to stop Ryan's momentum, and looked up to the left. Complete darkness.

"What are you going to do?"

"I captured about ten seconds of video on my cell phone from the television feed upstairs before I killed the power. I'm going to re-wire the camera to loop this feed on my cell so we can search back here with some privacy. It will look like the aisle is empty."

"Who taught you this?" Gabe pulled out a box from the shelf, stood on it, and began messing with the surveillance camera.

"Signal guys in Iraq are some of the brightest tech dudes on the planet. It's pretty simple. All you have to do is pull the lead off the back of this camera, plug it into the connecter on my cell phone, then head into the tools on my phone to ensure the security programs are willing to accept the feed, and then it's just...."

As confidant as Gabe professed himself to be, his explanation trailed off to silence. Two minutes passed as Ryan paced up and down the central aisle to watch for Ethel's return.

"Ryan!" Gabe broke the silence. "Ryan," he said again.

"What?" she snapped and leaned her head around the shelves.

"Do you have any lipstick in your pocket?" She patted the outside of her pants.

"Yeah."

"Drop it onto the floor right there."

"Why?"

"Just do it!" Gabe jumped down and pushed the box he had been using back onto the shelf.

"Okay, okay, you need to relax."

"I need to make sure this is working," he said as he passed her, then grabbed her arm to move her back towards the tables. A loud buzz cut through the building, and the power burst back on. If his jerry-rigged experiment wasn't working, the camera might have caught the lower part of her leg before she got around the corner.

"You're just gonna leave your phone there?"

"We'll get it before we leave, but for now, yeah. Who's gonna check?"

"I'm coming back down, you two," hollered Ethel from upstairs as her heels clicked on the concrete steps.

"I'll be right back," Gabe said as he met Ethel partway up the stairs. They collided more gently than they had six minutes before. "I was using the bathroom when the power went out, so I need to go wash my hands."

"Not a good place to be caught with the lights out," Ethel insisted with a smile as Gabe continued up the stairs. Moving past the front desk, Gabe stopped, looked around to ensure no one else had entered the library, and leaned over the desk to view the video feed. The lipstick was not in the picture.

CHAPTER 19

ATTICUS

The most painstaking play in any lengthy ruse is to carry it out successfully over an extended period of time. As well, whether short or long, no matter the level of planning for any contingency, there always was a wrench in the works. The wrench in Renovo was Ethel.

After the events with the power outage, Ethel and the pair spent the next three hours dusting off long-forgotten cemetery records. Each time Ethel burst out of her seat Gabe and Ryan hoped their moment of freedom had arrived, but she always returned. The name 'Miller' had unknowingly been the surname of some of the founders of tiny Renovo, and as Ethel pulled out mounds of information about them, Gabe glared at Ryan each time for not coming up with a more eclectic name. Her stares informed him of her dissatisfaction with his stares as well as her displeasure with not being given enough time to find a better name that may have led to less information for Ethel to find. Fortunately for the pair, lunchtime was soon upon them and a chance to escape Ethel's clutches with it.

When she offered to take them to lunch, Gabe began to moan until she recalled her need to prepare for her afternoon reading with local school kids. Ethel would have to remain behind. Feigning disappointment, the two requested directions to the best restaurant and accepted Ethel's offer to phone Sam's Tavern with their order. Gabe insisted on driving.

* * *

"Don't make me regret letting you have food down there now, you two," Ethel said from atop the stairs. Gabe grabbed the bag from Ryan, held it up to eye level, and assured Ethel there would be no trace of lunch when they were finished. It was a promise easy to keep since both of them had horsed down almost everything on the return trip. For once, Gabe, with no protest from Ryan, decided against their daily routine of eating slowly to get as much free time from Ethel as was possible.

"Sit here!" Gabe said as he pulled out a chair and placed the food bag on the table.

"What are you doing?"

"You're on lookout."

"Ethel's too busy to come down here, Gabe." Her point was bolstered by the din of a herd of third-graders gallivanting about the main floor.

"Neither of us can say for certain." Even though she wasn't happy with being left as the sentry, Ryan conceded. Gabe recognized her displeasure and turned back to her.

"You stay here and let me grab some boxes from the back row. I'll bring them up here, and we can mix them with this genealogy junk we've been sorting through with Ethel. That way, if she does come back, we won't make her suspicious." Ryan nodded, sat down, and opened the bag.

Gabe turned and headed down the central aisle. At the last row, he stooped over to pick up Ryan's lipstick tube and glanced up one more time to ensure his phone remained in place. The entire row across the basement was thirty feet long by thirteen feet high, and with some quick math, Gabe figured that around seventy boxes were within the camera's purview. He began to scan the box labels. Topics ranged from '1700's Soil Studies' to 'Water Volumes from Natural Springs in Pennsylvania' and just about every other useless topic one could imagine. While Gabe was sure some of the boxes were legitimate, his past experiences provided him with little doubt that the information would be scattered throughout the boxes. They would have to check them all.

Ryan was focused on nibbling on the remains of her turkey sandwich when Gabe dropped a box onto the table. He said nothing, disappeared, but returned in less than half a minute with two more.

"Get started on these two," Gabe directed as Ryan wrapped up the final piece of her sandwich and pulled the lid off the box. "Keep these two boxes right next to those cemetery records for cover and just take out a little from a box at a time." Ryan nodded and examined the topics of the boxes he left for her. Less than thrilled with 'Rainfall Averages in the Lower Valleys of Pennsylvania' and 'Renovo High Class of 69', she was nevertheless happy to look at anything other than grave records and census logs.

As minutes turned to an hour, neither Gabe nor Ryan found anything interesting. Despite Gabe's insistence to maintain speedy precision while reviewing the complete contents of each box, Ryan soon realized their pace was quickening as results were not forthcoming, and angst grew. Still, despite faltering to less than perfect searching techniques, the pair were unrelenting as they pulled, examined, and put away new boxes for hours undeterred. As Ryan leaned back in her chair to stretch and take a moment to smile about Ethel's prolonged absence, Gabe raised a hand.

"Got it!" he whispered.

"What is it?" She stood up and established a position over Gabe's shoulder. "Well?" Grasping a document titled 'Project Crimson Rage', Gabe pointed to a name in the middle of the paper.

"This name here...this Atticus Heacox..." Gabe had difficulty holding the document steady.

"You alright?" Ryan asked.

"I love it when crazy comes together," he grinned and took a deep breath.

"Amen!" Ryan put a hand on his shoulder and leaned in.

"This document is from the Secretary of State's office in 1820 and says here Atticus Heacox was put in charge of a new program to study the effects of a disease they called ocular pigment distortion."

"Seems logical this Project Crimson Rage could have led to the ROBE group Svetlana told you about then," Ryan said.

"It does, and it says here that Heacox was a doctor that suffered from the ocular problem himself...just like Svetlana indicated."

He put down the paper and grabbed the next.

"So what else is in there?" Gabe saw nothing, dropped that page, and grabbed another. Quickly the next page fell, and he reached for the third page in the stack.

"It's the only thing here…" he continued to flip each page of the stack onto the table "…the rest of these papers are about migrating bird studies and besides," he rubbed the papers between his fingers, "the paper quality of that first old document and these bird study pages is evidence it's the only old document here."

"Speaking of that," Ryan said, "how is this item in such good shape after all this time?" She picked up the letter assigning Heacox and handed it to Gabe. He turned it over and examined it with precision suggesting he had some expertise in dating documents. His look revealed the fact he had no idea.

"It looks damn good, though, doesn't it, Ryan?"

"Good amount of brown and fading, and if I tried to fold this, it might crack, but yeah, it's been well preserved," Ryan said.

"Until they put it in here anyway," Gabe said as he pointed at the box in front of him. "These are acid-free boxes which might help a little, but we can probably assume this document was in some sort of protective covering for years before it was brought here."

"I would have to agree." Ryan watched as Gabe looked at the staircase leading up to Ethel.

"We've got to slow down," he said.

"Why?"

"If they took the time to stuff just one letter in this entire box, we've likely missed things already. I have to admit I've gotten a little bit careless reviewing the last few boxes." Ryan nodded. "This might take a little longer than we thought."

PART 5

FRUITS OF LABOR

CHAPTER 20

ADAMS

Gabe was thankful Ethel didn't turn out to be quite the obstacle he first feared. Still, even without her as much of a distraction after the first morning, their comprehensive search of every box was meticulous and slow. As each day ended, the two placed the documents they found into Ryan's briefcase, mixed them with copied pages of useless census and marriage materials, and walked them out the front door. By noon on the fourth day, their search was complete. They had pieced together over seventy pages of notes, parts of a journal, medical documents, and correspondence between Atticus and the Secretary of State's office from sixty-three boxes. They were happy to leave Renovo behind.

* * *

"Ethel acted like she'd be standing by her mailbox waiting for our wedding invitation," Ryan said as she bit into her tenderloin sandwich. Gabe turned off the radio and focused his eyes on the road.

"She's just lonely, Ryan; try to have a little compassion."

"Yeah," Ryan said, "this coming from the guy who kept rolling his eyes each time she came down to check on us in the basement."

"She put so much effort into helping us, Ryan. She honestly seemed like she was going to miss us when we left."

"You did lay it on a little thick there when you grabbed her in that bear hug, Gabe."

"Being nice, Ryan. I was being nice."

"I think I saw a tear."

"Knock it off."

"In any case, I'm still a little queasy about this," Ryan said as they reached the outskirts of Dayton, Ohio, and slowed due to construction.

"I told you not to order that sandwich?"

"No, Gabe, about what we took back there."

"Oh, come on, Ryan, who's gonna know?"

"That's not the point...I just...I just don't like to steal stuff. We could have copied these pages as we did with all that census garbage. I guess my conscience as a law enforcement officer feels a little violated."

"You know I agree with you, Ryan, but if this information is what Svetlana says it is, we need to have the originals. If these tie into the El Paso murders and we have to reveal these documents as evidence, you know the originals would be long gone before we got anyone there to recover them. It had to be this way."

"Yeah," she put down her sandwich and closed the box, "but aren't you worried that dear old Ethel will get into trouble if this ROBE group finds out we took their information."

"What are they going to do, Ryan, bound and gag her and have a loop of Black Bear, Brown Bear read to her until she cracks? Come on. There's no way they'd assume she's complicit in it. They won't touch her."

"Think so?"

"Of course, and besides, I doubt she has any clue that the documents were even in there."

"Really?"

"Of course, Ryan. A little old lady with complete deniability about secret files hidden in her library is the kind of person I'd want watching over my stuff."

"Did anyone else besides you and your boss ever know what was inside the boxes you were delivering?"

"No one. Every box I delivered was already labeled and pre-approved for placement in each library, storehouse, and school. The people getting the boxes were often so happy to be getting their hands on real government documents they never took the time to do much more than quickly leaf through them."

"Yeah…"

"I just had to drop them on whatever shelf they had cleared for me."

"…that's probably true," Ryan said.

"Besides, we took enough precautions on this trip to avoid any tails, and I'm sure my loop trick worked, so no one is going to find out."

"I guess," Ryan said, "but there's…"

"Look," he stopped her. "Svetlana put her teams' life on the line to lead us to this information, and trust me, when I was hiding documents, my bosses were confident no one would ever dig up enough stuff to put together anything of relevance. Heck, even with my experience in hiding these documents, I completely passed over several pages of Atticus' journal in that first box I looked through."

"That's true…"

"So, relax, and let's just be glad about what we found and hope there's something to all of this." Ryan nodded and placed her sandwich box in the back seat.

"Speaking of those journal pages…"

"Yeah?"

"…did you get a chance to make it through any of those yet?" Ryan asked. Atypically, the pair worked themselves to the point of exhaustion every evening in Renovo and had taken little time to catalog, review or even analyze the contents of the items they were taking. Gabe assumed Ryan stayed up late each night to work as she often did. Apparently, she had not.

"Well, about the only thing I've gotten to so far is organizing the loose journal pages by date, and if you want, you can chronologically place them in between the pages that are still attached to the brown journal." He pointed towards her feet at the stack of journal pages. "The journal is in the back if you want to start organizing."

"You want me to drive so you can do it?" Ryan asked.

"No, I can't read when I ride; I get carsick."

"Oh, you ninny." Ryan reached over the median between the seats, grasped the pile of papers, and pulled them onto her lap. She shuffled through the loose journal pages to ensure Gabe had correctly ordered them, then placed them on the dash. She opened the brown journal that contained several dozen pages still affixed and ordered the loose pages with those in the binder. Ryan spent a good ten minutes placing all dated entries in chronological order.

"We're still missing quite a few pages from this journal Gabe," Ryan said.

"I noticed at least two dozen parts in that binder that had pages ripped out, but we'll just have to make do with what we have." She worked for a while longer, and once satisfied she had all of the journal sheets by the date; she began to read.

"Hello…a little volume, please?" Gabe asked.

"There are over twenty entries here, Gabe. Why don't you give me a few minutes to scan through these, and I can read the ones that may have something for us."

"We've got the time, I guess. Read away."

Within a few minutes, Ryan pulled out one of the loose pages and held it up. "This one's pretty good.

> September 4, 1824: The election of Adams is nearing and is a necessity for Crimson Rage to continue. His time as Secretary permitted my research regarding the madness of the eyes, but the program will be disbanded should he not win the day. My underground seclusion remains a source of contention, but I have been told it will continue until a cure is discovered. The rage of my subjects towards anything in red is absolute. New subjects arrived not less than a week ago, and already four of six have exhibited behaviors too violent and were removed. After six months underground, only my aide Dave Mitchell and I have the discolored vision but have not turned to madness as every other subject has. Will this change? Is there some answer in my body or Dave's holding the cure? What catalyst makes all of these others so violent after obtaining the visions? Signed…"

"He's talking about the 1825 election of John Quincy Adams!" Gabe said.

"How do you know that?"

"History major. My college thesis was on the Monroe Doctrine."

"And what does Monroe have to do with anything?"

"Not a ton Ryan, but when Monroe was President, Adams authored the Monroe Doctrine. The Doctrine was one of Adam's great achievements while Secretary of State. It basically warned the rest of the world to stay away from America and the Western Hemisphere since European countries kept trying to colonize parts of North America. It was a warning shot to the world not to try and colonize our lands. The Doctrine was hailed across the land and was the main reason Adams ended up being elected President a few years later."

"But what does any of that have to do with our search?"

"A bunch of those documents we found at the library had the seal of the Secretary of State's office from well over a hundred years ago, Ryan. I saw multiple dates from the eighteen and nineteen hundreds, which must mean ROBE worked with or at least under the authorization of the Secretary of State, even after Adams became president. From that entry, it sounds like Adams might have started or greatly expanded this ROBE project when he was Secretary of State and that Atticus needed Adams to win his Presidential bid to keep the research funded."

"What in the world would Adams be doing with this group?" Ryan asked.

"Maybe his position as an isolationist made him recognize the internal threat these Seers presented. I don't know; maybe he was friends with Heacox and was doing what he could to help him."

"Sounds like Atticus and his partner were being held prisoner, though."

"It does," he said. "But keep going; what else you got there?" Ryan took several minutes to find something more of interest.

"This is about six months or so later, Gabe, and it's pretty faded, but listen to this.

> March 10, 1825: Have studied over twenty persons afflicted and can confidently establish that only four colors exist for those seeing auras. Although we could attest to such from our own sight problems, sufficient numbers were necessary to prove the colors and their effects absolutely before Adams was willing to let us move forward with

our research. We established the very essence of a living thing determines what color we see. Criminals, vagabonds, guards, and politicians are most often consumed in red and draw the ire of those stricken by madness. Dave and I, not suffering from the rage, have noted over the months that the ones we also see in red are the ones our patients always try to harm. Neither of us has witnessed or heard of attacks on those with auras of the other three colors. Animals and children appear green or blue and are treated as gently as lambs by all subjects. Orange draws minimal or no angst amongst some subjects, and no attacks have resulted. Differences in the colors are firmly established and will report findings accordingly. Adams, now President, is still unwavering about the need to find an immediate cure to stop the murderous rages."

"The problem's not the eyes distorting then," Gabe said, "rather that most of these people get enraged and try to kill things they see cloaked in some kind of red aura."

Ryan shook her head.

"What, Ryan?"

"This just seems so far-fetched. This...this whole idea of auras has certainly moved from the outer fringe of the paranormal this century but could this possibly have been going on back then? I mean, people that see auras and become afflicted with some sort of madness? Really? You don't think it's a coincidence you met with Svetlana in Roswell, New Mexico, of all places? Could this all just be some elaborate hoax to get us off the real trail?" Her voice dropped off as she placed her hand on the journal pages.

"Heck, Ryan, I don't know any more than you do. Is it possible this is a hoax? I guess it could be, but look at what we've got. A bunch of bodies back in El Paso each killed from similar knife wounds, two more from a poisonous mushroom, others we can tie to odd phone numbers that don't exist, a crazy soldier who acted a lot like the ones you're describing in those journal entries and now these documents exactly where Svetlana told us they would be. Quite a lot of work for a hoax...you think? No matter how impossible something may seem, until you disprove it, it's possible."

"Yeah...I guess you're right for now," Ryan said.

"Don't for a minute think I don't cringe every time you start talking about auras and the crimson rage and some guy trapped in a cave named Atticus. It sounds like a fairy tale, but until we run all of this to ground, we need to keep at it."

Ryan smiled and reached for the page she had just read. "We can hit the internet tonight and see what's gone on with any modern scientific research about energy fields. It would seem that's what these auras are after all." Gabe nodded.

"Yeah, but you have to admit, even if we find anything, both of these guys probably had the best insight into this whole get-up," Gabe said.

"What do you mean?"

"Well, when Atticus and Dave didn't develop the desire to kill people in red, they were sort of like cogent rats inside a maze. They could see the affliction from the inside and study it logically. Being a doctor and suffering from the disease had to give Atticus great insight."

"I hadn't thought about that." Ryan shuffled through more pages and took even longer to find one of interest.

"May 1827: Program continues with no success at stopping the attacks on red auras, and we have now had over thirty-five subjects from all over the country. All but my partner and I have been removed from the cave. We have all of the scientific tools we need at our disposal but cannot discover what causes the visions or the rage. There are no obvious indicators as to why Dave and I obtained the visions, nor why we do not feel the urge to attack the red auras as all other subjects do. I would be quite alone without Dave and I have been lucky to find some peace with my friend. Continuing in solitude in this cave would drive even the sanest person crazy, but I must keep searching for an answer. We are meeting to discuss the project in Washington next month."

"It seems the eye disease was affecting people around the country, but I don't recall anything in the history books about this, Ryan, do you?"

"Maybe it wasn't a big outbreak. Besides, weren't we hanging witches around that time as well?" Gabe smirked.

"Wouldn't be the first time our government hid something from the public," Gabe said.

"But as of this entry date, there were at least thirty-five people who had been rounded up and brought to Heacox and Mitchell. It seems hard to believe nobody noticed."

"Well, we didn't have the internet back then, and nobody had a cell phone able to capture video and stills with the click of a button."

"Yeah, I guess with just word of mouth or other limited media of the times, any news of someone going crazy and trying to kill people probably didn't travel too far," Ryan said.

"And heck, Ryan, if one of these eye sufferers acted out and tried to kill somebody in our little town, would either of us have cared if one night the problem just disappeared or died?"

"Yeah, I can't imagine there were a lot of tears when the town crazy was taken out." Ryan flipped to the next journal entry and read entry after entry for the next half hour, finding very few helpful. Towards evening, Ryan came to the last attached page of the journal.

"That's all I've got here, Gabe, but I've got to be honest…I still don't see what Adams had in this fight. Why would he care about funding this project while he was Secretary of State and then President? I don't see his angle."

"I don't know, Ryan, but I'll take a look through those later. Maybe there's something that will give you some answers in the rest of the papers we have in the back."

"My boss is going to want something more than Svetlana and these documents to give this group the historical significance that's indicated here. Right now, this reeks of an early attempt by some science fiction writer to create a fantastic story for a sci-fi rag."

"Yeah, those journal pages don't help much to explain…"

"Hold on a minute," Ryan said.

"What's wrong?" Gabe slowed the car.

"There's something written along the seam of the binder where the remaining part of the final journal page was torn out. I guess I hadn't flipped past the last attached page before." Ryan turned the binder on its side and placed the journal just under the overhead light in the middle of the console. Distracted, Gabe pulled over to the side of the highway and parked.

"The pencil has faded so much that I can't quite make it out," Ryan said. Gabe pulled out a small pocket flashlight and illuminated the crease of the binder further.

"Adams taken by Mitchell to Gov. Jennings (In.)."

"What the heck does that mean?"

"We came across that Mitchell guy in one of those entries. He was that aide to Atticus while they were in the caves," Ryan said.

"Yeah, and I think we can assume I N is for Indiana?" Ryan flipped through the journal and inspected the tattered remains from pages that had been removed. She found no other words.

"Looks like some more research on the web tonight," Ryan said.

"And since we're just past Richmond, we could make a run to the Hoosier state capitol and rest for the night," Gabe said.

"Indianapolis it is then."

* * *

Far away from where the detectives stopped, in a nondescript building a half-mile from the White House, a door swung open, and two people strode across the red cherry floor. The clack of his assistant's high-heeled shoes was the only indication of their presence; it was just enough of a welcome to get the attention of the graying man behind the desk. With a slight shove from the older man's right arm, the chair spun without a sound.

"A little late for you to be at it," the man said to his aide.

"I'm here as long as you are, sir," the assistant responded. "This," she pointed to the man standing at her right, "is Mr. Thomas."

"Little flag popped up, sir, at one of the storage bins in Renovo," Mr. Thomas said before pleasantries could be exchanged.

The seated man instructed his assistant to see her way out.

"What is in Renovo?"

"Some reports about the Lusitania and about one-third of the items for project crimson rage, sir. Few journal pages, medical items, and other pieces," Mr. Thomas said.

"And I assume the articles located there were intermixed appropriately in various boxes."

"As per protocol, sir. But for someone knowing what to look for, there's quite a bit to find."

"Well, then what seems to be the problem with this site?"

"Our tech guys caught a glitch in one of the cameras."

"Can they fix it?"

"It's already fixed, sir, but per protocol, I reviewed the last two weeks of reels we have and came across this." Mr. Thomas dropped photographs onto the desk.

"And why is this problematic?"

"See here." Mr. Thomas picked up two photos, pointed to the bottom of the first one, and then pointed to the bottom of the second after shuffling them.

"Enlighten me here, son. What am I looking for?" The photos were placed side by side on the desk, and Mr. Thomas pointed to the bottom.

"Right there..." he pulled forward his other hand "...and there."

"So, what, this one's got a border, and this one does not?"

"The border is the bottom of a television screen. See here; if you look close, you can see the word Sanyo. Someone tampered with the camera and had this bordered picture looping over the camera for almost a week."

"It could just be the picture changed?"

"No, sir," Mr. Thomas said. He handed him a third picture. "This is what it looks like again today, and the picture on your left is what it looked like one week ago." Mr. Thomas couldn't tell if it was anger or fear creeping across the Secretary of State's face, but his concern over the breach was immediate.

CHAPTER 21

SOLACE

As the harvest moon's light replaced the sunset, Ryan reminisced about her falls spent in Indiana. In celebration of the three-day celestial event at the end of every September, she and her family prepared a late-night feast on the last night of the harvest moon for everyone in the community to enjoy. Farmers, their workers, and everyone else in her hometown came out to her home to celebrate the ending of another growing season and to admire the colors and images that formed along the skyline only at that time of year. As she continued about her memories, Gabe too was taken back to an easier time before stress, wars, and murders consumed him, a time when the most significant threat in a day was running out of daylight and hearing the call of his mother. As Ryan talked, the moon rose, morphed into a tiny ball, and darkness consumed the land by the time Gabe and Ryan arrived in downtown Indianapolis. And although three different Motel 6 lights flashed 'Vacancy' as they drove along the interstate, Ryan insisted after their four-day stay in Renovo, a four-star hotel in downtown Indianapolis was in order.

While Ryan targeted the sauna tub and had the water running before Gabe had chosen a bed, she instructed him to give her "maybe an hour or so" to wind down and get cleaned up. Determined not to waste the chance to see the city, Gabe donned his running shoes and trekked out on a five-mile run. Although he had never been in the city before, its' parallel streets and prominent buildings made it easy for him to take a loop around Conseco Fieldhouse, Lucas Oil Stadium, and over to the minor league baseball stadium on the southwest side of town. He and Mike had talked about visiting all of the sports venues in every metropolitan city when they were in college, and although Gabe had tried to keep up on his end, Mike had given up a long time ago. As he aged, Gabe no longer kept his interest in buildings to just the monoliths dedicated to sports, though, as now, whether historical or modern, he marveled at the intricacies of construction from gargoyles atop skyscrapers to the crown molding over any door.

He finished strong under the atrium located over the intersection next to the hotel and pushed his way through the glass doors. The concierge recognized Gabe and held out the gym bag he had left behind the front desk. After a quick shower in the hotel gym, Gabe found a small tub of free water next to the concierge desk and plopped into a comfortable leather chair.

"Pardon me, sir, but are you Gabe Moss?" Gabe pulled the bottle from his mouth and caught his breath.

"I am," he said, screwing on the lid.

"Ms. Rebecca Ryan ordered the food on the cart that is waiting over by the elevator. We were instructed to notify you that 'the coast is clear…and to bring the food.'" Gabe smiled, walked over to the cart, and wheeled it into the elevator.

* * *

"You order something for me in all of this, I hope?" Gabe asked as he pushed the cart through the door. He reached under the white drape and grabbed his duffel bag and wet towel. The cart rolled a few feet on the wood floor towards Ryan as Gabe plopped onto his bed.

"I got you a burger and some fries. Wouldn't want you to break from your fast food diet or anything." Ryan moved to the cart, shuffled lids and plates around, and handed Gabe two trays. She grabbed a small bowl, placed it on her bed, and then stacked several pillows to lean against. Once settled, she pulled off the lid from the small bowl revealing an assortment of cooked vegetables. Gabe flipped on a Pacers game that was being played about four blocks from their hotel and dropped the remote on the bed.

"We going to relax and enjoy the game for a little while?"

"Just for a minute while I polish off these veggies, but then I've got some work to do."

"Ten minutes isn't going to change the world, Ryan."

"I had enough downtime in Renovo, Gabe."

"Just because we came home each night and passed out doesn't mean we were goofing off Ryan."

"No funny guy, I just mean that I'm refreshed after our time there, the trip, and of course that nice soak I just had. Besides, sitting in that tub and tuning out the world, I developed some new ideas on things to search for."

"Well, I'm gonna take a few," Gabe said as he inched back to the headboard and settled in. As the clock in the second half wound down towards halftime, the human jackhammer to his right shoveled food so quickly into her mouth that peaceful coexistence was impossible. With his food barely touched, he watched as Ryan shoved every last piece into her mouth, dropped the tray on the floor, and pulled her laptop onto her knees. Gabe shook his head as she began to type and returned his attention to his food. He wedged himself further into the pillows and turned up the volume.

"You know there's something about you I just haven't quite put my finger on yet?"

Gabe reversed direction on the volume.

"What mystery do you need to solve now?"

"Why you're here?"

"Well, we shared several little cramped rooms on our trip so far, so I didn't overanalyze why one more night with each other in this much larger suite was that big a deal."

"No, not that. Here, or wait, I guess there…you know…in Texas?"

"What do you mean?" He propped himself up.

"What is a guy with all of your talents that spent so much time in a desert overseas doing in Texas of all places? Shouldn't you be out defeating the next Kim Jung whatever or dismantling nuclear threats in old Russia?"

"Told you I was tired of the rat race. I had to get away for a while."

"Well then, if you're tired of the Bondesque life you were leading, why on earth did you request a gig in the desert rather than anywhere else in the United States?"

"Come on, Ryan," Gabe turned his attention back to the game.

"No, I mean, we've talked several times about my life and my sister, but I haven't heard anything from you that leads me to understand why you're in the Texas desert right now."

"You needed my help."

"No, not that company line…there's got to be more to it."

"Why does there always have to be more Ryan?"

"Because in this instance, there is. It just doesn't seem right for you to be in the Texas desert, I guess…that's all."

"It's where I relax. It's the only place I can escape."

"Why's that?"

"Well, unlike our lives here in the States, our days overseas were not mundane and ordinary with a dash of excitement here or there."

"So?"

"So…unlike the ability of people in the United States of America to just shut down for a bit, take a peaceful nap, or to go home early from work if they want to, we rarely had that ability to escape. Jumping from city to city in search of our missing soldiers, in constant fear of every man, woman, and child, and never being able to wind down…that sort of existence wears on you."

"I guess that could suck."

"It did. The few times we got away from the cities and headed out into the desert were the only times we could relax. Thirty or so miles into nowhere, we'd circle the wagons, rip off our body armor down to our boxers and enjoy the sun and sand. Some guys would stretch out in the shade of the Humvees; some settled enough to write civilized letters home, while others spent the time tossing whatever ball we brought with us that day. The shift in attitude was amazing, and the men felt complete and absolute relief out there in the vast nothing."

"So, you needed an escape. I get that. But couldn't you just take a long vacation or find a cushy job somewhere in Wyoming or Montana?"

"I wish, but the FBI wouldn't just let me wander off and defend a two thousand acre range, so I had to find somewhere that I could work every day but still escape to a quiet night."

"And El Paso was the best you could do?"

"It was quiet for a few good months anyway since at first all they had me doing was some office work. I had lots of free time to head out to the White Sands Air Base to hike or just hang out in the hills or desert, and that's the very reason why the house I'm renting is up there near the border of New Mexico…to escape."

"This place your final destination then?"

"No. When I'm done working, I plan on disappearing onto one of those ranges you were talking about somewhere in Colorado."

"Until then, I guess we get to keep at these conspiracy theories that seem to be a large part of your life?"

"Someday soon, we'll talk about everything I've done…"

"Hold on," Ryan put up a hand.

"I don't get to…?"

"No. Here!" She patted the bed next to her. He put down his burger, got up, and nudged Ryan with his butt. Her movement destroyed her throne of goose feathers.

"What have you got?"

"While you've been talking, I was doing searches on President Adams."

"And?"

"Well, as you can imagine, there's way too much stuff online about every former President."

"Of course."

"So, I punched in Governor Jennings and Indiana, and although there are a few hits on here about him being the first governor, not much else popped up."

"Ok?"

"But I have been able to establish that the journal entries we read in the car all coincide with Jennings' life."

"Yeah?"

"So, it's very likely he is the one mentioned in that journal crease."

"Well, we sort of figured out in the car, didn't we?"

"Yeah, but the really cool stuff popped up after I added in the name Dave to my search." She pointed to one of the results on the bottom of the page. "Governor Jennings had a brother in law by the name of David Mitchell?"

"The same guy from the cave?"

"Well, I'm not sure, but it's the same name we found in the journal. And what's more, this one article says David Mitchell was a physician."

"I don't recall the journal entries indicating he was a doctor, though?" Gabe said.

"But it would make sense that both he and Atticus had medical training since they were the ones trying to cure the Seers." Gabe nodded.

"So now that we might be able to tie up David Mitchell to Governor Jennings, what's that get us?"

"Well, there's more."

"I'm all ears."

"When I added Adams' name back into the cross-references, it seems that Jennings and Adams knew each other rather well."

"Really? How well?"

"After being Governor of Indiana, Jennings was elected to Congress and was an ardent supporter of Adams when he first put his name in for president. Later though, for some reason, Jennings changed his mind and threw his support behind Henry Clay before finally backing Andrew Jackson when the final votes were counted."

"Guy jumped allegiances quite a bit. Why'd he bail on Adams?"

"It's not exactly clear as Adams had Jennings's support early on in the race, but when it came time to vote in the House, Jennings backed off for some reason," Ryan said.

"Still though, Jennings's vote didn't end up mattering much since, as we know from history, Adams eventually won the presidency that year."

"Figured you knew that, but that's what it said on here," Ryan said.

Gabe grabbed the brown journal and flipped to the back.

"So then, looking at the wording on the spine here, what do you think it means that Mitchell took Adams to the Governor?"

"Well, if I had to guess, Dave Mitchell took something from this journal or ROBE and delivered it to his brother-in-law, the governor."

"But what could possibly be his reason for doing that?" Gabe asked.

"Posterity? Leverage? Protection? Who knows?"

"So, if this Dave Mitchell is who we think he is, then we have to try and find what it is that Mitchell brought to the governor." Gabe stared long at the journal.

"What is it, Gabe?"

"This sounds impossible? Where would we even start?"

"Welllll…that might be a problem were it not for the industrious Governor Jennings!"

"He create the very first website preserving all of his secrets?"

"No funny guy, but one of his main goals while in office was the establishment of the first Indiana State Library."

"And you think whatever Mitchell delivered might be there?"

"Well, I can't say for sure, but I do know that every state library keeps the personal notes and logs of every governor for future generations to review and enjoy."

"Another library?"

"Something a little bigger this time, though." Ryan pulled up a minimized window. "State library is just a little north of here. We can hit it in the morning."

CHAPTER 22

PREFERENTIAL TREATMENT

The clerk behind the desk rested her hands on the granite counter. She watched as a dapper man dressed in black maintained a fair distance, moving slowly, mouth agape at the atrium sixty feet overhead. His grin and childish spinning drew the attention of several patrons, with one parent redirecting her child away from the spectacle.

"Knock it off, you fool," Ryan whispered as she brushed past Gabe, disturbed his balance, and nodded for him to follow.

"What?"

"I knew I shouldn't have gone to the bathroom before we at least got in here and found you something to do."

"But look up there," Gabe said, pointing.

"Yeah, yeah, great," Ryan said, "but how about you look over there at the not so entertained mother and child you scared off."

"You know I love these places."

"Maybe I'll build you a dome in your living room when we get back."

"That'd be cool."

"Morning," Ryan said to the patient clerk.

"What can I do for you folks?"

"We're hoping to see the historical archives of former Indiana governors."

"Well, this is my first week here, so you need to let me look, but I'm pretty sure anything you might be looking for would be on the second floor."

"That's what my search indicated on the web last night," Ryan said, "but this place is pretty big, so we kind of hoped you could direct us where we needed to go."

"Even I get lost in here sometimes, so just let me verify my belief."

Gabe leaned over to Ryan.

"I think it's Ethel's sister."

Ryan pushed him away.

"Here you go, folks. Yes, you need to head up to where the Indiana Collection is preserved, and they can help you out. Just take those stairs, turn left at the top and go down to the double doors at the end of the hall."

"Thanks," Gabe said. The pair moved up the stairs, turned, and headed for the double doors.

"So why wasn't any of this information we're seeking online?"

"Well, the website said most of the older documents are unable to be photocopied or microfilmed for fear that the process itself might cause some damage."

"By the microfilming?"

"Any light can cause damage, Gabe. Old document handler like you should know about preserving historical papers."

Gabe frowned. "Just delivered 'em…had nothing to do with preserving 'em."

"Oh, and by the way…" Ryan asked, "…what's up with all of your tourist behaviors in these libraries? I'd hoped we left that in Renovo."

"The history in these places is fantastic, Ryan. You know I love that."

"Well, obviously, but why? Maybe you missed your calling as an archeologist or historical preservationist or something?"

"No, my interest didn't start until I was in Nasiriya."

"Why there?"

"It's where the Babylonian Gardens are, for God's sake Ryan, and the birthplace of Abraham. The history was just oozing out of the ground."

"And that's all it took? Your presence in the dusty old grounds of the most famous greenway ever constructed and a rickety old home?"

"It was the first time I saw the destruction, Ryan. So much history in that country was gutted, destroyed, and stolen up to that point. But when we got there, a small band of people had taken up arms to defend their greatest treasures."

"I read about that. They did lose a lot of historical stuff over there, didn't they?"

"Almost made me cry at times. Thousands of years of history, epic documents, and statutes stolen or ruined."

"And so, from these preservationists was borne your bizarre behavior every time we enter one of these places?"

"Not just libraries Ryan. Last night I got to see several sports monoliths around this town and even took a loop around a war museum and an old Masonic Temple that was pretty cool." Ryan chuckled. "Never know when these buildings and pieces of our history will be gone, so we need to admire and appreciate them while we can."

Gabe pulled open a door at the end of the hall.

"Well, I guess since you have a decent enough reason for the behavior, I'll do my best to deal with it." He smiled and followed Ryan into a large room lit by a bank of windows reaching from floor to ceiling across the wall ahead of them.

"Afternoon, folks," a man said as he approached the pair and fumbled with his glasses. "What can I help you with?"

"Hello. We're looking to access old records on one of Indiana's governors," Ryan said.

"Well, we have hundreds of books, biographies, and articles…just about anything you could imagine back there, so what exactly do you need?" The aide postured as he scanned the room full of materials.

"Well, we need to see the private collection of Indiana's first Governor Jonathan Jennings."

"You two are reaching back quite a bit. I don't recall ever having anyone needing information about him."

"Well, we'd love to be the first then. Can we see it?"

"Sure, but we just don't let anyone search through the old private notes and compilations from our governors without prior approval."

The man walked to his desk and produced a blue sheet of paper.

"We have a form here that you need to complete so we know what you'd like for us to pull out. After you're done with that, hand it to me, we'll put together what you need, and then I can give you a call to come back and review the information. Shouldn't take but a week."

"Why all the cloak and dagger?" Ryan said.

"Sorry?"

"Why the process. Why can't we just get in there and look at the items?"

"They're buried deep, ma'am. First, we have to make sure we even have the items you're seeking, and then it takes some time to get those things out. And of the things we do find for you, we'll have to assist you so as not to damage anything."

"Any way to speed up the process?"

"Not unless you're with the government." Ryan smiled and waited for Gabe.

He said nothing.

She turned and found Gabe spinning once more as he squinted at the artwork located around the ceiling.

"Libraries fascinate him," she whispered to the clerk. "Hey. Agent. I need some of that authority you claim to have." Gabe wasn't listening. Ryan repeated it louder.

"Sorry, but this place is really cool," he smiled as his eyebrows raised.

"We know, we know, now help me out here."

"What do you need?"

"Your badge. Pull it out."

"Why?"

"Not the time for a moral stand on abuse of authority, Gabe. We need to see those items, and he needs to see that you're someone of authority."

Gabe reached for his badge and hated that, for the second time in this investigation, he called upon the mighty shield to try and work his way through a situation.

"FBI credentials get us some access?" Ryan asked.

"Should have said something when you came in, folks. That's as good a magic ticket as we get around here, but you have to give me a minute to shut up shop."

"Why?"

"I'm the only one in here, and we're going to be behind closed doors for a time. Give me a second to call downstairs and lock that door so we can go back into the vault."

"Can't just bring it out here?"

"No, ma'am. As I said, this will take some time. The stuff's all locked down and has to be carefully handled. Just hold on."

"Shutting down the world with all that power, eh Gabe?" Ryan said.

"You're the one that told me to pull it out. You know I hate using it, Ryan, but your little piece of tin wasn't going to get us anywhere."

* * *

After the aide returned, he motioned for Gabe and Ryan to follow him to a door located under a spiral staircase leading to the second floor. The clerk waived a magnetic key card, punched in a few numbers, and the door swung open. The aide held the door open, and once they all were inside the square room, he closed and sealed the door with the card.

"Planning on keeping us here forever, sir?"

"Enough with the sir. My name is Greg, and no, I don't plan on keeping you guys here. The stuff we hold back here in the vault is valuable, and we have to make sure it stays safe."

"This room fireproof?" Ryan asked.

"No, but the one that holds all of the items is." He pointed to another door with a window through which they could only see darkness. Greg directed the pair to a metal table in the center of the room and instructed them to leave their coats and briefcases. "Come on through here," he walked to the door with the window and grabbed a small box on a shelf. "First though, I need you to put these on, please."

Gabe and Ryan pulled small plastic wads from the tiny box in Greg's hands and snapped on the rubber gloves. Another wave of the card and the door opened into a large storeroom where automatic lights flickered on down row after row of stacked items. Plastic containers, polyurethane folders, and simple cardboard boxes consumed every inch of space, and Gabe noticed fresh oxygen being pumped into the room.

"This room holds all of the historically significant documents from all of our governors and most of the United States Senators and Congressmen elected from Indiana. There's also quite a bit of other information in here, but as you can tell, we're starting to run out of room." Greg turned the corner and walked to a point farthest away from the door.

"So, everything we need should be in here?" Gabe asked.

"Well, you haven't told me exactly what you're seeking, agent," Greg said. "But I know everything we have that belonged to Governor Jennings is right here." He stopped and pointed at the first box on the floor against the wall. "Easiest boxes to find. Being the first governor and all sort of takes out the necessity of having to sift through the items in here to find who starts where."

"So, if we need to look through everything on Governor Jennings, how many boxes are we talking about?" Ryan asked.

"I looked up the numbers on the computer before we came back here, and he has section one through four on top, one through twelve in the middle, and then one, two, and three on the bottom."

"Where do we start?"

The aid scowled and put an arm out to stop Gabe.

"There's a process I think even you can appreciate here, agent." Gabe stepped back with his hands up. "If you need to see everything on Governor Jennings, then I will bring all of these items out to you one at a time."

"Out to that little room where we left our stuff?"

"Yes, and we can sort through things out there."

* * *

Over the next several hours, Greg delivered box after box and personally pulled each item from inside the container for the pair to review. His pride in his work was evident as he donned a fresh set of rubber gloves before unloading every box. Greg initially required the officers to allow him to flip through each book, loose page, and item, but soon he realized the process might take days if he did not permit Ryan and Gabe to have more freedom. After ensuring clean gloves with each box opened, Greg allowed Ryan and Gabe to be more involved in the process. Towards afternoon, Greg headed back for the last box on the bottom shelf.

"I sure hope this isn't like what happened in Renovo," Gabe said.

"What do you mean?"

"What we're looking for here is so particular that we could have missed it when we were whipping through some of those notebooks earlier."

"True, but I think we've been pretty good with our search up to this point."

"Maybe it was crazy to believe the governor or the people that collected up his stuff when he died might keep around some torn-out page from a journal that he didn't even write," Gabe said.

"Have faith."

Gabe looked at his watch and realized they had worked through lunch and even now past their regular dinner break. Greg placed the last box onto the table.

"This one's lighter than the rest, so we should just about be done," he said.

"Sorry we've taken up your day, Greg; we can at least buy your dinner when we're done here."

"No need for that, folks. I enjoy looking through these old documents like this, and I don't get to come back here and do this very much."

"Then I guess we're glad we could help," Ryan said as she smiled.

"This one had a good amount of dust on it, so I'm not sure too many eyes have seen what's in here." After donning new gloves, Greg began to pull out the contents. He held up a few flat items bound by a string and a black book with fraying paper. After laying those items on the table, he reached inside once more.

"This shouldn't have been kept like this!"

"What's that?" Ryan asked. He pulled out a half-inch thick parchment folded over in several corners. He placed the item down flat on the table and inspected the folded-over parts of the document.

"What's the problem?" Gabe asked.

"Things need to be kept open and flat, agent. Someone should have unfolded this letter, or these parts will decay more rapidly and fall apart if they are ever opened."

Greg picked the item up from the table and flipped it. "This is the first thing we've run across that wasn't flat...Oh..." Greg said.

"What?" Ryan asked.

"The seal on here hasn't been broken." He pointed to a red wax seal holding over the folded letter.

"Looks like an easy way to avoid having to use an envelope," Gabe said.

"Wait, though," Greg said as he reached into the box. "There's a stamp right here that probably made this seal."

He held up the stamp.

"That's kind of cool," Gabe said.

"It is, and my guess is this was a family seal that was particular to Governor Jennings. The wax seal on this parchment might have been the only intact seal they found when they collected his items. I don't recall seeing any other sealed items in any of the other boxes today."

"Me neither," Gabe said.

"So you know about these stamps and seals?" Ryan asked.

"I've run across them in the past when I found broken seals on some letters of correspondence from a U.S. Senator to his wife and on one special letter from one of our governors to the President of the United States, but I've never found an intact wax seal and the actual stamp used to make it before."

"These wax seals used to be common then?"

"Yeah. These were quite common in the old days and were used on high-status or ceremonial papers. Today, of course, we use ink or rubber stamps to identify things, glue-based tack, or even tape to seal letters, but this was how it was done well into the early nineteen hundreds," Greg said.

"You a notary or something?"

Greg laughed and tapped his head.

"Thousands and thousands of useless facts up here, agent."

"So, this folded over paper item with the seal must have been important to the governor then?" Ryan asked.

"Most likely," Greg held up the stamp. "But I believe this little stamp here might be the real find if it was created just for the governor. Add to it this one remaining wax seal on the folded paper, and the pair of these items are pretty valuable together."

Gabe grabbed the sealed item and held it up to the light. He squeezed the envelope on its folded ends, and the creased corners popped. The pressure on the edges of the document permitted light to pass through the middle of it.

"I think we need to open this," Gabe said. He held the document into Ryan's line of sight and squeezed the edges once more.

"See that in there?"

"That loose page in there looks awfully familiar," Ryan said.

"Don't think that's going to happen, agent."

"Honestly, Greg, we don't have time to waste right now. This is what we've been searching for all day. We've got to get this open."

"Not without a court order," Greg said.

"For once, you and I are in total agreement here," Ryan said as she nodded to Gabe.

"I can't let you…"

Gabe cracked the lipstick red seal and unfolded the document.

The clerk's eyes widened.

Several documents dropped to the table from the middle of the parchment, including one journal page matching the ones they had recovered in Renovo.

"That's unacceptable, agent. You can't just…you can't just do that. I have to report this."

"Do what you have to, Greg. I assure you I will take full responsibility for this and will even help you fill out your report when we're done here."

"I've never…"

"You'll be cleared of any wrongdoing here, but now you need to let us work."

"No agent, I think it's time for you two to go."

"Not gonna happen just yet, Greg," Ryan said as she held up the journal page.

"But I can't…"

"You need to find somewhere else to be right now," Ryan said as she shot Greg a stern look. "Why don't you go get that report started, and we'll be with you when we've finished."

Greg pulled in a deep breath, slapped his card against the card reader by the door under the stairs, and exited into the library.

"Dinner with Greg is probably out of the question," Ryan said.

"Just read."

> "January 1828: The sad horrors we men create. I shared
> with the President news of no progress in my research and
> reported after almost five years there was no cure forthcoming. Upon requesting a return of the subjects taken from the

cave for more testing, I was caustically informed they had been eliminated as they were too dangerous. Anger consumed me as I was led to believe those taken from the cave were hospitalized. President Adams discussed forming an official program to track and kill Seers, the name given to the afflicted. Mitchell challenged the request but was rebuked by a Senator whose name was not revealed. He informed us Seers had killed two Congressmen in just the past two months. One is Pettis from Missouri, and another, Johnston from Virginia. The former was shot in a duel with a Seer, Major Biddle, who also died. Adams declared all Seers an immediate danger to the country and ordered anyone possessing the crimson rage to be killed to prevent the senseless loss of life. He ignored my research showing one of every fifty of those afflicted will never go mad, such as Dave and me. Funding for the new group will come from the same monies used for our research over the past five years. I fear I have made my own grave."

Ryan and Gabe read over the document once more in silence and said nothing for a long moment.

"After all of their effort and research, they just…"

"The technology of the time wasn't advanced enough to do the type of studies like we can today. Atticus' end was ROBE's beginning," Gabe said.

"So, Adams ordered both Dave and Atticus to be killed?"

Gabe shrugged.

"Not sure, but I think we can surmise that Dave Mitchell got away since this document is right here in Governor Jennings' items," Gabe said.

"If so, then Atticus or perhaps even Dave put that cryptic little message on the page crease in the journal."

"True."

"But why?" Ryan said.

"What do you mean?"

"Well, besides the fact that this page reveals the creation of ROBE and its mission to hunt down and kill Seers, what's so special about this one page?"

"It implicates Adams in government-sanctioned killing," Gabe said.

"But that just doesn't seem to be enough of a reason to tear out this one page of the journal, deliver it to the governor, and for him to preserve it in this fashion all these hundreds of years." Ryan reread the document while Gabe leaned back in his chair for insight. As she continued to whisper the words of the journal, Gabe dropped forward and grabbed hold of the other papers enclosed inside the sealed parchment.

"You've got to be kidding me."

"What?" Ryan said.

"The name George Washington Adams ring any bells?"

"First part yes, last part, no." Gabe pushed aside the top paper and grabbed another as Ryan waited for a response.

"He was the son of President John Quincy Adams."

"And you know this how?"

"John Quincy Adams had a firstborn and named him after the first President of the United States much to the ire of John Adams, his father and second President of the United States."

"Okay."

"And these two documents," Gabe pushed aside the second and grabbed a third, "and I'm guessing all of the rest of these that were folded up are in regards to George Washington Adams." Ryan dropped the journal page and reached for two pages that remained folded. Between those folded pages, another journal page dropped onto the table.

> "April 13, 1827: Patient #1108 shows no improvement in his behaviors towards the guards and others in the cave. I discovered the source of Adams's interest in patient #1108 as Mitchell accidentally saw medical records that the patient is Adams' son. Adams has now asked that we care for his son in particular and is permitting us to utilize him in whatever manner we see fit for testing. Still, it is clear that, like the others, nothing is working. It is of note that Adams has dispatched us to utilize new opiates and other numbing drugs to dissuade the Seers and his son from carrying out their

rages. Further study of the drugs is required, and effects will be noted."

"His son was the catch," Gabe said.

"Of course! President Adams was interested in what was going on with Atticus and the Seers when he discovered his son was one."

"It does seem to fit. What do the other documents say?" Gabe held up three bluish pages, listing all of the drugs injected into Adams' son. Blazoned across the top of one document was 'Geo. Washington Adams,' with dates listing back to 1826. Flipping to one of the last two pages, the more extended sheet identified the son of Adams as patient #1108 with an admittance date of February 9, 1826. The last page contained more writing.

"This page is dated like our journal pages but written on different paper," Gabe said.

"What do you mean?"

"It's just on a regular piece of paper here, not like the other two you have there and back in the car." Ryan began typing on her laptop while Gabe read.

"It's dated just before Atticus' foreboding journal entry we found first when we cracked open the seal.

> December 1827: We have been pressured to inject #1108 with dozens of concoctions to nullify the effects of the rage. While we have found that extremely high levels of an opiate-based compound mixed with chemicals used by morticians to preserve bodies are adequate at dulling the subject, he has become a gloomy character consumed by constant paranoia. Adams' visit did not go well when the patient lunged at him before #1108 sulked off to a corner and cried for well over four hours. While the patient did not injure Adams or anyone else, it is clear this chemical mixture is not the answer we seek as this subject is a shell of a human being and cannot function in this way as a member of society. Adams still believes there is hope the patient can be released, but we are not convinced."

"The president was using his son as a test dummy!"

"It seems he was desperately looking for answers to the Seers but not getting any Ryan. And from what we know from that journal entry from over a month later, he must have given up hope as he essentially ordered his own son to be killed."

"Wow!" Ryan tapped on her computer screen.

"What'd you find?" Gabe asked.

"My web search on George Washington Adams reports not only that he was a troubled fellow with bouts of paranoia in the mid-1820s but that he also died mysteriously," Ryan said.

"How?"

"Says he disappeared from a ferry named, get this, the *Benjamin Franklin* one night. He didn't arrive at his planned destination, and his body washed up on the shore on June 13, 1829. Papers called it a suicide." Ryan frowned. "What is it Ryan?"

"That date is a little removed from the January termination order though, isn't it?" Ryan said.

"It's doubtful Adams was super eager to kill his own son Ryan, so it's possible he tried to let him out and about one more time with all of the drugs in his system before he let him be put down".

"That's awfully cold Gabe...put down," Ryan said.

"Cold or not Ryan, maybe it was a suicide with all of those drugs in him, but my guess is someone from ROBE was finally ordered to take him out," Gabe said. "So, then Dave Mitchell brought these items to the governor of Indiana for leverage to cover his own backside."

"No doubt Ryan, and once he takes the evidence of ROBE's creation to Indiana, he sends word through the governor that if anyone from ROBE came after Dave, then the documents about the President's son would be released for public consumption."

"Smart guy," Ryan smiled. "What's more, thanks to that research we did last night in the hotel room about the governor's souring on his relationship with Adams, it's possible that this whole episode with Adams ordering all Seers to be killed was the catalyst for Jennings shifting his support away from Adams' presidential bid."

"The timing of all of that is not just a coincidence," Gabe said as he nodded. Ryan rubbed her forehead.

"My brain hurts."

"It's almost too much, isn't it, Ryan? But still…"

"What, Gabe?"

"When did ROBE's plan to kill all of the Seers change?"

"You've lost me," Ryan said.

"From what Svetlana told me, her job for ROBE is to detain Seers and hand them over to be cured, right?"

"Yeah, so? Maybe they found a cure after Atticus was gone and stopped having to kill the Seers," Ryan said.

"But that's not what Svetlana was taught when she was brought to the cave and trained with her two partners."

"You're gonna need to explain that to me," Ryan said.

"Svetlana was told Atticus found a cure, and ROBE was then created to collect up Seers so they could be cured. From what we've read in these last journal entries, Atticus discovered nothing. Even if a cure was found years later, why would Svetlana not have been told when and who created the cure? Why teach her this Atticus fellow discovered a cure when clearly he didn't?"

"Because maybe there is no cure?"

Gabe nodded.

"And if there is no cure, then these Seers are just being rounded up and killed then," Ryan said.

"Except there's still the issue that Svetlana was pushing about how Seers like Carlisle in Florida and Mazar at the wedding got out. Could ROBE have found a way to corral these crazy guys and turn them into government assassins?"

"You did say that Carlisle killed some American with a connection to Al-Qaeda terrorist Al-Zarqawi after ROBE captured him, right?" Ryan asked.

"That's what Svetlana said, but it doesn't explain why someone like Mazar just started shooting up a wedding," Gabe said.

"Not yet, but when we get back to El Paso, I think we need to take a closer look at the guest list."

CHAPTER 23

FUNGUS

As Gabe welcomed the calm of the morning with his usual routine of coffee and Labrador lap time, he refused to peruse the documents Ryan had given him from Renovo to spend time in the quiet of the moment. He had looked over all of the papers rather quickly when he arrived home the night before but found few new ones of interest other than a three-page lab report written by doctors proud of using big words. Unable to discern most of the medical jargon before he tired and headed to bed, he set the information on his cell phone, which resulted in a frantic search for the vibrating device when it broke his peaceful morning.

"You just can't let me have ten minutes, can you?" Gabe said as he reorganized the papers that had been atop his phone.

"Cunningham set up that meeting with the fungus person for us today. Did you forget?" Ryan asked.

"How can I forget about someone that plays with mushrooms and calls themselves a Mycologist?"

"Be nice, Agent Moss of the Federal Bureau of Investigation. If you have a title, everyone deserves one."

"I'll be nice. Meeting's at ten, right?"

"Yeah, and we're meeting with Doctor McClary, who is a friend of Cunningham's from college, so let's try to be nice. Do you need me to pick you up?"

"You've got your car back?"

"Yeah, I had a voicemail when I got home last night, so I got up early this morning and went and got it."

"I think I'll drive myself today. I'm not sure how bad your skills are now that you've gone so many weeks without driving."

"Fine by me. I'll see you there."

* * *

Gabe had envisioned something a bit more dark and mysterious as he pulled up to the strip mall occupied by a grocery store and several business offices. Thanks to time in theater where the dangers of biological and chemical warfare were beaten into his skull, he had a hard time imagining anything positive about a place that prided itself on teaching young children about the joys of fungus. From what Gabe remembered of the doctors who taught him of these dangers, their personalities were non-existent. It was clear they preferred analyzing the proliferation of fungal dispersions to actually holding a normal conversation with the living. As he opened the front door to the business, an intense aroma caused him to shiver.

"Says out there that this place has a petting zoo?" Gabe asked. Ryan, standing by a large poster with a smiling mushroom, walked towards her partner.

"It's an educational facility, Gabe. The Center for Disease Control and Prevention runs it in conjunction with the department of natural resources. I think it looks kind of cool."

"Not sure what your idea of fun is, Ryan, but this place gives me the creeps."

"Aw, come on, Gabe, look at the joy on those little kids' faces." Gabe watched as a class of half a dozen kindergartners followed a woman dressed as a tree around a corner and into the depths of the building.

He grimaced and shook his head.

"Don't tell me the all-powerful Army warrior is terrified of a little fungus?"

"Handful of fears I've got Ryan, and this stuff just happens to be one of them." She laughed and pointed at the smiling moss creature dancing on the floor next to her. "This place is probably gonna kill everyone…" Gabe caught himself before uttering his next words as a woman of fair stature and thick glasses appeared seemingly out of nowhere and extended a hand.

"I'm Doctor Tamera McClary," she said.

His fears of the Mycologist were genuine.

"I'm Gabe...sorry...Gabe Moss. I assume you already know Ryan here from previous field trips?"

Ryan glared.

"No, no, I don't think we've ever had the pleasure." She extended a hand to Ryan. "Besides, I try not to mingle with the tours and folks coming through. I just stick to the fungi."

"Rebecca Ryan, we spoke on the phone."

"Of course, of course, dear, come on along, and let's get this little quest of yours going." The three walked around the corner where the school group had disappeared. The narrow passage expanded into a larger hallway with multiple learning stations for visitors to enjoy on either side. Information about different types of fungi and quotes from famous woodland types were plastered on the ceiling and walls. The mood lighting and forest interior did not ingratiate Gabe to the museum.

"I overheard your opinion of our little slice of heaven here Agent Moss as I approached, but I didn't quite catch that last part."

Gabe smiled.

"I can't lie to you, doctor. Is it okay to call you doctor?"

"Yes, yes, doctor or Mac will work just fine."

"I've never heard of a Mycologist before, and I've never told anyone, but mushrooms and their progeny make me nervous."

"You are very funny, agent, but I assure you there is nothing to fear here."

"Sorry, but I've seen too many of the wrong effects of spores and black mold and the like over the past dozen or so years, and when I think of these things, they stress me out." Ryan punched Gabe on the arm and shook her head.

"Quit being negative," Ryan whispered. "Try to show a little interest."

"I will do my best to be gentle," the doctor said.

"So...who thought of putting a CDC location in this place, doctor?" Gabe asked and shrugged while looking at Ryan for confirmation that he had asked an appropriate question. She nodded, satisfied.

"CDC has locations all over the country agent, and they needed one in the southwest here, so we offered up some space in the back for their lab."

"So, you work for the CDC then or the DNR?" Ryan asked.

"I was with the Texas DNR in their forestation sciences but jumped at the chance to join the CDC when this joint venture popped up. They sent me to the mothership in Atlanta for a few years for training, and then I moved back out here and took over this place. I'm still also licensed by the DNR, though."

The trio entered a spacious circular room with dozens of more stations and interactive shows in every free space. They walked towards a fake tree trunk pushed out and away from the wall, upon which a glowing orange sign read 'Mushroom Hunting can be FUN, but Avoid the NO FUNGI'S.' A low-cut rough opening at the side of the tree trunk forced the detectives to duck into a small cave-like room located inside the trunk. Inside, two long wooden benches arched along the back wall, and the doctor directed them to take a seat. An automatic projector kicked on, and the doctor walked up to the screen.

"Fungi and a movie, how quaint," Ryan whispered.

Gabe fought his grin.

"Doctor Cunningham told me you needed some information about a certain type of mushroom that was found in the bloodstream of some murder victims."

"That's pretty much it," said Gabe.

"He also warned me I needed to keep this simple for Detective Ryan's sake," she chortled oddly as she turned to face the screen.

"Now she's after you too," Gabe whispered.

"Just so happens the little guy you see here at the start of this movie is the genus of the amatoxin that was sent to me by Cunningham." She pointed to the screen and nodded. A voice came over the loudspeaker.

"In the wonderful world of mushroom hunting, there are dozens of species that are edible for both animals and man." The video flipped to various other forms of mushroom. "Unfortunately, dozens of people eat the wrong mushroom every year and end up in an emergency room. Because of these dangers, you must know what you are doing before hunting for nature's little fungi. Let's start at the beginning..."

As new images appeared on the screen, the doctor pointed and nodded at four other different mushrooms. Not until the part of the video where the doctor herself was on screen did she shut off the presentation.

"This video goes on for a time pointing out bad things to look for, but I wanted to draw your attention to the four fungi in particular that can typically be found within sixty or so miles of El Paso."

"So that first mushroom you pointed out and mentioned something about an amatoxin, is that also found around here?"

"No, it just happened with luck to be there in the introduction. And while the Galerina species are found worldwide detective, you cannot find that species naturally anywhere within a hundred miles of here. Most species of mushroom cannot grow in the desert, and that is why I wanted to show you those four particular types on that video."

"So, if that first mushroom cannot be found around these parts, can we assume that no market or street vendor is picking and pawning these off on people?" Ryan asked.

"That is most likely true detective. I cannot imagine that any vendor or market owner would have these products for sale, particularly since most of those types of sellers grow their own products."

"Then what about restaurants?" Gabe asked.

"Improbable, Agent Moss, since those establishments are well regulated, particularly when it comes to having foods that can kill people."

"So, if that species of mushroom cannot be found locally and could not be sold in our restaurants, how can you explain the presence of this strain in our dead guys?"

"I surmise that someone is growing these locally."

"But I thought you just said the climate here can't support that species of mushroom?"

"No agent, I said the Galerina species does not grow naturally in these parts. I never said anything about being able to grow them on your own."

"Like a hydroponics set up then?" Ryan asked.

"Exactly. For this item to be found in this region, someone is growing it at their place of residence or business."

"And for what purpose?"

"Hard to say agent, but whoever is growing this particular species knows what they are growing and likely is growing these for a nefarious purpose."

"How can you say that?" Gabe asked.

"People involved in hydroponics are meticulous about what they grow in their private gardens. They have thousands of dollars invested in equipment for particular purposes like, for instance, growing marijuana or their own organic goods. Hydroponics owners would never just be growing this particular random mushroom without knowing what it was for."

"But even if that's true, how do you conclude it must be for a nefarious purpose then?" Gabe asked.

"Because if this particular type of mushroom were served at, say, a dinner party, where the cook accidentally got ahold of this poison, this would have played out quite differently."

"How so?"

"Well, the dinner guests wouldn't have ended up in the street dying, but rather would have found their way to a hospital complaining of the great pains they were having in the hours or days before their deaths."

"Good point," Gabe said.

"So, to answer your question more succinctly, I have to surmise from what I know about this species, our location in the country, and what Doctor Cunningham told me, someone knows what they are growing, and they purposely placed this amatoxic mushroom into the bodies of your dead people."

"Sounds logical," Ryan whispered to Gabe.

"Come, come," she insisted as she ducked out through the door of the video room. The three exited the theater and walked across the center of the open atrium as teachers worked to corral eager children. The trio pushed through a set of swinging doors and headed down a dimly lit hallway. Coming to a large steel door, the doctor revealed a red key card which permitted entry into an area denoted 'Employees Only.'

"This not part of the tour, I assume," Gabe asked as they entered a laboratory with various test tubes, liquids, and row after row of glass cases with various plants and molds.

"This is where we keep all of the species that can be found in the States, agent."

"Even the dangerous ones?"

"Yes, even the dangerous ones." Gabe slowed his pace. "Not to worry though, filters are pumping out everything of danger in this room. It's clean, I promise you."

He caught up to the pair of women.

"So, do you have our bad fungus in here then?"

"Right here," she turned and pointed to a little brown cap, enclosed in glass, on the table next to a microscope. "We used this exact specimen to match the amatoxin with blood that Cunningham sent me."

"So, since we're on that topic, help me understand why we keep using the term amatoxin rather than just saying mushroom. What's the difference?"

The doctor pointed to a chart on the wall next to them.

"As you can see here, amatoxins are a subgroup of at least eight toxic compounds that are found in many different types of poisonous mushrooms."

"Then you're saying that amatoxins can only be found in this particular species then?" Gabe asked.

"No, they can be found in several different species, but for our purposes here today, this particular species that was found in your deceased is always poisonous."

"And we sort of gleaned over this a moment ago with the dinner discussion, but how is this mushroom normally ingested?" Ryan asked.

"You eat them, Ryan," Gabe said.

"Well, actually, you can eat them, they can be inhaled, or they can be absorbed through the skin, detective."

Ryan smirked at Gabe.

"So, it's possible that someone could crush these to a dust, and you could inhale it without knowing and then die?"

"Possible but not likely. You would have to be in an enclosed space with pounds of this stuff being pushed up your nose for days for it to be fully ingested to the point at which your intake could result in death."

"But it's possible these people didn't know if they were inhaling it, though, right?" Ryan asked.

"Possibly, but again, they would be feeling miserable for a few days before they died, so it only seems logical that even if you didn't know you inhaled these, the pain you were feeling as your body shut down would have resulted in you seeking out immediate medical treatment."

Ryan nodded.

"And once absorbed, what does this amatoxin do exactly?" Gabe asked.

"If these species were completely absorbed, which most often would be through eating them, then the liver would be the first victim. As well, in your scenario detective, if enough were inhaled, the lungs, kidneys, and heart would be infected first."

"And what happens after ingestion?"

"The affected organs begin to fail which in turn leads to exhaustion, diarrhea, headaches, coughing, back pain, and a variety of other unpleasant maladies too long to list."

"And would eating just one of these mushrooms do all that?" Ryan asked.

"Only takes a few caps to start your internal organs on a downward spiral."

"And then this leads to death?" Gabe asked.

"Almost always if untreated."

"How long does it take from time of ingestion to time of death in an average-sized man?" Gabe asked.

"The side effects will start in a matter of hours and organ failure not long after that. Then it could be a matter of one to three days before death."

"If you were able to get to a hospital in time, could you be saved?"

"It is possible, but often an infected has waited too long, and their organs have succumbed to the poison by the time they seek help." The pair looked down at their notepads in search of other questions. Gabe stepped back from the mushroom when he realized he had moved too close for his comfort. Ryan looked up from her notes.

"Did you get anything else from the sample Cunningham sent over?" Ryan asked.

"Just that this strain was highly concentrated which even more so negates any street vendor or food establishment from being the cause, as well as the innocent inhaling we spoke about a moment ago."

"Why is that?"

"The blood sample was thoroughly laced with amatoxin, which suggests that someone fed a bunch of these mushrooms to the men that died."

"So, you're able to tell then, in this case, that ingestion was by eating them?" Ryan asked.

"Yes, detective, and while there was always the possibility by injection into the bloodstream, Cunningham told me the victims did not have any evidence of track marks."

The detectives looked at one another and nodded.

"I think that's all we need, for now, doctor," Ryan said.

"Well, while I can't say I'll ever come back here again to learn more about my fuzzy and furry friends, you've been a real help." Gabe extended his hand.

"Just make sure to wash your hands after you leave," the doctor said. "I've been working with that stuff all day," she pointed to the brown cap.

The three walked back through the lab to the door leading into the atrium. As the door closed behind them and the doctor disappeared, Gabe dodged the young children as he raced for the hand sanitizer dispenser on the wall. He hit the dispenser, rubbed his hands together, hit the dispenser again, and then rubbed his hands dry on his pants. Once outside, Ryan burst into laughter.

"She was joking, you moron!"

CHAPTER 24

RAGE

Strong hands grabbed Uriah by his bound wrists. He lurched sideways into a seated position and felt a muscle tear in his shoulder as the ties were cut and his arms swung loose to his side.

"It's time, Uriah. It's time to take out your target and finish this," a man whispered to him. The blindfold sapping all light jerked off his skull, and the sun's rays blinded him. Still unfocused, a heavy shove into the small of his back forced Uriah to stumble onto the sidewalk as the van door slammed behind him and the vehicle sped off. As he rubbed his eyes, the assault on his ocular nerves relented, and his vision began to clear.

"He's in red," Uriah mumbled to himself as he caught sight of a hot dog vendor ten yards away.

Kill the red.

"You need to die!" The vendor making change for a customer glared at Uriah. "You need to..." Uriah snarled then stopped as his focus moved from the vendor to the others standing in line encased in a rainbow of colors. Uriah lurched towards the cart as a blinding pain cut into his side. He reached out and found a brick pillar beside the hot dog cart, permitting him a moment to balance and collect himself.

Not the right one. He's not the right one.

Uriah took in a deep breath as the pain subsided, pushed off the pillar, and redirected his momentum to the sliding doors at the building entrance.

Must focus on the one. Must find him and end this.

Looking up at the letters above the sliding door, the words 'Exchange, General Cline and KILL' flashed as one in his mind. Tears formed from the force he exerted on closing his eyelids, but neither the pressure nor the darkness eased the visions. He slapped his head several times as civilians exiting the PX modified their movements to avoid Uriah. After one final strike to the back of his head, Uriah kept his hand on his skull, pushed his chin to his chest, and marched through the entrance. To find his way, Uriah darted his eyes side to side along the tile floor and was able to make out kiosks in the center of a long hall with larger shops on either side. Multiple colors consumed the legs of the people he could see, and the words in his mind crashed into his psyche more prominently. He closed his eyes tight once more and felt another pain inside his stomach which crippled him. He put out an arm and fortune found one of the kiosks.

"Sir, can I help you?" a woman said.

"This isn't why I'm here!" he said to no one in particular. Annoyed patrons turned.

He gripped the post holding up a kiosk selling dog tags more tightly.

"I'm sorry, sir, but are you ok?"

Uriah looked up at the young girl bathed in blue, and he felt at ease. His breathing slowed.

"I'm not here for you," he said with precise diction.

"Can I help you find who you're looking for then?" Uriah gave an odd stare that made the girl uncomfortable, then grinned.

"Just trying to find the food court." His voice strained. "Can you help me find the food court?" She raised her arm and pointed down the hall. Uriah's eyes followed down the corridor, and he prepared to move.

"This soldier bothering you, ma'am?" asked a sergeant who appeared over the employee's shoulder.

Uriah looked up and red stabbed at his eyes.

"It's not you. You're not a part of this!" Uriah screamed.

The sergeant stiffened.

"Your tone is unacceptable private. Do we have a problem here?" Uriah looked down towards the employee's waist seeking the blue, and he calmed.

"It's not you," Uriah said softer. "I just need to get to the food court and find the general." Uriah raised his hand in the direction the girl had been pointing and willed himself not to look at the sergeant.

"Then make it quick…" the sergeant said, "…and if he causes you further problems, ma'am, you need to report his conduct to the MP's."

"He's been fine, sergeant, thank you."

"Yeah, thanks," Uriah grumbled as he pushed away from the kiosk and made his way back into the flow of foot traffic. To his left and right, the mash of too many colors turned everything sepia, and he fought the urge to stare too long in any one direction. Uriah opened and closed his eyelids, trying to fight the color sensations, but the strobe effect created by his fluttering offered no solace. Finding no remedy, Uriah shot his eyes up to the skylights after every third step that he took. The leaking yellow rays pulled his attention from the people around him and permitted momentary respite. The routine, albeit slow in getting to his destination, calmed him.

"I've been here," Uriah muttered to himself as he reached the food court.
I remember being here the first day of basic.

Uriah stood alongside a large square room with a half dozen food establishments lining the walls. In the middle of the restaurants were rows of sturdy black chairs lined up along ghost-white tables. Soldiers in and out of uniform were everywhere as the dinner rush was just beginning.

He's here. They promised me he was here.

Uriah repeated the phrase over and over in his mind as he took time intermittently to scan the room, then look up to the skylights.

Got to find him and end this. Have to end this now. The pain is unbearable.

With no success from a distance of fifteen yards, Uriah moved closer to the dinner tables and pushed past several soldiers that did not take kindly to his intrusion.

He's here. They told me he was here.

Uriah stopped at an empty table, leaned over, and tried to compose himself. His right eyelid began to flutter, and the bulge pushing against the right side of his abdomen forced him to jolt sideways and almost drop to the floor. Catching himself on a table, the pain became too much, and he collapsed into an empty chair. On the far side of the food court, Uriah's actions had not gone unnoticed by the MP's, as a few patrons had reported the odd behavior. Once Uriah had been pointed out, one MP moved towards the tables.

He's here…I know he's here. They told me he was here.

Uriah banged his head on the table, and more patrons stared. Following three more head slams, Uriah stood up and forced himself to look at the soldiers around him. The colors flooded over every free corner, and for the first time, a new concern arose.

They're all dressed the same.

"They all look the same," he said aloud as more soldiers turned. Uriah lumbered towards the table full of soldiers nearest to him. He placed his shaking hands on the clear white surface and didn't look up.

"See the general?"

"Sorry, what?" a specialist asked.

"See the general today?"

"Which general are you looking for private?"

Uriah jerked his head up and stared at the chests of the assembled soldiers. He squinted as he tried to read the names on each soldier's nameplate through the colors. His eyes twitched, and his head swung side to side. Two of the female soldiers turned away.

"Not here," Uriah mumbled. "Not you."

"You got a problem, buddy?" one of the male soldiers said as Uriah pushed off of the table and moved to another.

"General Cline?" Uriah whispered as he held onto a new table and shook.

"Do you need help?" one of the female soldiers said as she looked back to the table from which Uriah had just come. The soldiers at the first table shrugged their shoulders and shook their heads.

"Your names. What are your names," Uriah asked as he again tried to identify each of them at the table by their nameplates.

"Haircuts are all the same. Uniforms all the same. Colors all the same," Uriah said aloud. "I know he's here, and I need to find him!" Across the room, more MP's stood and moved towards Uriah. Two went left, while another went to the right and caught up with the MP closest to the scene.

"Can't find him! How do I stop this?" Uriah yelled as he moved away from the tables and stumbled to other patrons walking by the food court as they departed from a grocery store.

"General Cline?"

The frightened man shook his head.

Uriah moved on.

"General?" The soldier in Uriah's grasp pointed to his rank on his chest.

"General Cline?" Uriah said again and again as he moved from person to person. The MP's surrounded Uriah as he got more crazed, became more frantic and his questions grew louder for all to hear. Uriah grabbed at a tall man dressed in fatigues.

"General Cline!?" Uriah yelled.

"You need to step away from that man, private, and do it now!" ordered one of the MP's. His hand rested on his holstered weapon.

"We can help you out, soldier, but you need to calm down," said another.

Uriah didn't notice the military police presence as he pulled the rigid man close to him to look at his name. "Simpson!" Uriah yelled. He pushed the man in his grasp to the ground. Other patrons retreated to the exits as the MP's and a few other soldiers stepped in to help form a cordon. Uriah's attention snapped to the men surrounding him.

"I can't find him!" Uriah yelled.

"We can see that. We can help you out, but you're going to have to calm down. We need you to relax and get down on the ground."

"Can't end this way! Have to end this now, or the pain won't stop!"

"I don't understand," said an MP.

"Just sit down on the floor, son, and we can figure this whole mess out together," said another. Uriah looked at the men surrounding him and saw a sepia mix of colors along with a few cloaked all in red.

"You're with him!"

"We're here to help, son, that's all."

"He's with you!" Uriah screamed.

"We're MP's son. We just need you to calm down."

"I can't do this," Uriah mumbled. He realized his mission was compromised. His goal to find and kill the general was not going to be met, and worse, the pain would not end. Hands at his side, he stood stiff as a board and forced his eyes up to the skylights. A broad streak of light highlighted his face, and he opened his eyes for one more moment of calm. The light evaporated the rainbow of colors surrounding him, and his thoughts conflicted.

This isn't who I am.

"This isn't who I'm supposed to be," Uriah yelled as he continued to look up.

"Just calm down!"

It's not supposed to be this way. I'm a soldier!

"Not like this!" Uriah yelled. Without breaking his eyes from the sky-lights, he reached down to his waist and pulled out a pistol. The muzzle pointed at the ground. Screams of panic consumed the food court, and several unarmed troops surrounding Uriah scampered for safety. The MP's drew their weapons, and with all of the commotion, several seconds passed before each MP had a clear line of sight.

"Put it down, soldier!"

"Drop your weapon!"

"I can't find him," Uriah muttered. "The pain won't stop!"

"Nothing you have to do, son, but put the gun down!"

"This isn't me!"

Uriah dropped his gaze from the sunlight as a sharp pain in his side forced him to jerk sideways. The movement was slight, but he felt the grip on his weapon slip.

I can't find him. I can't get it done.

"Drop the weapon!"

I can't take living like this. I was not meant to be like this.

"Drop the damn weapon!"

"I won't let it end like this!"

Uriah pulled up the handgun, raised it over his head, and fired into the ceiling.

CHAPTER 25

CLEAR SIGHT

"This is Moss."

"We've got another one."

"Do you have me on speed dial for a wakeup call at seven every morning?" Gabe asked as he rolled over after seeing the time on his clock.

"Sorry. Good morning. Now, where are you?"

"In bed, of course; where are you?"

"Leaving the office."

"You've been to work already?"

"Did some follow-up research online on the fungus issue, and I spent an hour or so pouring over those journal entries one more time," she said.

"You're gonna need a long downtime meal today, aren't you?"

"We'll see."

"What've we got?"

"Happened last night, but just found out about it because the detectives didn't know we were back in town. The scene has been cleaned, and the body is already down at the morgue."

"You heading that way?"

"Yeah, I'm getting off the elevator now."

"Well, I did need to see Cunningham," Gabe said.

"You find something?"

"Yeah, I have that three-page lab report that I've been pouring over, but I need him to look at it and decipher some things for me."

"We know what that says pretty much, though?"

"Yeah, but an unbiased and fresh look might help us out," Gabe said.

"Need some java?"

"Large would be great!"

"I'll see you in twenty."

* * *

"That coffee's really not for me?" Gabe heard Doctor Cunningham groan as he stepped off the elevator by the morgue.

"I thought you people who work in offices with operating tables had endless supplies of coffee at your disposal, so no, again, this isn't for you," Ryan said.

"She brought coffee for you, but not me," Cunningham said to Gabe as he walked into the morgue. "I don't get this girl. She thinks the coffee here is remotely palatable. This isn't a design firm, you know. You ever see an espresso machine in this place?" Gabe shied away from responding to the barbs as he realized Cunningham was genuinely offended by the slight.

Not only was Ryan not catching on to Cunningham's awkward mating rituals, but it was becoming quite clear that she wasn't even considering extending standard niceties, such as purchasing his coffee. While Gabe long ago conceded that a Ryan/Cunningham pairing was never in the offing, it was only now that he believed Cunningham was starting to see the light as well. He threw a hand in disgust towards Ryan and walked towards a body. "I shouldn't even let you in here after you ruined my trash can last time."

"I had been up all night, doctor, had an empty stomach, and told you I was sick."

"So no regurgitating today then?" he asked.

"I got a bagel before I got here, so I promise, no vomit. Anyway, I washed out the trash can myself." Gabe walked up beside Ryan.

"Here's your coffee!" Ryan shoved the steaming cup into Gabe's hands.

"Thank you." Gabe turned to Cunningham. "I got coffee," he whispered to try and redirect Cunningham's stewing. The doctor scowled and tightened his grip on a chisel.

"We had just finished with the chest," Cunningham said, diving back to business, "when those detectives covering for you found out you two were back in town. Once they got hold of Ryan, we stopped and decided to wait."

The detectives approached the body while Doctor Cunningham tuned out the world and resumed where he had left off. The skin that had protected the man's skull for the duration of his life was pulled down over the bridge of his nose, evidencing that the good doctor had been preparing to remove the skull. The skull had been separated before their arrival, and Gabe was relieved to have avoided the piercing hiss of the band saw as it separated bone and wafted mists of powder into the air that both he and Ryan found so disturbing. The doctor tapped along the cut around the top of the skull and popped loose the cap without much effort. The sucking sound as the cap came loose caused Ryan to wince, and Cunningham glared at her while he dropped the top loudly onto a metal tray. Returning to the body, the exposed brain took a few moments to pry loose as dangling tendrils remained, but in less than half a minute, Cunningham held the pink mass in his hands and placed it on a scale.

"Kids name is Kent, Uriah Kent, and he just got into town from Utah," Ryan said.

"What was he doing here?"

"He arrived for basic training, disappeared a week ago, and then showed up last night, in uniform, at the PX," Ryan said.

"Any obvious cause of death yet?" Gabe asked.

"Primarily death by cop," Cunningham said. "The kid has a dozen bullet holes in him."

"The detectives omitted that bit of information on their way out," Ryan said, pointing to the sheet covering all but Uriah's head.

"So if he's dead from lead, why are we here?" Gabe asked.

"I said the primary reason was death by cop, Gabe. We ran some blood tests when they first pulled him in here to try and shed some light on why he just showed up at the Fort Bliss PX and stood there shooting into the ceiling."

"They think he was high on something?"

"Was a possibility," Cunningham said.

"Was?" Ryan asked.

"Well, Kent here has the amatoxin in him like those other two you had in here a few weeks back."

"The same mushroom poison you found in both Mallon and Wade?"

"Best I can tell, it's exactly the same. Mallon's blood was a little dated, and it was hard to pull out the specifics of the poison in his blood, but the poison in Specialist Wade's body was from the same strain as the poison in this kid's body."

"Anything abnormal about his eyes?" Gabe asked.

The doctor stopped and looked up, clearly unprepared for the shift in focus.

"Well, no, but I haven't gotten there yet…on him anyway."

"Sorry," Gabe said.

"Well, no, I mean, I haven't gotten to Uriah's eyes yet, but I did check the eyes on Specialist Wade as you asked me to. His mother hadn't arrived from Detroit to identify the body yet, so it was still here. I compared his eyes to what I found with Kay Farr's and found both of them had scarring."

"Scarring from what?"

"Well, as I told you before, Farr's was from contact with histo, but there are several possible explanations for Wade's."

"Such as?" Gabe asked.

"Well, anything from exposure to sunlight, punches to the face, or even herpes."

"Why is it so hard to pinpoint a reason behind Wade's scarring?"

"Most of the fluids from Wade were long gone by the time I got to revisit his eyes so that I couldn't check for the histo, but it is possible that both he and Farr may have both suffered from it."

Gabe gave a long, defeated breath.

"Look, I've told you before, Gabe, I'm not an eye guy. You asked me for anything interesting about the eyes in those other folks, and I told you I'd look. Before Farr and Wade, I wasn't ever told to be looking at the damn eyes for scarring, so there's nothing for me to review. You asked me to look, that's what I did, and that's what I found." Gabe backed off. "But I'll take a look at this kid's eyes right now if you really need me to."

"Before you do that, would you mind reading this for me?" Gabe handed Cunningham the three-page lab report.

"What's this?"

"I'm hoping you can tell me." Doctor Cunningham removed his gloves and grabbed the documents. While both Gabe and Ryan were aware of most of what was contained in the lab report, they said nothing of what they knew, hoping to get a fresh perspective from Cunningham. The doctor's expression changed quickly as he read.

"Huh?"

"That a good 'huh' or bad 'huh'?" Gabe asked.

"An interested 'huh.'"

"Care to enlighten us?" Ryan asked.

"It sort of answers some of those questions about that histo stuff you guys keep tossing in my face."

"Well, what does it say?"

This is a paper hypothesizing about Histoplasmosis capsulatum and people called Seers. Like I told you a few weeks ago over the phone, Ryan, histo has to do with a fungus afflicting people all over the globe..."

"Yeah, the bird and bat poop...we remember." Gabe glared at Ryan to remind her to act ignorant. "Sorry." She shrugged.

"So, this paper goes a step further and postulates that the fungus might cause even bigger issues beyond just basic eye deformations or vision problems."

"Such as?"

"Well, beyond the usual damage to various organs, the author's theory in here discusses how certain people called Seers gain the ability to see auras or colors around living animals."

"And so just having this Histoplasmosis causes these visions then?"

"Well, no, not without help."

"What kind of help?" Ryan asked.

"The writer isn't sure, but he seems pretty convinced that how a person gains the ability to see colors has something to do with the histo fungus mutating in the eye and damaging the macula. He postulates that the mutation might occur naturally at times, as he surmises the trigger is caused by prolonged exposure to the histo or particularly strong strains of the stuff. Pretty sophomoric thinking, I'm sorry to say, but from the age of this paper, it was written well before most of today's technology even existed. My guess would be overexposure to the sun, radiation, or contact with some volatile chemicals, you know, something along those lines is what can cause the mutation."

"So, some unknown trigger mutates the histo, and then what?"

"Well, once this damage occurs, he proposes a person's wavelength absorption changes, and after that, they can see colors around live animals or people."

"Wavelength absorption?"

"Think of it this way. Those with normal eyesight perceive the visible light spectrum because that is the wavelength range our photoreceptors absorb. We call these photoreceptor cells cones, and when they are working properly, we see them in the visible light spectrum. These cones are located in the macula, and if they get damaged, you can lose your eyesight."

"Makes sense."

"Then for these people gaining the ability to see auras, it would seem the photoreceptors in the macula are not being destroyed, but instead mutate, so the eye now perceives a different wavelength such as the infrared spectrum."

"And that's why affected persons see different colors?"

"Well, this paper touches on that topic, but the writer believes all living things give off some sort of electromagnetic aura that persons with the mutated infrared spectrum vision can see as different colors."

"What colors?" Gabe interrupted.

"Sorry?"

"What kinds of colors can be seen?"

"I would imagine many colors, but this paper here talks about only red, green, orange, and blue."

"Any sense as to why those four?"

"It seems when this was written, these were the only colors seen by those suffering from the mutated histo."

"And those people with mutated vision sort of could tell what kind of mood someone was in then?"

"Not quite," Cunningham pointed at the last page. "The hypothesis here suggests the colors indicate the very nature of a living thing as it evolves over time. For instance, take Al Capone, having laid a trail of crime and murder across Chicago; his color would be red. A puppy or even a young child, save they weren't born possessed by the devil, would be green or blue. That's what this is talking about."

"So, you're not born with any other color than green?"

"Well yeah, I guess…" Cunningham said. "…or at least the writer interpreted it that way. This Atticus guy goes further to hypothesize that while all living things start the same, once you've attained a certain level of deceit or dishonesty, you're stuck with orange or red and never go back. The soul is stained if you will."

"Is this like a Karma thing then," Ryan asked.

"Didn't either you ever take a philosophy class?" The detective's heads turned. "Philosophers have forever posed questions about the inherent nature of beings. There's the whole nature versus nurture argument for how people turn out, and of course, there's Karma which is simply that what you get in this life is a culmination of whatever deeds you've done in your past lives. Then, of course, it gets a tad confusing with the Buddhists, who allow that even in what appears evil, there may be some higher good."

"A medical examiner with a side of religion…how intriguing," Ryan said as she turned away and placed her coffee cup on an empty table.

"Comparative religious studies," Cunningham puffed up his chest. "We pathologists spend a lot of time with bodies in transition, life to death, and we often start to wonder what's next? Is there truly anything to this life, and why exactly are we here, for good, for bad? Atticus believed there was some conclusive, undeniable nature of each living thing, related to these auras, which these Seers could judge."

"Sort of a terrifying prospect," Gabe said. "To think these Seers are so certain in what they are seeing around a person that they want to kill them."

"I didn't say that."

Ryan glared at Gabe.

"Sorry, it's on some of the other documents we have," Gabe said. "According to what we've discovered, Seers almost always turn dangerous when they see red."

"Turn?"

Ryan gave him another look.

"Turned," Gabe said. "Turned," he repeated. Cunningham massaged his chin as he glanced over the last paragraph once more before he looked up.

"It's all just a rather fantastic hypothesis, guys."

The detectives looked at one another.

"Wait a minute; you don't think this hypothesis here is driving someone to commit all these deaths around El Paso, do you?"

"No…well no…not exactly," Ryan said.

Gabe now shot her a glance.

"Hey doc," Gabe sought to distract the doctor, "could you do us a favor?"

"Of course."

"When you're checking Kent for scratches to his eyes, could you also test him for the Histoplasmosis?"

"Sure."

"And can you dig through the records from our earlier bodies and determine if they had the histo as well?"

"As I said earlier if you were listening," he shot Gabe a disappointed look, "Wade's fluids were all gone making it impossible to find the histo strain in his body, and I didn't look for eye scarring on anyone else other than Farr and Wade, so probably not."

"What about that Benito Mazar guy from the wedding? Do you still have him around here somewhere?" Ryan asked.

"You think he's part of all this…this…Seer business of yours?"

"Not sure, but could you look for us anyway?"

"He's been in the freezer for over a week, so I might only find scarring as I did with Wade, but I'll look. I'll let you know what I find."

* * *

As the pair waited for the elevator outside the mortuary, they flipped through their notes taken regarding Uriah Kent. Ryan's phone vibrated.

"This is Ryan."

"Ma'am, this is Captain Kyle from Fort Bliss."

"Of course, Captain, what can I do for you?"

"You heard about the incident at the PX last night, I assume?"

"Matter of fact, we were just leaving the autopsy. Was he one of yours?"

"No, ma'am, he was just getting into basic and hadn't been assigned anywhere yet, but I have some information you might find useful."

"Mind if I put you on speaker for Agent Moss to listen in?"

"No problem at all." The elevator door opened, Gabe apologized to the patrons for the unnecessary stop, and the door closed without them aboard. Ryan leaned against the wall of windows across from the elevator and tapped her speaker button.

"Go ahead, captain."

"Late last night, my brother called me about the incident at the PX. He is aware of the whole McCollum mess, so he thought what he found out might be of interest to you."

"Was he there?"

"No sir, but his wife was working, and she saw the whole thing go down."

"She okay?" Ryan asked.

"She's fine, well, it's just, I guess I should clarify. She did not see the end game of what happened, but she saw this Uriah guy when he came into the building."

"How does she remember him?"

"She works at a dog tag stand inside the entryway, and this soldier came up to her and was acting all crazy."

"Crazy like McCollum?" Gabe asked. Ryan frowned at the callous description. "Sorry."

"No, I get it, but no, he wasn't attacking her or anything. Anyway, he talked to her for a bit, and he was acting all skittish. Said he was mumbling about finding the food court."

"Never got angry with her?"

"No. She said he just kept looking at the ground and just seemed like he might be drunk."

"He was calm with her the whole time they spoke then?"

"Well, he did get angry when a sergeant walked up to ensure my sister-in-law was alright."

"Is that when the MP's got involved?" Ryan asked.

"No. The sergeant was not an MP but must have seen Uriah in his disheveled state and was just making sure there were no issues. She said when he looked up at the sergeant, he did lash out at him, but then dropped his eyes back to the ground and calmed down."

"So the sergeant didn't do anything else?"

"No, he just chastised Uriah to move on, and that's when Uriah started stumbling on towards the food court. She said as he walked away he just kept looking up and sort of back and forth across the ceiling of the PX. She found it odd."

"And that was all he said to her then?"

"Well, no, sir, that's really why I'm calling."

"What'd he say?"

"He wanted her help in finding a general."

CHAPTER 26

WIRETAPS

"Ryan! What the hell is in Pennsylvania?" the chief said as Gabe rose from his desk with his arm extended to greet him.

"Well, hello to you to chief," Ryan said as she returned to her desk with a fresh cup of coffee.

"Skip the pleasantries, you two. I want to know what's going on!"

Gabe returned to his seat without a handshake.

"Just trying to say hello."

"Cut it, Ryan," the chief held his finger to his mouth. "I want to know why I'm getting calls about the two of you doing illegal things."

"Not really sure what you mean about…"

"You know what I mean," he said.

Gabe raised his hand.

"I said I'd pay for breaking the seal."

"Not the time to be the funny guy Agent Moss." Gabe shrugged his shoulders. "What went on out east?"

"I met with you last week, sir," Ryan said. "I know we talked about the fact we were taking a car and heading out east to pursue some leads."

"You said you were going to Washington. You never said anything about stopping off at some library in Pennsylvania."

"Wait a minute, sir, don't you mean Indiana?" Gabe asked.

"No, Pennsylvania…some little town called Renusit or Rolover, or…"

"Renovo," said Ryan.

"Yeah, Renovo."

Ryan's eyes grew wide.

"Somebody knows we were there!" Gabe said calmly.

"All I know is I got this call from some county yokel claiming one of my detectives took things from their library. Any truth to that?"

"Did you get a name?"

"What?"

"A name? Did the person who called you give you a name?"

"Yes, he left a name and number." The chief walked to Gabe and held up the note to read. When finished, Gabe picked up a pen and a pad of paper on Ryan's desk and began to write.

The chief looked at Ryan. She shrugged her shoulders. When finished scribbling, Gabe stood next to the chief and held up the notepad.

"I just don't think..."

Gabe raised his finger to his mouth then tapped on the last sentence.

"Seems unlikely," the chief said.

Gabe scribbled again and once more held up the pad.

"Well, you'd better be right."

The chief turned and headed out the office door without another word. Gabe motioned for Ryan to follow as he grabbed his keys and headed out of the office. The pair snaked through a maze of cubicles in the squad room, with Gabe slowing for a moment to scribble a note and drop it onto Jenkins' desk. He weaved his way to the elevators and held the door as Ryan tried to keep pace. Once inside, he pushed the bottom button and stared forward without a word. Not halfway through the intro of a trumpet rendition of the *Love Boat*, the door dinged, opened, and Gabe headed towards the guard cage in the center of the parking garage.

"Key to any pool car, please," Gabe said.

"ID," the guard responded. Gabe handed his card to the man. Slowly, words were transferred from card to form, and once finished, Gabe scribbled his name on the bottom. "Here's your keys. 313 is the first slot around the corner." Gabe turned and walked along a row of parked vehicles before finding number 313, hitting the key fob, and unlocking the car.

"Inside Ryan."

She climbed into the passenger seat, and they made their way out onto the El Paso streets. Not twenty yards from the exit, just in front of the station, Gabe stopped, released the locks on the car, and the back door flew open. The chief, looking confused and angry, plopped into the back seat.

"I'm sure I'm going to get a great story out of this?!"

Gabe didn't say a word and drove along the streets at a fast yet respectable speed. Once through town, he began to ascend into the mountain range towards north El Paso.

"Sorry, sir," Gabe said as he mixed with traffic. "I had to get some distance from the office."

"This had better be good," the chief said.

"Amen," whispered Ryan.

"Chief, do you have the information about the caller from Renovo?"

"Here's the message." A chiseled hand reached over Ryan's left shoulder, and she took the note.

"Sheriff Timmy Holden," Ryan read. "The number he left is (586) 445-6586."

"That's not from Renovo," Gabe said.

"Well, that's what he told me."

"It's a fake number, chief. The first three digits are the same as the last three. Government types give out numbers like this when we don't want someone calling us back." The chief stared at the note in Ryan's hand and whispered the numbers.

"How was I supposed to reach him then?"

"Well, they're either sending us a message, or they'll call back…trust me," Gabe said. "So, do you recall what this guy said exactly, chief?"

"He said he was a Sheriff from Renovo, and he was all friendly and cheeky to start with before demanding that I return whatever it is you two took from his town's library."

"Did he tell you what was taken?" Ryan asked.

"No, he just needed me to recover what you have and return it. Did you two take property belonging to the library?"

"Well, a massive ongoing government cover-up sort of required it," Ryan said.

"A cover-up? In this little town in the middle of nowhere? What on Earth are you talking about?"

"A cover-up that, if proven true, could provide critical information about our recent murders in El Paso, chief."

"And this critical information was just lying about in a little library in Renovo?"

"Old tactic chief," Gabe said. "The government gets around the laws regarding requests for information by simply not having possession of important or classified information. They remove sensitive information from confidential holds to hundreds of old libraries or old buildings around the country which are accessible to the public and can then plausibly deny the possession of information when it's requested."

"And who made you privy to this practice?"

"I worked as a delivery boy years ago," Gabe said.

The chief didn't look surprised. "So, what led you two to this particular library?"

"An informant."

"Somebody reliable, I hope?"

"Mostly reliable," Ryan said, refusing to meet the eyes of her boss in the rearview mirror.

"Mostly or completely?"

"Like I said, chief, it's still early to tell, but for now, I'm sticking with mostly."

"So, how did you meet this informant?"

"After we found the knife in Kay Farr's neck three weeks ago, we were contacted by a woman who knew about the knife. Gabe met with her, and she directed us to Renovo."

"So, this informant works as a delivery person for the same people in the government you used to work for Agent Moss?"

"Well, she used to work in that business, but now she's involved in something with a little more teeth on it. Something that doesn't make what we're about to tell you easy to believe."

Tired of looking through the rearview mirror, Gabe pulled onto a runaway ramp near the bottom of the hill leading into north El Paso and parked. Gabe flipped open the back of his cell phone, pulled out the battery, and popped out the memory chip. He removed a small clear plastic case from his jacket and opened it, revealing a red chip. He pulled the red chip from its cover and inserted it into the memory slot on the phone. Gabe reinstalled the battery and hit the power button.

No one said a word.

After a minute, the phone rebooted, and Gabe hit a green button appearing on the screen, followed by a series of twelve numbers on the keypad. Jumpy screeches and pulses could be heard through the earpiece as Gabe put the phone back up to his head.

"I'm in a car near north El Paso," Gabe said. "You told me I had one opportunity to use this chip if they were onto us. Well...they know." There was silence. "Yes, we had to bring Ryan's chief into this after he got a call today about our trip." He paused. "Yes, we found a lot of good information." Gabe listened for a moment more, pulled the phone from his ear, and hit the speaker.

"Hello, chief," a husky voice said.

"I take it you're the informant that led my detectives to Pennsylvania?"

"Call me Svetlana chief, and yes, they worked off of my lead. Chief, the chip Gabe installed will be worthless in about three minutes, so I need you to listen closely. You received a call from someone named Holden, Hayden, Hobart...something with an H, correct?"

"Go on," the chief said.

"And he asked you to return the information Gabe and Ryan took?"

"That's right," he said. "But what does any of this have to do with my murders here in El Paso?"

"I worked for the group responsible for some of the bodies you've been finding around El Paso."

"Wait, then..."

"Just listen to me for a minute, chief, and then when I hang up, Gabe can fill you in on the rest. This will all sound fantastic, I know. It's even hard for me to believe at times, but your people had to get to Renovo to verify what I've been telling them. I believe the killings in your town are being done by a covert group working deep within the government. This group collects up Seers who have the unfortunate ability to see auras around all living things. As Gabe will tell you, these people are enraged by the color red and often kill people they find cloaked in that color. My team was assigned to pick up these people to be cured, but it would seem a more nefarious plan is now afoot. I'm hoping with what Gabe found, along with my testimony and evidence from the bodies there in El Paso, we can bring this group down."

"Then turn yourself in, and we can start putting this together," the chief said.

"I can't come in right now, chief. There are still a lot of loose ends to tie up, but we're getting close. If I come in too early, there'll be little chance to piece this all together before the group gets wind of what we have. My surrender to you is going to have to be timed perfectly. This group I work for has extraordinary abilities to twist the media and create evidence when they have needed to for many years. We're just not safe anywhere right now. Besides, there have been some recent developments…" the call began to cut out, "…regarding…other night…Vegas…"

The line went dead.

Gabe flipped over his phone, pried the battery from the back, and flipped out the red chip. A small hole burned through the middle of the chip and formed a gooey blob. Gabe plopped the red chip back into the plastic case and threw it onto his dash.

"Good lord," the chief said, "do you really think this girl and her little group are responsible for our murders?"

"Yeah, chief, and it's becoming evident this group she used to work for has been doing this sort of work for the past two hundred years or so."

"What in the world have you two stumbled onto here?"

Over the next half hour, Gabe and Ryan relayed all of the information they had learned about ROBE, Seers, and how these entities had worked together since the time of John Adams. Although Ryan and Gabe had just recently discovered the historical blueprints creating ROBE, the chief was impressed with their dissection of the information and how it might tie into the local murders. Fantastic or not, the chief had to admit the story wasn't as crazy as when Svetlana initially pitched it over the phone.

"So that I have this straight, we've pieced together that this ROBE group has existed for a few centuries and was formed to round up people called Seers?"

"Correct."

"And members of this ROBE group now believe that they have been collecting up Seers so they can be killed and not cured?"

"You pretty much have it, sir," Ryan said.

"So, this ROBE group lied to your contact all these years, has been collecting up Seers to kill them, and got sloppy with dumping too many bodies in my streets? I don't see the mystery here. Sounds like we pick up Svetlana, have her identify members of this group, and our cases are closed."

"Well, sir, the nefarious part of the story that Svetlana did not get into detail about a few minutes ago on the phone is that we believe ROBE is using some of these Seers as assassins."

"Wait, wait, wait...I thought you told me these people went crazy and essentially started killing on their own without any need for provocation or direction?"

"That's true, chief, but from what Svetlana has pieced together and some information she gave us about a few Seers, it seems ROBE might have developed a way to use some of the Seers to kill government targets."

"Which ones?"

"Sorry?"

"Which of the bodies here in El Paso are you talking about?"

"The Mexican wedding massacre a few weeks back was one incident," Ryan said. "First time they met, Svetlana told Gabe that she caught a man named Mazar and turned him over to ROBE a few weeks prior. We verified Mazar was the shooter at the wedding, and Cunningham is compiling the identities of all the victims to see who of interest might be lying in the morgue."

"Might have just been one incident where this Mazar guy got loose and went wild, though, right?" the chief asked.

"Well, we're also checking on another Seer, a Specialist Carlisle, who was involved in a killing in Florida after Svetlana grabbed him in Seattle. He took out someone linked with Al-Qaeda before he was captured and then committed suicide a few days later," Gabe said.

"While we have sufficient proof that this group exists, we haven't identified the players here in El Paso, and more importantly, we haven't yet been able to show that ROBE is turning these Seers into assassins. Before we met Svetlana and headed out east, we were nowhere close to where we are right now, but we're still sifting through information. You just have to give us some more time," Ryan said. The chief leaned back against the leather seat and took a deep breath.

"They're pretty pissed about what you two took?" They nodded, and the chief fought a smile.

"Yeah," Gabe said. "But these guys aren't just blowing smoke here. They won't just let this die."

"And Svetlana and her team will have their backsides on the line if they get picked up before you two fully flesh this out?" the chief said. They nodded.

"This ROBE group is good chief. We paid cash everywhere we went. We never used our last names and only spoke to the librarian and a few people at the local deli. I've been running covert ops a good portion of my life, and our cover was rock solid in Renovo. Still, they discovered us," Gabe said.

"Well, I think they're only onto Ryan since they called you two 'my people.'"

"Perhaps."

"Heck, we obviously missed some traffic camera or security tape from a gas station in town that got a good look at us," Ryan said.

"And it won't be long before they identify you, Gabe."

"You're right, sir. I figure my cover as an FBI agent runs a little deeper than Ryan's, but they'll figure out who I am sooner or later. The call you received was just the first step in getting their information back quietly. Without compliance, there's bound to be an escalation."

"And that's why we're out here on the side of the highway having this little chat," the chief said, "to avoid bugs at the office?"

Gabe nodded.

"So, where do we go from here?"

"Well, the coroner is working on the science end of this eyesight issue. He's compiling proof with all of the bodies in his morgue about a type of mutated fungus to confirm we're dealing with Seers."

"Mutated how?"

"Not sure, but Cunningham thinks it could have something to do with the biochemistry of nature, oversaturation of the fungus in a given system, contact with the sun, radiation…nothing substantial just yet."

The chief massaged his chin.

"You both need to keep this information between the three of us and the coroner. Don't share it with anyone else until you have something more to go on."

"We'll do that, sir," Ryan said.

"And if you're concerned about the police station, we can get a sweep of the offices going."

"Already on that, sir," Gabe said. "I dropped a note on Jenkin's desk before we left. He's just waiting for your call to get started."

"If this is as big as you say it is, you'd better find more concrete evidence if we're going to go up against some federal agency that's been doing dirty work before any of us were even a thought."

PART 6

THE FINAL PIECES

CHAPTER 27

EYE IN THE SKY

Ryan punched at random buttons on the device in her hand as she wandered around her kitchen and into her family room. As she dropped onto her couch and sat back, she began humming the refrain of *One Day More* from her favorite Broadway musical as she held her phone high in the air seeking a stronger signal. As the signal indicator dropped, she pushed herself up and away from the couch and walked to different corners of the room. A creature of few comforts, zig-zagging across the room took little time as only the television and sofa were set in the twenty by twenty space. Unable to increase the bar levels, she headed down a long hallway past the guest bedroom and burst into several parts of other songs that danced in her mind. She made her way into her bedroom, avoided a laundry basket collecting dust, and crossed over the threshold into the bathroom. Ryan shut the door, dropped the lid on the toilet seat, and sat. Her phone rang, and she withdrew the noisy device from her left jacket pocket.

"Hello?"

"Ms. Ryan, this is your neighbor, Will."

"Oh hi, Will, what's going on?"

"The television you ordered arrived earlier today, and you weren't home, so the UPS guy brought it over here for us to hold. We've got it in our garage."

"Well thanks, Will. Can I come over and pick it up?"

"That would be great, and if you can get here soon, the cable guys are finishing up connecting my new service, and they said they not only can get your television over to your house but also set up your dish right now if you've got the time."

"Sounds great, Will. I'll be over there in a few minutes. Tell the cable guys I would love to take them up on their offer."

"See you in a minute." Ryan hung up her cell phone, put it in her left pocket, and headed out to her garage. She opened the door and could see the white van of the local cable company in Will's drive. She walked down her drive, past the half dozen empty lots consumed by sand and grass, and enjoyed the quarter-mile stroll to her neighbor's front door. She knocked and waited for Will.

"Rebecca, so good to see you again. Come in, come in; the guys are just finishing up in the living room." She entered the home, and once the front door was closed, pulled a device out of her right pocket and handed it to Will.

"We've never formally met Detective," Will extended a hand. "I'm William Carlson, former 'tech nerd' is the term I think Jenkins said you like to use."

"Nice to meet you, sir. I had no idea we were neighbors."

"I like to keep a low profile because of some of the junk we got involved in with the cartels during my time with the force."

Ryan nodded. "Sorry to intrude on you with this charade."

"It's alright. Jenkins knew he could rely on my acting skills since, when he was a rookie, he created the bright idea to have our tech department take acting classes."

"Acting classes?"

"He believed we needed to be more social…you know, able to perform for the public in jury trials or when dealing with crime scene victims."

"Seems smart?"

Will waived for Ryan to follow him. "Most guys hated going to those classes, but he and I enjoyed our time there and really hit it off…which of course leads us here today."

"Again, thanks for doing this."

"No worries, detective. I don't get much excitement anymore, so it's nice to be included." She smiled. "Besides, Jenkins kept saying we'll get lunch, so when he called today, I made some sandwiches, and here we finally have that lunch." Will pointed to the kitchen table where Jenkins and his men had set up a half dozen gizmos making various bleeps, whirrs, and whistles.

"That thing I handed Will there just kept vibrating Jenkins, and for the life of me, I have no idea what any of that meant. Is my place hot or not?" Ryan asked.

Jenkins smiled and took the device from Will.

"I would say hot," Will said.

"Really?"

"From the information gleaned from this transmitter you had with you, there are at least a half dozen listening devices in your house," Jenkins said.

"You've got to be kidding me. What about video?"

"We checked over the readings two times already, and from what we can tell, there are no video capabilities in your home."

"How were you able to differentiate the audio from the visual? I don't get that."

"Well, you see…" Will started but then looked to Jenkins for approval. Jenkins nodded to his mentor. "…these devices can detect RF signals that are sent out by audio or visual bugs. It tracks one megahertz to 6.5 megahertz and allows us to figure out what type of devices are in your place."

"So, it can tell for sure what is audio and what is visual then?"

Jenkins walked toward the pair. "Well, there's also some new tech on the top of that transmitter that sent out various flashes to detect lasers and other types of infrared lights that often come from cameras," Jenkins said.

"I never even noticed any flashes," Ryan said.

"Too small and brief for the human eye Ryan."

"Those are new," Will said.

"Times they are a-changing boss. You've been out of the loop for almost ten years now. Every magazine I pick up anymore is like reading some new foreign language. These things…"

Ryan raised a hand. "Can I be excused from the nerd reunion here so we can get back to the bugs in my house?" Will shrugged and smiled.

"Right, sorry. Anyway, nothing on the frequency bands and nothing from the flash nodes on the transmitter indicated any cameras, so we should be good to head in there and fix your place up."

"So, what's the holdup?" A garage door slammed, and one of Jenkins' men approached.

"It's clear, sir," he said.

"Complete radius check?"

"Grabbed the Falcon on my second loop around. Hit a quarter-mile the first time, and the second was around three quarters. We've covered more than a sufficient distance. No one is listening remotely."

"I don't understand…" Ryan said, "…what's a Falcon?"

"Used to be a balloon we'd send up to grab signals from the air, but now we use a drone to do a sweep."

"You better not let Gabe get ahold of that," Ryan said as Jenkins smiled. "And what's all that about a radius check? I thought my little routine with the device you gave me was all we needed to do to find bugs?"

"There's even more advanced tech out there right now that permits a person to utilize a laser to hear your conversations from a good distance."

"Just a laser?"

"It's tied to other electronics Ryan, but yes, we can sit about a half-mile from your home, use an instrument that shoots a laser at your window and hear everything that's being said. Cool, huh?" Ryan shuddered at the smile on Jenkins' face.

"So, where do we go from here?"

"We'll load up the television we have in Will's garage and take our two work trucks to your house to install your satellite package."

* * *

After packing up their items from Will's kitchen table, Ryan, Jenkins, and his assistants carried a big-screen television out of Will's garage and placed it into the back of one of the fake cable trucks. As rehearsed, Ryan thanked Will for holding onto her television and then walked back to her home with the two white trucks in tow. Arriving in the drive, the truck with the television backed into Ryan's garage before they unloaded their tools and the tv into her home. As the other men carried the television inside,

Jenkins signaled Ryan to step into the truck in her garage. He closed the doors behind her.

"Why are we in here?" Ryan said.

"Just giving those two guys a little time to bump around the house a little more to make sure we know what's all in there."

"But you said the garage didn't have any bugs; why are we in here?"

"Just a precaution Ryan. This truck also has jammers along the inside of these walls, which will cut out any listening devices that might still be able to pick up out here."

She nodded. "So, what's the plan for these devices? Can you guys get them out ok?"

"They need to…" Jenkin's phone rang. "It's Gabe." Jenkins turned away to take the call, and Ryan watched out the side window in anticipation of the other men returning. She couldn't hear Gabe's end of the conversation, but it was clear he was instructing Jenkins on how next to proceed. "I've got it. Let me check with my guys, and I'll let you know." He hung up the phone as the men came out to the garage, opened the side doors on the box truck, and stepped inside.

"Pretty advanced stuff in there," one of the men said.

"No visual like we thought, so we can move about as we need to," said the other.

"That's good," Jenkins said, "but what sort of 'advanced stuff' are we talking about?"

"These aren't run-of-the-mill, bought-off-the-net things. Seen these used by some of our special forces in Bosnia a few years back. The items inside are a little more advanced than those, but basically, it's the same tech with some more bells and whistles."

"You're former military too?"

"Isn't everyone around here?" Ryan shook her head, and the man smiled at her. "Don't worry, detective, Jenkins isn't either." Jenkins scowled. "Sorry, my extremely talented boss isn't either," Jenkins smirked.

"I assume there are alarms on the devices in the house?" Jenkins asked.

"Yeah, they're gonna know if we tamper with them."

"Recommendations?"

"Leave 'em in place."

Ryan glared. "And what am I supposed to do then?"

"Just a minute, Ryan," Jenkins said. "Gabe recommended the same, so we..."

"Oh, he did, did he?"

"Hold on, Ryan. Guys, did we bring those timers and recording devices along in the other truck?"

"Trip lights, some water operators, and a few devices that can record a couple of hours of conversations, yeah."

Jenkins pointed to one of the men. "Ryan and I will get working on the tapes in here while you head outside and get a ground pole for the satellite dish we need to install."

"Got it."

Jenkins pointed to the other tech. "And I need you to get moving on setting up the water and electricity timers. We'll put the tapes in last."

"No problem. I'll go get those recording devices out of the truck out front."

Ryan sat speechlessly, brow furrowed as the men went to work. She watched Jenkins take a seat towards the back of the van and punch at random buttons to turn on the equipment inside the truck. She realized what the men were doing was the best course of action but leaving devices in her home was not a solution she appreciated. In a matter of moments, one of the techs opened the door, dropped in the recording devices, and headed back into her home.

"You and I need to go inside for a few minutes and talk about your television and what we are going to install for your cable. Can you ad-lib on this one, or do you want a script?"

"I'm not really humored about this Jenkins, but you know, I can wing it if need be." Jenkins smirked, realizing she had no self-awareness of her inability to properly 'wing' anything. Ryan had wandered her home humming the refrains of seven different songs for over fifteen minutes but never any of the more intricate parts. She clearly knew nothing more than the refrains, doubtfully having ever spent any real-time listening to, enjoying, or even dissecting any song. Her time was never spent just killing time, and therefore, when forced to ad-lib or create action within a moment, she simply was unable to do so effectively.

"Well, you just had some problems coming up with something more to do than hum some random lyrical refrains from songs when you were looking for bugs earlier, so I just want to make sure you can do this without knowing what needs to be said." Ryan glared. Jenkins shrugged.

"Just lead the way, Jenkins!"

The pair headed into her home and made casual speech about watching the Cowboys on Sundays and made sure to include the fact she was not home very much due to long work hours. Ryan did an adequate job, for whoever was listening, of solidifying the fact that her office was her residence as of late, but when she did come home, she usually just showered and went to bed. After a five-minute discussion, the pair headed back to the truck and continued recording.

CHAPTER 28

FALLOUT

A s Gabe suspected, ROBE wasn't on to his identity just yet.

"All clear," a tech said after a search of his residence lasting less than fifteen minutes.

"Nothing at all?" Gabe asked.

"No. Just like the office downtown. Your house and the office are clean."

"Have you heard from your other team about Ryan's house?" A white van pulled up before the tech could answer, and Jenkins waived at Gabe. "All done over there, Jenkins?"

"Yeah, just one of my guys finishing up with the timers on the water and electricity around the house to make sure those kick on at random times."

"Only very late and very early, I hope," Gabe said as Jenkins laughed.

"Yeah, and her new television turns on only Sunday, Monday, or Thursday night when the Cowboys are playing."

"You gonna let her keep that new tv when this is all done?"

"I don't think she's letting that seventy incher go…should've brought her one of the forty-fives."

"Your guys here told me you found nothing visual over at Ryan's house, right?"

"Nothing at all," Jenkins said. "Not sure if they didn't have time or just don't trust the noisy little video buggers. Maybe they were concerned with you being in her home for visits and finding the devices."

"Why is that?"

"I'm guessing since they haven't been able to identify you yet, they're assuming you're someone with special skills or training. Perhaps until they know more about you, the video devices were just too risky."

Gabe nodded. "She get the recordings done okay?"

"Yeah, they were a little canned at first, but we went back and dubbed over some things. We also put in some background water noise to cover up her less than stellar singing I had her do for shower times."

Gabe chuckled. "You going to trust her to keep an eye on all of those expensive gadgets you've got..."

Gabe's cell phone rang. "Hello."

"I'm coming over," Ryan said.

"Not anxious to sleep at your place tonight?" he asked.

"I'll be staying with you for a while, Gabe. Don't be coy about this." Before he could respond, her car pulled up and parked on the street. In the seconds between hanging up the phone and arrival at Gabe's home, Ryan had begun a conversation with herself inside the vehicle.

"...no sir...not letting those creeps listen in on me," Ryan said as she slammed the car door, dropped her bags on the walkway, and called for Stump.

"Heard you got a new television." Jennings struggled with his composure.

"When have you known me to watch television, Gabe?"

"Sorry."

"Well, you're the one that told Jenkins' guys to leave those listening devices in there."

"We don't want them to know we're on to them, Ryan?"

"I can't imagine it'll take them long to realize they're being tricked by all of the goofy devices set up by Jenkins and his boys."

"You'd be surprised, Ryan. Those should keep us clean for at least a week as long as you swing by from time to time so anyone watching can at least see a car out front," Jenkins said.

"You can't just have one of your guys borrow my car and hang out there for me?"

"I'll see what we can do, Ryan, but right now, I've got to get back to the department to run these serial numbers located on the audio equipment we found at your place," Jenkins said. "I'll call you with exact specifications of the items and let you know if we can backtrace 'em."

"Thank you, Jenkins," Ryan said as she turned to Gabe.

"Well, I guess you have a roommate for a few days."

"You'll be safe here," Gabe said.

"You know I don't need protection."

"Oh, come on. Stump loves sleepovers," Gabe said. He pulled open the screen door and waited for Ryan and the dog to enter.

"You know I wasn't super prepared for this," Ryan said.

"I figured you hadn't unpacked from Renovo yet, so at least you had a suitcase ready to go. So, see, after your long trip, you now get to spend a few relaxing days at casa de Stump."

"You're taking me shopping for some comfortable clothes, Gabe." He smiled and nodded, indicating she needed to pick up her own bag.

"No concierge service?"

"No, but I'll get you some clean sheets. I think Doug slept in that bed a few weeks ago after a game. That's the best you're going to get."

* * *

A half-hour later, Ryan was fast at work at Gabe's kitchen table, dancing her fingers on her laptop. As had been her routine throughout the current murder investigations, she entered and searched the names of the dead men they had been finding in hopes of digging up relevant information. Rarely did anything new come from an obituary or death notice from a local paper. Still, online comments from friends and acquaintances or featured stories about the deceased occasionally provided something of interest.

An online search of Benito Mazar only returned one protected article. She hated the online paywalls popping up more often, generally with the more prominent city newspapers, as they struggled to find ways to make a dollar. Her search permitted access only to Mazar's date of birth, date of death, and part of his street address in upstate Washington. Nothing helpful. Undeterred, Ryan turned the page in her notes and plugged in the name of the most recent of the dead even though she knew the report of Kent's suicide was likely too fresh. To her surprise, the search returned four hits led off by a detailed and lengthy eulogy consuming the front page of the St. George Bee. Ryan read with interest.

"Gabe," she yelled. There was silence. "Gabe!"

"What?" He shut off the water running in the bathroom sink.

"You need to get in here," she said. "With some clothes on, please."

"Yes, ma'am," he said, lumbering in with pinstripe pajama bottoms and fighting with a double XL Georgetown jersey.

"I'm not your mother," she said, "so kill the ma'am."

"Can do." Gabe put his hands on the back of her chair. "What's up?"

"This is a story about Uriah Kent," Ryan said. "You know, the kid killed at the PX?"

"Yeah, I know."

"Says his mother died about five years ago."

"So?"

"Well, she died of cancer."

"Sooooo?"

"So, she got cancer from excessive exposure to nuclear radiation." Gabe leaned closer to the screen and began to read.

"From a nuclear bomb?"

"No, it was radiation from a bunch of nuclear bombs."

"A bunch? I don't get it." Ryan pointed halfway through the article.

"In the late fifties and sixties, there were hundreds of nuclear tests out in the deserts of Nevada," Ryan said.

"And she took part in the tests?"

"Well, not exactly," Ryan scrolled further down the page and pointed again, "but this little town of St. George, Utah was the unlucky recipient of a bunch of the fallout after the tests, and that's where she lived her entire life."

"Seriously?"

"Yeah," she clicked back to the original search page and jumped to an article entitled 'Valley of Death.' This article says this little town is located east of where dozens of nukes were tested, and ever since the tests took place, they've had the highest rates of cancer and birth defects of anywhere in the States. Years ago, the government tried to move the people out of there, but most townsfolk chose to stand their ground. Uriah's name was referenced in that article because his mother was a vocal advocate for staying in St. George and building up the tiny town. They interviewed him not long after she died."

"So, I'm assuming by your excitement here you're buying into Cunningham's speculation that radiation exposure might be the catalyst behind the altered visions of Kent and the others?"

"Well...yeah...I guess since this is the first dead person we've been able to tie up to direct contact with nuclear radiation. I think it's time for a little more digging on that aspect of Cunningham's hypothesis." Gabe reached across Ryan and started typing as she melted back into her chair and waited for him to finish. The search term 'St. George Utah murder' worked across the web.

"Hit the third article on there," Gabe said. Ryan moved the mouse to the hyperlink and clicked once. The St. George Bee from April 12, 1963, appeared with the bold headline 'Death in St. George.'

"Well, look at that," Gabe pointed.

"Says a man killed four random people in the town in one night and then took his own life the next day."

"Keep reading," Gabe said.

"The police didn't have a clue who had murdered the four people until they got an anonymous call the next morning on where to find the killer's body. When they arrived, they found him along with a suicide note."

"Yeah, but look..." he pointed to the bottom of the article, "...it says he had self-inflicted knife wounds to his neck. Who commits suicide by chipping away at their own neck?" Gabe asked.

"Well, this could be a case where a Seer went crazy before ROBE was able to arrive and properly deal with them."

Gabe nodded. "Yeah...perhaps, but first go back to the main search page again and scroll through those other articles." Ryan returned to the page regarding deaths in St. George and clicked on the fifth article.

A church publication from 1967 stated how a local priest went crazy one night and bludgeoned to death two members of an alcoholics anonymous group meeting at his church. He struck so fast the others at the meeting couldn't stop him.

"They had an initial hearing the next day where he was threatening everyone in the courtroom, so they locked him up in a mental ward," Ryan said, "and then they found him dead four days later in his room. There's another possible Seer."

"Starting to fit into a little pattern there in St. George, isn't it?" Gabe said.

The two searched through four more articles about suspicious murders followed almost religiously by suicides or sudden deaths of the killers in the town of St. George. After half an hour of scanning all of the stories, the search ran dry.

"There are no more articles after the turn of the century," Ryan said.

"I guess it's possible ROBE positioned a team nearby to handle the situation better," Gabe said. "Svetlana informed me they do that sometimes, even more so recently as Seers keep popping up around military bases."

Ryan nodded. "All of these murders in St. George can't be a coincidence, Gabe. Still, though, there's nothing in those articles to lead us to believe ROBE was using anyone there as an assassin in any way. St. George doesn't offer any answers to that part of our investigation," Ryan said.

"But what about the Kent kid?" Gabe asked.

"What do you mean?"

"Unlike his townsfolk, Uriah Kent went crazy here in El Paso. Why here? Why did it take until he got here to turn? I mean, just a week after disappearing from basic training, he turns into a Seer before stumbling into the PX with a gun looking for a general? Something doesn't click."

"Yeah, and if he were there to kill someone, I would like to know why Kent was just shooting at the..."

A loud rap on the front door startled Ryan.

Stump growled as Gabe exited the room.

He swept back into the kitchen with his service weapon in one hand and a finger raised to his mouth with the other.

"You expecting anyone?" she whispered.

"No," he said. Gabe moved to the window above his kitchen sink and leaned forward, straining to see who was at the door.

No luck.

He looked back at Ryan as she too pulled her revolver from its holster, rose from her chair, and took cover in the hallway.

CHAPTER 29

VISITORS

D oug and Phil were not amused with the gunpoint greeting. Card night had snuck up on Gabe.

"You expecting burglars?" Phil asked as he inched past an apologetic Gabe. The game had been postponed several days due to his trip to Pennsylvania, and evidently, Mike let everyone but him know the new date. After closing the screen door behind the pair, Gabe returned his weapon to his bedroom and arrived in the kitchen to find them setting up for the game.

"Mike on his way?" Gabe asked as they established a seat at the table across from Ryan.

"He just texted he was a few minutes out," said Phil as he nodded in the direction of Ryan.

"They found a scorpion nest inside a wall of her house, and she needed a place to stay while they clean it up."

"Chose Gabe over the scorpions? Brave lady," said Doug. Not at all willing to give up on a chance to push Ryan off her game early, the two chirped at Ryan for making up the story about her house just to stay with Gabe. She ignored them, shuffling the cards, and accepted a beer Gabe pushed across the table.

"We're partners, you losers. I'm helping her out, that's all," Gabe said in her defense. "Besides, I need someone to do my laundry and cook for me."

A bag of chips on the table flew from Ryan's hands.

Gabe caught the bag, opened it, pulled out a few chips, and held up the bag. "As I said, she cooks for me."

Ryan glared.

"Hey, when Tommy gets here, remind me to ask him if he ever fought in any mixed martial arts matches," Doug said.

"Are you nuts?"

"No, Gabe. The other night I watched some old reruns of those television shows where guys fight to get into the house and then fight for a contract. Guy named 'T-Rex' was supposed to be this great fighter that was a shoo-in, but he didn't even make it past the qualifying round. Looked like Tommy...that's all."

"Doug brought the damn video over to my house and played it for me three times, and honestly, I don't see much of a resemblance. Besides, that show was about seven years ago, and that kid that keeps slapping us around in cards is just that...a kid," Phil said. Doug conceded with a slight nod.

"No wonder you donate your money to us every week; that fighting crap has fried your brain," Gabe said.

The screen door pulled open amidst the laughter.

"Where's your sidekick?" Doug asked Mike as he maneuvered his cooler through the door.

"Tommy said he'd be here to collect up our weekly wages when he's finished with some work." Mike dropped his cooler and took a seat next to Ryan. "What's she doing here in pajamas? I didn't get the memo, so I guess I'm overdressed."

"She's living here now," Doug said.

"Gabe's new best friend," Phil said. Mike smiled and looked to Gabe for the truth.

"She's having some fumigation work done on her house. She's just here for a few nights."

"I could have put her up."

"You already have a roommate Mike," Ryan reminded him. "Besides, I've seen you eat and know how well you clean up after these games. I'd kill you after just a few hours cohabitating with you."

* * *

The games played out much as they had before. Ryan confirmed at her second time at the game that Doug and Phil were the perpetual losers, Mike often broke even, and Gabe usually won. This was, at least until she showed up. Not wanting to lose her welcome on her first night at Gabe's, though, she'd thrown away half a dozen good hands, allowing her partner to win a few substantial pots. However, this plan soon revealed a flaw as Gabe's bravado got the better of him. After a little too much peacocking by Gabe, she decided to let loose her gaming experience, and had Tom not rolled through the door after an hour, slightly altering her winning streak, things could have gotten ugly.

"About time you showed up; I thought you were scared," Doug said to Tom without looking up from his hand.

"Never of you compadre."

"No sprekensy espanol," Doug said.

"Given your difficulty with English, I thought I'd try something new." Tom patted Doug on the shoulder as he searched for something to drink in the kitchen.

"Get your stuff done?" Gabe asked as he retrieved a bowl from the cabinet and handed it to Tommy.

"Had a few hiccups, but it's sorted out," he said.

Ryan looked up just in time to catch Mike staring uneasily at Tom. The crow's feet leading to his temples crinkled, and an eyelid quivered as his gaze followed Tom to his seat and remained on him for several seconds.

* * *

After two hours of continuous play, the table called for a bathroom break, and the gentlemen permitted Ryan first dibs. As each player took their turn, Mike approached Ryan and Gabe, standing by the sink.

"I came across some interesting information about the eye issues you two asked me about a few weeks ago," he said.

"Go watch some of that ninja warrior junk you morons enjoy so much," Gabe shooed the other three from the table. Doug and Tom scrambled through the ice for the last two Molson's inside of Mike's cooler.

"Don't mind if we do," Phil said as he picked up his lukewarm bottle and dashed into the living room to claim a couch. The two in search of the cold beers arrived in the living room simultaneously and wrestled for the right to spread out on the one remaining couch.

"So, what did you find?" Gabe asked Mike as he sat back down at the poker table, and Ryan hopped up onto the kitchen counter.

"I called Doctor Cunningham the other day and got some information about those vision problems."

"What did he say?" Ryan asked.

"He didn't have much information and kept telling me I was the one you guys should be harassing about eye issues."

"Sounds like him," Ryan said.

"But I did take some of his ideas, did a little digging, and found some items regarding older people that start to see things."

"What kind of things?" Gabe asked.

"Well, there were three different studies about the elderly who develop color blindness and then start to have sudden visions."

"What kind of visions?"

"Memories of how they used to see images, you know, of what their eyes used to see before the colorblindness occurred."

"Sort of phantom images then?"

"You could say that. See, when a colorblind person sees a familiar object they used to see in color, their brain recalls how the object used to look, forces the image into the eye, and then the damaged or missing photoreceptors fire off at a rapid rate trying to create the image in the color the brain remembers. This results in a distorted vision."

"Does the distorted vision continue forever then?"

"Likely not," Mike said. "But if you spent forty years seeing the colors of a pine tree and then one day it's just black, it could take years for you to get over what your mind used to see."

"So the distortion might make you see things that weren't really there, but your mind makes you think they were?" Ryan asked.

"Yeah."

"I hadn't heard that before…gives us something else to ponder." Ryan knew from Gabe's voice that he was disappointed in Mike's discovery. In the moment, and despite the warning from the chief to keep the information close to the vest, she decided to try and rehabilitate Gabe's confidence in his friend.

"Have you ever heard of anything about a mutated fungus in the eye that could cause a person to see on another wavelength?" Ryan asked.

Mike's brow furrowed, and Gabe set down his drink.

"More particularly, have you heard about some sort of fungus or genetic marker that mutates with exposure to a certain chemical, biological or radiological component that could cause distorted visions due to a change in wavelengths?" Gabe said.

"Some...sort...of fungus mutating?" he said. "I know you asked me about histo at the last game, but mutated? I don't think there's anything out there like that."

"A friend found an article on the web suggesting people who suffer from exposure to histoplasmosis and then later come in contact with some unknown organism might form an ability to see on another wavelength. We ran it by Doctor Cunningham, but his expertise is in the dismantling of the dead, not the voodoo of the eye."

Mike bit his lip.

"Don't hurt your brain," Gabe said.

"I'm just trying to think," he said. "I know a lot about histo, but…" The shake of his head started slow and increased in speed. "No."

"No, what?"

"No, I've never heard anything about a mutating fungus, histo or otherwise, that might give a person the ability to see on another wavelength. What kind of study was this?" Mike asked.

"Just something another detective stumbled across. He didn't tell me where he got it, but maybe I can get my hands on it."

"Sorry, Gabe, but without seeing the article, I can't help you there."

"Well, I can…"

"Ryan," Gabe glared. She noticed Gabe's head moving slightly back and forth.

"Hey, I'm just thankful that you even looked into this for us, Mike," Ryan said. "I think Gabe owes you a six-pack for taking the time to do what you did."

"I spotted you another twenty about half an hour ago, Mike; I think we're even," Gabe said. Their discussion came to an end, and with the rest of the card sharks now engrossed in a classic heavyweight Tyson boxing match on the television, the night of cards was over.

"I think I'm off to bed, guys," Ryan said. It was after midnight, and she was exhausted. Although the group mocked her as a lightweight, Gabe knew she couldn't have had more than a few hours of sleep since their return from Renovo. Gabe offered to help her find some bath towels, and the two strolled down the narrow hallway. Reaching the guest room, they turned left as Gabe flipped on the bedroom light and opened the bedroom closet.

"Why didn't you want to share those documents we found in Renovo with Mike, Gabe? He might be able to help us flesh out what Cunningham talked about when we were at the morgue."

Gabe reached high for some towels.

"I'm a little jumpy right now with what went on today," he said. "Your house was bugged...the phone call the chief got...Svetlana's call. I just can't shake the feeling things are about to get worse. I don't want my friend endangered by this, and he honestly seemed to have no idea about a mutated fungus causing wavelength distortion. Besides, that entire color-blind information in old people that he did tell us about just seemed way off base."

"I understand," she said. "And you're right; Mike wasn't very helpful." As she placed her towels at the foot of her bed and rubbed her eyes, Gabe walked to the door.

"Goodnight, Gabe."

"Night, Ryan."

As Gabe closed the door, Stump's nose wedged between the door jamb as he wrestled his way through the tight space, into the bedroom, and onto the guest bed.

"You good with my traitor lab there?"

"Yeah, I'm good. We'll see you in the morning."

CHAPTER 30

CRASHER

"Another good game, my friend," Mike said as he walked with Tom towards their cars parked in the street.

"Same time next week?" Gabe asked.

"I'll try to be on time," Tom said.

"And maybe you can get me a copy of the report about the mutating fungus?" Mike said.

"I'll try to get my hands on it." Gabe waived and waited as his friends drove off before turning to make small talk with Stump, who was not there. With the front door locked, Gabe finished picking up the last few remnants of beer bottle caps and other small items overlooked by the crew in the kitchen and contemplated the comments his friends made throughout the night about him and Ryan.

Discussions about romantic relationships were taboo at poker games, as his friends long ago accepted Gabe's excuses of being overworked and too tired to pursue women. He always appreciated their unwillingness to challenge his statements on the topic since the real reason he shied away from female companionship was the burns he received from the fire in college. No greater hurdle existed than the thought of finding a girl to like him first, love him next, then accept him later when he brought up enough courage to introduce her to the horrendous scars covering his legs and back. No one at the games, not even Mike, knew about the emotional impact the burns had on his psyche and, thus, the ability to find relationship comfort with members of the opposite sex. At war, battle scars were accepted. At home, he was more a pitied sideshow. Still, as his body warmed his sheets, he wondered if the thought of something more between him and Ryan had ever crossed her mind. What little she had said about men in her life was negative, and it was clear her sister's relationship left permanent marks on her as well. Perhaps they were a perfectly scarred fit. Maybe it was just the barley and hops playing their mental games.

* * *

Gabe hadn't intended to be awake at three in the morning, tiptoeing along the creaky floorboards in his hallway. He pushed open the guest room door as a low rumble rolled from the foot of the bed.

"Ryan," Gabe whispered. "Ryan, you awake?" She stirred and rolled over, her eyes trying to focus on the figure next to her bed. "Ryan, it's me."

"I figured as much." She rubbed at her eyes, and the top covers fell to her waist as she sat up. "What're you doing?"

Gabe fumbled with the light on the end table.

"I need you to come out with me to the kitchen for a minute."

"Do what?"

"I just need you to come out to the kitchen." He stood for a few moments to ensure she didn't drop back into bed, then moved to the door as she pulled on a sweatshirt and found socks for her feet. She caught up to Gabe and shuffled along towards the kitchen. At the kitchen entrance, Ryan was startled when she caught sight of a sinewy woman sitting at the kitchen table, drawing hard on a cigarette. The woman set down a lighter and released a wisp of smoke that danced around her head.

"Who...is...that?"

The lady stared at Ryan as Gabe pulled out a chair.

"Meet...Svetlana," Gabe said. He took the seat between the two women. Ryan took a concerned breath.

"Svetlana?" Ryan asked. "The golf course Svetlana?"

"Yes, the golf course Svetlana," the woman said.

"And what...exactly...is she doing here?" Ryan asked.

"I'm running."

"From whom?"

"From the same people that are after you."

"That doesn't make any sense," Ryan said. "If they're after us, then why would you come here to Gabe's home?"

"I didn't say they were after Gabe, Ryan; I said you." Ryan's fog cleared as she internalized the direct statement.

Svetlana inhaled.

"My contact in Washington informed me earlier this evening ROBE hasn't identified Gabe yet. Your place is bugged, though, right?" Ryan nodded. "And as you know," Svetlana drew heavy once more and exhaled, "they've been after me for some time now, but the noose has tightened since last we spoke."

"I thought you and your team were in hiding. What are you doing here?"

Svetlana looked at Gabe for permission to speak, and he nodded.

"They killed my partner, Argyle."

"I'm sorry," Ryan said.

"It was inevitable, detective. ROBE is good at what they do," Svetlana gestured at herself with her half-burned cigarette.

"How did they find him?"

"It seems someone recognized him when we were moving through Vegas. He went out to buy some food for us one evening, and when he wasn't back in an hour, we evacuated our hotel as was our normal routine. I held onto his cell for another twelve hours and received a call from ROBE informing me he'd been taken care of."

"Taken care of?"

"The 'buried in the desert' kind of taken care of," Svetlana glared and released the smoke from her nostrils. Ryan felt a nervous chill consume the room and suddenly saw the chiseled ROBE agent as something less than invincible.

"Tell her what happened to your other partner, Tyler," Gabe said.

"He went back to the fold."

"He what?" Ryan asked.

"They sent us a photo of Argyle's filleted body, and he panicked. Tyler decided he'd go back to ROBE with his tail between his legs in hopes they'd welcome him back after all of our years of dutiful service. I tried to talk him out of it, but he wouldn't listen. He didn't want to spend the rest of his life running, and he didn't want to end up like Argyle."

"And you?" Ryan asked.

"I can't go back to being a part of ROBE anymore, detective, even if it means running until I drop. I won't be a puppet anymore. Gabe and I have even been discussing the benefits of turning myself in while you were sleeping."

"So that's why you're here then?"

"Well, no, I actually came to warn you both in person."

"You don't think we know the danger? Couldn't have just called with your warnings?" Ryan asked.

"I tried to tell you this yesterday when you called me with the chief, but the chip burned up too quickly. And of course, thanks to the sort of thing that's happening over at your place, I can't use the landlines because I don't know who's listening," Svetlana said.

"Tell her the rest about Tyler," Gabe said. Ryan shot an eager glare at Svetlana.

"The reason I'm sitting here now is that I followed Tyler from Vegas to El Paso before I lost him. He's here in the city right now, probably syncing up with the ROBE group here. He'll fill in the gaps about Gabe being your partner and then help get a plan in motion to eliminate you both."

"You really think he'll tell them everything about Gabe and what we've uncovered?"

Svetlana nodded and smirked. "Tyler will do what he needs to get back in good graces with ROBE. He's a good man and a great soldier, but death scares us all in different ways. Argyle was like a brother to him, and his death impacted Tyler in ways I had never seen. He may roll it out slow, but sooner or later, he's going to tell ROBE everything he knows about you, Gabe, and this investigation."

"So, if this plan to take us out could be in place as we speak, was it really that smart for you to head over here? Why put yourself at risk?" Ryan asked. Svetlana's steel demeanor melted some more.

"I don't entirely know." Svetlana looked at Gabe. "Could I get something to drink?" Gabe went to the refrigerator and brought her a bottle of water. "I guess as I was following Tyler here, I started thinking that with the information you obtained from Renovo, along with my testimony and what you have from Doctor Cunningham, maybe we have enough to move on ROBE. The only thing missing is a clearer view of this radiation angle Gabe was telling me you two have been digging up as well as figuring out whether or not Seers are being used for assassinations."

"She's seen everything then?" Ryan asked Gabe.

"I showed her everything we've found in Renovo while you were asleep in there..." Gabe said, tapping the stack of files, "...and I filled her in on Doctor Mike's and Cunningham's theories."

"It's more than I expected you'd find," Svetlana said. "I figured you might get some journal pages or even half a dozen medical pages in Renovo, but someone got messy by leaving so much of the ROBE reports in one building."

"There was a lot," Ryan said.

"And what you two pulled up in Indianapolis was just priceless...nice work."

"Thanks, but is there enough here to bring down this; I don't know what to call it, institution?" Ryan asked.

"My sympathetic ear in Washington feels they might able to get us a hearing before Congress with what you've got." Gabe shook his head.

"I don't know if I agree," Gabe said as he began to flip up fingers to count the issues. "We've got Kay Farr killed with one of your knives, several others where the same or similar knife could have been used, a few bodies with a mushroom poison, an alleged suicide at a military base, a strange telephone number in some phones we found on or near dead bodies, several soldiers who disappeared for a time and then reappeared to carry out murders and a few others found dead in the streets after being detained by ROBE. Those seven things and no substantial medical evidence or something explaining how these all tie together don't leave me with a real warm feeling about taking this to Washington. I'm not sure who you know out east wanting to fight ROBE, but from what we know, some extremely powerful people have coveted and protected this group for hundreds of years. Speculation and hypotheses are not going to win the day."

"What about Mike?" Ryan asked. "We could share the rest of the evidence with him and see if he could help us come to some more definitive medical conclusion?"

"Possibly," Gabe said, "but like I told you last night, I just don't know I want him too involved in this."

"What about Cunningham?" Svetlana asked. "Could we get him to review all of this and see what he comes up with?"

"As I told you, Svetlana, he's not an expert in this area, even though he was able to pry some useful information from Atticus' report that we showed him."

"Yeah, he is the one that keyed us in on the idea that radiation may be what causes the mutation of the fungus in Seers," Ryan said.

"That…actually might explain all the soldiers we've been grabbing over the past few years," Svetlana said.

"What do you mean?" Ryan asked.

"Radiation is everywhere in the Middle East deserts, Ryan. Kuwait's our staging ground for most of our troops overseas, and the soil there is one giant graveyard of irradiated material. Heck, all the stuff we destroyed in Kuwait in 1991 is still half-buried there, and Iraq and Afghanistan have as much if not more of that crap lying around. There's enough radiation in those countries alone to light up half of Europe."

"Still doesn't help explain Seers that are not soldiers, though?"

Ryan jumped up from her chair. "Where's the laptop?"

"On the counter over there," Gabe said.

"And where are those notes from Captain Kyle about his unit?"

"Over here," Gabe grabbed the notes as she hit the power button.

"What was the name of the little town south of Baghdad where Kyle's unit worked at? It started with a T…." Gabe walked up behind Ryan's chair and flipped through the pages of the notepad as she entered her computer password.

"Anything harder than water in this house," Svetlana asked.

"Beer is in the fridge," Gabe pointed without looking away from his notes.

"I'm more of a Bordeaux girl, but I guess a Pabst will do for now."

"There it is," Gabe moved the notepad over Ryan's left shoulder for her to read, "Tuwaitha." She typed in the name.

"Where's that?" Svetlana asked as she reached into the refrigerator.

"It's where Captain Kyle told us his unit was stationed in Iraq...there!" Gabe said, pointing to an article with an image of two men wearing bio-hazard containment suits standing next to a battered Iraqi city sign.

Ryan sighed. "Why in the hell didn't we look this place up before?"

"We only had one of our dead people that had been there Ryan...it wasn't a priority," Gabe said.

"What'd you find?" Svetlana asked as she and her beer hovered over Ryan's right shoulder.

"It says here that a nuclear facility in Tuwaitha was destroyed years ago during an attack by Iran." Ryan continued reading. "Tests from the Iraq site in 2003 showed radiation levels equaling those of Nagasaki just after the bomb was dropped. It says here in 2004 we cleaned the place up, and now the levels of radiation there are acceptable."

"Acceptable to whom?" Gabe asked. "The same geniuses who cleaned up St. George?"

"That little town in Utah you were telling me about earlier?" Svetlana asked.

"Yeah, but what I didn't get to tell you was that our most recent body in the morgue is another dead soldier that grew up in that little town. We think he might have been captured and used by ROBE."

"He kill anyone in particular?" Svetlana asked.

"Didn't get the chance."

"Why not?"

"He was apparently sent to the PX to take out a general, but after an apparent unsuccessful search to find his target, he ended up standing in the middle of the mall shooting at the ceiling. MP's took him out," Gabe said.

The three read the remaining articles about Tuwaitha for several moments before Gabe and Svetlana found their seats at the card table.

"It's been about radiation exposure all along," Svetlana said.

PART 7

MISSTEPS

CHAPTER 31

CLOSE TO HOME

While the recent trip to Pennsylvania and Ohio provided Gabe insight into the 'rolling out of bed in the morning Ryan,' where she hit every single dawn with vigor and an overabundance of energy, this morning produced a much more jaded character.

"Stump keep you from your beauty sleep?"

"Need java," she said.

"You didn't try that magical blend Svetlana whipped up?"

"Girl spooks me. She's as dark as her coffee."

"I doubt she poisoned the coffee," Gabe said. "She's scared too now that her partners aren't with her; you need to give her a break."

"You left a killer in your house with poor Stump."

"She's not going to eat him."

"She better not. I want my electric Labrador in one piece tonight. He kept me warm."

"Yeah, well, it was a little cold last night."

"Before or after you let her into the house?"

"Be nice."

"Do you honestly feel safe with her around, Gabe? I mean, she might have been working for ROBE this entire time for all we know, and she's just finding out what we know before she kills us."

"That doesn't make a whole lot of sense, Ryan. Why would she lead us to Renovo if she wasn't on the up and up? It wouldn't make sense to give us the proof about ROBE so that she could then come back to kill us once we found it. If ROBE realized how much information there was in Renovo, they would have just gone and picked it up themselves."

"Yeah, but how do we know she didn't go back to the fold like her partner Tyler and the two of them aren't just stringing us along right now until they figure out a clean way to kill us? Poison in our bedsheets...pipe bomb on the water heater...serving up some Stump soup..."

"Knock off the paranoia, Ryan. Before I woke you up last night, it was pretty clear from what she said that she's not there to harm us."

"What could she possibly say that was so convincing?"

"She spoke about death and dying and how she wanted to do something right before that day came. They weren't the words of someone that believed there was some shiny happy ending to all of this mess. I've heard similar talk and witnessed the same somber demeanor with men from my unit in Iraq before we went outside the wire. The quick calls home from the satellite phones; the last-minute letters dropped in the mail bin, the trailing voice... you recognize the signs. You can't hide that kind of fear from me. This is her last chance at redemption." Ryan pursed her lips.

"I'm not sure any amount of help she gives us is going to get her a ticket on the elevator going up."

"What's all this talk about Heaven from you?" Gabe said. "I haven't seen you heading off to a holy house on Sundays. She's working her own course, and it's not our place to judge. If she can bring some resolution to these murders, and we can end the bloody history of a couple of hundred-year-old secret society, I think she can at least make a case at the pearly gates."

"I just don't trust her," Ryan said. Gabe realized there was no convincing Ryan and thought momentarily about the woman he'd just left behind at his residence. He understood Ryan's concerns but felt it was unlikely Tyler or ROBE knew Svetlana was in El Paso, and for now, his house was the smartest place to hide her. His vibrating phone broke his concentration.

"Can you grab that, Ryan?"

"Hello," Ryan said. "Oh, sorry, sir, I didn't recognize the number." Shrugging her shoulders at Gabe, she whispered "chief" as he continued to talk.

"You're kidding," she said. "When did this happen? And how do they know? And they got them both? Where's the scene? Alright, we're almost there now. Thanks, sir."

"Sounded like he was still talking," Gabe said as she dropped the phone on her lap.

"We'll be there before long, Gabe, and besides, they've got another body...with a knife."

"A knife?"

"A knife with a whalebone handle and an eye at the base of the blade, just like the one stuck in Kay Farr. Chief told me there are two dead bodies..."

"Two?"

"Yeah, it appears the one that used the whalebone knife succeeded in killing his target, but the target killed the knife-wielder as well."

"So, where am I going?"

"The bodies are already at the morgue."

* * *

The crowds massing within the administration building housing the morgue was a substantial annoyance as Ryan and Gabe were beset by a gauntlet of police, press, onlookers, and medical services personnel blocking their access to the elevators. The city had been on edge with all of the recent murders, so it was of little surprise to see such attention if word had leaked about the significance of the bodies in the morgue. Ryan tucked close behind Gabe as he pushed through the crowds and into an open elevator. The car ascended four stories in moments, and Ryan's excitement peaked as the car dinged and the door swung open. Her momentary high became an immediate concern as she turned the corner and was met by some policemen surrounded by a sea of yellow tape.

Gabe pulled out his badge, and a uniformed officer held up the plastic barrier. The two moved down the hall towards the morgue's open doors, which were guarded by two decked-out members of S.W.A.T. Passing the guards, Ryan gasped and stepped back at the sight. Silver tables splattered and smothered with blood were scattered about the room in disarray. Band saws and minor instruments used to scrape matter from bone were strewn about the room adrift in pools of red and black liquid. A few bodies in varying states of decomposition were flung about the room, several on top of one another, while several with their skulls partially detached remained strapped to examination tables.

"What the hell happened here?" Gabe asked one of the young detectives scribbling on a notepad.

"I'm Detective Peeler, and I work with the mayor's task force. And you are?"

"I'm Agent Gabe Moss, and this is Detective Rebecca Ryan with the El Paso P.D." Ryan moved past Gabe and Peeler and approached one of the sheet-covered bodies surrounded by officers.

"What are you doing here?" Gabe asked Detective Peeler.

"We always get called out when someone gets killed in a government building."

Ryan lifted the sheet.

"Gabe!" she rose and stammered sideways. "It's Cunningham!" The sheet dropped as she stepped back to distance herself from the body. Gabe approached, bent down, and pulled the sheet down to Cunningham's waist. He hovered over his friend's body for long moments as was his norm and did his best to carry out his routine. Numerous wounds on his friend were exposed and substantial, and try as he might, he could not keep his composure. He covered his friend and walked to Ryan. He held her arm as the pair stared down at the floor without a word. Gabe felt Ryan's body tense as she fought back the tears. He pursed his lips and did his best to funnel her some strength. After long moments Gabe worked his face into her sightline.

"You all right?"

"I will be in a second," she nodded.

Other officers, technicians, and morgue officials went about their business while the detectives took their time. The orchestrated movements around Cunningham's body frustrated Ryan. She internally lashed out at how these men and women could so coldly go about their business as if nothing was wrong. Although she knew they were just doing their job, and it was a disturbing dance she had carried out a hundred times at other murder scenes herself, her soul screamed. Gabe realized Ryan needed more time, so he tapped her on the back and released his grip on her arm.

"I'll be right back," Gabe said as he approached the Mayor's office detective. "Peeler, can you fill me in on what happened here."

"Hold on," the detective held up a finger and finished speaking with a photographer who was snapping photos of Cunningham.

"Sorry about that."

"No worries. I don't want to step on your investigation."

"I appreciate that agent. So anyway, we got a call about an hour ago of a disturbance in the morgue. The caller was a young tech who came to work this morning and saw the tables overturned and tools everywhere. With everything the way it is in here, he didn't even know the doctor was among the dead at first."

"What time was the call?"

"About zero six hundred this morning."

"Any idea when this took place?"

"Once we identified that two of the bodies in here were not supposed to be here, we were able to get some initial temperature readings. Indications are the deaths occurred somewhere around nine last night to one or two this morning, but those times are still just speculative."

"And what was the cause of the doctor's death?"

"Knife wounds for now," the detective knelt over Cunningham and pulled down the sheet that the photographer had set back down. "As you can see, he has slashes here, here, and another one here. There are also a bunch of defensive wounds on his arms and hands, but the final one there in his chest is what finished him. That's also the wound where we found the weapon."

"Where is the weapon now?" The detective turned right, then left, in search of the knife.

"On that table right there," he pointed. Gabe walked over to the plastic bag containing a knife, held it up, and spoke loud enough for Ryan to hear.

"It's the same," Gabe said.

"Same as what agent?" the mayor's detective asked.

"We had a knife just like this one pulled from the neck of one of our unsolved murders about a month ago. Same eye design, blade length, and one-of-a-kind whalebone handle." As he had hoped, the knife piqued Ryan's interest, brought her back to the logic of her work, and she moved to Gabe's side to get a closer look.

"What else have you got so far?" she asked as she took the bag from Gabe and examined the knife.

"Well, during the struggle, the doctor got in at least one good jab with a scalpel to the perpetrator's neck. So even after the perp killed the doctor, he didn't stumble too far before bleeding out himself."

Gabe pointed to the other bloodstained sheet. "That him over there?"

"Yes, sir."

"Any identification on him yet?" Ryan asked.

"No ma'am, we found nothing except his fingerprints on that knife, a cell phone over there next to Cunningham, and the clothes on his back." The three stepped around Cunningham's body. Eager to see the killer, Gabe didn't wait for Ryan as he knelt over and pulled back the white sheet. Numbness consumed him, and he lost his balance, finding a wall behind him to stop his fall.

"You okay," Ryan asked as she caught up and gently pushed his back with her knee to aid his support.

"I'm fine. I'm ok," he said in a fading tone as he dropped the sheet.

"You don't look fine," insisted Ryan. "What is it?" He shook his head at Ryan, stood up, and ignored her overtures as he walked briskly across the room. She let him go and continued to obtain information from the mayor's detective about the unknown male.

"Can I get a better look at the wound on this man?" she asked Detective Peeler. The pair leaned over the body of the assailant.

"Looks like he got it in the neck just under the right side of his voice box there, see? Best we can tell, Doctor Cunningham was using a scalpel to defend himself and the blade sunk in just under there." Ryan leaned over and identified a decent-sized hole in the neck of the assailant.

"That the only wound you've found on him?"

"We're working on finishing with the doctor's body first, and then we'll get a better look at this one, but from what we've found so far, it's the only wound he has."

"Thanks," she said as she walked back towards Gabe, who was examining the bagged-up cell phone.

"Is it alright if we get his phone to a lab tech friend of ours that has been working on other phones to compare their memories?" Gabe asked Peeler as he held up the bag.

"Just make sure it's properly logged," Peeler said. Gabe turned to an evidence tech from the local PD.

"Check this at the door, then take this back to the headquarters and get it to Jenkins," Gabe said. The tech took the bag, stopped to verify the item had been logged at the front door, then headed out of the morgue. As Gabe sorted through other bags of evidence, his movements were jittery and stilted, exhibiting an anxiety Ryan didn't often see in her partner. Leaning close into Gabe, she began her interrogation.

"What's up, Gabe?" she whispered, "Why'd the assailant's body over there spook you?"

"That's Tyler," he said.

"Tyler, who?"

"Svetlana's partner!"

CHAPTER 32

END IN SIGHT

Ryan had never seen Gabe more focused as he weaved through traffic. The initial shock of finding Cunningham and then Tyler had consumed Ryan's and Gabe's focus for over an hour as the scene was scrubbed and the bodies were examined more closely at the morgue. It was only after the adrenaline and anger began to fade that thought of the danger facing Svetlana and perhaps even Stump flooded his mind. Ryan tried to lighten the mood by joking that Svetlana really just wanted a Labrador companion while she was on the run, and Stump was her only real target. Gabe wasn't willing to acknowledge his partner's attempt to diffuse the tension.

The chief fidgeted in the back of the car and was an additional source of strain on Gabe's heightened state as the pair had argued for several minutes at the morgue over whether he should be included in the run to Gabe's home. Of course, Ryan's logic won out as the reasons to include the chief were many, none of which was more important than having a third-party witness on hand should they find Svetlana dead.

The car crept into the drive.

Leaving the car doors open, the three drew their weapons and moved in formation towards Gabe's front door. Gabe ascended the steps and began to slide the key in the lock, Ryan took up point on the opposite side of the door, and the chief knelt at the bottom of the stairs. Ryan peered through a small window leading into the kitchen and shook her head side to side. The lock turned with ease then Gabe pushed open the door and swept his weapon into his home.

Across the room, on the couch where she had slept the night before, Svetlana perked up. Stump, resting on her lap, came over to greet his master. Upon seeing Ryan and the chief follow Gabe into the residence with their weapons drawn, Svetlana rose with her hands level with her chest.

"Put 'em away, please," Gabe asked Ryan and the chief. He looked at Svetlana and shook his head.

"I thought you might be dead."

"Who's the old guy?" she pointed to the chubby gray-headed man at the door, still working to holster his weapon.

"That's my chief," Ryan said.

"Why's he here?"

"We need to talk."

Svetlana pulled out the kitchen chair closest to her, sat down, and placed her hands on the table for all to see. Gabe walked to the fridge, grabbed the five bottles of Pabst left, and dropped them in front of Svetlana.

"I've got harder stuff over there when we need it," he pointed to the liquor cabinet.

"So, what's going on?" Svetlana asked.

"Chief needs to hear about your partners."

"My partners?" Svetlana looked puzzled.

"Sorry to be so blunt, but Tyler's dead."

Svetlana's expression tightened. "How do you know?"

"He died as he took out our friend Doctor Cunningham last night."

"Doctor Cunningham? The one that's been working on the radiation theory?"

"The same, but there's something else?"

"What?"

"Ryan and I are pretty sure Tyler wasn't there alone," Gabe said.

"Wait a minute, Agent Moss," interrupted the chief. "Didn't you just get done explaining to me on the way over here that detectives believe Cunningham got in one stab to the killer's throat just as he was being stabbed in the chest?"

"Yes."

"And didn't you tell me the weird knife with the eye was found sticking out of Cunningham and had the fingerprints of this Tyler guy?"

"Yes."

"And it is the exact same type of knife used to kill Kay Farr and possibly used in three other of our unsolved murders?"

"Yes," Gabe said. "That is what I told you, but there's more. ROBE clearly wants us to believe Tyler was responsible for all of the recent murders around El Paso."

"It most definitely appears that way," said the chief.

"That's just it, sir…it does too clearly appear that way."

"What are you saying?"

"While Ryan had a look at Tyler, I took a trip down to the lobby and hit up a few of the contacts I've made in the press. It seems at least half of the outlets got calls around six-fifteen this morning informing them that the man responsible for the killings in El Paso was in the morgue. That's why all the press was there when Ryan and I arrived."

"The press did some good work, so what?"

"These calls didn't come from the police and obviously didn't come from the morgue, so it had to be from someone that knew Tyler was lying up there with a knife in his neck. It's not a stretch to believe the calls came from ROBE."

"That's all fine and dandy, but how does any of that suggest Tyler, who works with Svetlana and therefore ROBE, wasn't the one responsible for all of our murders?" the chief asked.

"Because he's been with me, and we've been nowhere near here," Svetlana said.

"Every waking moment?"

"Almost chief."

"How is that possible?"

"My three-man team always traveled together on every op. When we went somewhere solo, we had GPS trackers on our phones, cars, and even chips in our shoes. Anyone flying solo had an extremely tight window to be gone, and after we bailed on ROBE, our time window closed even further such that our time away from one another was almost non-existent."

"So, he figured out a way to give you the slip. What's so hard to believe about that?"

"Benito Mazar was the last of four men we delivered to ROBE here in El Paso well over a month ago. Shortly after dropping off Mazar, we split with ROBE, and since that time, we've been hiding and haven't been within a hundred miles of this town."

"Explain to me then if you two were avoiding ROBE, and nowhere near El Paso, what're you doing here, and what's Tyler doing in my morgue?"

"ROBE found our other partner, Argyle, and gutted him."

"Argyle?"

"Not important," Gabe said.

"Tyler got spooked after Argyle was killed, and he determined it was best to return to the fold in hopes that ROBE would welcome him back and spare his life. He knew an active team was here in your city, so he came here, and I followed him to El Paso yesterday."

The chief crossed his arms. "Seems a little too convenient. It still seems very possible this Tyler guy is who we've been looking for."

"Well, even if you don't buy her story, chief, Ryan, and I are convinced that Cunningham didn't make the wound on Tyler's neck."

"And exactly how is that?"

"We're pretty sure someone came up from behind Tyler and sunk a knife in his neck while he was stabbing Cunningham," Ryan said. "Tyler never knew what hit him."

"And just where does this come from?" the chief asked.

"Once the scene was processed, and I was down milling with the press, Ryan had one of the other medical examiners put Tyler onto a table for a closer look."

"And?"

"We first assumed the scalpel found in Cunningham's grasp was the instrument used to kill Tyler," Ryan said.

"Okay."

"So next, I assumed this scalpel, which had a straight blade on one side, and a sharp edge on the other, was likely being held by Cunningham with the sharp end out towards his attacker." Ryan took out her pen and ran her finger along the pocket clip to identify the part of the side of the scalpel with the blade.

"I'll buy that."

"Therefore, any successful thrust he made to Tyler's neck should have caused the cleanest cut where the blade end went into the neck on the side of the wound closest to Tyler's spine."

"I'm not sure I follow."

"Chief, if the blade side were pointing towards Tyler when it went in," Ryan pressed it against Gabe's neck for a better example, "then the smoothest cut side would be on the side of the cut that was closest to the back of Tyler's neck."

"Got it."

"The medical examiner opened Tyler's wound and determined the clean end of the cut, where the blade was sharpest, was along the side closer to the chin side of the wound, not along the part of the wound closer to the spine."

"That's it?"

"Well, no chief, there are three more things that convinced us completely."

"Which are?"

"First, the diameter of the hole and depth of the wound on Tyler show that something other than the scalpel found in Cunningham's hand was used."

"It was that obvious of a difference?"

"Based on the size of the scalpel in Cunningham's clutches, it couldn't have gone that deep into Tyler's neck, and the actual hole was a little wider in diameter than what that blade could have made."

"What else?"

"Second, we also found that the wound on Tyler curved around his throat."

"What's relevant about that?"

"If it were from the front side, or in other words, from Cunningham's hand, the arc would have most likely been opposite the curvature of the throat."

"And third?"

"Cunningham was right-handed," Ryan said.

"And the entry wound in Tyler's neck was on his right side," Gabe said. The chief rubbed his chin as Gabe rose from the table and went into the hallway to respond to his vibrating phone.

"This still doesn't mean Tyler didn't kill the doctor," the chief said.

"No. Like we said, we're pretty sure he did," Ryan said. "But while he's stabbing Cunningham, someone came up from behind and killed him."

"Your hypothesis seems plausible," Svetlana said. "Tyler was one of the best hand-to-hand tacticians I ever worked with, and I just can't imagine he'd let Cunningham get anywhere close to his neck with a knife. The only way he was ever going to be killed was by surprise."

"But if there was another player, then this thing isn't over?"

"Well, we…"

"Hold on!" Gabe burst into the room, dropped his phone on the counter, and made his way to the living room.

"What's wrong?" asked Ryan. Gabe ignored her, grabbed the television remote, and punched buttons. "What is it, Gabe?" she asked again.

"Just listen!" The words 'Breaking News' flickered across the screen, and a salty brown-haired man sitting behind a news desk held his ear.

"…say they have solved the rash of mysterious deaths plaguing El Paso for the past several months. For more on this story, we head to Trisha Walker, who is down at the police station. Trisha?"

"Thanks, Edward; we received word a few moments ago from the El Paso Police Department that the man in this photo, Anthony Dickson, has been identified as the killer terrorizing El Paso."

"That's Tyler," Svetlana said.

"Last night, in a successful attempt to kill Doctor Aaron Cunningham, Dickson was fatally stabbed by the doctor in self-defense. Moments ago, the police began releasing evidence that Dickson is the main suspect behind over half a dozen deaths in El Paso. As our listeners know, our local law enforcement has been working for some time trying to solve multiple homicides around the city, and it looks like they may have found their man. The chief of police has scheduled a press conference for six this evening, and we'll be here to update you as…"

Gabe shut the television off.

"What the hell was that!?"

"This has all been orchestrated," Gabe said.

"Nobody in this town ties up murders without my say so. The Good Lord and you three know I've been sitting here with you for the past hour, and I haven't gotten so much as a phone call from my office or the press about this."

"It's ROBE, sir," Svetlana said.

"Of course it is!" the chief said, slapping his hand on the table.

"But the good news, sir, is that this is a clear indication the mission in El Paso is about to end," Svetlana said.

"And how would you know this?" asked the chief.

"Well, with this information being fed to the press, ROBE is likely done here."

"How so?"

"When a hotspot has died down, ROBE looks for a clean exit. Tyler has provided that. I can promise in the next few hours; the press will have enough information to tie Tyler to every single murder you've had here to date. With that done, this El Paso op is all wrapped up into a nice tidy little package, and it'll be time for the team to move on."

"What do you mean by 'hotspot'?" the chief asked.

"In recent years, as the wars have raged on in the Middle East, more and more often we've been sent to military bases when soldiers return home from overseas. Once at these 'hot spots,' outbreaks of Seers always seemed to follow, so we captured them and turned them over to ROBE. We'd remain in a hotspot for at least a week or two after our last Seer was captured, looked for a clean exit story, then we moved on."

"But some of these Seers Gabe and Ryan have been finding are just run-of-the-mill citizens. Who takes care of them when they pop up?"

"They're usually handled by a sleeper agent or people working for them."

"A what?" Gabe asked as he turned to Ryan. She shrugged her shoulders and shook her head.

"Good Lord, we've been so busy focusing on my team I hadn't realized we didn't get into that yet."

"No, no, we have not," Gabe said as he shook his head in disbelief.

"Well, a few years back, rather than call my team in initially or call us back to a 'hot spot' location to pick up a single Seer or two, ROBE came up with the idea of planting sleeper agents in major cities and at all military bases."

"Yeah, you definitely forgot to mention this," Ryan said as she too began to shake her head.

"I'm sorry…it's just…"

The chief's index finger circled in the air. "Just get to it!"

"So anyway, these sleeper agents are ROBE's eyes and ears on a day-to-day basis. They may have to gather up one or two Seers every couple of years and are often in positions to identify Seers and hopefully get to them before they turn crazy and hurt anyone. They can usually handle small outbreaks, but they will call in teams like mine when Seers start showing up in bundles or, like I said, when hundreds of soldiers return from theater."

"Is there a sleeper in El Paso?" Gabe asked.

"I have no idea, Gabe. We never meet the sleepers and often do not even get to speak to them directly."

"How's that possible?" Ryan asked.

"What do you mean?"

"When you are called in to help a particular sleeper agent, how do you not know who they are?"

"Once ROBE orders us to a spot, we set up shop and wait for a call. I have never spoken to a sleeper agent and only ever have discussions with people working for the sleeper. We do meet the helpers once we have captured a Seer and need to turn them over, but to the best of my knowledge, I have never once spoken with or met one of the sleeper agents."

"So, the sleepers hire minions to do their dirty work?" Ryan asked

"Yes, detective."

"Any reason why the sleepers are not involved in the dirty work?" the chief asked.

"I've honestly never even asked why they weren't involved. Maybe they're high-level politicians, cops, or people in power that need to lay low to do their job."

"Then, from what you're telling us now, if our assassin hypothesis is true, the minions or the sleeper agent must be the ones that are either turning these Seers into assassins or killing them, right?" Ryan asked.

"Again, since we thought Seers were being cured, Ryan, I can't say. If our idea is true, though, it is either them or someone they hand the Seer off to after we've done our part."

"Perhaps the placement of a sleeper agent is what caused the drop in the murders in St. George in the nineteen nineties," Gabe said.

Svetlana nodded.

"What's in St. George?" asked the chief.

"It's a small little town that was downwind from a bunch of nuclear blasts."

"In Russia?"

"No chief," Ryan said. "Nevada."

"And we think that kid that shot up the PX, who came from St. George, was a Seer," Gabe said.

"So, I'm guessing from this talk about radiation you've found evidence that is what has been causing these Seers to appear?"

"We spent most of last night determining where all of our dead soldiers were located overseas and assumed anyone near Kuwait, Iraq, or Afghanistan has had enough radiation for several lifetimes, so linking them was easy. However, except for the kid from St. George, we haven't had as much luck with the civilians."

"Cunningham was helping you flesh out the radiation angle, wasn't he?" said the chief.

"Yeah, chief, and maybe that's what made him a target?"

"So back to the assassination issue, where is…"

A cheery ring tone unnerved the chief. Ryan picked up her phone and raised a finger. "Ryan. Oh hey, Jenkins, what's going on? Hold on a second," she pulled her ear away from the phone and tapped the screen, "go ahead." She placed the phone on the table.

"Calling about that news report Jenkins?"

"No, chief, I tried to call your phone, but I think you left it here in the office. We've got something from Will."

"Will?" Gabe asked.

"Yeah, Ryan's neighbor," Jenkins said.

"What's the news, son?"

"He had a hit," Jenkins said.

"Do tell, son."

"There was a breach of the cordon, he was able to identify a target, and then he followed the source out west of town to the warehouse district. Once the target stopped at a building in the yard, Will doubled back to the yard-master to check on who was renting it."

"What the heck is he talking about?" Gabe asked.

"This is my contribution to the fight," the chief smiled before shushing Gabe, picking up the phone, and turning off the speaker.

"So, did he find out who owned the building? And do we have anything on them yet? Ok, tell Will to back off and get our SWAT team out there now, but do it quietly. Call Assistant Chief Cason and tell him I want plain-clothes officers in the buildings surrounding the warehouse where the target is located and not to move before I get there. Keep the trucks at a distance and use civilian vehicles for anything within a half-mile—nothing with officer plates. Stealth is the word on this one, Jenkins. Got it?"

The chief hung up the phone and got up from the table.

"Spill it, chief," Ryan said.

"Yeah, what's going on?" Gabe asked.

"We need to move now. I assume Svetlana will be alright here?"

She nodded, and just as fast as the three had swept into the home, they left. Once in the car, as Gabe again raced down his neighborhood streets towards the warehouse district, the chief revealed his operation.

"Back when we had Jenkins put in those devices at Ryan's house and ran that little charade with her neighbor Will, it got me thinking that we should have someone keep an eye on Ryan's place."

"So, Will's been working for us again?"

"No, but I convinced him to keep an eye on your place and, in exchange, let him borrow some new tech toys to play with."

"What kind of toys?"

"Jenkins filled you in on some of the new listening technology that's out there today, right Ryan?"

"Yeah."

"Well, one of the things Jenkins set up around your home can identify any lasers shot at your house or detect any intrusions into a defined space."

"Couldn't just set up an alarm system at my house?"

"Alarm wouldn't pick up the laser, Ryan. So anyway, he set up that satellite dish at your house plus one at Will's house and another down the street in a lot under construction."

"What for?"

"They act as a triangulation system around your house, and the energy field that is generated can identify when someone either uses a laser to break the barrier or does it in person."

"And Will has just been sitting around watching this monitor all day for intrusions?"

"No. He has an actuator that keys him in if anyone breaches the space. The program on his phone or computer then directs him to what type of intrusion is taking place, and from that information, he can pinpoint where the break-in is or where the laser intrusion is coming from."

"That's too cool," Gabe said.

"So anyway, it would appear he's followed someone that was intruding on your home in some manner, Ryan. Maybe there wasn't enough noise coming from your house, and ROBE sent in one of their guys to check it out? Maybe with all this going on this morning, they were tidying up and picking up the devices they put in your home? In any case, our SWAT team is heading out to the yard right now, and Jenkins is trying to find out more about Adam's Construction, so…"

"Wait a minute, chief," Ryan interrupted. "Who did you just say?"

"Adam's Construction."

Gabe grinned at Ryan through the rearview mirror.

CHAPTER 33

CAVE

Despite the heavy traffic and a distance of over fifteen miles, Gabe pulled up to the entrance of the warehouse yard in less than ten minutes. He parked his vehicle amidst a dozen abandoned police vehicles located outside the main gate. The three exited the car and were directed to the yard master's office. After climbing some steps, Gabe held open the door to the modular mobile home, and a blast of cold air greeted them. Once inside, he was taken by the size of the interior as another mobile home that could not be seen upon approach had been attached to make the room sixty feet across and eighty feet wide. The room reminded him of several TOCs or tactical operation centers he had been in overseas as smaller cubicles lined the room's walls while a ring of square tables formed a conference space in the middle. Images from a projector held the room's attention as the incident commander utilized a red laser pointer to identify important elements.

"Everyone set up, sergeant?" the chief asked as he approached the incident commander. He nodded to the chief as the projector clicked to a bird's eye view of their current location.

"This is a photo taken five minutes ago from one of the two drones we've got up. As you can see, we have snipers on every building surrounding the target warehouse and a man in every warehouse in this yard. This particular drone has been here since ten minutes after Will arrived and has remained hovering over the target warehouse ever since. Our intel is solid that the target is still inside."

"What's the approach?" Gabe asked.

"We've got a team arriving by a tactical vehicle which will move from here," the incident commander indicated a course between the buildings, "to here, followed by a turn down this short stretch, then it's a straight shot to the main door. The approach will be silent, and after arrival, the team will stack here," he pointed to the central warehouse door, "where half will wait until the leads breach."

"Is there a standard floor plan for the inside of this warehouse?" one of the team members asked.

"Each warehouse is different." The team member shook his head. "You'll be at the mercy of the layout that has been established by the persons renting this particular space."

"Could be a little testy for just six with an unknown layout," the chief said.

"Well, we'll be adding Agent Moss and Detective Ryan for greater numbers and some rear security."

Gabe nodded, and Ryan even more so.

"Tactical assessment of what we're up against, sergeant," the chief asked.

"No intel on weapons or capabilities, sir, but we ran a threat assessment based on the information we obtained from Will and Jenkins about these cases of yours, so we're assuming the occupants of the warehouse are armed and dangerous." The incident commander looked around for further issues and, seeing none clapped his hands together.

"Let's get to it." The room's silence was gone as dozens of people scattered in different directions.

"Will Ryan be all right with you, Gabe?" the chief asked.

"I'll keep an eye on her." Slightly annoyed but too nervous and honestly appreciative of Gabe's experience in these types of situations, Ryan simply nodded and followed Gabe and the incident commander out the door. The three did not follow the team of six, yet instead were directed to the open back end of an SUV that was parked forty yards away. Once at the vehicle, Gabe reached inside the tailgate and grabbed the smaller of two body armors hanging inside. He handed the trim frame to Ryan, and although he kept the larger one for himself, as was usually the case with his long torso, the bottom of the armor didn't cover his belly button.

Early in his military career, he was made aware that the bottom part of his stomach would never be fully protected for his particular body type, despite the size of armor utilized. After that, to cover his entire torso, Gabe developed a penchant for slouching forward when involved in tactical maneuvers, making him a small target and protecting essential organs. Fortunately, in all of his missions, the only shots ever making contact with his body were to the plate along the right side of his back and a glancing blow to the outside of his unprotected left leg.

After sealing the last Velcro binding, Gabe pointed to the M4's lined up inside an open case and received consent from the incident commander to obtain one. He strapped the weapon to a carabiner dangling from his body armor before pulling back and locking the charging handle, grabbed hold of a loaded magazine, and inserted it into the weapon. A bullet jumped into the chamber as he slapped the side of the firearm, pushed it to safe, then let the M4 hang in front of his body. He looked at Ryan to see if she wanted a rifle, but she tapped her sidearm.

"You know your roles?" the incident commander asked as he led them towards the insertion vehicle.

"Special forces, FBI, and multiple tours busting down doors in the Middle East sergeant, I should be good."

"Probably should be leading this parade."

Gabe smiled. "Thanks, but I'll hang back with Ryan and fill her in on her role."

"Excellent," the incident commander pointed to the insertion vehicle and left the pair to make their way over the last thirty yards as he headed back to the command center. Ryan fiddled with the earpiece that dangled around her neck, and Gabe reached out to help her with proper placement.

"This piece is just a receiver; you know that, don't you?"

"I can't talk to anyone?" Ryan asked.

"You're the caboose, Ryan...if you run into trouble, you're best just to yell it out because it's likely we all just walked into an ambush."

"That's comforting."

"Never been the caboose before?"

She moved her head side to side. "I ran a few drills in front and middle, but never the back. You know me…hate not to lead."

Gabe smiled. "We move through any door; you simply stop in the frame, set up, and cover our tails. We move in to clear a room; you move into the door and cover the hall. We stop any time; you spin and cover where we just were. Easy enough?" She nodded.

"Covering your ass…got it. Just do what I've been doing for the past few months." He smiled and patted her on the shoulder as they reached the tactical vehicle. Six men decked out in full regalia held onto a railing atop a jet black Explorer and rested their feet atop an extended running board.

"You two can hop on the back next to me," one of the team members said. Gabe jumped up on the running board before noticing Ryan messing with her body armor.

"Why in the world won't this come off," she struggled with a piece dangling in front of her.

"It's a nut protector," Gabe laughed.

"And how does it come off?"

"It's there to protect your cojones, Ryan; just leave it alone."

"I don't have cojones, Gabe!"

"Excuse me, ma'am," said the officer next to Gabe, "but if you're coming along with us, you've got cojones." Ryan smiled and let the piece be as Gabe reached down to help her onto the running board. Once set, the officer thrust a thumb in the air, and the vehicle accelerated.

Ryan held on with both hands as the vehicle turned tightly around a corner and made its' way onto a long straightaway. Her palms were damp with the sweat of excitement, and although she could feel her heartbeat against the body armor, Gabe never looked more serene.

She had seen his calm reactions to dozens of stressful situations that would disrupt citizens and soldiers alike but had yet to witness Gabe in any moment of true 'warrior glory.' It seemed the vehicle's speed didn't register with Gabe as he held on with one hand as they whipped past dozens of warehouses with increasing speed. He remained locked onto his surroundings as he scanned the rooftops, the buildings, and even the side roads to understand the entire battlespace. He looked into the sky to locate the drones flying overhead and identify the exact locations of the snipers as they neared the target building. It was clear his interest was not out of curiosity or excitement for the task, as was hers, but instead was for an understanding and awareness of what assets and detriments awaited them. At this moment, flying along on the back of the SUV heading towards danger, his training as one of America's finest was most evident.

The SUV slowed then rounded a final corner. The car shifted into neutral, and the vehicle glided the last two hundred yards to the main entrance of the target warehouse.

"Move!" whispered the officer by the driver's side window. The command was so quick and sharp Ryan was delayed in hopping from the vehicle and taking her place in line. The rest of the team moved in perfect formation towards the warehouse door, and the officer at the end of the stack motioned for the detectives to fall in behind him once he reached the building.

The four officers up front moved to the door and the man toting the battering ram approached, turned, and permitted another to pull it from his backpack. The two without the ram covered two angles of the door while the man with the device placed it gently above the bolt lock atop the door. Slowly, he began to swing the ram back and forth to build momentum, and on the fourth thrust, with the ram level with his head…the door pulled open.

The momentum of the ram carried the officer across the threshold with the metal device leading the way. The stranger who had opened the door stepped to his left, the officer fell, and the ram hit the ground with a deafening clang.

"Get on the ground!" two of the officers yelled over the metallic din. The man that opened the door thrust his hands high into the air.

"Down, down!" hollered the officers outside the door as the officer laying inside the building reached out, grabbed the legs of the unknown male, and toppled him. The subject didn't struggle as the others outside quickly joined in subduing the stranger. The remaining stack members entered the building and covered angles while Ryan, as instructed, stopped in the open door and spun around.

"Clear!" one shouted.

"Clear!" said the others. She didn't see the final moments of the man being subdued and cuffed but got a look at him after she was ordered to move aside so they could bring him through the front door. Once past her, she again stationed herself in the door frame and watched as the three SWAT team members released their captor to awaiting officers.

"Coming in," radioed one of the men that had taken the fugitive outside. Ryan eased off her position and once more took a step away from the door. Once the team was back inside the building, the team leader whispered "move" over the comms, and Ryan turned to follow.

"Guy was quick to lawyer up when we handed him over to the chief," one of the SWAT members informed the team over the headset.

"Did say he was the only one here, though," said another.

"Keep sharp," the team leader instructed, "we don't have the cloak of silence or surprise anymore, and we have no idea what's ahead."

The team moved in rhythm through a long hallway with no doors, which simplified Ryan's role. A door frame without a door attached was at the end of the hall, and the SWAT team members flowed through. As Ryan reached the door frame, she turned and covered the long corridor from which they had just come.

Gabe and the others scanned the vast room they had entered as the team had gone from the confines of a tight hallway into a space the size of a football field. A majority of the area inside the warehouse was nothing more than bare concrete, but taking up a space of approximately forty yards, in the middle of the warehouse, stood a large white canvas tent. A ghostly yellow glow emanated from a floodlight centered atop the canvas, and from somewhere inside the giant circus tent, a recorded yet indiscernible voice escaped. The team leader instructed the men to collect on him, and he called Ryan from her position covering the door. They backed towards one another, kept a slight distance, and continued to scan angles.

"Can't we get some lights in here?" Ryan asked as she kept her focus on the hallway door.

"Told Jenkins to be ready with lights if we need them, detective. With this much open space, though, we're better off in the shadows." Ryan nodded.

"I see an entrance to that tent right there," said one of the team members, pointing his laser sight attached to his M4.

"Split up in fours and form up again, there," the team leader pointed with his tactical flashlight, "and there," he pointed again, "but keep some spacing." Gabe tapped Ryan on the shoulder, assuring her she could relinquish her watch in the hallway, and the pair joined up with two team members. The four waited for five seconds before Ryan's group followed the lead group and set up on the opposite side of the canvas door. The team leader nodded then pulled back the giant door flap.

"Need two of you to remain here," the team leader pointed to the two men with Ryan, one of which grabbed the canvas door flap, "and you two stay with us," he pointed at Ryan and Gabe.

The leader's team entered first, followed by Gabe and Ryan. Gabe ducked his head through the low-hanging entrance and peered into the darkness. The floodlight in the middle didn't provide much more light inside the tent, as even now, he still was barely able to make out the team leader who was less than four feet ahead of him. The door flap dropped behind them, and the team leader pulled out a small pocket flashlight illuminating a massive steel cage that arced to the right and left as far as the light extended. He motioned towards the space from where the audio was emanating, and the team moved left, following the right arcing bars towards a large white tarp that formed a wall.

Ryan was reminded of her days working at the county fair as a concessionaire on the merry-go-round as her job required circling the entire ride to ensure everyone was on board before starting it up. Although the bars to her right didn't allow movement up onto what would be considered the entertaining part of the merry-go-round, the space from the bars to the circus tent to her left was reminiscent of a path she had walked a thousand times.

As the team of six shuffled forward towards the recording, they inadvertently inched closer to the cage's steel bars to their right.

"Holy crap!" Ryan yelled as she jumped into Gabe.

The team leader thrust his weapon and light towards Ryan and then to the space where she was pointing. Encased in a small pie piece of a jail cell, a waif of a man straining to speak grasped at the air where Ryan had been. The team leader and others shined their lights on the figure, and the man inside the cell began flailing wildly. His head crashed over and over into the cell bars in a building crescendo, and blood poured from his nose and forehead. Gasping from the blood filling his mouth, the man fell forward with his hands still extended.

"We need a medic in here!" Ryan yelled to the guards outside the tent. "Who's there?"

Startled by the whisper in the darkness, Ryan grabbed her flashlight and shined it into two empty cells to the right before finding the whispering man. Located only a few feet from where the team had entered moments before, Ryan noticed tears streaming from his eyes as he too began to scream and convulse against his cell. The other officers illuminated him further.

"I'm gonna kill you. Gotta kill you!!" The bars creaked as he rocked violently back and forth against the metal cell.

"Turn them off!" Ryan yelled.

"What?"

"The light's setting him off. Turn them off!" Gabe and the team leader dropped their lights to the ground, and immediately the thrashing and threats dulled in the darkness, trailed off, and the men in the dark pled for help.

"Jesus, Gabe, I think these are Seers."

"Yeah, Ryan, and I think there's another one in there," Gabe pointed with his flashlight against his hand in the direction of the audio recording.

The team leader ordered his men to stay with the bleeding man in the cell in front of them and directed Ryan and Gabe to follow him towards the audio recording. They quick-stepped until stopped by the tarp-covered wall that extended out and away from the cylindrical steel cage. Gabe grabbed hold of the tarp covering the wall and pulled it down. Bars from a square steel cage blocked their path to a bug-eyed man strapped to a chair who began to shake violently as the light from the video outlined Gabe and the others. The figure screamed and thrashed, but his head remained restrained by a leather strap.

"Get some light in here now!" Gabe shouted.

"But the light drives them nuts," Ryan said.

"Now!"

The team leader keyed his mike and ordered Jenkins to illuminate the building. Gabe scrambled along the barred wall to try and find a way to get to the man in the chair. The audio continued,

"...the one causing all of your pain. The General doesn't care about your problems. He has done wrong by you and everyone around him. He is the cure. He is your cure, but he must be eliminated. Tell him you want him to put a stop to your pain. Tell him you need him to die so that you can be at peace. General Cline..."

Daylight seeped through the thick canvas as bay doors were raised, then abruptly the video and audio flickered off as a string of yellow caged work lights lining the interior of the tent ignited. At the moment of illumination, all three detained men slammed against their bindings and cages, and the voiceless one on the ground spit blood in place of words. Chaos ensued as medical personnel arrived and tended to the mute man through the bars as he scratched at them.

The search to find keys to the cells took on the highest priority as each SWAT team member swarmed the warehouse. Gabe was analytic in his search for an entrance into the cells, and finally, once able to see the entire structure with the light, he had an answer.

"It's a turnstile jail," Gabe yelled over the commotion as the man in the chair began bleeding around his wrists and head.

"A what?"

"Look for a crank! A giant crank!"

As the caged men became more enraged, the officers scampered around the metal cage, searching for a crank while other officers pulled at the main tarp covering the entire structure. Ryan moved towards the man in the cell that wasn't being tended to and tried to calm him down. He seemed incapable of reason as he reached desperately for her through the bars.

"Got it!" an officer yelled.

"Don't touch it," Gabe said as he ran to the crank. "We need them all inside the cells."

"He's out of control!" Ryan yelled. Gabe looked over at the securely seated man, and the man spitting blood that had shrunk into a fetal position inside his cell and realized they were not the issue.

"Get your guy inside his cell Ryan!" Gabe said.

"Do what?"

"Get his arms inside now," he yelled louder. The man strained to grab Ryan.

"But he won't just…"

"Do it!"

Ryan turned and grabbed an AR from the officer next to her, dropped the clip, cleared the chamber, and thrust the butt end of the weapon through the cell bars.

* * *

Ryan sat in a corner, took in a half-hour of deep breaths, and watched as all three of the men were sedated, treated, and taken from the warehouse.

"Quick thinking Ryan, that was really good," Gabe said as he approached her after aiding with the man bound to the chair.

"I gave him a concussion Gabe. Not sure that was the smartest thing to do."

"No, but it was the right thing."

"Mind explaining to me why you had me do that?"

"The cell structure here turns on an axle Ryan. When you spin it, you have to make sure that no one has any arms or legs hanging out, or they'll lose 'em. Better a concussion than a missing limb."

She shrugged. "And just how did you know about that crank up there, Gabe?"

"I've seen these before, Ryan."

"In Iraq?"

"No, believe it or not, this is an ancient relic from early American history. I once took a road trip to see one of these when I was in college."

"They have tours of these things?" Jenkins asked as he walked up.

"Somewhere in Iowa there's a big one, but the one I saw was smaller and was located in a little town west of Indianapolis. A couple of Hoosiers came up with this design in the fifties so that you could use minimal staff for warehousing your bad guys."

"How so?" Jenkins asked.

"Well, the prisoners were placed in their own little piece of the pie with a toilet in the middle of the pie and the door on the outside of the pie. On one of the sides, or even on several of the sides, the jail could construct little rooms for eating, for exercise, to release them, and of course, as you see there, a room to brainwash them." Gabe pointed to the chair inside of the square cage.

"So, each little piece of cell could be turned to the door or exit you wanted by that crank?" Ryan said.

"Exactly. Just sort of like a Lazy Susan in a kitchen."

"And they used these a lot in the past?"

"No," Gabe laughed. "They found out pretty soon that prisoners were losing their limbs when these things turned without notice, and prisoners also discovered that you could escape by pushing out the toilets and crawling through the sewage drains."

"Gross."

"Desperate men do desperate things, Ryan."

"How many of these things were made?" Jenkins asked.

"Not a bunch and I wasn't aware these were even mobile. That's why this one here is so fascinating."

"I don't share your enthusiasm, Gabe. At least not after what we just went through."

One of Jenkin's men approached. "We found several military uniforms in a bin over there, but they don't have any identification on them."

"Nothing to ID these guys at all?" Jenkins asked.

"It's been impossible so far, so we're going to have to take their prints when they're at the hospital."

"Okay, but let us know what you find," Jenkins said.

"Hey, have you guys inventoried the videotapes in that square room over there yet?" Ryan asked.

"Yeah, we found several with various names on them. The one in the machine was titled General Cline, and there was another couple with some Hispanic names on them that I don't recall offhand."

"Thanks," said Ryan.

"He was supposed to finish the job," Gabe said.

"What?" Jenkins asked.

"The job that Uriah Kent started a few nights ago at the PX. He was there to kill a general. Kent failed, and the one in the chair was going to be sent to try and complete the job." Ryan nodded.

Another officer approached before Jenkins could inquire further. "Guy outside started talking," he said.

"Sorry?" Gabe said.

"Brandon. The guy we grabbed at the door when you first came in. He started talking."

"I thought the SWAT team said he lawyered up right away," Ryan said.

"Well…we might have accidentally started to put one of those crazy guys you found in here into the wagon with him, and he didn't take it too well. Started screaming that he'd do whatever we wanted if we just didn't put them inside with him."

"So, what'd he say?"

"A whole bunch of gibberish at first, but then he gave us some names." The officer handed Ryan the list.

"Oh my God, Gabe!"

CHAPTER 34

EXPOSED

"Good morning, Westside Optometry."

"Hi, I'm not sure if you can even help me or not, but I'm having a problem with my eyes."

"Well, I'm sure we can help you but first, have we seen you here before?"

"No."

"Who do you normally see for your eyes?"

"I don't, I mean…sorry, I've never been to an eye doctor before."

"That's ok…"

"Well, wait, I guess the military eye doctors have looked at me a time or two, but I've never been to a real eye doctor before."

"I'm sure they are properly trained, sir, but let's see if we can figure out what's going on. Can I have your name and address, please?"

"My name's Carl Sanders, and my address is 361 Landover Lane, here in El Paso."

"Okay, Carl, what seems to be the problem?"

"I woke up this morning and flipped on the television, and all I could see was this weird sort of sepia glow coming from the screen. The television is old and all, so I didn't think much of it, but when I got out of the shower and pulled my towel off my head long enough to see my dog, he was all green."

"And I assume your dog is not normally green?"

"No, ma'am," he laughed. "I paid good money for my Husky, so I'm pretty sure he's not a defect."

"Do you have a headache or fever?"

"No, neither of those right now, but I had a panic attack earlier."

"No need to panic over this," she said. "We have a doctor who just finished up with a patient, so could you hang on for a moment?"

"Sure." The music piping along the telephone line offered little comfort as the moments turned into a five-minute wait.

"Hello, sorry for your wait; this is Doctor Collins. I understand you're having some problems with your eyes."

"Yeah, doctor, I guess I just need to know if this is something you might be able to help me with or is it something I need to go to the hospital for."

"Well, give me a few moments to look over your file here, and I might have some more questions for you." Carl waited. "Now, when did this start exactly?"

"Just this morning."

"And you've never had eye problems in the past? No glasses, contacts, no surgeries?"

"Nothing."

"Says something on here about military doctors. Have you seen them about these eye problems?"

"No. I just answered yes when she asked me about military doctors since they have looked at my eyes before and after my deployment. I'm not even sure they were doctors since all they had us do was look into one of those little machines and read off the bottom line."

"And when did they do this?"

"They've done that a couple of times. I guess most recently was when I returned from Iraq a month ago. Are those guys really doctors?"

"Doubtful they were, son, but I can assure you they were trained to conduct the tests they gave you."

"Did you ever report problems to them during any of those tests?"

"No, nothing."

"And it says here your television was going bad this morning...and your dog was green?"

"Yes, my dog was green, and yes, the television was all discolored. Sort of like those old photos people sometimes take when they're trying to age their picture."

"And can you see your dog right now?"

"Yes."

"And what color is he?"

"Still green."

"Do me a favor."

"Sure, doctor."

"Is there anyone at your residence with you?"

"No."

"Well then, are there any neighbors or kids playing out in your neighborhood?"

"I guess I can look." Carl opened his front door and stepped onto the front porch.

"Do you see anything?"

"There's a kid across the street who's digging around in his mother's garden. He's sort of bluish-green. That's not normal."

"Keep looking around, Carl, and tell me what else you see."

"The mailman just pulled up and is getting out of his..."

"What is it, Carl?"

"A bright orange glow is coming from the guy."

"Good Carl, that's helpful."

"Is that all you need?" There was no answer. "Doctor, are you there?" Carl asked again.

"Sorry," he said, "I'm just writing this down. Now you said you'd been to Iraq."

"Yeah."

"Where were you exactly?"

"Well, I was in Kuwait for some time helping troops go on leave, and then I spent some time in a little dump on the south side of Baghdad for about four months."

"The little dump have a name?"

"Tuwaitha was nearby, but it wasn't much to see."

"And what unit were you with?"

"I'm with the 11ᵗʰ ADA Brigade out of Fort Bliss. But sir, why do you need to know that?"

"Don't worry, son, it's standard practice when we deal with soldiers to make sure we know where you've been. You might have come in contact with someone or something over there, so we may have to call your unit if there are issues."

"Roger, sir."

"So, are you still outside?"

"I am."

"Anyone else come into your sight?"

"Postman just dropped off some mail at the first house, but he's the only one...wait. He's knocking on Brian's door across the street."

"Just tell me what you see?"

"I can't see around the postman, but his orange color just went almost completely red when Brian opened the door. That's not right," Carl said. "Is any of this helping?" There was silence again. "This sort of reminds me of a scene from Carrie," Carl tried to lighten the mood.

"I'm pretty sure you're one of a select few able to see auras, son."

"See what?"

"Someone who can see energetic fields around living things."

"And you can fix this?" Carl returned to his home.

"Well, there is a way to manage the ability, so you don't feel so at odds. We don't call it a cure, but you could think of it that way."

"Doc, I really don't care what you call it. I'll do almost anything to make this go away. I can't function seeing these...these...what did you call them, auras?"

"Can you hang on for just a minute and let me check on something?" Carl's heart raced as blood pounded through his neck and rushed into his brain. Worried about getting the help he needed and panicked over the thought of having to live with this affliction, it seemed an eternity before the doctor returned to the phone. "Carl, are you still there?"

"Yes, of course."

"I was contacting someone to come over and pick you up because the visions can be dangerous for you if you try to drive. Do you have a problem with me sending someone over to get you?"

"Really?"

"Yes, really. I've been in touch with one of my assistants running an errand for me, and he's pretty close to your address. He should be there in a minute or so if that's fine with you?"

"That'd be great. So, who am I supposed to be looking for?"

"He's on the other line here, so just let me…yeah…alright then." Carl could hear the doctor conversing with his assistant. "Carl, he should be pulling…"

"I see someone in the drive right now," Carl interrupted. "That was fast."

"GPS is a wonderful thing." Carl stared at the man as he climbed from the vehicle, scanned his surroundings then shut his car door.

"The guys all cloaked in red. Is that normal too?"

"Don't you worry, Carl, we're going to take care of this problem you're having." Carl watched through his living room window as the red-cloaked man approached.

"I guess I'll see you in a bit then, doctor." Carl hung up the phone, went to his front door, and opened it. "You're from Doctor Collin's office, right?" Carl asked as he swung open the door. The man in the ball cap and dark leather jacket smiled and nodded.

"Afternoon, sir, the doctor sent me to get you. Your eyes bugging you?" the driver asked as he walked into Carl's home.

"Yeah…yes…uh-huh," Carl stuttered and began to shake. He turned to get his cell phone and keys while trying to continue to carry on a conversation with the driver. Amid the pleasantries, Carl stopped talking and froze. The man at the door stood and waited for Carl to turn around for over a half minute, but Carl didn't move. The driver stepped to his left to get a better look at Carl's face in hopes of producing a response.

"You're not going to take me," Carl whispered.

"Sorry," the driver asked.

"Not going to take me anywhere. I'm not letting you take me," Carl shouted. "I'm going to kill you." Carl threw down the items he had picked up and spun towards the driver. However, before Carl could entirely turn, the driver grabbed hold of Carl's arm, twisted it into a joint lock, and threw him onto the ground. The driver's full weight dropped onto Carl's back.

"I'm taking you in, Carl. I was hoping to get to you before the rage kicked in, but now we'll have to do this the hard way. You need to relax."

"You're a dead man," Carl yelled as the driver forced each of Carl's hands behind his back and bound them with a zip tie.

"Shut up, crazy man," the driver said as he pulled out a syringe. Carl struggled and knocked over a stool with his foot, startling the driver. As the driver turned to see the stool, Carl hit the driver's baseball hat askew with his foot, and the driver shook his head to get the dangling cap off of his head.

"Freeze!" Gabe shouted as he and Ryan entered the room with their nine millimeters rigidly pointed and ready to tear through the driver's leather jacket. Wild-eyed, the driver dropped the syringe, rose, and spun at the two officers with a knife in his right hand. He worked his frenzied vision back and forth between his knife and the handguns pointed at his body.

"It's over," Gabe said. "Come on, Tom, drop the knife!"

"It's not over, Gabe. You have no idea what you're doing here. You have no idea who I work for." Tom's grasp tightened on the knife.

"Drop it, Tommy!" Ryan shouted. Shaking his head side to side as his nostrils flared, Tom realized he had brought the wrong weapon to the fight and tossed it away. He thrust his hands into the air.

"Knees!" Ryan said. Tom dropped, slowly, to the ground.

"Now, face down on the floor!" Again, he complied with a casual pace. Ryan reached him first, followed by Gabe, who knelt on his legs. Ryan pulled each hand behind his back and took little care in ensuring the zip cuffs weren't too tight. The sound of sirens approaching drowned out the commotion at the scene, and once finished, she pulled Tom to his feet as Gabe cut the ties from Carl Jenkins.

"We can take it from here," the chief said as he rushed up the steps to Carl's residence, along with four other uniformed officers. Tom was drug down the stairs none too gently by the men and into the yard that was filling up with other members of law enforcement. Looking back over his shoulder as he was led away, a crooked smile smeared across Tom's face, and he began to laugh. Annoyed, Ryan dropped down the steps towards Tom, but Gabe grabbed hold of her arm.

"You just going to leave the knife lying in there?" Gabe said.

She smiled and eased. "I might."

The pair headed back into the residence.

"You guys took long enough," Carl said as he rubbed his wrists.

"I'm not sure you're going to get an Emmy nod for the best crazy man performance Carl. Laying it on a little thick there, don't you think?" Ryan chuckled.

"I thought it was pretty well played. Those acting skills Will and I told you about the other day really came in handy, huh?" Carl said.

"For a tech guy, I guess."

"Hey, at least he didn't get the chance to use the knife," Gabe said.

"Funny, sir."

"And we got here in time to save that beautiful yellow shag rug from your blood Jenkins."

"Like I said, sir, funny." Jenkins shook his head as he walked along the hallway to where the techs and recording equipment had been set up for the sting. Neither noticed the chief re-approach.

"Knife look familiar?" They turned and looked to where the chief was pointing.

"The whalebone handle and eye on there are unmistakable, sir."

"I was thinking the same thing," the chief said.

"Hey Jenkins," Gabe called down the hallway moments after he turned out of sight.

"I said I was done," he hollered.

"Where's your phone?"

"I left it on the counter for you."

Gabe picked up Jenkins' phone, opened it, and pushed the button to recall the last number. Even though the cell phone had been wired and the entire conversation taped, Gabe just had to see the numbers one more time.

"A set of similar numbers on there?" Ryan said.

"Yeah, but this time we know where they're coming from."

CHAPTER 35

NO APPOINTMENT NECESSARY

A t the most prominent business complex in downtown El Paso, Gabe pulled himself up three stairs at a time with the aid of the handrail. While the others were taking the elevator, Gabe's patience ran thin with the day's delays necessary to solidify the case against the primary target. Ryan did her best to keep up and was glad Gabe waited at the door to the sixth floor and held it open. Once through the stairwell door, Ryan returned the favor and insisted that Gabe reassume the lead. The two moved so fast down the hallway that the names of attorneys, accountants, and businesses were unreadable. The bell from the elevator dinged behind them as they reached the last door at the end of the hallway. Gabe stopped, inhaled, and opened the door.

"Hey Gabe, I didn't know he was expecting you this evening?"

"I assume he's in?" Gabe said to the receptionist. He didn't wait for her answer as he walked around the desk and moved towards the patient rooms lining a hallway. Only one door was closed.

"He's with his last appointment of the day, Gabe. I'm sure if you can just wait..." her voice trailed off as he arrived at the last room on the right. Both drew their weapons as Ryan moved to the opposite side of the door and prepared to breach. Gabe nodded, turned the doorknob, and entered the room.

"Good evening Doctor Collins." The man administering eye drops to a patient in the dimly lit room turned.

"Gabe, what in the hell are you doing?" Noticing the weapons focused on his head, the doctor dropped the bottle.

"Get out," Ryan said to the patient. The man scampered out of the chair, caught himself on a counter, and bolted through the door.

"What the hell is going on, Gabe?"

"Sit down, Mike!" Gabe pointed with his weapon. Throwing his hands in the air, Mike sat on a stool next to the patient's chair as Ryan closed the office door and turned on the lights. Gabe lassoed another stool with his foot from under one of the smaller desks and rolled it over to Ryan. Instead, she ignored it and kept her weapon trained on Mike's head with steely precision.

"Do you mind explaining what's going on?" Mike asked.

"Right after we talk about your buddy Tom."

"Tom? What are you talking about?"

"Where did you meet him?"

"He, you know, he's my intern this summer."

"That's a crock," Ryan said.

"What do you mean?"

"What school did he come from?" Gabe asked.

"Texas Tech...you know that!"

"And you're sure about that?"

"Positive."

"And exactly what does he do for you here?"

"He follows me around...shuffles some papers...you know, intern stuff."

"Anything else?"

"Nothing else...well, wait, he stays at my place...but you know that."

"What about ROBE?"

"What...are...you talking about?" Mike moved his gaze from Gabe to Ryan.

"You heard me. Don't make me repeat it!"

"I don't understand what you're talking about, Gabe. Did something happen to Tom?"

"You know more than you're telling us..." A knock on the door broke the rhythm of the interrogation. Ryan stepped back, lowered her weapon, and opened it.

"It's Jenkins," Ryan reported. "He says they found it in the other room. Do you want him to bring it in?"

"Sure," Gabe replied. Ryan opened the door further, and Jenkins entered, carrying a small metallic box with a green button on top. Various colored wires leading to internal and unseen places decorated the sides. A tiny speaker, the size of a half-dollar, was located to the left of the button. It was unlike anything either of them had ever seen before. Mike's right eyelid quivered.

"You can't just search my office!"

"Something wrong with your eye there, doc?"

"You can't do this…this…whatever this is you're doing here, Gabe."

"We've got a warrant, Mike. You know me, I don't like to leave loose ends. Now, do you want to change your story and tell us about Tom, this gadget here, or your involvement with ROBE?"

Mike didn't respond.

"How about we fill you in, and you tell us when to stop?" Ryan said. Mike's eyes strained, and the weird creases Ryan noticed at the card game when Tom arrived late formed.

"You and Tom work for a group called ROBE, and the two of you have been responsible for most of the deaths occurring around El Paso for the past couple of months." Gabe leaned over and nodded his head as he stared into Mike's eyes.

"You don't know what you're talking about."

Mike looked away.

"You've been working with this ROBE group for years."

"I don't…"

"In fact, these scared people that call you for help are captured against their will and then are killed by this ROBE group, isn't that right?"

"No…Gabe…what you're saying isn't right," Mike insisted.

"These people have the fungus we discussed a few times, that histoplasmosis capsulatum from the bird droppings. Sometimes for no reason, but most often when they come into contact with radiation, the fungus mutates, and these people develop the ability to see auras or colors around all living things." Mike's attention peaked.

"Yeah, Mike, Gabe and I believe we discovered the catalyst causing the visions in people. We're pretty sure exposure to radiation is the main cause, and that's the reason we have so many soldiers coming back from overseas with these problems over the past ten years," Ryan said.

Mike looked up. "You don't know what the hell's going on!"

"Seers, Mike. Name strike any chords?" Ryan asked.

"You get a call from a potential Seer, trace the call and then send out Tom or some other team member from ROBE to pick these people up. Sometimes the pick-up is quick and easy. Other times the Seers are more violent, and Tom either has to kill the Seer since they're already dangerous, or he has to kill some innocent person who unwittingly interferes with the pick-up. After the telephone call, you hit that little metallic gizmo there, and the memory on the phone shows some random number you've programmed into it so they can't trace the call."

Mike shook his head defiantly.

Gabe pulled out his cell phone and dialed. "Ryan, tell me the extension on that phone."

"Two, Five, Seven, Five."

Gabe waited for an answer.

"Westside Optometry, how can I help you?"

"Gloria, this is Gabe. Can you send this call to extension two five seven five?"

"Aren't you in that office with Mike now?"

"Just do it, please?" The extension rang, and Ryan picked it up and said, 'hello.'

"Ryan, can you put the headset of the phone up to the speaker on that little box?"

"No problem." Gabe looked at Mike as she placed the headset onto the device.

"You want to stop this?" Gabe asked his friend again. Mike's gaze did not move from Ryan's hand.

"Hit the green button for me, Ryan; I've got him covered." Ryan laid her weapon on the counter and then hit the green button on the machine. A loud buzzing consumed the room, and Gabe pulled the cell phone from his ear. Without looking at his cell, he showed the readout to Ryan.

"A bunch of fours," she smiled.

"That's...there...there's an explanation," Mike broke his silence.

"We're all ears."

Mike took a deep breath and then looked up at his college friend. "I do work for ROBE Gabe. I have been since my sophomore year in college. All those internships in the summers that I used to disappear for were spent in Pennsylvania training for this important work I do for them."

"Killing innocent people?" Ryan said.

"This is about our country Ryan! Our government! Our way of life! I would think the two of you, of all people, would understand that. These infected people are extremely dangerous. They've killed off dozens of innocent people and even some of our greatest leaders, politicians, and business tycoons throughout history. ROBE is necessary to capture and cure them."

Ryan frowned.

"Yeah, well wait, look, I know sometimes ROBE agents have to kill their targets when they've reached them too late, and they're dangerous or when someone interrupts a pick-up, but that's the exception and one our country is willing to live with. You two should be more than willing to live with that as well," Mike said.

"So we're just supposed to accept the innocents caught up in the killings then...innocents like Doctor Cunningham!?"

"I didn't know Tom was going to kill him, Ryan, honestly I didn't."

"Both your eyes are twitching now," she said.

"You know Mike, our country might be willing to live with the whole safety of the country bullshit you just recited if there really was a cure," Gabe said.

"Wait! What are you talking about, Gabe?"

"No, first, tell us about the assassinations carried out by the Seers?"

"I don't understand?"

"The fact these Seers were being corralled and brainwashed into carrying out assassinations on high-value targets for our government."

"What in the world are you talking about, Gabe? I'm in charge of helping find these Seers, leading ROBE agents to them, and then they're cured. That's all I know. What's all this about assassinations?"

"Tommy told us everything Mike and then when we interviewed his ROBE partner Brandon, he verified each detail. Do you really need me to keep doing this?"

"I don't follow you, Gabe."

"Once you call Tom and direct him to a Seer for capture, ROBE takes them to a centralized location and subjects them to images of a particular target our government has deemed expendable. Operatives in third world countries, drug lords, undesirables, people asking too many questions…"

"Like General Cline at Fort Bliss!" Ryan said. Mike shook his head.

"And once the brainwashing is complete and a Seer shows signs of uncontrollable rage towards a target, the Seer is released to kill them."

"I didn't know this," Mike said. His head fell into his hands.

"Then, when these Seers successfully kill their target, ROBE agents sweep in to take out the Seer or ensure their death looks like a suicide just in case they might be able to talk."

"You have to believe me, Gabe; I never knew that. I would never have taken part in what you're describing. I thought we were helping these people and saving lives when we could. What you're talking about is an atrocity. I…I…I didn't sign up for this."

Gabe stared for long moments into his friend's eyes then crouched down.

"You know Brandon told us one of these Seers was used to take out Lincoln back in the day? Guy named John Wilkes Booth?" he said, nodding.

"And even though Brandon was a former Marine and Tommy turned out to be that 'T-Rex' fighter from that MMA show Doug was asking about the other night, do you really think we're going to believe some stooges like those two know about the assassinations, and you don't?"

"Honestly, Ryan, I can't begin even to tell…"

"We found three alive, you know?" Gabe interrupted.

"Found what?"

"Seers. We found three down at the warehouse just before noon. Remember the guy from the military base I told you about a few weeks back that was pronounced dead before we could get in to see him?"

"Yeah."

"He's alive. ROBE exchanged another corpse for the soldiers' body and then took him to the warehouse. Specialist McCollum was in one of these cages erected by Tommy and his buddy. He was being subjected to all sorts of images of General Cline stationed at Fort Bliss. Is that who you sent Uriah Kent to kill the other night?"

Mike shook his head.

"Kent failed and was killed by the police at the PX, so you moved onto another more willing Seer, didn't you?" Ryan asked.

"I don't know who you're talking about," Mike said.

"McCollum and the other two couldn't talk much because of the things you did to them, but I'm sure they'll come around after a few days once we get them some real medical care."

"I had no idea." Mike dropped his head once more.

"What about the rest of the Seers or those who didn't show signs of a willingness to carry out an assassination?" Ryan asked.

"What?"

"The Seers you capture but for some reason are unable to be turned loose to carry out an assassination. What do you do with them?" Ryan asked.

"I told you, we were curing them. I didn't know about anything else."

"Work with me on a hypothesis here…you doctor types are good at these kinds of things."

Mike glared.

"You would agree with me if there was no cure, then something had to be done with Seers unable to be utilized as assassins, right? I mean, if a Seer wasn't of any use to ROBE and there was no cure, then where are all of these Seers located right now?"

"I didn't know they were doing that, detective; I thought they were curing them," Mike's face flushed red. "How many times do I have to repeat it?"

"Stay with me here, Mike. On top of the question of where are all of these Seers that have been captured, I'm also at a loss to understand why ROBE was willing to take such a risk releasing a Seer to assassinate someone when it was likely the Seer would be captured for their crime."

"What do you mean?" Mike looked up at Ryan.

"Well, you have to agree with me once captured, the Seer was a massive liability for ROBE, right? I mean, if somehow a Seer could describe what he was subjected to or God forbid lead the police to a ROBE hideout after carrying out an assassination, then that would be a disaster."

"So?"

"So essentially then there had to be a way around that possibility. Something to ensure ROBE that a Seer would never survive long enough after their capture to tell his tale."

"I told you, I didn't know this. How can I answer you?"

"Horticulture, right?" Ryan asked.

"Horticulture?" Mike's voice turned raspy. "What are you talking about?"

"You and Gabe told me about the interest you had in horticulture back in college when you made the aloe for his burns."

"Yeah, so?"

"You ever play around with mushrooms, doc?"

Mike stared.

"A team searching your house as we drove over here found three trays that looked an awful lot like the ones we found at the warehouse where Tom and Brandon were corralling Seers."

"I don't…"

"Shut up, Mike! Just shut up!" Gabe said. "You created the idea for ROBE to feed Seers poisonous mushrooms to infect them so they would die within a few days of ingestion. When you had a Seer looking promising to carry out whatever assassination came down from your handlers in Washington, you held off on feeding that Seer any mushrooms until a few days before they were assigned their assassination. Tom told us Harris, Caldwell, and Wade all escaped one night, and although Tom caught up with them and killed each of them, you told him he only needed to worry about Harris since you hadn't been feeding him the mushrooms yet. The other two would have died within a day or so anyway since you'd fed them the poison. Harris was supposed to carry out the hit at the Mexican wedding the following week, and that's why he didn't have the poison in his system yet. Is any of this ringing a bell?"

Mike stopped moving altogether, lowered his head, and shook.

"You came up with the mushroom idea back in college, didn't you?" Ryan said.

"We also found the poison in the Mazar kid who did carry out the Mexican wedding killings, along with Kent who didn't carry out his mission to kill the Fort Bliss general. Tom believes the Kent kid must have had some mental struggles in his mind before he was supposed to kill the general, and that's why he shot at the ceiling of the PX. Gunfire or not, the kid was going to die from your poison, wasn't he?"

"I'm done." Mike's voice went up several pitches. "I want a lawyer."

"Perfect timing Mike since we're done with you." Ryan moved towards the door. "And I can promise you no lawyer in the world is going to get you out of this one."

"They'll protect me from this."

"What did you say?" Ryan asked.

"I'll get out of this...you'll see." Gabe took two steps towards his oldest friend.

"No, Mike," Gabe motioned for the officers in the hallway to come in. "They won't come to help you."

"You'll see Gabe. I'll be out in a matter of hours."

"Not when they hear you're cooperating with us."

"But I'm not...I won't...I haven't said anything!"

"That's not what Ryan is going to tell the press when we step outside. Your ROBE group isn't the only one able to push through false stories to the media."

"I'm really believable when I want to be." Ryan smiled. "You've seen me play poker." Her eyebrows rose.

"They won't believe you...you...your lies won't sell," Mike said.

"Oh," Gabe poked his head back in the room as the officers forced Mike to his feet. "You're also coming to Washington with us tonight. Ryan's leak to the press and your willingness to come along to some emergency hearings we set up on Capitol Hill should be enough to convince your ROBE buddies you've turned state's evidence."

"See ya on the plane," Ryan hollered as she neared Gloria at the front desk.

No sooner had Gabe turned the corner into the pale white hallway than Mike's pleas for mercy rushed out of the room.

"They'll kill me! You can't do this to me! Gabe...Gabe!!" They could hear Mike struggle with the cops. "They'll think I'm helping you. You can't do this!"

His whining faded as Gabe and Ryan pushed past a dozen officers and a handful of employees from other businesses working late. They reached the elevator, hit the button, and the door opened. Gabe waived Ryan into the waiting car, and just as he crested the elevator door, he made brief eye contact with the doctor being dragged from his office. Trying not to stare, Ryan caught Gabe's smile as he turned and stood next to his partner.

EPILOGUE

"That was a heck of a lot faster than the little jaunt we took across the country a few weeks back," Ryan said, happy with the quick flight to Washington, D.C.

"We could have driven here if you wanted to, but the whole 'my life is in immediate danger' thing kind of turned me off of that idea," Gabe said.

Ryan nodded. "No, this time at least, with all the baggage we had with us, flying was the right thing to do."

"Little help," Gabe said, pointing to the silk mess hanging down just below his neck. Ryan smiled as she faced him and took apart the disaster. Pulling the larger end of the tie-down to his waist, she ensured the tie was lying flat before she began the flips, twists, and turns to form a perfect Windsor knot just below his neckline. She pushed down his hands, grabbed each button-holed collar, and placed them delicately over the tiny white buttons. Patting his chest to let him know she was finished, his cheeks raised and flushed from his smile.

"Ready for this," the chief said as he came into the room through a large wooden door.

"Bands all here, chief," Ryan said, "I haven't seen this much security since the inauguration two years ago."

"You two are about to take down the Attorney General of the United States, Ryan."

"Or at least a group working under him, sir," Gabe said.

"Whatever comes of this, some serious heads are gonna roll. You guys know you're walking targets for a while, don't you?"

The two shared a confident gaze.

"Tom and Brandon sing for the committee like they did for us in El Paso?" Ryan asked.

"After they both got done blathering on about protection and immunity, they got their point across. Of course, what they lacked in experience and knowledge about ROBE, your friend Svetlana filled them in," the chief said.

"How'd Svetlana do, chief?"

"She was nervous at first, but when she got going, she had every ounce of their attention. I've seen enough of those congressional inquiries to know that Congressmen would rather hear themselves talk than listen, but not one of them interrupted her for the first two hours of her testimony. It was amazing."

"It helps her dad is the Chairman of the committee."

"Yeah, she could have told us earlier that her father was her contact in Washington," Ryan said. "So anyway, she's safe now?"

"I've been assured she'll be well cared for."

"That's great, chief, thanks."

"Any news about McCollum or the other guys we found?"

"They're not able to testify and so far, show little in the way of overcoming the aura issue, but the doctors are working with them. They showed the videotape of McCollum back at Fort Bliss that Captain Kyle commandeered for you a few weeks back and then had a live feed into where he is being held today. The images were disturbing, and clearly, there's a danger there, but from the comments made around the room after watching McCollum, the solution was not ROBE."

"Keep us posted on them if you could, chief?"

He nodded. "Well, if you're almost ready, I'll get out there to the chambers and tell them you're coming," the chief said.

"Two minutes, chief."

Gabe whistled out a short breath.

"You sure we're ready to do this, Gabe?"

Gabe dropped his right hand and pulled up Ryan's chin until her gaze caught him straight in the eye. Her face lit up at his assuring glare, her posture stiffened, and she smiled at her friend.

"As you told me when we talked about the death of your sister Ryan, this is what we do. We bring resolution. Let's have no more mysteries…no more questions," he winked and returned her smile.

Spinning with ease on the slippery floor, Gabe moved towards the large wooden door and opened it as the room was inundated with flashbulbs. Gabe took a step back as the roar from the collected press consumed him, and Ryan pushed him on the small of his back. He took a deep breath, looked over at her big smile, and they walked out into the fray together.

ABOUT THE AUTHOR

Matthew Hanson is a former trial lawyer, former lobbyist, former adjunct professor, current judge in Indiana and a retired JAG Major having served a tour in Iraq. He enjoys combining historical facts into his stories utilizing elements from all of his experiences and is currently working on completing two other books. Matt enjoys spending time with his family, Labrador Moose, and visiting the mountains out west.

For more information on this book and what's coming find him on Facebook and Instagram at "authormatthewhanson".